MICHELLE KIDD

Seven Days

First edition

This book was professionally typeset on Reedsy.
Find out more at reedsy.com

# Acknowledgement

To Lexi and all at the Cambridge Writer's Retreat - this book would not have been completed without you!

And thanks to oliviaprodesign.com for the book cover!

# Chapter One

Time: 7.35am
 Date: Friday 20<sup>th</sup> July 2012
 Location: Southeast corner of Hyde Park, London

If the grass had been any longer, he might not have seen it.

And if the diamante buckle hadn't caught the early morning sun, glinting lazily through the light summer dew, he might have carried on walking and missed it completely. DI Jack MacIntosh knelt down in the ankle deep wispy grass at the edge of the park and parted the fronds with a gloved hand.

"Over here," he called, turning his head over his shoulder. "I think I've found something."

Careful not to disturb the scene, Jack straightened up and took a step back, letting the scene of crime officers approaching from behind take over; the crime scene manager already making a bee-line for him. The shoe was gently lifted from its resting place on the bed of grass, and slipped into a waiting polythene evidence bag.

"Wait." Jack held up a hand and took a step forwards. With the beginnings of a frown threatening the edges of his forehead, he motioned for the officer holding the evidence bag to pass it to him. Taking the bag in his still-gloved hands, and with his frown deepening by the second, Jack cast his eyes down on the newly found shoe. "Shit," he muttered.

With a nod of his head, Jack returned the evidence bag and carefully retreated back towards the outer cordon, allowing the scene to be secured and processed. He knew the drill. He had been through it often enough. He made his way back across the grassy wasteland, retracing his steps towards the small white tent that had quickly been erected, the area already buzzing with white-suited bodies.

As was true of most murder scenes, in Jack's experience, the atmosphere was heavy and subdued. There was a calm, respectful silence as people went about their jobs; whether it was out of respect for the dead, or for the living, Jack was never quite sure.

"DI MacIntosh." A tall, wiry-framed man, dressed in a well-fitting light grey suit, complete with waistcoat and bow tie in an oddly contrasting burnt orange, stepped out of the tent and nodded his balding head at Jack. "You know how to keep a man busy on his day off." He handed his protective white suit to a waiting officer.

Jack nodded in response and offered a brief smile. "Can't have you taking it easy with a boiled egg and the Daily Telegraph, can we Doc?"

Dr Philip Matthews, the Metropolitan Police's senior pathologist, returned the smile, his light blue eyes twinkling. "Indeed we cannot, Detective Inspector, indeed we cannot."

Jack self-consciously rubbed a hand over the three-day stubble on his chin, trying not to notice the immaculately shaved and presented facial features of the police pathologist in front of him. He inclined his head back towards the white tent. "Anything?"

Dr Matthews headed away from the tent, making his way towards his car parked illegally by the side of the road. At just after seven thirty on a Friday, the area was already building up with traffic; bad tempered drivers leaning on their horns as they negotiated around the well-polished Volvo that was hampering their crawl to work. He motioned for Jack to accompany him.

"Just the preliminaries. You will get my full report tomorrow, after I have had a chance to look at her properly. But for the moment – white female, approximately twenty to twenty-five years of age, slim build. Well nourished. Obvious ligature marks to the neck, but I will need a closer look for any other injuries before committing myself to the cause of death." Dr Matthews paused by the driver's side door to his car, and caught Jack's gaze.

"And yes, just the one shoe on the victim."

"Like the other one," murmured Jack, feeling the all too familiar clenching in the far reaches of his stomach.

"Indeed," concurred Dr Matthews. "Just like the other one."

With a curt nod, the pathologist slipped into the driver's seat of his car, no doubt returning home to Mrs Matthews to explain, once again, that his leisurely day off was to be disrupted with another urgent post-mortem.

Jack sighed and made his way back towards the tent and its surrounding hive of activity. He could do with a strong coffee......and right now, a cigarette.

"Boss?" A ginger-haired officer broke away from the crowd and headed in Jack's direction. "The crime scene manager says you found the shoe?" DS Chris Cooper raised his eyebrows, expectantly, at Jack.

"I found *a* shoe, Cooper, *a* shoe. But not *the* shoe." Jack motioned for DS Cooper to follow him back to their car, stripping off his white protective suit as he walked. "A black stiletto type shoe. A good four-inch heel. Velvet I think, with a diamante style buckle."

"But the victim - they say she was wearing flat shoes, not heels," stated DS Cooper, walking round to the passenger side of the car. "And white ones, too."

"Indeed she was, Cooper. Indeed, she was."

"So, if it wasn't her shoe that you found, whose was it?"

Jack let the question hang in the air, unanswered. Slipping into the driver's seat, he waited for Cooper to join him. Starting the engine and pulling out into the ever-building traffic, Jack wound down the window to let in some cool morning air. "Let's go and get some coffee."

* * *


Time: 8.15am

Date: Friday 20th July 2012

Location: Isabel's Café, King's Road, London

The Acaso coffee machine gave out a forceful yet satisfying rush of hot steam, causing Isabel to take a hurried step back.

"Whoa!" she exclaimed, wafting her hands vigorously through the thick curtain of vapour that was quickly enveloping her. "That's more like it!" Reaching for her cloth, Isabel began wiping down the stainless steel casing to the coffee machine, deftly securing the steam wands back in place. She slotted the drip trays into the recesses until they gave a satisfying click, and wiped her forehead with the back of her hand. Taking a step back, the vapour having now dissipated into a light mist, she gave her handiwork the once over. The machine was her pride and joy; the single most expensive investment she had made – she couldn't afford for it to be out of action.

Wiping the last of the damp vapour from around the workspace, Isabel tossed the cloth into the bucket by her side and tilted her head back towards the rear of the coffee shop.

"Dom, I think I've fixed it!"

Moments later a tall, somewhat gangly looking figure popped his head through the archway that separated the coffee shop at the front from the rest of the building at the rear.

"That's good news," he remarked, nudging the thin wire-framed glasses higher up onto the bridge of his nose. "Can't run a coffee shop without coffee."

"Indeed we can't, Dom," smiled Isabel, reaching down and picking up the bucket of soapy water and heading towards him. "How did you get on with the ordering?"

Dominic pulled a notepad from the rear pocket of his faded jeans and flicked the pages with a long, delicate finger. Pianist fingers, his mother had always called them. "Order complete. 7.52am. Delivery scheduled 6 -7am tomorrow, Saturday 21$^{st}$ July, 2012. Order reference TXT52017."

"Perfect. I knew I could rely on you." Isabel put the bucket of soapy water down and slipped herself behind the front serving counter, resting on one of the tartan covered stools. "Thank you so much for coming in extra this

4

morning. I really do appreciate it."

Dominic lowered his eyes and his pale cheeks began to flush pink. "I don't mind; it was no trouble. Mum said you needed my help."

"All the same, I do appreciate it."

Dominic nodded but continued looking at his feet, shifting the weight from one foot to the other in a regular rhythm, counting to three on each foot.

"What do you have planned for the rest of the day?" continued Isabel, pulling a plate of homemade chocolate brownies towards her. She had missed breakfast, what with the malfunctioning coffee machine emergency.

"Planned?" Dominic raised his head and frowned for a second. He slowly rubbed a well-manicured finger over the neat ginger-toned goatee beard that hugged his chin. "Well, it's Friday. I walk the dog at 12.30pm, help Mum with the cooking at 4.00pm – we have fish on a Friday - and then load the dishwasher at 7.00pm."

"Wow, that sounds like a busy day, Dom," smiled Isabel, unwrapping the cling film from the plate of brownies. "You had better pop off home then."

Dominic nodded and opened his notebook again, retrieving his pen from his back pocket. Leaning on the counter, he bent over and methodically began to write in his neat, carefully constructed handwriting. Isabel strained her eyes to decipher the printed lettering. "Friday 20$^{th}$ July 2012 – Isabel's coffee shop. Time of departure 8.21am."

Placing the lid back on his pen, Dominic slipped both pen and notepad into his back pocket. Without a further word, he collected his jacket from the coat stand by the front window and left, the bell jangling as he closed the door behind him.

Isabel took a large bite out of the chocolate brownie in her hand, and chuckled to herself. Dominic was such a sweetheart. Insanely clever, with an almost photographic memory, Dominic Greene was the twenty-one-year-old son of a friend of a friend, brought in for a milkshake by his older sister one afternoon not long after Isabel had opened her coffee shop. The rapport she had felt with him was instant. His mother had popped in not long afterwards, filling in the background to her son's engaging behaviour and idiosyncrasies. "Somewhere on the spectrum" had been her explanation, giving Isabel a smile and a shrug, folding her hands around the cinnamon flavoured latte in front of her. That had been as far as they had managed to get towards a "diagnosis", Sacha Greene had later explained. With an almost obsessional desire for routine, occasional repetitive rituals, such as the hopping from foot to foot and note taking, and being unable to pick up on a lot of social cues and expressions from others, Dominic Greene had merely been placed "on the spectrum" by his GP. And that had been that. Whereabouts on the spectrum was either a very closely guarded secret or no one quite knew.

With such a helpful nature and a surprisingly sarcastic sense of humour, ever since the day he had stopped by for a milkshake, Dominic had slipped into the role of Isabel's personal assistant. A few hours here and there to begin with, more to keep him occupied than anything else, had then led to a more permanent three days a week job offer. Plus more when she was busy. Like this morning.

And Isabel now couldn't do without him. Although without the social skills to serve behind the front counter, he was a whizz behind the scenes. He ordered all the stock for the kitchen, making sure a steady stream of baked goods came out of the ovens. The cleaning rotas were planned to within an inch of their lives, and he kept the art studio well stocked and organised. In short, Dominic Greene was her saviour.

For "Isabel's" was not just your regular run-of-the-mill coffee shop. Yes, it sold coffee, and pretty good coffee by all accounts, but it was a whole lot more than that. The café area at the front of the shop housed two comfortable leather sofas, several well-loved armchairs, plus some beanbags and bar stools. In addition, there was a large bookcase covering the far wall, rammed full of books and magazines. Customers were encouraged to relax at the front of the shop, put their feet up and immerse themselves in a novel while sipping their cappuccinos. Books could be borrowed and returned at a later date; donations of other unwanted books were gratefully received and added to the groaning book shelves.

What made "Isabel's" unique, however, lay through a low archway behind the serving counter, where the café turned into a small art studio. A surprisingly large space housed several drawing tables, and some free standing easels which could be rented by the hour. The art studio was flooded with natural light from two large ceiling windows, and a concertina style patio door that when it was fully retracted opened out into a small courtyard at the rear. Customers were encouraged to view the artwork that adorned the walls, some of which was for sale.

Isabel wrapped the plate of brownies back up and pushed herself off the stool. Although she usually opened the café seven days a week, the malfunctioning coffee machine had forced her to hastily erect a "sorry we are closed" sign on the front door earlier that morning. Picking up the bucket of soapy water and disappearing behind the counter into a small kitchen space, she tipped the water into the sink, while contemplating opening the café for the final push of the working week.

Just at that moment the bell jangled over the top of the front door.

"Just a minute," called Isabel, sloshing the rest of the water down the plughole and replacing the bucket underneath the sink. "Sorry, we're closed at the moment. Had a bit of an emergency."

Wiping her hands on a tea towel, and tucking several stray strands of hair behind her ears, Isabel emerged from the kitchen to find out which of her customers couldn't quite read the closed sign.

* * *

Time: 8.30am
  Date: Friday 20<sup>th</sup> July 2012
  Location: A cellar in London

Using his shoulder against the ageing wood, the heavy oak door opened slowly. Peering into the inky blackness that infiltrated the musty cellar, he paused to let his eyes adjust to the dark. The thin, fluid-stained mattress in the furthest corner lay empty. The blanket, riddled with holes and frayed around the edges, so rough it merely scratched and scathed the skin, lay crumpled by the side. A solitary wooden chair in the opposite corner hosted a plastic tumbler of stale water and the remnants of last night's supper; thin crusts of bread, now curled and stiff.

Where was she, he thought to himself? A momentary flicker of panic welled up inside him, his heart beginning to race at the thought he may have lost her. Although he knew that there was no way out of the dank, dark prison cell of a cellar, other than the stairs he had descended, the feeling that she had managed to escape filled his veins with ice-cold fear.

But then he saw her.

The outline of a huddled figure, almost hidden behind the heavy oak door, appeared through the blackness. He turned towards her, and even though the darkness lay heavy and suffocating, sucking out any source of light and seeming to squeeze the oxygen out of the air, he could clearly see her quivering form. Clutching her knees up to her chest, she hugged her arms tightly around herself, although nothing was quite able to quell the shaking terror that rippled through her body.

"Now now," he murmured, a broad, reassuring smile crossing his tight lips. "Let's get you back over to the bed, shall we?" He stepped towards her, silently amused at how his mere presence seemed to cause her to shrink even further back into the cob-web filled corner. Reaching out, his hand grasped firmly around her wrist. Feeling the coolness of her skin beneath his fingers sent familiar jolts of electricity through his body. He heard a faint whimpering emanating from her lips. "Sssshhhh now…. I'm not going to hurt you."

Two wide, doleful eyes peered up out of the dimness, a look that he recognised. Wariness, trepidation and fear, tinged with just a flicker of hope.

"That's better," he murmured, coaxing the quivering form out from the shadows and across the roughly hewn concrete floor towards the makeshift bed. The sound of the weighty metal chain clunking against the floor filled the silence. He checked that the clasp on the metal cuff attaching the chain to her ankle was still secure. It was. The other end of the chain wound its way through the dust and dirt to a lone radiator fixed to the wall opposite; a radiator that had long since ceased to emit any form of heat or comfort.

Satisfied his captive was secure, he bent down and reached out to stroke her hair, gently brushing the strawberry blonde wisps away from her beautiful, yet tear-stained face. He felt her flinch underneath his touch. "There, there," he breathed, letting the once soft and silky strands caress his fingers. "You get yourself some rest."

His soothing tones seemed to do nothing to quell the simmering fear coursing through the girl's fragile shape. He watched as her narrow shoulders shuddered with each sob that quietly escaped her mouth. He let a small chuckle tease his lips.

"I'll be back soon, my sweet," he murmured, backing away towards the door. He had picked up the plate of stale bread crusts from the wooden chair and replaced it with a bowl of cereal, smiling at the tinny sound of pops and crackles filling the dank air between them. "Have your breakfast, Jess – there's a good girl. It's your favourite."

* * *

Time: 8.30am
 Date: Friday 20th July 2012
 Location: Isabel's Café, King's Road, London

Isabel placed two cups of steaming coffee down onto the low table in front of one of the sofas, and slipped herself into a neighbouring armchair.

"It's so good to see you," she smiled, reaching behind her onto the serving counter and bringing down a plate of Sacha Greene's homemade biscuits. With Sacha's skills at home-baking, Isabel's coffee shop now had an assistant *and* a regular supply of homemade cakes, biscuits and pastries. "I wondered when you might drop by; it's been ages. Please, help yourselves." Isabel nodded at the plate of biscuits which she placed next to the coffee cups.

"Thanks, don't mind if I do," replied DS Cooper, reaching forwards and swiping two homemade cookies from the plate. "Missed my breakfast this morning," he added, while stuffing a generous portion of a chocolate chip cookie into his mouth.

"I can't take you anywhere, Cooper," chided DI Jack MacIntosh, grinning in Isabel's direction as he reached for his coffee. "So, how have you been?". As soon as he had said it, Jack realised the foolishness of his question and inwardly kicked himself. How have you been? Did he really just say that? How did he think she had been, after discovering her parents had died for the second time, burying them for the second time? Then discovering a long lost brother was also dead? Although several years had passed, Jack knew the grief still lingered. He felt his cheeks colour beneath the stubble that encased them, and flashed Isabel an apologetic look.

"Things have been OK really, Jack," she replied, her eyes softening. "Mac's been in a few times since I opened – he has a thing for my hazelnut latte."

Jack nodded and sipped his coffee. "Yes, he told me. Said it was the best thing he had ever tasted."

"How long have you been here?" asked DS Cooper, brushing the crumbs from his shirt and swallowing the final piece of cookie. "And how come I never knew about this place? These cookies are amazing."

"The café's been open about three months now. I've had a few teething troubles along the way." Isabel gave a sideways glance at the coffee machine which was now, thankfully, happily purring away. "But things are going quite well so far."

"Well, I'm definitely coming back," said DS Cooper, reaching for his coffee and taking a large gulp. "Coffee's damn good too."

Isabel smiled and nodded her thanks. "So, you guys. What's going on in your world?"

DS Cooper leant forwards and lifted another chocolate chip cookie from the plate, ignoring Jack's raised eyebrows. "I told you, I haven't had any breakfast yet," he explained, breaking off a chunk and taking a bite. "And my blood sugar is low."

Jack sipped his coffee and avoided the gaze he knew Isabel was casting in his direction. He fixed his eyes on the trail of crumbs leading from DS Cooper's breakfast plate to the edge of the coffee table. He began counting them as if he were conducting an inventory. An inventory of cookie crumbs. A very important inventory that needed to be completed without delay.

"You still living in that sweet little mews flat?" Isabel wasn't giving up. She shifted in her armchair, and Jack could still feel her penetrating gaze searching for his own. He eventually glanced up and shrugged.

"Yes, still in the flat. Same place."

"On your own?" Isabel's eyes narrowed, challenging him to look away. Which he didn't; not this time.

"Yes," Jack replied, cautiously, wondering where the conversation was heading. "Still on my own. The way I like it."

"Eternal bachelor," cut in DS Cooper, draining his coffee cup to wash down the last of the cookie. "That's our boss. We can't live without him, but it seems nobody is quite brave enough to live with him." He chuckled at his own joke, eyes twinkling between his fair, ginger eyebrows. "Isn't that right, guv?"

"So some would say, Cooper," conceded Jack, feeling a smile twitch at the corners of his mouth. "No one quite brave enough to take me on." He turned his attention back to his coffee which was cooling in his cup.

"Well, that's a shame, Jack," continued Isabel, placing her own coffee cup back on the table. "You need a good woman in your life. You deserve some happiness. Someone to look after you."

Jack gave a conciliatory nod in Isabel's direction, eager to change the direction of the conversation. His eternal bachelorhood was not something he felt especially comfortable explaining over coffee. It was something he was more than content with himself, but for some reason others, usually women it had to be said, and well-meaning women at that, seemed to beg to differ. He deserved happiness apparently. And happiness it would seem could only be achieved with the company of another. But was he not happy? Did he not feel happiness in his outwardly solitary life?

I don't need mothering or looking after, thought Jack. I'm more than capable of ironing my own clothes and doing my own housework. He glanced down at the more than slightly crumpled suit trousers that he had on, together with the barely matching socks, and images of the pile of dirty dishes in his kitchen sink flashed through his mind. He hastily pushed the thoughts away and turned his attention to DS Cooper.

"Well Cooper here is tasting the single life once again, too." He nodded at his partner, hoping that at least one of them would take the hint and leave Jack's personal life out of the discussion. "He's the one you really need to watch."

"Oh, really," enquired Isabel, turning her attention away from Jack.

DS Cooper nodded. "Yeah, divorce finally came through. I've moved out of my parents' house and into my own place now. Plenty of room for the kids to come and stay."

"That's good. How old are they now?" Isabel got to her feet and began clearing away the empty coffee cups and now-empty plate of cookies. She had noticed two potential customers hovering outside, perusing the menu in the window. "I can't remember. You have two, don't you?"

"Yes, Thomas and Chloe. They're nine and seven now. Growing up fast."

"Well, it's nice that they're still local to you and they can come over and stay." Isabel moved back behind the serving counter. "Are you going to be taking them to any of the Olympic events? Are they into any of that?"

"Oh, don't get them started on the Olympics! They're obsessed." DS Cooper followed Jack's lead and got to his feet. "I blame the schools. It's all they ever talk about now. Thomas is really into cycling, so hopefully we'll get to go and watch something at the velodrome. And Chloe loves her swimming – so I'm hoping to buy a few tickets for that too."

The bell above the door jangled noisily, as the hovering customers stepped inside, clearly enticed by what they had seen on the menus outside.

"We'll leave you to it," said Jack, nodding towards the couple making themselves at home on one of the sofas. "We need to get back anyway. We have a new investigation to launch."

Isabel smiled at her new customers and gave a wave towards Jack and DS

Cooper as they departed. "See you both again soon. And don't leave it so long next time."

Jack returned the wave and stepped outside onto the street, closely followed by DS Cooper. Although it was still early, they could both feel the heat rising from the already-baked pavement underneath, the sun steadily rising into the now-cloudless sky – the early morning clouds having been scorched into oblivion as the temperatures began to soar. The heatwave that had begun some two months ago showed no signs of abating.

"Come on, Cooper." Jack began to stride quickly in the direction of his car, parked on a double yellow line outside the café. "We need to get back. This guy has killed twice now."

"Twice?" DS Cooper jogged to keep up with Jack, a frown forming on his brow. "What do you mean twice?"

"Our victim from this morning wasn't this killer's first - and unless I'm very much mistaken, she may not be his last."

* * *

# Chapter Two

Time: 10.30am

Date: Friday 20<sup>th</sup> July 2012

Location: A cellar in London

She thirstily gulped down the tepid, stale water, her throat dry and itchy from breathing in the musty, mouldy cellar air. She eyed the bowl of now-soggy cereal, but not even the painful hunger pangs that clenched her stomach could force her to eat the mushy brown lumps that had settled in the bowl. No longer snapping, crackling or popping, the sight made her feel nauseous.

She returned to the threadbare mattress, dragging the metal chain attached to her ankle in her wake, and resumed her position in the corner, hugging her knees tightly to her chest. Her body trembled beneath her touch, fear continuing to rush through her veins at agonising speed.

Was anybody looking for her?

Had anybody even realised she was missing?

They had to.

Surely they had to.

Surely someone would have realised something was wrong when she didn't turn up to collect Hope from her day nursery.

Hope.

Fresh tears brimmed as she thought about her daughter's wide, innocent eyes, her toothy grin, and her tiny button nose. Her happy gurgles and her tiny fists; the sweet smell of baby shampoo in her hair.

Not that it would have been the first time she hadn't shown up at nursery.

Maybe no one was out there looking for her. Maybe they all thought that she had just done a runner – like the last time. And the time before that.

She had had her last warning. Social services had told her in no uncertain terms – no more mistakes, Hannah. You must put Hope first. Her welfare must be your one and only priority. This is your last chance.

Your *very* last chance.

Even if she managed to get out of this god forsaken cellar, she was unlikely to see Hope again. As the memory of her daughter's face filled her consciousness, Hannah sank down beneath the stained blanket covering the mattress and sobbed.

* * *

Time: 10.30am
  Date: Friday 20<sup>th</sup> July 2012
  Location: Metropolitan Police HQ, London

Jack placed the plastic evidence bag containing the black stiletto shoe with the diamante buckle onto the table in the centre of the investigation room. DS Cooper and DC Cassidy both stood facing the whiteboard which now adorned the main wall.

"Patricia Gordon," stated Jack, turning his attention to the whiteboard too. A small photograph of an attractive brunette appeared in the top left hand side and, with a quick touch of the screen, this was followed by a series of known facts. "Age forty-five. Lived alone. Occupation – housekeeper. Smoker. No tattoos or body piercings. Birthplace – Worcester. Height – 1.70m. Weight – 75 kilos. Hair – brunette. Skin – fair. Distinguishing features – none. Date of death – 12<sup>th</sup> July 2012. Location of body – 13<sup>th</sup> July at St James's Park. Cause of death – strangulation."

Jack paused and looked at the series of bullet points that had materialised on the screen. Taking a marker pen from the table in front of him, he stepped up to the whiteboard and wrote in large capital letters above the first bullet point - VICTIM NO 1. Then he underlined it. Twice.

"Getting used to our new toy?" grinned DS Cooper, taking a step backwards towards the makeshift table behind him which was housing an array of assorted mugs, mostly chipped and unwashed, plus a hot water urn. He selected the cleanest of the mugs he could find, deposited a few teaspoons of ground coffee into each and filled them with hot water from the urn. The resultant murky, swirling liquid looked unappetising, with a greasy film on its surface – Isabel's hazelnut latte it was not.

Cooper placed the coffee mugs on the investigation table, and nodded towards the screen. "Good, isn't it? The way you can pull up all sorts of information from your computer, send it to the screen and add all sorts of other stuff, pictures and the like – and you can still write over the top of it with a marker pen. It's amazing."

Jack grunted and reached for one of the mugs. Amazing was not a word he would use for this new piece of high-tech equipment the Metropolitan Police had invested in. He glanced behind him at the far end of the investigation room, his gaze falling almost longingly on the now forgotten and apparently old-fashioned pin board. The board was now gathering dust in the corner, amongst a collection of boxes and broken chairs. He didn't share Cooper's enthusiasm for this latest piece of technical kit foisted on them by the Chief Superintendent. He longed to reach for a drawing pin and press it into the new whiteboard screen in defiance.

"So – Patricia Gordon. Definitely linked to the one found this morning then?" DS Cooper sniffed his coffee before taking a tentative mouthful. His gaze rested on the words written by Jack at the top of the screen.

Victim No 1

And underlined.

Twice.

"Without a doubt." With a sigh, Jack managed to tear his eyes away from the beloved pin board, and reached for the computer mouse. He clicked the whiteboard screen, the right hand side now populated with another series of bullet points. "The second body was discovered earlier this morning, and as yet we do not have a positive identification." Few details had made it to the screen, other than the date of discovery and location. Hair colour was documented as blonde. Age was estimated at twenty to twenty-five. The only photograph that was available was a head shot, hastily taken in the white tent earlier that morning; not a particularly pretty sight. Jack again picked up the marker pen and wrote "VICTIM NO 2" in large letters at the top of the screen.

"How can we be sure they're linked, boss?" DC Amanda Cassidy had been watching the screen intently, ignoring the mug of coffee DS Cooper had nudged in her direction. "There's quite an age gap between them. And we don't yet know the cause of death of the woman found today. I know they have both been found in parks, and parks that are close to each other, but the word on the grapevine is that the shoe found at the scene today didn't belong to either of them."

Jack nodded and turned his attention to the slightly-built DC perching herself on the corner of the investigation table. DC Cassidy was a useful addition to his team, someone he knew he could rely on to accurately assimilate the evidence and come up with credible arguments and theories. "That's entirely correct. We don't yet have much to go on for victim number two. But the crimes are definitely linked."

"How so?" persevered DC Cassidy.

"The shoe," replied Jack, simply, placing the marker pen back down on the investigation table. "The shoe."

"But we've just established that the shoe found today didn't belong to either of them." DC Cassidy reached forwards and picked up the plastic evidence bag containing the black stiletto with its diamante buckle.

"I don't mean *that* shoe." Jack reached forwards once again and clicked the computer mouse. "I mean *this* shoe."

Underneath the details for the first victim, Patricia Gordon, another picture flashed up onto the screen. Jack stepped forwards and tapped the whiteboard, the image instantly enlarging.

"This shoe was found seven metres away from Patricia Gordon's body in St James's Park. Initial DNA samples do not link the shoe with her. Also it wasn't her size." Jack paused while DS Cooper and DC Cassidy took in the enlarged picture of a single, flat, white, imitation-leather slip-on shoe. "This shoe has now been matched by the naked eye as being identical to the remaining shoe worn by our victim from this morning. DNA tests will obviously be carried out, but I am confident it will show that it belongs to our victim number two." He paused, casting a glance over at DS Cooper and DC Cassidy. "So, what does that tell us?"

"That the killer left the shoe of his *next* victim at Patricia Gordon's body site," replied DS Cooper, slowly nodding his head.

"And?" prodded Jack.

"And so, whoever killed Patricia Gordon also killed our Jane Doe from this morning," added DC Cassidy.

"Indeed it does. And that also means that we have ourselves a serial killer," confirmed Jack, taking the evidence bag out of DC Cassidy's hands.

"A serial killer?" DC Cassidy frowned.

"Yes, a serial killer," replied Jack, solemnly, turning the evidence bag over in his hands. "Because this shoe here belongs to his potential and, as-yet unknown, third victim."

\* \* \*

Time: 11.30am
Date: Friday 20th July 2012
Location: A cellar in London

Hannah heard his footsteps descending the damp, stone cellar steps before the sound of the grating key in the lock and the heavy oak door being pushed open. A thin chink of bright light opened up into the inky blackness, but she turned her head away and hid her eyes, not wanting to see his face, or his eyes. She especially didn't want to see his eyes.

She heard his footsteps echoing further into the cellar, his boots scraping over the roughly hewn cellar floor towards her. Shrinking further back into the musty corner, she crouched in a huddled ball on the thin mattress, hugging her knees tightly to her chest. She heard his knees creak as he bent down by her side, hearing the soft rasping of his breath as he edged closer, reaching out towards her. She stiffened, as she always did, for she knew what was coming next.

His touch sent rivers of ice coursing through her veins, her limbs trembling uncontrollably as she felt his fingers dance slowly along her forearms and up towards her shoulder. Fingers that were so light they barely touched her, but so terrifying that they felt as though her skin was burnt and scorched. She could taste the bile beginning to rise up into her throat.

"No need to be frightened, Jess." His fingers continued to stroke her shoulder, then moved spider-like up to smooth her hair and lightly caress her tear-stained cheek.

More uncontrollable shaking and retching caused her to shrink back even further into the dusty corner of the cellar, cobwebs clinging to her hands as she scraped fruitlessly at the walls – she would dig her way out if she had to, through stone, through concrete, through anything to get away.

"Sssshhh now, Jess," he continued, his voice barely more than a whisper. "Don't be scared. I've brought you something to eat. Can't have you going hungry now, can we?"

With a rush of relief, she felt his fingers leave her skin. The sound of rustling paper and something being placed on the mattress beside her made her turn her head slightly and open one eye cautiously. She saw him walking away, back towards the cellar door, leaving a sandwich in a paper bag and a bottle of water by her side.

After a few soft murmurings that Hannah couldn't quite hear, he disappeared back up the stone steps, pulling the heavy cellar door closed behind him, the sound of the key scraping in the lock echoing around the damp walls.

Hannah reached for the water bottle and drank, thirstily, not caring that water dribbled down her chin and onto her knees. She eyed the sandwich wrapper, but her stomach turned nauseously at the sight. She had no idea what time of day it was – or was it night? Time meant nothing anymore.

After draining the bottle dry, she dropped it back down onto the dusty floor, and thought, not for the first time - who was Jess?

* * *

Time: 12.45pm

Date: Friday 20th July 2012

Location: Metropolitan Police HQ, London

"Coffee?"

"No, thanks, Sir." Jack shook his head and let his eyes sweep around the Chief Superintendent's office. Although he had been in this room many times over the last four years, some for good reasons, some maybe not so, Jack couldn't help but see the body of Malcolm Liddell, the previous Chief Superintendent, slumped over his desk with half of his head missing.

Since Liddell's suicide and the media circus that ensued, the room had been gutted and redesigned – new carpets, new curtains, new plastering and new paint on the walls; a new desk and other office paraphernalia filled the space. Nothing of the old Chief Superintendent's reign remained – but still Jack couldn't stop the images of Liddell's body lying face down on the desk flooding his brain. Images culminating in the river of blood leading from the gunshot wound at Liddell's temple, down to a congealed pool on the floor beneath. Jack shivered once again at the memory.

Chief Superintendent Douglas "Dougie" King nodded towards the vacant chair opposite his desk, causing Jack to break his thoughts and take his seat as instructed. The Chief Superintendent's six foot four-inch frame lowered itself into a generously-sized leather swivel chair, the leather sighing as it took ownership of its new inhabitant. He reached behind to pour himself a mug of coffee from the sleek looking percolator gently humming on the sideboard. Jack mentally compared the shiny, state of the art coffee machine and its accompanying row of gleaming white coffee mugs, to the aged and spluttering hot water urn and collection of chipped mugs with dubious hygiene that could be found two floors below in his own department.

Bringing the mug back to his desk, Chief Superintendent King methodically stirred in two sweeteners and a dash of low fat milk. "Do we know who this morning's unfortunate victim is yet?" he asked, taking a sip of the coffee and wincing as the scalding liquid hit his lips.

Jack shook his head. "Not yet, Sir. No apparent identification on the body – forensics will swab for DNA and such like."

Chief Superintendent King nodded, bringing his fingers together and propping up his chin, thoughtfully.

"This needs to be wrapped up in record time, Jack, you know that."

Jack nodded, "Sir,"

"In seven days' time, we will have the eyes of the world upon us, watching our every move. The world and his wife is going to be descending on London for the Olympics. We can't be seen to have a serial killer on the loose in the city." The Chief Superintendent paused, and locked his gaze on Jack. "And you are sure we have a serial? No question?"

Jack shook his head once again. "No question in my mind, Sir. Both women are the victim of the same killer. Or killers. And we have another potential victim out there."

"Shit." The Chief Superintendent leant back in his chair and rubbed his eyes. "Shit. Shit. Shit."

Jack let a small smile cross his lips. He liked the new Chief Superintendent. "Dougie" King was a man of the people. He was a copper's copper. He hadn't had anything handed to him on a plate, or received promotion just because he went to the right school, wore the right tie, knew the right people or could perfect the correct handshake. He had earned his rise through the ranks by sheer hard work and being a damned fine policeman. The first black Chief Superintendent the force had ever seen. It was a well-deserved accolade, and most people were congratulatory. Most... but maybe not all.

"I need you to put your best officers on this one, Jack. Your best team. No holds barred. No expense spared. Whatever resources you need, you have them."

"What about the cut backs, Sir?" The Metropolitan Police had been hit hard by austerity measures just like every other force in the country. "The ban on overtime?"

"Sod the cutbacks, Jack. You have my word." Chief Superintendent King took another sip of his coffee and gave a half-hearted smile across the desk. "Find me the killer, Jack. Preferably before the Opening Ceremony."

Jack nodded and pushed himself up out of his chair. He had a feeling the meeting was at an end. As he turned to leave, Chief Superintendent King caught his eye. "One more thing, Jack. I've drafted in another pair of hands to assist. Tomorrow you will be joined by DS Carmichael from Sussex Police."

"Sir?" Jack hesitated, his hand reaching for the door handle. He turned and faced his superior officer with eyebrows raised, questioningly. "My team is more than capable....."

"I know," cut in Chief Superintendent King, raising a hand in solidarity. "I know. It's just an extra pair of hands; an extra brain cell or two. Orders from above." He motioned skywards with his eyes, meaning the order had come from his own superiors.

Jack nodded. "Sir." He turned to leave and give the good news to his team. Following him out of the door and into the corridor were the departing words of the Chief Superintendent.

"You've got seven days to find me this man, Jack. Whatever it takes. Seven days."

\* \* \*

# Chapter Three

Time: 1.45pm
Date: Friday 20<sup>th</sup> July 2012
Location: Isabel's Café, King's Road, London

As the bell above the door jangled with the last departing customer, Isabel sighed and flopped down into one of the armchairs. It had been an extremely busy lunchtime, and she secretly wished she had asked Dominic to stay on. Her last customers had brought a smile to her face, however - Don and Jean from Illinois. The two Americans had breezed in, dressed in their matching "I love London" t-shirts and Bermuda shorts, baseball caps pulled down firmly over their heads, and cameras swinging from their necks.

Isabel had served them her best cappuccinos, with a large slab of Sacha's homemade chocolate fudge cake – which judging by the expressions on her new customers' faces, had gone down a treat. Having only just arrived in London the previous evening, Don and Jean immediately started asking Isabel about where they should visit during their three week stay. Isabel had trotted out the usual suggestions – the London Eye, Trafalgar Square, Big Ben, Buckingham Palace, London Zoo, the Changing of the Guard. Although here primarily for the Olympics, Don and Jean quickly began to pore over their London A-Z tourist guide in between polishing off another serving of fudge cake.

As they got up from the sofa, leaving a hefty tip under one of their napkins, they asked Isabel if they would get to see the Queen if they visited Buckingham Palace. Isabel smiled as she took away their empty coffee cups and plates – assuring them that if the flag was flying at the Palace, then the Queen was at home, and who knows what they might see? Don and Jean quickly gathered up their belongings and bade Isabel a cheery goodbye, chattering constantly about their chances of seeing the real Queen of England as they stepped out into the heat of the afternoon sun.

Sighing once more, Isabel pushed herself up onto her feet, knowing that she only had a brief lull before the café would be filling up again. Somehow she had managed to cope alone with the steady stream of customers wanting their mid-morning and lunchtime caffeine hit, and the empty display cases on the counter proved just how popular her cakes and pastries were becoming.

Taking a dustpan and brush, she quickly swept the crumbs out of the display cases, ready for the fresh batch that she was about to place in the oven. If Dominic were here, he would have the ovens humming already, she mused, smiling to herself as she worked. With the counter now crumb-free, Isabel stepped back into the kitchen and selected some fresh trays of sausage rolls, Danish pastries and cookies, and pushed them into the waiting ovens. Setting the timer so that she didn't forget about them, she returned to the café and began straightening the tables and plumping the cushions.

Stepping briefly outside, she straightened the menu board on the pavement, shielding her eyes from the glaring sun as she did so. It was another scorching day, with not a cloud in the sky. She could almost feel the heat radiating from the ground through the soles of her shoes. Anticipating a run on cold drinks later, Isabel returned inside to make sure the milkshake and frappe glasses were lined up in readiness.

As she closed the front door to block out the heat of the day, she felt something brush past her legs. She smiled as she looked down to see Livi, her beloved tabby cat, winding herself around her ankles and brushing her head against her skin.

"Come on, Livi," she laughed. "Let's get you some milk. It's too hot for you outside today. Let's get you upstairs before the afternoon rush starts.

\* \* \*

Time: 3.15pm
 Date: Friday 20th July 2012
 Location: Metropolitan Police HQ, London

With the investigation room now set up as he wanted, Jack eased himself back into his chair. DC Cassidy had managed to commandeer two floor fans from somewhere, and both were now whirring away on their highest setting – but despite this, the room still felt warm and stuffy. Two more computers had been brought in, plus a printer – they were ready to go.

"I've linked everything from the Patricia Gordon investigation, boss," said DS Cooper, clicking the mouse and bringing up a series of files onto the whiteboard screen. "Everything recorded so far, plus the post mortem report."

"Good work, Cooper," replied Jack. "Both investigations are now going to be run from this room. We need to set out our initial strategy and get the preliminaries underway. We will need to look at everything in the Patricia Gordon case with a fresh set of eyes."

DC Cassidy sat down next to Jack and opened up her notebook. "What's first up then, guv?"

"A priority needs to be analysing the phone records." Jack nodded for DC Cassidy to start taking notes. "I'm sure this has already been done for Patricia Gordon, but we need to double check. Once we have an ID for the body found this morning, we will need to access any phone records for her too. Focus on the weeks leading up to both their disappearances." Jack paused, mentally going through the checklist he had constructed in his head. "Then we need to access any CCTV. Check what CCTV has been gone through already for Patricia Gordon. And then go through it again. We need images around both St James's Park and Hyde Park. Check what cameras we have in both locations."

DC Cassidy nodded as she made bullet point entries in her notebook.

"And check the system for any known recently-released prisoners that flag up as a cause for concern. It's a long shot, but it's worth checking." Jack got to his feet. "I'm going to go and see if I can get hold of Dr Matthews – see when he's likely to get the post mortem done for the body found this morning. For the rest of the afternoon, I want both of you to familiarise yourselves with the Patricia Gordon case – you need to know it backwards. We'll meet bright and early at seven AM tomorrow – with a full briefing at ten."

"Boss." DS Cooper immediately began pulling up the files relating to Patricia Gordon.

For now, all they could do now was wait for a positive identification on the second victim.

Jack stepped out into the corridor and felt the temperature rise several degrees. He headed back to his office with the sole intention of ignoring the ever-growing pile of paperwork that he knew would be there. He needed to focus on Dr Matthews. Entering the office, he headed across to his desk and picked up the telephone receiver, which was miraculously still visible in amongst the towering files and folders. As he dialled the mortuary number, his mind couldn't help but wander towards the new DS that was arriving tomorrow. An extra pair of hands was always welcome, but Jack couldn't quell the sense of disquiet that was settling in his stomach.

\* \* \*

Time: 3.10pm
Date: Friday 15th May 1998
Location: Arundel, West Sussex

He had parked on the opposite side of the road, fifty metres away from the main entrance. She wouldn't be expecting him to be there, so he was quite sure she wouldn't notice him.

He looked at his watch.

She was late.

Drumming his fingers against the steering wheel, he kept his eyes trained on the main front doors.

Come on, Carol. You finished work ten minutes ago. What are you doing?

Yes, Carol. *What* are you doing?

He could feel the anger welling up inside him already, like a carefully stoked fire, blazing away in the depths of his stomach. It was becoming a familiar feeling, this anger; this fire. He steadied his breathing in an effort to quell the flames.

Stay calm, he muttered to himself. Stay calm for Jess.

He glanced at his watch again and grimaced. He needed to leave soon if he was going to get across town in time to pick up Jess from school.

Five more minutes.

He would give Carol five more minutes.

He tapped the steering wheel, rhythmically, as if counting down the seconds one by one. The street was quiet, with not a lot of through traffic, so he had an uninterrupted view of the main entrance.

The entrance Carol should have walked through fifteen minutes ago.

He felt the anger building once again.

He needed to go. Jess would be waiting.

He turned the key in the ignition, the roar of the engine matching the anger growling inside him.

And then he saw her.

Carol.

And Brian.

Carol and Brian, leaving work together with smiles on their faces; their shoulders touching briefly as they both squeezed through the door at the same time.

He thrust the car into first gear and stepped heavily on the accelerator.

He had seen all he needed to see.

\* \* \*

# Chapter Four

Time: 9.00pm
  Date: Friday 20<sup>th</sup> July 2012
  Location: Kettle's Yard Mews, London

Jack dropped the empty Indian takeaway cartons into the sink, and pulled another chilled bottle of Budweiser from the fridge. He eyed the black bin liner sitting by the door, waiting to be taken down to the communal bins in the narrow alleyway behind the row of mews houses. A black bin liner full of the remnants of his bachelor existence – an unhealthy abundance of foil takeaway cartons, empty pizza boxes, crushed beer cans and the odd hamburger wrapper.

Although Stuart was to blame for a fair proportion of it.

He ran a hand through his hair and across his chin. He would shower and shave before bed. History told him, and everyone around him, that Jack was not a morning person. Leaving ritualistic tasks such as that to the hours following yet another fitful night's sleep, if you could even call it that, would be a fool's errand.

His last therapist had told him about the importance of routines. To get into the habit of the early morning shower, the early morning shave, the early morning jog before work. She had lasted just the one session, and Jack had not been back. That had been three years ago. He didn't need lectures on routines and time keeping. He could tell the time. He could plan his day. He wasn't a child.

But what he couldn't plan for were the nights spent searching for elusive sleep. Sleep that teased him, pretending to be within reach, within his grasp, only to slip mischievously out of sight night after night.

After night.

Jack eased himself down into the comfort of the sofa and took another mouthful of ice cold beer, savouring the coolness as it slid down his throat.

Alcohol was another thing the therapist advised against. Probably another reason Jack didn't go back. Sometimes alcohol, rightly or wrongly, was his only saviour in the midst of another sleep-deprived night.

At least he was trying to stay away from the hard stuff these days. Jack glanced down at the almost full bottle of single malt standing, forlornly, by the side of the coffee table. Within reach, but out of bounds.

For now.

A brief hint of a breeze rippled into the room from the open window opposite. The air outside was quiet and still, the temperature slowly cooling down as the sun dipped lower and lower in the evening sky. Although there were dozens of people living in the streets outside his flat, Jack could hear nothing, nothing at all. It was as if all life had been extinguished and he was the lone survivor in some post-apocalyptic world. The heat made people retreat into their houses, the streets emptying after the end of the working day. Everyone was too lethargic to move far. Of course, the bars and restaurants in the West End and other trendy night spots would be full to bursting with shiny-cheeked, sunburnt faces; but here in the quieter neighbourhoods you could hear the proverbial pin drop outside. There was nothing and no one to disturb the sultry slumber of the evening air.

A sharp beep cut through the silence, making Jack flinch and tighten his grip on his almost empty beer bottle. He reached across to his jacket, which he had slung across the back of the sofa as soon as he had arrived home, fishing out his mobile phone.

A reminder from his appointment calendar.

8.30am Saturday 21st July.

Dr Evelyn Riches.

Psychotherapist.

Jack grimaced and drained his bottle.

* * *

Time: 10.00pm
  Date: Friday 20<sup>th</sup> July 2012
  Location: A cellar in London

Hannah stirred at the sound of scraping. Her eyes flickered open, struggling to focus in the darkness that surrounded her. She could feel her heart thumping faster and faster in her chest; the sound of her blood whooshing as it raced through her veins.

Was he here?

Had he come back while she had been sleeping?

Hannah's stomach tightened in fear, her skin feeling cold and clammy underneath the scratchy blanket. She squinted again through the darkness, but couldn't find any shapes to focus on. She felt tired and groggy, her eyes heavy as though made of lead.

Maybe it was rats.

She shivered beneath the blanket at the thought. Rats. Rats scurrying across the stone floor, nibbling and biting at everything in their path, their claws scraping over the concrete.

Hannah drew her legs up towards her chest at the thought of rats nibbling at her exposed toes.

And then she heard it again.

Scraping.

As the fog in her mind began to lift a little, she realised what it must be. It was just the chain attached to her ankle scraping across the floor as she moved. She reached down and ran a quivering finger around the cold metal clasp – feeling her skin chafed and sore beneath. Pulling at the chain only made it feel tighter.

A tear trickled down her cheek as she closed her eyes and thought of Hope.

* * *

Time: 8.00pm
  Date: Friday 15<sup>th</sup> May 1998
  Location: Arundel, West Sussex

Jess had been waiting for him outside the school gates. He had mustered a smile for her, pushing the anger he really felt beneath the surface as he listened to her chattering about her day and what homework she needed to do that night.

The evening at home had been tense. Carol had acted as though nothing was wrong. Cooking their dinner as usual, quietly humming to herself as she stirred the bolognese on the hob. It took all of his restraint and resolve not to confront her there and then. But he had to think of Jess.

Jess mustn't see.

Jess must never see.

But now Jess was up in her bedroom, no doubt oblivious to the world around her with her headphones clamped to her ears while she listened to some rock group or other.

Now it was just them.

Now it was just the two of them – alone.

Carol had some questions to answer.

* * *

Time: 10.01pm
 Date: 5<sup>th</sup> April 1971
 Location: Old Mill Road, Christchurch

The kitchen window was cracked in several places, and the hinges didn't quite fit – so the howling wind outside was able to rush inside, unguarded and unchallenged. Angry raindrops pelted against the glass, accompanied by the occasional flash of lightning and deep rumble of thunder.

Whether it was the surge of wind that flooded through the chilled air of the kitchen, or some other unseen force, Jack looked up from where he had been crouching and watched as his mother's body swung to and fro above him. Her arms hung limply by her sides, brushing against her nightdress as it billowed in the arctic breeze.

The creaking of the light fixing, as it took the strain of her thin frame, echoed eerily in time with the rhythm of the wailing wind. Creaking backwards and forwards. Backwards and forwards.

Creaking.

Creaking.

Creaking.


\* \* \*


Time: 10.35pm
 Date: Friday 20<sup>th</sup> July 2012
 Location: Kettle's Yard Mews, London

Jack woke with a start, his body jolted as if by an invisible bolt of electricity. The light summer breeze outside had strengthened a little, enough to cause the blinds across the small window in the kitchen to rustle and creak.

Creak.

Jack shuddered, instantly feeling a chill wash over him despite the clammy heat of the day still clinging to the air. A quick glance at the window confirmed it was dark outside. He must have fallen asleep on the sofa – again. As he sat there, blinking rapidly to clear his head, the blinds began rattling and creaking once again.

Rattling.

Creaking.

He got to his feet, collecting the three empty beer bottles from the coffee table, and crossed the room to snap the kitchen window shut.

He could do without the creaking tonight.

Tossing the empty bottles into the sink to join the remnants of the earlier Indian takeaway, Jack returned to the sofa, sweeping up his phone as he passed.

He looked again at his calendar.

8.30am.

Dr Evelyn Riches.

Rubbing methodically at his temples, he wondered if Dr Riches knew what she was taking on. This would be his third, maybe fourth, therapist in as many years; he had lost count. He rarely made it past the first session, but both Stuart and the Chief Superintendent had been persuasive enough to talk him into trying again.

One last time.

Jack picked up the business card that had been sat on the coffee table. It had been over six months ago that the Chief Superintendent had pressed the card into his hand and given him a knowing look.

"Just try it, Jack. For your own sake."

Jack had, dutifully, nodded and pocketed the business card – but in true Jack MacIntosh style had done nothing about it. It wasn't until Isabel had returned from her travels around the USA and Europe, full of enthusiasm for her next venture, the next chapter of her life, that Jack had stopped and had a cold, hard look at himself. After unimaginable trauma, Isabel had managed to turn her life around.

So why couldn't he?

So Jack had taken the business card for Dr Evelyn Riches, Psychotherapist, out of the drawer where it had been unceremoniously discarded, and made the call.

8.30am.

Dr Evelyn Riches.

Tomorrow.

* * *

Time: 10.45pm

Date: Friday 10<sup>th</sup> May 1998

Location: Arundel, West Sussex

The evening had progressed in silence. Carol had taken a shower and washed her hair, then caught up with one of her favourite soaps on the TV. He had sat in the corner of the front room watching her towel dry her hair, noticing how she occasionally looked at her phone as she did so. Although she had put her phone on silent, he could see the screen light up from time to time with what looked like an incoming message.

And not just one message.

There seemed to be several, one after the other.

Brian.

It had to be.

Carol was flaunting it right in front of his eyes, and the expression on her face proved that she didn't even seem to care.

They were now standing together in the kitchen. Carol had begun the washing up, sliding the pile of plates, splattered with remnants of bolognese sauce, into the bowl of hot, soapy water. He watched from the doorway as she began squeezing and wiping the sponge over the dishes, her hands dipping underneath the foaming bubbles.

Her hands.

He had always loved her hands.

"You could come and help rather than just standing there staring at me

– it's creepy." Carol flashed him a look as she stacked a plate onto the draining board. "Here, start drying." She picked up a tea towel and threw it across the kitchen.

He caught the tea towel with a snatch of his hand, but remained motionless in the doorway. He continued to watch as she dropped a saucepan into the water and began to scrub the sides. He glanced at the pile of crockery at the side of the sink, still waiting to be washed. One more dinner plate, a chopping board, and Jess's glass with remnants of her strawberry milkshake still in the bottom. Two wine glasses rested by the side – glasses that he and Carol had sipped from, the alcohol having done nothing to thaw the chilled air between them.

His gaze then came to rest on a large bread knife Carol had used to slice up the fresh French baguette that had accompanied their spaghetti bolognese. He had sharpened it especially beforehand, honing the blade so it glided effortlessly through the crispy crust of the bread.

He liked the feel of it in his hand; the way it made him feel centred and in control. Not taking his eyes from the knife, he took a step towards the sink, feeling the invisible pull of the blade. Twisting the tea towel in his hands, he silently crossed the kitchen floor until he was standing close to Carol's shoulder. He noticed that she was wearing a thin-strapped vest top, which exposed the pale skin of her delicate neck.

Such an exquisite neck, he mused. Like a swan – a very elegant swan.

Carol had picked up the bread knife and was carefully washing it free of breadcrumbs, leaving it on the draining board when she was done. The metal gleamed in the low-level lighting of the kitchen. Unconsciously, he felt his hand reaching out towards the knife, eager to feel its power within his grasp.

Images of Brian and his wife danced at the edges of his vision. It made his fingers twitch.

It would be so easy.

So easy to bring an end to it all.

He felt his fingers stretch out towards the blade, drawn to it like a magnet.

It would be very quick – one slice and it could all be brought to an end.

So very quick; and so very easy.

Suddenly, a figure appeared behind him in the kitchen doorway.

"Have we got any lemonade?"

Jess.

His hand recoiled from the knife and he plastered a smile on his face as he turned towards her. "Of course – in the fridge." He glanced towards Carol who was rinsing a selection of spoons. "I'm just helping your mother with the washing up."

With one last look at the bread knife, he reached for a plate and began to wipe the tea towel over its surface, sighing as the opportunity disappeared along with the soap suds.

* * *

# Chapter Five

Time: 6.30am

Date: Saturday 21st July 2012

Location: Metropolitan Police HQ, London

Jack picked up the envelope that only minutes before had landed on his desk. Dr Philip Matthews had been true to his word and produced his post mortem report in his trusted expedient fashion, couriering the final version over to Jack's office not long after daybreak. Although the same copy would have been sent by email, Dr Matthews was a traditionalist.

Jack sliced the envelope open with his finger, full of admiration for the dry-witted pathologist who must have spent much of his Friday evening dictating and then typing his own report, and then ensuring it was biked over in time for Jack's early morning arrival.

He quickly skimmed through the preliminary description at the beginning of the report, briefly looking up and nodding at DS Cooper who had entered the office bearing two mugs of coffee and what appeared to be a paper bag with something greasy inside.

"Is that the post mortem report on our Jane Doe from yesterday?" DS Cooper nudged aside some scattered paperwork and files that littered Jack's desk to find a suitable space to deposit his coffee mug. "Anything useful?"

Jack silently nodded, flicking the report over to scan down to the conclusions at the very end. He reached for his coffee mug and took a long sip before replying. "Cause of death, strangulation. As we suspected." He paused and took another sip of coffee. "Superficial injuries to the left ankle, suggestive of some sort of restraint."

"Tied up?"

"Looks that way."

DS Cooper perched himself on the side of Jack's desk, leaning over to take a look at the pathologist's report. He waved the greasy paper bag in Jack's direction. "Fancy half of my bacon sarnie?"

Jack shook his head and held up a hand. "I think I'll pass, thanks." He turned his attention back to the post mortem report, re-reading the conclusions at the final paragraph. Although his stomach was growling at him, reminding him that he had yet to eat anything this morning, reading these "death reports" as they were sometimes colloquially known amongst the team, always managed to dampen down his appetite. "No signs of sexual assault."

DS Cooper nodded while taking a large bite out of his sandwich, a thick globule of tomato sauce dripping from between the thickly cut bread slices and landing on Jack's desk. Or more precisely on the envelope that had housed the post mortem report.

"Go and make a mess of your own desk." Jack flapped his hands towards the desk opposite. "We have a visitor coming this morning."

"Ah yes, the infamous DS Carmichael." DS Cooper hopped off Jack's desk and returned to his own chair, resuming the devouring of his sandwich. "Remind me, why are we being landed with him?"

Jack shrugged. "Who knows? Officially, it's to give us extra support in this investigation – orders from up on high, apparently." Jack raised his eyes to the heavens, and the offices above them. "But who knows what the real reason is. All I've been told is that we have to play nicely." Jack paused and watched DS Cooper push the final wedge of sandwich into his mouth. "And don't speak with your mouth full."

\* \* \*

Time: 6.30am
Date: Saturday 21st July 2012
Location: Isabel's Café, King's Road, London

Open.

Isabel smiled as she flipped the sign over and tugged the door towards her. Stepping out briefly onto the wide pavement, she closed her eyes and took in a deep breath. It was a glorious morning, the sky already clear and bright. Only a slight breeze tickled her face as she turned her head upwards to feel the gentle warmth of the early morning rays.

Traffic was already slowly filling the streets around Isabel's, as the city came to life. One of the reasons she had decided to open her café this early was to catch the early morning commuters as they hurried past, stopping off for their double espresso, skinny latte or flavoursome cappuccino with extra chocolate on their way to start their day.

The tantalising smell of freshly baked croissants, pastries and breads filled her nostrils as she turned back inside and closed the door behind her. Although it meant getting up while it was still dark to put the ovens on and create her own masterpieces, Isabel wouldn't change her life for the world. With a small flat upstairs over the café, she felt, for the first time in a long while, settled. Putting behind her the events of four years ago had been a struggle at times, but she finally felt at peace with the world and ready to begin life once again.

As she turned to head into the kitchen, she heard the familiar tinkle of the bell over the door announcing her first visitor of the day.

She knew exactly who it would be.

"Morning, Dominic," she greeted, without turning round. "I'm just getting the pastries out of the oven."

Dominic, smartly dressed in dark blue jeans and a white polo shirt, headed straight through to the kitchen, picking up his apron and deftly tying the strings around his small waist. He turned towards the kitchen sink and deposited exactly three squirts of antibacterial hand wash into the palms of his hands and began to rub vigorously. Switching on the hot tap he continued to scrub his hands and nails for exactly sixty seconds. Isabel smiled in his direction before turning her attention to the front counter, placing a fresh supply of paper napkins, knives, forks and spoons within her customers' reach.

With the morning ritual complete, Dominic dried his hands on a disposable piece of kitchen towel, before turning his attention to the two ovens. Expertly donning a pair of freshly laundered oven gloves, he opened the oven doors and began extracting the sensuous delicacies that had been browning inside.

Although Isabel bought in some ready-made goodies for sale in the café, she would also hand bake a selection of treats for her customers each day. And it was Dominic's job to ensure that the first batch of early-morning pastries were ready for her first customers of the day. With Dominic's mother also supplying homemade cakes and biscuits, Isabel's café was fast attracting an excellent reputation.

Bringing the first tray of freshly baked sausage rolls and croissants through to the front counter, Dominic slid the tasty treats into the display case. Turning back to the kitchen, he hurried back to collect the second tray. Isabel arranged the baked goods inside the heated display case to entice and tempt her early morning customers. As if on cue, the bell over the door tinkled once again.

"Morning, Isabel," greeted Angus, Isabel's regular 6.45am customer. Every morning, without fail, except for Sundays and Bank Holidays, Angus McBride would stop by for his regular white coffee with two sugars and a sausage roll. His deep, gravelly, coarse-sounding Glaswegian accent masked a gentle soul beneath. A broad smile split the greying beard that hugged his chin, and deep, cavernous laughter lines caressed the edges of his twinkling grey eyes. "It's a lovely day." He swung the heavy Royal Mail post bag from his shoulder, letting it drop by his feet while he reached into his pocket for some change.

"Morning, Angus," replied Isabel, slipping the freshly baked sausage roll into its greaseproof paper bag and passing it across the counter to join the takeaway coffee cup already standing there. "All ready to go."

"Ach, you're a sweet girl, Isabel." Angus dropped his change onto the counter and swept up the coffee cup, taking a quick sip. "Hits the spot every time, hen. Best coffee in toon." Although Isabel's coffee menu listed all manner of exotic choices, from lattes to espressos, cappuccinos to mochas, Americanos to a macchiato, Angus's choice was always - "Just a coffee, hen. Nothing fancy." Turning his nose up at all the different flavours and fanciful syrups on offer - crinkling his nose and frowning at the "sheer nonsense, hen, it's just coffee," - Isabel would have his ordinary white coffee and two sugars - "white sugar, hen, none of that brown nonsense" - ready for his 6.45am call.

"See you Monday, Angus," smiled Isabel, scooping up the change. "Have a good day."

"Aye, you too, hen." With that, Angus hauled the Royal Mail post bag high up onto his shoulder, and after picking up the greaseproof bag housing his sausage roll, he turned with a wink and disappeared out into the street.

The departure of Angus always heralded the start of the breakfast rush. For the next two hours Isabel would be rushed off her feet fulfilling orders that came thick and fast. The coffee machine would be humming and spouting steam constantly as office workers, taxi drivers, shop workers and yummy mummies on their way to nursery stopped by for their caffeine fix. With a lucrative spot just around the corner from Sloane Square, Isabel benefited from the high-end, up-market shops and businesses that stretched along the Kings Road. With Isabel at the front of the café serving, Dominic would be working hard behind the scenes keeping a regular supply of freshly baked goods coming.

At just after nine, Isabel slipped herself onto one of the bar stools by the counter and let herself inhale the aroma from the mug of steaming Americano coffee she had poured for herself.

The lull.

For the next hour, the steady stream of customers would reduce to a mere trickle, and Isabel could afford to take the luxury of a quick break before the mid-morning tea break brigade would descend.

"Dom?" Isabel sipped her coffee and eyed a buttery croissant in the display case in front of her. "Come and get yourself a drink and take a break."

Dominic's head dutifully popped through the archway that led to the small kitchen area behind the counter. "In a minute. I'm just finishing up."

Isabel smiled and nodded, her resolve finally faltering as she reached into the display case and extracted the still warm pastry. Slipping it onto a paper napkin she broke off a section of the crumbling, flaky pastry and popped it into her mouth. She knew Dominic would be recounting his morning activities in his notebook, recording exactly how many croissants, pain au chocolat, Danish pastries and sausage rolls he had supplied to the front counter. Isabel popped another morsel of fresh croissant into her mouth and smiled again. Better than any accountant, Dominic was the most wonderful addition to her enterprise.

"Thirty-two sausage rolls, fifty-five croissants, thirty-five pain au chocolat, but only eleven Danish pastries so far." Dominic appeared behind the serving counter, replacing his notebook in his back pocket. "Last Monday we had done eighteen Danish pastries by now. But not as many sausage rolls."

Isabel pulled off another tantalising corner of croissant and popped it into her mouth, smiling as she chewed. "Well I'm not sure I would want a Danish pastry for my breakfast either...more of a mid-afternoon treat that one."

Just then the bell tinkled over the door, announcing another customer arrival. Isabel swivelled on the bar stool, ready to greet her visitor. But when her gaze registered on the slightly built figure backing in through the doorway, struggling with two over-sized canvases, one under each arm, she beamed.

"Patrick, let me help you!" She jumped off the stool and strode over to the front door, holding it open with one hand and taking one of the awkward, heavy canvases with the other.

"Thank you, Isabel. Much appreciated." Patrick Mansfield stepped through the doorway and into the café, slightly out of breath from his exertions. He leant the remaining canvas that he had under his arm up against one of the sofas, and from his other shoulder he let a large, canvas rucksack swing to the floor. "I'd forgotten quite how far it was on the tube." Still panting a little, he took a hand to brush away the fringe that had flopped across his forehead, his bright emerald green eyes twinkling as he smiled at Isabel.

"You took these on the tube?!" Isabel raised her eyebrows at the enormous canvases. "Are you mad? I bet you were popular."

Patrick grinned, and gave a small shrug of his slightly built shoulders. "What can I say? Mad artist, guilty as charged. I didn't think it would be that busy, this time of the morning on a Saturday."

Isabel chuckled, picking up one of the canvases and making her way towards the back of the café and out into the artist's studio. "Patrick, this is London. It's always busy!"

Following on behind with the other canvas and rucksack, Patrick grunted, ruefully. "Next time I'll get a taxi. Honestly, you should have seen some of the looks people gave me when I tried getting into a carriage with this lot."

"And what is "this lot", exactly?" enquired Isabel, leaning a canvas up against the art table in the centre of the studio. "What are you up to?"

"It's a commission." Patrick deposited the rucksack at his feet and leant the second canvas up against the first. "Local advertising agency liked my work, and have asked me to design them something for their brand new offices, something for their front reception area. Big, they said." Patrick nodded at the canvases. "So, I've gone big."

As the resident artist at the café, Patrick Mansfield paid Isabel a weekly sum to rent the studio space at the rear. Some of his paintings adorned the walls of the café and were up for sale, others he exhibited at local independent art galleries to eke out a living. Arriving on Isabel's doorstep three months ago, dressed in cut-off denim shorts and sandy espadrilles despite it being a chilly April, Isabel immediately warmed to the softly spoken, unassuming artistic character that later introduced himself to her as Patrick Mansfield, travelling artisan. In his early forties, Isabel guessed – although he was always vague about his actual birth date – "age is just a number my dear" – he had the longest fingers Isabel had ever seen, long and exquisitely elegant, with perfectly manicured fingernails. Originally only calling in for a cup of Earl Grey to take away, once Patrick had seen the studio at the rear of the café he had immediately offered to rent the space. And with the rent so high along the prestigious Kings Road for her newly opened café, Isabel had accepted immediately.

And so, along with Dominic, Patrick had become one of the family.

"What's the theme?" asked Isabel, nodding once again at the canvases. "For the commission."

"Apparently I have full artistic licence." Patrick raised his fair coloured eyebrows.

"How dangerous!" laughed Isabel. "They obviously don't know you very well!"

"Indeed. All I have to do is make sure it reflects their company ideology – "Innovation. Inspiration. Ideation.""

"Well, good luck with that one! I'm just having a coffee before the mid-morning rush. Tea?"

Patrick flashed Isabel a warming smile. "An Earl Grey would be perfect." He shrugged off the light jacket he had been wearing and sat down at the artist's table, eyeing the canvases as he did so. With a frown, he reached for a sketchpad and pencil. "I guess I had better start getting some inspiration while I have an hour or so to spare."

\* \* \*

Time: 8.35am

Date: Saturday 21st July 2012

Location: St James's University, London

"Now, Jack, before we start I will just ask a few questions about yourself, so I can get a feel as to the best approach to your first session."

Dr Evelyn Riches, Consultant Psychotherapist, sat back in her leather chair and studied Jack with a pleasant, relaxed smile. "It's nothing to be worried about." Her voice was calming and reassuring. "Tell me what you like to do, what makes you feel happy?"

Jack looked up and stared blankly back at Dr Riches. What makes me happy? Jack tried to think back to the last time he had felt happy. When had that been? Could he remember? His mind whirred incessantly, searching and searching for even the faintest indication of a time when he had felt happiness, true happiness, but it failed to connect to anything.

Have I really never been happy?

Jack fidgeted in his seat.

"Don't worry," smiled Dr Riches. "Everyone finds that question hard to answer. Try thinking about something you enjoy doing."

Again Jack felt his brain whirring, the cogs turning faster and faster as they searched for another elusive answer.

What do I enjoy doing?

Jack felt a frown darken his brow. Do I actually enjoy anything?

Work.

I enjoy my work.

"Work," Jack heard himself say, his voice sounding disconnected. "I enjoy my work." He looked up and met the gaze of Dr Riches, allowing himself a sheepish smile. "I guess that sounds very sad."

"Not at all, Jack." She rewarded him with another smile. "Not at all. If your work wasn't important to you then you wouldn't be here. Let's try and focus on somewhere that makes you feel safe. Can you close your eyes for me and think about where you feel at your safest? Where nothing can hurt you. Where do you feel safe, Jack? Think back to happy times – holidays, time spent with family and friends."

Jack closed his eyes, and sank back into the soft armchair.

Where do I feel safe?

Jack let his mind wander.

But he felt the same void building inside his head.

Where do I feel safe?

Dr Riches' words echoed inside his head. "Think back to happy times –

holidays, time spent with family and friends."

Jack didn't go on holiday.

He didn't like beaches.

He didn't like the sand.

And wasn't keen on lakes, forests or the outdoors either.

He couldn't swim.

And he didn't have anyone special in his life.

No wonder.

There was only one place that he felt safe.

"Old Mill Road in Christchurch." The words had escaped Jack's mouth before they had registered in his brain. "When I was four."

"OK, Jack. This place will be your safe place. Is there a particular room there where you felt happiest?"

Jack's mind transported him back in time – back to Old Mill Road. The flat had several rooms. He had a bedroom he shared with Stuart. Their mother had her own room, next to the bathroom. There was a large living room plus a smaller box like room filled with junk.

But there was only one room that he really remembered.

The room he would never be able to forget.

The kitchen.

The kitchen where he had found his mother's lifeless body.

"The kitchen," Jack heard himself say, his voice sounding small. Quite why he had said that, he wasn't sure, but the words had escaped his lips before his brain had a chance to catch up. Before he could give it any more thought, Dr Riches moved on.

"Ok, so that will be your safe place, Jack. A place where nothing can ever hurt you." Dr Riches consulted the brief notes in front of her and then continued, her voice taking on a measured and lyrical tone. "I want you to relax now, relax every bone and every muscle in your body. Starting at the top, from your head and neck, down through your shoulders, across each arm and down to your hands and fingers. Feel your muscles relax, feel how weightless you are."

Jack allowed himself to sink further backwards into the armchair, feeling it pulling him in, inviting him to sink further and further. He felt his neck and shoulders relieve their pent- up tension, felt his arms sag as their weight evaporated.

"Good. Feel the muscles in your chest and abdomen relax, spreading out down each thigh, across each knee and down towards your feet and toes. You feel so relaxed now, Jack. Every muscle in your body is slack."

At Dr Riches' suggestion, Jack felt all tension in his body subsiding. His body felt instantly lighter, as if he were weightless and floating in the breeze. He couldn't hear anything. There was no sound at all. Nothing except the rhythmical, soothing tones of Dr Riches, floating in the nothingness.

"Now, Jack, I want you to imagine you are descending a staircase. There are ten steps. There is a rail on one side to hold onto. You are descending slowly, slowly, slowly - taking one step at a time. With each step you take your body feels even more relaxed; with each step you take, you are one step closer to your safe place."

Jack found he could see a staircase in his mind; he moved instinctively towards it, feeling himself gliding weightlessly through the air.

"You are at the top of the stairs, Jack. Taking your first step. Down you go. Nine. Your body is feeling lighter, Jack; your safe place is getting closer. Eight. Slowly, down you go. Control your breathing with every step; breathe in, and then breathe out. Feel your lungs inflate with every breath. Seven. One more step - further towards your safe place. You feel even more relaxed, now, Jack. Six. Keep breathing. In and then out. In and then out. Five. Halfway there, Jack. Keep going. One more step. Four."

Jack's chest rose and fell steadily. With each breath he felt lighter, with each breath his muscles felt as though they were no longer attached to his body. His body had no weight at all; he was floating gently within his own mind.

"That's it, Jack. One more step. Three. Nearly there now, Jack. Keep breathing, in and then out. In and then out. One more step. Two. You are so relaxed now, Jack. Nothing can hurt you. You are nearly at your safe place. Just one more step to go, Jack. Take that one final step."

Jack felt himself take the last step. He was surrounded by nothing, yet he could feel everything. He felt lighter than the air itself, as though he were wrapped in cotton wool.

"You are nearly at your safe place now, Jack. Can you see it? Nothing can hurt you now. You are completely safe. You are in control at all times. No one can make you do anything you don't want to do when you are in your safe place."

Jack reached out into nothingness. His safe place. A place where nothing could hurt him.

Apart from what was behind the door.

* * *

# Chapter Six

Time: 9.45am

Date: Saturday 21st July 2012

Location: Metropolitan Police HQ, London

Jack jogged up the stairs to the second floor, heading towards the investigation room he had commandeered opposite his office, and glanced at his watch. Running a finger along the inside of his shirt collar and loosening his tie, he could feel the temperature outside was already creeping up, heralding yet another baking hot day on the horizon.

With very few offices at HQ having the benefit and luxury of air conditioning, that particular invention of the 20th century having yet to make an impression on the Metropolitan Police budget, Jack could foresee another uncomfortable day ahead.

Arriving on the second floor, Jack pushed open the door to the investigation room with his shoulder, grunting at the wall of heat and stagnant air that greeted him. And the three pairs of eyes that looked up, expectantly, in his direction.

Three pairs of eyes.

Three.

Two pairs whom he recognised.

One unfamiliar.

"Glad you could join us." The voice belonging to the unfamiliar eyes had a clipped tone. Jack's own gaze remained fixed on the cool, hard, almost expressionless eyes, noticing how they darted up, bird-like, to the clock on the wall and back again. "Tut, tut. Time keeping not one of your fortes, Jack?"

Jack paused in the doorway, holding the stranger's stare. He noticed DS Cooper and DC Cassidy were both seated on the far side of the investigation table, closest to the open window that was barely affording any infiltration of cooler, fresher air; the air outside already humid and breathless. DS Cooper momentarily caught Jack's gaze and offered a slight raise of his tufty, ginger eyebrows. Next to him, DC Amanda Cassidy merely sat silently, wide-eyed, a small smile catching on her lips as she watched the theatrical display play out before her.

"I had a meeting." Jack's reply was equally as clipped. "And it's Detective Inspector MacIntosh."

Letting the door swing shut behind him, Jack stepped into the room and headed towards his seat at the table. As he lowered himself into the vacant chair, he again fixed his gaze on the man leant up against the far wall.

"You must be DS Carmichael."

The man nodded, slowly, turning his thin face towards Jack and affording him a good look at the smooth, almost translucent pale skin, beak-like hooked nose and beady, bird-like brown eyes that fixed Jack with a humourless stare. Jack wondered whether if he put bird seed out on the table, the man might start pecking.

"Indeed, I am." DS Carmichael pushed himself away from the wall and stepped forwards towards the table, hand outstretched towards Jack. Jack hesitated a moment, maybe a moment too long, before briefly shaking the proffered hand, wincing slightly at the dampness of Carmichael's palm. "Been to see the shrink?"

Jack dropped the handshake and held Carmichael's gaze in his, feeling the initial tentative feeling of instant dislike morphing into something stronger.

"It was a psychotherapist. And also none of your business."

Despite the rising heat from the blazing sun outside, the temperature inside the investigation room dropped several degrees. Silence enveloped the room like a musty, suffocating curtain, seeking to squeeze every ounce of oxygen out of the humid air.

DS Cooper rose, hurriedly, to his feet, his chair scraping noisily on the cheap linoleum flooring. He cleared his dry throat, eager to dispel the creeping sense of hostility that was quickly filling the space around them.

"Boss, I've printed out everything on the Patricia Gordon case, including her post mortem report." DS Cooper pointed at the bundle of papers sitting in the centre of the investigation table. "And here is everything we have so far on yesterday's victim." His hand shifted to a much smaller pile. "And we now have a name for her."

Jack jerked his head away from DS Carmichael's stony stare, and raised his eyebrows at DS Cooper. "We do?"

"Yes," nodded DS Cooper, reaching for the remote control to activate the whiteboard. After a few clicks, the whiteboard was illuminated with a passport style photograph of an attractive young woman with blonde hair.

"Georgina Dale, or Georgie as she was known to her friends and family. Aged twenty-one. Lived alone in the halls of residence at St James's University. We've got officers going round there today to see what other information we can gather."

"How come we got her identified so quickly? She didn't have any ID on her. Missing persons come up with something?" Jack's eyes scanned the scanty details on the screen.

DS Cooper shook his head. "No, it was DNA. The lab managed to rush through the DNA samples yesterday, and she was already on our system. Flagged it up this morning, just after you left for your…. for your appointment." DS Cooper hesitated, flashing a wary glance in the direction of DS Carmichael, but the new addition to the team remained silent. "She was on our system after a minor drugs offence two years ago."

Jack nodded, appreciatively. "Good work, Cooper. So what do we have for both of them? Any similarities?"

It was DC Cassidy's turn to get up out of her chair this time. As she rose, she noticed DS Carmichael remained on the far side of the room, leaning against the wall, watching proceedings with a haughty expression. She didn't like the way his gaze dropped to the curve of her skirt around her thighs as she stood.

"I've compiled a comparison list, boss. With all the facts we know about both victims so far." She took the remote control from DS Cooper and after a few clicks the whiteboard was filled with a table. "The left side is victim number one, Patricia Gordon. The right side our latest victim, Georgina Dale."

Jack's eyes scanned the details on the screen, frowning slightly against the glare. He afforded himself a quick glance to the back of the room, where next to DS Carmichael rested his beloved noticeboard, complete with drawing pins. Dragging his gaze back to the screen, Jack read through the list of comparisons. Height; weight; hair colour; age; home address; ethnicity; employment status; marital status; distinguishing features.

Nothing seemed to match.

Not one single thing.

Other than the fact they were both female. And both dead.

"Damn." Jack rubbed his eyes and re-focused once again on the screen. "So, apart from the fact that they were both strangled, we don't have any links."

DC Cassidy shook her head and clicked a button on the remote control to turn off the whiteboard. "It doesn't seem so, boss. Not yet." She reached forwards and took a couple of sheets of paper from the small pile in the centre of the investigation table. She handed one across to Jack, and read from the other. "So, victim number one was aged forty-five years. Five foot seven inches tall. Weight eleven stones. Dark brown short hair with green eyes. Divorced. A smoker, living alone in St John's Wood. Worked as a housekeeper in a care home. Cause of death - strangulation." She paused, before continuing. "Victim number two. Aged twenty-one. Five foot three inches tall. Weight seven stones. Long blonde hair with blue eyes. Single. A non-smoker, living alone in the St James's University halls of residence. Full time student, no part time jobs we are aware of as yet. Cause of death - strangulation."

Jack studied the paper in front of him, scanning through once again the comparison of their two victims. Nobody spoke, and the silence hung heavily in the breathless air.

"I'd say that's not much to go on." DS Carmichael's nasal tones cut through the silence. The other three pairs of eyes in the room flickered towards him, causing a crude smile to cross his thin lips and his beady eyes to glisten. "Apart from the cause of death, you have no connection."

"There is always a connection." Jack spoke quietly, casting his eyes back to the papers in front of him.

"Looks pretty random to me," continued DS Carmichael.

"Murders are never random. There is always a connection, always a reason." Jack looked up and held DS Carmichael's gaze in his. "We just have to find it."

* * *

Time: 11.00am
Date: Saturday 21$^{st}$ July 2012
Location: Isabel's Café, King's Road, London

Using a shoulder to push open the door, Sacha Greene stepped into the café weighed down with several trays of homemade goodies.

"Coming through," she trilled, quickly making her way behind the counter and into the small kitchen.

Isabel was stacking up used baking trays and dirty plates by the side of the dishwasher, and turned to beam at her best friend.

"You're a lifesaver, Sacha," she smiled, nodding at a vacant area of worktop. "Just down there would be great."

Isabel had sent an urgent plea requesting more baked goods, after an especially busy Saturday morning. Dominic's expert stock taking had highlighted that they were running very low on Sacha's homemade cakes and biscuits - and, with still the rest of the weekend to go, she had sent out a mayday message for assistance.

And assistance had appeared less than two hours later.

"My pleasure," replied Sacha, depositing three trays of cookies and two more of home-made cakes onto the worktop. "I can stay for the rest of the day if you like? I don't have anything planned."

"Oh, would you?" Isabel visibly breathed a sigh of relief. "Even with both me and Dom here this morning, it has been non-stop. Patrick has gone out so I can't call on him to help."

"I'll just go and move my car – I'm on a double yellow outside. Give me half an hour and I'll be back."

Isabel smiled gratefully as Sacha turned on her heels and headed for the door, crossing paths with Dominic as he headed back into the kitchen with yet more used coffee cups and plates piled up high, one on top of the other. Stacking them with the others by the side of the dishwasher, he pulled on his rubber gloves and got to work.

"Thanks, Dom," acknowledged Isabel, wiping her hot brow with the back of her hand – hoping she wasn't smearing herself with chocolate frosting or cake crumbs. "If you crack on with loading the dishwasher, and then get some of these cakes and biscuits set out, I'll be out front."

Isabel slipped back behind the counter and smiled warmly at the building line of waiting customers. Whether it was the scorching-hot summer weather, or the Olympic effect, her café had never been so busy. Briefly wondering if her American visitors from the day before had managed to see the Queen, or if they were currently suspended above the Thames in a pod on the London Eye, she reached for a coffee cup and once again disappeared in a cloud of steam as the coffee machine fired up.

\* \* \*

Time: 12.15pm
Date: Saturday 21$^{st}$ July 2012
Location: The Shard, London Bridge Street, London

He craned his neck and gazed skywards, shielding his eyes from the scorching sun's rays that bounced off the mirrored glass and sent sharp stabs of light towards him. The architecture was magnificent. So sleek. So clean. So elegant.

So tall.

The Shard, as it was tentatively being called in the media, towered some three hundred metres above him. A master of design. A thing of true beauty; if indeed a building could be described as beautiful.

He felt a stirring inside, a quickening of his heart.

This was the place.

It had to be.

He knew it the moment he saw it.

This was where he would find Carol.

\* \* \*

# Chapter Seven

Time: 12.30pm
    Date: Saturday 21<sup>st</sup> July 2012
    Location: Metropolitan Police HQ, London

Jack sat alone in the investigation room and ran a hot hand through his hair. The two fans were working at maximum capacity, but merely seemed to be circulating the already sticky, sultry air. He had switched off the whiteboard monitor, the constant humming it gave off getting underneath his skin. He had also switched off both the computers, convinced that all three screens were contributing to the uncomfortable heat of the room. Without the artificial glare from the monitors, and with the blinds shut, the room sat in semi-darkness.

A quick glance towards the pin board at the back of the room caused a small smile to flicker on his lips. Pin boards don't hum, thought Jack. Pin boards don't need plugging in and re-booting. And pin boards definitely don't get overheated.

Jack turned back towards the stack of paperwork on the table. DS Cooper had done a good job at printing everything off for the Patricia Gordon case, plus everything they had on Georgina Dale. It wasn't much. The plastic evidence bag containing the black stiletto shoe was still in the middle of the table. It's mere presence reminding Jack that the life of a third woman was hanging in the balance.

DC Cassidy and DS Cooper were both off chasing phone records and CCTV footage, leaving Jack alone to collect his thoughts. DS Carmichael was nowhere to be seen, something which was already grating on Jack's nerves. He had been in the team for little over an hour before making some excuse about needing to sort out his ID badge and access.

And then he was gone.

And Jack had no idea when he would be back.

The new addition to the team was not making the greatest first impression mused Jack, as he leafed through the Patricia Gordon paperwork. Not a great impression at all.

\* \* \*

Time: 12.35pm

Date: Saturday 21st July 2012

Location: The Shard, London Bridge Street, London

He leant against the corner of the brick wall that housed an organic vegetarian bistro, nursing a takeaway pot of whole-wheat noodles with quinoa. Stirring the contents absentmindedly with a biodegradable cardboard fork, he inhaled the vaguely unappetising aroma.

He hadn't wanted noodles.

He hadn't wanted quinoa.

He didn't even know what quinoa was.

Or how to pronounce it.

He had merely stabbed his finger at the first entry on the takeaway menu, one eye still on the building under construction across the road. Would he like a cardboard fork with his noodles? "We don't stock plastic due to its impact on the environment," he had been informed when he let his eyebrows raise in response. He had agreed to the noodles; and the cardboard fork.

And now he waited.

He pulled the brim of his cap further down across his brow, shielding his face from any prying eyes. But no one was paying him, or his noodles, any attention. He was just another face in the crowd; just another customer eating his quinoa noodles with a cardboard fork.

The main door to The Shard was flanked by sturdy protective barriers, a large "no entry" sign hanging at an angle. Although practically complete on the outside, there were still some finishing touches inside that were necessary before the first tenants could take up occupation. As he watched from the shade of the awning outside the bistro, he saw the main door open and send a searing flash of reflected sunlight towards him. He held his breath as she exited the smoky mirrored front doors, heading purposefully towards London Bridge tube station. She had some form of portfolio tucked underneath her arm and was hurrying through the general melee of midday office workers escaping from their cages and wide-eyed tourists consulting tube maps.

Dumping the unappetising and uneaten noodles in a nearby bin, he adjusted his cap and set off in a gentle jog across the street.

Carol.

* * *

Time: 2.00pm
    Date: Saturday 21st July 2012
    Location: Metropolitan Police HQ, London

"A press conference, Jack. This afternoon." Chief Superintendent Dougie King eased his ample frame into his chair and nodded at Jack to sit opposite. "Liaise with Pippa in Public Relations – you know the score."

"This afternoon?" Jack sat down as he was bidden and raised his eyebrows. "Doesn't leave us much time to put something together, Sir."

"Indeed, Jack. Time is definitely something we do not have. With the

Opening Ceremony in less than a week, millions of pounds of taxpayer's money is being spent here, there and everywhere. They're saying it's going to be a sight to behold – the best opening ceremony ever. There is even talk of James Bond, the Queen and some corgis making an appearance. The mind truly boggles. So, we can't afford for this to become a problem; for the killer to still be out there. You understand me, Jack?"

Jack nodded.

"Then it's a press conference at 4.00pm." The Chief Superintendent inclined his head, indicating to Jack that he was free to go. He caught his DI's eye and gave him a small smile. "Maybe smarten yourself up a bit though – get that DS of yours to lend you a tie."

Jack returned the half-smile and rose from his chair. He left the Chief Superintendent's office and made his way downstairs. A press conference. Jack inwardly groaned as he jogged down the steps, two at a time. He hated them. Detested them. Although acknowledging they were a necessary evil in today's modern world, where social media infiltrated every corner of every person's life, the public ever hungry for the twenty-four-hour hamster wheel of non-stop news, Jack found them nothing but a waste of time. You could never say what you truly wanted to say at a press conference – salient points of the investigation had to be withheld from the public to prevent scores of time wasters who enjoyed nothing better than clogging up the phone lines.

So what was the point? Send out a press statement, by all means. But a live press conference on national TV? Jack gave an involuntary shudder as he reached the bottom of the stairs. He ran a finger around the inside of his shirt collar, feeling the sweat prickling at his skin in anticipation. He would need to get that tie. And he probably could have done with a shave this morning, running the same finger over the short, sharp prickles hugging his chin. Too late now. He had two hours to come up with a suitably short and uninspiring press release. Plus, he needed to check one of the evidence rooms was ready for the defence lawyers coming to view the unused evidence in the McArthur case; a people-trafficking case which was due to start at The Old Bailey in September.

Glancing at his watch and lost in his thoughts, Jack rounded the corner and almost collided with DC Amanda Cassidy walking towards him and carrying a takeaway deli sandwich bag.

"Sorry, guv," she smiled, sidestepping out of his way just in time.

"Amanda, just the person." Jack came to a halt in the corridor and indicated for her to follow him. "Can I borrow you for a minute?"

DC Cassidy paused for a moment, eyeing the sandwich in her hand, her stomach growling impatiently, then spun round on her heels and followed Jack back the way she had come.

"I need you to help me set up one of the evidence rooms – we've got the defence team coming in to look at the unused material for the McArthur case."

DC Cassidy nodded and quickened her step. "Will it be Anthony Saunders? Defence solicitor?" she enquired, following Jack as he turned down a small corridor that housed three evidence rooms. He unlocked the door at the far end and pushed it open to reveal a tight space packed to the rafters with boxes and boxes of evidence.

"Saunders? I'm not sure. Probably." Jack stepped into the room and quickly surveyed the contents. There was a small, battered table that had seen better days pushed up against the far wall. Surrounding it from floor to ceiling were cardboard boxes stacked up one on top of the other, each marked with an identification tag and date, and, as far as Jack hoped, arranged in chronological order as set out in the schedule of unused material disclosed to the defence some weeks ago. A copy of the schedule sat on the battered desk. Jack gave it a cursory glance and nodded to himself. "Why?"

"Why, sir?" DC Cassidy raised her eyebrows.

"Saunders. Why are you so interested in whether he's coming?"

DC Cassidy gave a small chuckle, her eyes sparkling as a broad grin crept across her lips. "Anthony Saunders? You really have no idea, do you?" She shook her head and tucked a stray strand of her jet-black hair behind her ear. "He's only just about the hottest looking defence lawyer there is. And I think he's single. You wait until Mary on the front desk clocks him." DC Cassidy giggled again, watching Jack's bemused expression. "Do you want me to hang on here and greet him? I don't mind." She lifted up her sandwich bag and waggled it in front of Jack. "I'm on my lunchbreak."

Jack felt a smile cover his lips and slowly nodded. "OK, yes, you hang on here and greet our wonder boy. Make sure everything is in order here first; put paper in the photocopier and such like. Check the boxes are all here. They'll be here about half past four. I need to go and pen a press conference. But behave! I'll see you upstairs later."

With that, Jack pressed the key to the evidence room into DC Cassidy's hand and hurried back out into the corridor. He needed to start work on the damned press conference. He glanced at his watch and sighed.

He needed to find Pippa.

* * *

Time: 3.45pm

Date: Saturday 21st July 2012

Location: Metropolitan Police HQ, London

DS Carmichael pulled into the rear car park and instinctively checked his rear view mirror. The place was deserted, save for a lone PC sneakily having a quick cigarette by the back entrance. Another glance into his mirrors reassured him that he had not been followed.

After the initial briefing with Jack and the rest of the team earlier that morning, he had managed to slip away unseen on the pretext of needing to go and sort out his access badge with HR. Jack had looked mildly irritated, but had nodded his acquiescence, having more than enough on his hands to keep him busy. He was unlikely to have noticed his newly acquired DS had walked straight past HR and left the building.

DS Cooper had been busily organising the retrieval of information from the two women's mobile phone records, and DC Cassidy was looking more deeply into their backgrounds – neither had paid any attention to him slipping unnoticed, and unchallenged, out of the room.

DS Carmichael replaced his ID access badge around his neck, there never having been any problem with it in the first place, and exited the car. Another glance at his watch confirmed he was in good time. He had received a brusque message from Jack a short while ago, requesting his presence with regard to the press conference that was due to take place at four o'clock.

DS Carmichael smiled to himself. Although the message had been brief and to the point, he could sense the unwritten message that lurked beneath it.

Where are you, DS Carmichael? had been what Jack really wanted to say.

I'm right here, Jack.

I'm right here.

Jogging towards the rear entrance, he opened the door and used his fully functioning ID badge to swipe access to the building. He headed towards the stairs, noticing DC Cassidy leaning against the front reception desk, deep in conversation with another female officer. As he approached, DC Cassidy swung round and caught his eye.

"Jack wants you upstairs, right away. He's not happy." She nodded towards the ID badge hanging around his neck. "You manage to get your access sorted, then?"

DS Carmichael flashed her a smile and waggled the badge in front of her. "All sorted, thank you."

With another smile and a brief twinkle in his beady bird-like eyes, he pushed open the double doors and headed towards the stairs. Waiting until she saw the doors swing shut behind him, DC Cassidy then turned back to the reception desk to resume her conversation.

"As I was saying, Mary. Keep your eye out for Anthony Saunders – and let me know what you think." A mischievous grin crossed her face. "And buzz me the minute he gets here."

* * *

# Chapter Eight

Time: 4.15pm
 Date: Saturday 21st July 2012
 Location: Metropolitan Police HQ, London

Every chair in the conference room was taken. News about the hastily arranged press conference had spread far and wide, rippling through the journalistic community like a stone thrown into a stagnant pond, and it was standing room only. If that.

The air conditioning was struggling to cope with the demand of over 100 perspiring bodies jostling for position in the cramped media suite. If it was even working at all. Someone had opened the two side windows in the vain hope of locating some fresh air, but this only allowed more hot and humid air to seep into the already sauna-like conditions.

The main broadsheets and tabloids had secured the best seats towards the front, with sleeves rolled up and expensive digital recording equipment at the ready, they were good to go. The local newspapers and local radio reporters were relegated to the back benches, or standing propped up against the rear wall – most still relying on the trusty pen and paper.

A large TV camera was positioned to the left of the press conference table, which itself was on a slightly raised platform at the front of the room. Jack slid into the middle chair behind the table, flanked by DS Cooper to his left and DS Carmichael to his right. He could feel the hot, bright lights overhead, adding to the already sultry feel of the conference room. He took a sip of tepid water from the glasses in front of them and then nodded to Pippa Reynolds, head of PR.

Let's get this over with.

The TV camera began to whirr.

A tall, smartly dressed woman stepped forwards in front of the TV camera. Despite the rising temperature, she was perfectly presented; her long, blonde hair pulled back into a no-nonsense bun, high atop her heart shaped face. Light make-up dusted over a flawless complexion, and pale green eyes glinting out from beneath luscious lengthy lashes. She addressed her waiting audience.

"Good afternoon, ladies and gentlemen. Detective Inspector Jack MacIntosh will now address you. Please keep any questions until the end." With a glance towards Jack, she smiled briefly from perfectly shaped lips, and mouthed the words "good luck" before retreating back into the corner and out of the spotlight.

Jack liked Pippa. They had gone for a drink a couple of times, although nothing had ever come of it, as was usually the case when he went on a date these days. If it had even been a date. But he liked her company. And right now, looking out at the sea of expectant faces before him, and feeling the palpable tension in the air that was always present at a press conference, going for a drink with Pippa seemed like a much more attractive option.

All eyes now fell on Detective Inspector Jack MacIntosh. Clearing his throat, he ran a finger around the collar of yesterday's shirt and loosened the tie DS Cooper had produced from his desk drawer, then he picked up the single sheet of paper that hosted his hastily prepared notes.

"This is Operation Genevieve. As you will be aware, over the last week, two women have been found murdered in London. We are linking their deaths. Our first victim was Patricia Gordon, found on Friday 13th July in St James's Park." Jack paused while a large monitor on the wall behind him brought up a picture of the forty-five-year-old brunette. "Last seen on Friday 6th July as she left her job as housekeeper at The Briars Residential Care Home. The post mortem estimates she was killed sometime between six pm and midnight on Thursday 12$^{th}$ July, the day before she was found. Cause of death – strangulation. Yesterday, Friday 20$^{th}$ July, our second victim, Georgina Dale, was discovered in a quiet corner of Hyde Park." The monitor behind Jack changed to show a photograph of the attractive blonde student. "Last seen at her halls of residence at St James's University, we believe she was killed on or around Thursday 19$^{th}$ July, again between six pm and midnight. Cause of death, once again, strangulation."

Jack paused again, letting his eyes scan the faces before him. He knew that much of what he was saying would be going out on TV and radio news bulletins in time for the tea-time news reports, his words appearing in print in newspaper articles hot off the press first thing in the morning. Maybe even front page. He glanced back down at his crib sheet, at the scanty details they had so far.

Just as he was about to continue, a voice cut through the stuffy, stagnant air.

"Are there any links between the two victims? Bearing in mind they were both found in London parks?"

Jack raised his gaze from his crib sheet back out to the congregation, searching the many pairs of eyes trained on him, trying to identify the owner of the voice, and the question that he knew would be on everybody's lips. A question that Jack knew he couldn't answer.

"Jonathan," cut in Pippa, stepping forwards from the corner behind the TV camera. "All questions at the end, please."

Jack flashed a grateful smile in Pippa's direction, and then nodded at DS Cooper by his side. "Thank you, Jonathan," he replied, quickly catching the eye of the senior crime correspondent from the Daily Mail. "DS Cooper here will fill you in on the details we have so far."

DS Cooper quickly cleared his throat, his cheeks turning a stinging shade of pink. Public speaking was not his thing; his palms felt sweaty and he could feel his heartbeat thudding in his chest. He gripped his own sheet of prepared notes, such as they were, and felt his hands trembling.

"Yes, thank...thank you," he stuttered, deciding to place his hands palm side down onto the table to stop them shaking and to at least absorb some of the relative coolness of the formica table top. "At this present time there is no known link between the two victims, other than the cause of death. But enquiries are continuing."

"So, why are the crimes being linked?" persisted the Daily Mail reporter, lifting his hand held recording device high above his head to ensure he caught everything that was being said. Or not being said. Other recording devices were raised high above heads and shoulders, causing the press conference to take on the look of a pop concert. All we need now, thought Jack, is for them to all start swaying side to side in time with the air conditioning motor.

Pippa went to step forwards once again, but Jack caught her eye and raised a hand, giving her a quick nod.

"Due to operational constraints," he replied, directing his answer to the whole room but focusing his gaze on the Daily Mail reporter, "the reason for linking these two crimes cannot be divulged at this present time."

But the tenacious Daily Mail crime correspondent was not giving up that easily. "Is it DNA? Have you found the killer's DNA at both scenes?

Jonathan Spearing pushed his round rimmed wire-framed spectacles further up onto the bridge of his nose and brushed away the unruly mop of fringe that dressed his forehead. Jack had had several run-ins with him in the past, unsure whether he admired the lean framed reporter's dogged persistence or found him irritating. He was one of the new breed of investigative reporters that fancied themselves as a detective, something that often made Jack's hackles rise.

"As I have already said, Jonathan, the reason we are linking these crimes cannot yet be divulged publicly." Jack held the reporter's gaze a second or two longer than necessary, affording him a stony stare that let him know to drop that line of questioning.

"So, what lines of investigation are you pursuing?" This time it was a different journalist, seated towards the back of the room. Jack recognised him as a Sky News reporter.

"There are several active lines of enquiry ongoing at this time, Rob." Jack flashed an exasperated look at Pippa. The Chief Superintendent wouldn't be pleased at how the carefully constructed press conference had degraded so quickly into a free-for-all Q&A session. Thankfully "Dougie" King was not present, but he would no doubt catch the edited highlights on the evening news.

"But you can't divulge what they are for "operational reasons"?" Rob Haslet persisted, edging forwards in his seat, positioning his recording device so it was in Jack's eye line. Jack afforded the Sky News reporter a brief smile.

"Correct. Although we believe the two women were not known to each other, we would welcome any information from the public as to their last known movements." Jack glanced down at the notes in front of him and tried to steer the conference back on track. "Patricia Gordon was last seen around four o'clock in the afternoon on Friday 6th July leaving work at The Briars Residential Care Home – did anyone see her after this time? Maybe later that evening? Did anyone see her in the company of anyone else?" Jack paused and allowed his eyes to scan the room, watching as reporters scribbled their notes into their notebooks or merely held their recording devices higher to catch Jack's words. Although he despised these rituals with a passion, he knew that they could unlock the key to an investigation that would otherwise remain hidden. For that reason, and that reason only, he continued. "Georgina Dale was last seen at her halls of residence on Thursday 12th July. Did anyone see her leave? Was she with anyone? Even the smallest of details could be of crucial importance." Jack paused once again as the monitor behind him flashed up with images of both women, side by side. "Contact numbers for the investigation team here at the Metropolitan Police are on our website. Alternatively, information can be given anonymously through Crimestoppers."

Jack folded the piece of paper in front of him in half, and nodded at Pippa that the conference was finished.

"Are there any further questions?" Pippa once again stepped forwards in front of the TV camera which had now been switched off. Several hands shot up into the air.

Jack pointed at a young, female reporter with short brown cropped, boyish style hair, sitting on the second row. "Yes?"

"Rachel Wiseman, The Independent." The young reporter's voice had a slight Scottish lilt. "With a serial killer on the loose, what advice are you giving to women who might be out late at night on their own?"

Jack opened his mouth to reply, having anticipated this question would crop up at some point, but instead of his own voice he heard a voice to his right begin to speak.

"I think, Rachel, in the circumstances, women in the capital should be advised to remain vigilant at all times and not venture out alone at night until this murderer is found." DS Carmichael gave the young brunette reporter a smile. "These are extremely dangerous times."

"Are you saying that women should not go out after dark at all?" The young reporter stared wide-eyed at DS Carmichael, thrusting her hand held recording device out in front of her.

Jack felt the hackles at the back of his neck begin to rise. "I think what DS Carmichael is trying to say, is for everyone, not just women, to be sensible and not take any unnecessary risks." He turned and glared at DS Carmichael. "But what we don't want to do is create any panic." Jack returned his gaze to the floor and pointed at another reporter he knew, standing at the back of the room. "Will?"

"William Goldmyer of the Telegraph. What implications does this have for the Olympics? The Opening Ceremony is only six days away."

Another question Jack had been anticipating, and one that the Chief Superintendent had already briefed him on what reply he should give.

"No one is panicking, Will. This investigation is our top-most priority, and we will be working around the clock until we catch the offender."

"Before the Opening Ceremony?"

"That is certainly our intention, yes."

"But you can't guarantee it?"

Jack paused, and held the reporter's gaze. "Nothing in life is guaranteed, Will, you know that. But what I can do is reassure everyone that we will not stop until the person responsible for these crimes is apprehended."

A reporter next to the Telegraph's William Goldmyer now stepped in. A small, rotund man, dressed in a striped shirt and tie that looked more at home on the trading floor of one of the City's stockbroking firms, raised his hand. "With tens of millions of pounds of expected revenue to flood into the capital during the course of the Games, if the killer remains on the loose and people stay away, how will you explain that loss of revenue to the Government and the people of the UK?"

Jack recognised him as an economics reporter for the BBC. "My job is to detect crime and bring criminals to justice. I don't work for, or answer to, the Treasury." Several more hands shot into the air, but Jack waved them away and continued. "I think the people of the UK are more concerned about us removing a killer from the streets of London than whether there is an increase in the sale of floppy hats, cycling shorts or burrito wraps." Jack couldn't suppress the edginess entering his tone. "In fact....."

"And on that note, I think we will leave it there, ladies and gentleman." Pippa stepped forwards once again and raised her arms to the side to usher the congregation out of the rear doors, something akin to herding cattle. "Full details of the press conference and the contact details for the investigation team will be live on our website shortly. Thank you very much for your time."

Jack remained seated at the table until the last of the reporters had vacated the room. Then he turned to DS Carmichael who was still sat next to him. "What the hell was that all about? The last thing we need to do is create a wave of panic throughout London. What on earth were you thinking?"

DS Carmichael shrugged. "I just feel it's better to be honest. We have no idea what links these women, and we have no idea who else could be at risk. If any members of my family lived in London, I would have no hesitation in telling them not to go out after dark."

"Well thankfully, you're not in charge of this investigation....and I..." Jack's voice began to rise, but just at that moment he was interrupted by the door to the conference room opening. Pippa popped her head back around the door frame.

"Jack?" She looked hesitantly across the room. "The Chief Super would like to see you before you clock off. I don't think he's very happy."

* * *

Time: 4.30pm
   Date: Saturday 21st July 2012
   Location: Metropolitan Police HQ, London

"Hi, DC Amanda Cassidy." Amanda held out a hand towards her visitor, having stowed away the half-eaten warm roast beef and horseradish sauce deli sandwich under the counter at reception. She hoped the grease from the wrapper wasn't still clinging to her fingers.

"Pleased to meet you, Amanda," replied a deep, gravelly tone emanating from a neatly trimmed white beard that enveloped a full, round face with twinkling ice-blue eyes. A crop of equally ice-white hair covered his scalp. "John Fortmason."

Amanda felt her hand being engulfed in a warm, two-handed handshake, and noticed the gleaming and very expensive looking cuff-links glinting under the harsh overhead lighting. Sir John Fortmason was a well-known London-based QC, handling both prosecution and defence work, and recently represented the Metropolitan Police in a successful prosecution of twelve members of an organised crime gang operating in Central London. The gang received a record total of 272 years in prison. This time, however he was working for the defence.

"And this is my instructing solicitor, Anthony Saunders." The eminent QC stepped aside and nodded towards the figure languishing in his shadow.

DC Cassidy bit her lip as her eyes came to rest on Anthony Saunders.

"Hi, Amanda. Anthony." Anthony Saunders extended a hand towards DC Cassidy, which she grabbed potentially a little too quickly, marvelling in the softness of his grip. She glanced down and noted the immaculately manicured nails – and absence of wedding ring. His grip was firm and strong, and somehow transmitted a weakness that reached her knees. "But you can call me Tony." Her eyes strayed from his handshake up to a ruggedly handsome face. With a clean-shaven square jaw, and closely cropped dark hair that matched the chocolate-brown eyes that sparkled as a smile crossed his lips, she could smell the faint aroma of his aftershave lingering in the air between them.

"Nice to meet you both," squeaked Amanda, letting the defence solicitor's hand drop to his side. Get a grip, Cassidy, she reminded herself. Get a grip. "If you would like to follow me, I'll take you to the evidence room."

DC Cassidy turned on her heels and led the two lawyers back through into the building, turning sharply to the right to reach the corridor housing the evidence rooms. Unlocking the door with the key Jack had left her, she stepped back to allow the two men to step inside. Following on behind them, she snapped on the overhead light.

"You may need the light on," she explained, nodding towards the walls. "No windows, I'm afraid. Sorry, it was the only room available today at short notice that was big enough for all the paperwork." She gestured towards the boxes piled high, one on top of the other, along each wall.

Both lawyers quickly appraised themselves of their surroundings, instantly noticing the lack of daylight and oppressively warm and stagnant air.

"Not a problem at all," replied Sir John, flashing DC Cassidy another warming smile. "I know things are a little busy around here at the moment." He cast a look towards the boxes and grimaced. "These trafficking cases – they certainly know how to generate the paperwork."

"Yes, I see the press conference is in full swing," added Anthony Saunders, depositing his shoulder bag on the floor. "I think you're best off out of it; a messy business by all accounts, and so close to the Olympics too. I bet those upstairs are tearing their hair out." He grinned at DC Cassidy, a dimple forming on his chin.

DC Cassidy was about to nod and make a comment, but thought better of it. With the press breathing down their necks, the last thing the department needed was a gossip. "And there's a fan in the corner if it gets too stuffy." She nodded at the free-standing fan plugged into the wall in the far corner. "Apart from that, it's all yours. The unused material schedule is on the desk, although I'm sure you already have a copy. The boxes should be stacked in order, with the reference numbers on the outside. If you need to make copies of anything, there's a small photocopier over here." DC Cassidy nodded behind her, where an antiquated photocopier nestled behind the door. "Other than that, unless I can get you anything, I'll leave you to it."

Anthony Saunders nodded his thanks and strode over to the small table where he began unloading his laptop from his shoulder bag. "Thanks, Amanda," he smiled, turning his head towards her over his shoulder. "We'll be fine."

Sir John raised a hand to acknowledge his own thanks, while seating himself at the table and reaching for the unused material schedule. With a last look at the broad shouldered, slim waisted defence solicitor, DC Cassidy backed out of the room and closed the door behind her.

Anthony Saunders was in the house.

Tony.

You can call me Tony.

DC Cassidy grinned to herself like a teenager, revelling in the warm, fuzzy feeling that was hovering in her stomach, before climbing the stairs in search of Jack.

\* \* \*

# Chapter Nine

Time: 5.45pm
  Date: Saturday 21<sup>st</sup> July 2012
  Location: King's Road, London

Mac pulled off his motorcycle helmet and took in a gulp of air. Hot, humid, stale air – but it was, at least, air. He could feel his hair sticking to his scalp and ran a finger around the inside collar of his leather jacket, feeling a layer of sweat clinging to his skin.

His last delivery of the day.

Thankfully.

He swung his leg over the back of his motorbike and retrieved the final package of the day from the courier box on the back. Taking the helmet with him, as you never could trust anyone these days, especially in London, and activating the bike alarm from his key fob, Mac disappeared into the building at 111-113 Kings Road.

He was instantly greeted by a bank of cool air as soon as he stepped over the threshold, momentarily stopping him in his tracks.

Heaven.

Standing still in the doorway and closing his eyes, he allowed the chill from the air conditioning to wash over his sweat-matted hair and caress his burning cheeks.

"Can I help you?"

Mac's eyes sprung open at the sound of a pleasant female voice emanating from behind the sleek reception desk in front of him. His brief immersion into the heady coolness of heaven dissipated almost as quickly as it had arrived. Stepping forwards, he brandished the thick, padded brown envelope in his hand.

"Sorry, just enjoying your air conditioning for a moment. It's been pretty hot out there today." Mac stepped towards the desk, and was greeted by an equally sleek receptionist, dark chocolate brown hair cut into an immaculately kept bob at just below the jawline, her flawless skin sporting expertly applied make-up that had not succumbed to the hot and humid air outside. Mac placed his helmet at his feet and instinctively ran a sweaty hand over his rough, unshaven face. He avoided looking in the full length mirrors that adorned the wall behind the reception desk. "Package for HLM Recruitment."

Mac handed over the envelope, which was taken lightly by a well-manicured hand, sporting expensively filed and painted fingernails in a shade of ravishing crimson. Mac withdrew his calloused hand, complete with bitten nails, scars and scratches and quickly bent down to pick up his helmet. Pulling a delivery note from his back pocket, he watched as the same elegant, ravishing crimson fingernails acknowledged receipt of the package with a flourish.

"Thank you," the receptionist smiled, a perfect row of equally perfect white teeth beamed back at him. "Have a good evening."

Dismissed, Mac left the cool interior of HLM Recruitment and stepped back out into the baptism of fire that was the Kings Road on a Saturday afternoon. The atmosphere was thick and heavy, not a breath of wind to stir the already stagnated air. Traffic was crawling along the street, nose to tail, the odd blast of a horn from a frustrated taxi echoed in the stillness. Weary cyclists weaved in and out of the near-stationary vehicles, some with face masks on to protect them from the hot dust and pollution. Everyone had their windows down, arms hanging out, faces turned to the outside air in the vain hope of catching even the smallest hint of a breeze.

Mac kicked his motorbike off its stand and pushed it towards a nearby zebra crossing by Sloane Square. There was only one place he was going right now, and it wasn't going to be joining the monotonous stream of creeping traffic back to his flat. He gazed across to the opposite side of the road and sniffed the air, the faint aroma of coffee and pastry greeting his nostrils.

Isabel's.

\* \* \*

Time: 5.45pm
Date: Saturday 21st July 2012
Location: Metropolitan Police HQ, London

"So, Jack, what was that?" Chief Superintendent Dougie King nodded at Jack to take the seat opposite him, sighing as he lowered himself into his swivel chair. "The press pack getting all hot under the collar; just what we didn't need. God knows what the headlines will be tomorrow."

Jack slipped into the vacant chair and shrugged. "You know what I think of press conferences, Sir."

"A necessary evil, Jack, a necessary evil." Chief Superintendent King reached behind him to the sideboard that housed the coffee pot. "Coffee?" Jack shook his head. The Chief Superintendent put the coffee pot back down and reached for the drawer at the side of his desk, bringing out a half empty bottle of what looked to Jack like a half decent malt. "Something stronger?" Jack eyed the bottle but felt his head shake again.

"Best not, Sir. Still some work to do this evening."

Chief Superintendent King nodded, and replaced the bottle in his desk drawer with a somewhat regretful look. "I guess you're right." He paused, leaning forwards onto the desk and resting his chin on steepled fingers. "So?" Another weighted pause while he studied Jack's face. "Aside from the press conference, how are things shaping up?"

Jack knew that the Chief Superintendent didn't have it easy. The first black policeman to rise to this level through the ranks of the Metropolitan Police meant that it had not been a smooth ride. There had been more than a few barricades along the way, and still some who would bar his progress any further.

But Jack liked him.

And Jack respected him.

So Jack felt he could not lie to him.

"It's slow going, Sir. There's not a lot to go on. We have weeks of CCTV to trawl through, plus catching up with the FLOs in the morning, reviewing the victim's homes. Seeing what we can come up with."

"But at the moment?"

"It doesn't look good, Sir. I will be honest. It's early days but forensics are drawing a blank."

Chief Superintendent King nodded, Jack's answer being as expected. "Then I need you to include the forensic profiler on this, Jack."

"Sir, I...."

"No buts, Jack. Orders from above." The Chief Superintendent again raised his eyes heavenwards. "You know how it is. You need to send everything that you have onto the profiling team. And keep them up to date with any future developments."

"But.... profiling?" Jack sighed. Another bug bear. The force's profiler. It seemed to him that all police forces in the country were now employing criminal profilers, or criminal psychologists, to solve cases for them. Jack wasn't convinced, finding them more of a hindrance than anything else, their conclusions often being so vague that almost anyone, including half the police force themselves, could be highlighted as a potential suspect. But he wasn't such a dinosaur that he resisted all progress. Slowly, he nodded at Chief Superintendent King. "Sir."

"I know how you feel about profilers, Jack. But they can be useful. They have proved invaluable in several recent cases of ours." The Chief Superintendent paused and caught his senior officer's doubtful gaze. "At least hear them out. If you don't agree with what they say, then as the Senior Investigating Officer you have the right to disregard it. But we need to tick that box."

Jack nodded.

He understood box ticking.

He understood all too well.

"And DS Carmichael?" Chief Superintendent King continued holding Jack in his gaze. "Is he helping out?"

Jack let out a breath he hadn't known he was holding in. "I didn't like his input into the press conference, I will say that. The press will go to town over his comments that we advise all women in London not to go out alone. Talk about inciting panic. And he rushed off straight after the conference – he's barely been here today."

The Chief Superintendent nodded. "I hear you, Jack. Just let him settle in. Give him something constructive to do – keep him busy. Let him prove his worth." There was a pause before he continued. "But keep an eye on him."

Jack frowned. "You don't trust him?"

"It's not that." The Chief Superintendent shook his head. "I don't know the man. Orders came from above, you know that. But you know as well as I do, Jack. Nobody trusts a cuckoo."

* * *

# Chapter Ten

Time: 6.15pm

  Date: Saturday 21st July 2012

  Location: Metropolitan Police HQ canteen, London.

"Good work at the press conference, Boss." DS Cooper handed Jack a bottle of iced water from the fridge, and they both slipped into chairs close to one of the open windows at the back of the canteen. "What do you think tomorrow's headlines will be?"

Jack shrugged, taking the proffered bottle and instantly ripping the top off and taking a long gulp. "Depends which newspaper you're talking about. The Mail on Sunday will probably lead with how we have no idea what we are doing and they will then proceed to instil panic on the streets of London. The BBC will probably focus on how our inability to catch the killer will cost the UK taxpayer millions of pounds in lost revenue, and Sky will most likely claim that we are keeping vital information from the public."

"Which we are." DS Cooper pushed a packet of crisps across the formica table towards Jack, remnants of its last occupants still visible on the sticky, plastic covering. Some random grains of salt. A blob of ketchup. A pile of stale crumbs.

Jack pulled a paper napkin from the metal box on the table and brushed the crumbs and salt away, smearing the ketchup stains. "Which we are, indeed, Cooper." Jack took another swig of water and tossed the crumpled napkin onto a neighbouring table, piled high with dirty plates and mugs. "The shoes are our key evidence. We need to keep their existence away from the press as long as possible. If anyone rings in with information that they know about the shoes – we could have our killer."

"Something only the killer knows." DS Cooper nodded and twisted the cap off his bottle of cola. Bubbles instantly sprayed out of the top, and then ran down the sides covering his fingers and onto the table.

"Exactly, Cooper." Jack threw a couple of paper napkins across the table in the direction of his DS. "Who have we got on liaison duty with the family of Georgina?"

DS Cooper wiped his fingers from the stickiness and reached into his jacket pocket for his notebook. He flipped over a few pages. "DC Rachel McBride."

Jack nodded. "And for Patricia?"

"DC James Anderson."

"Good." Jack knew both DCs well, and knew that they were highly experienced FLOs – family liaison officers – a vital source of information and support for the family and an extremely important connection to the investigating team. "Let's catch up with them both first thing in the morning, see what they have. They will need to work closely together on this one. See if we can uncover anything that the two victims had in common."

DS Cooper nodded, pocketing his notebook. "I'll put in a call first thing. In the meantime, what should be top of our list? I've got Amanda setting up a trawl of the CCTV cameras around both locations where the bodies were found."

"Good. That's a top priority. Draft in some other bodies if we need the manpower. The Chief says there is no limit on resources. And get them to check CCTV from where the victims were last seen too."

DS Cooper nodded and made a mental note to tell Amanda she could have as much overtime and additional PCs as she needed. "Will do. Anything else?"

"I think it's time we caught up with our friend, DS Carmichael. Don't think I didn't notice him disappearing in the middle of the day. Some ruse about his access badge. I don't buy it – I don't buy it for a second." Jack rose from his chair, picking up his water bottle and the packet of crisps. "And then he did another disappearing act as soon as the press conference was over. I've got my eye on him. Let's go and see if he's made it back and put him to work. We have a potential victim number three out there somewhere, the owner of our black stiletto shoe. We need to find her – and fast."

* * *

Time: 6.30pm
 Date: Saturday 21st July 2012
 Location: Isabel's Café, Kings Road, London

Isabel's flat above the café, although small, was light and airy. Mac sat by the open window and closed his eyes, a full size floor fan behind him, emanating a welcome breeze at last. He had peeled off his bike leathers, leaving his t-shirt clinging to his skin as if bound by an invisible hot adhesive. The sound of the busy street below washed over him like a gentle wave rippling on a sandy beach. It was on the verge of lulling him into a light sleep when Isabel interrupted his meditative state and placed a tray of iced coffee and pastries down on the small rickety wicker coffee table.

"Nodding off?" she smiled, handing Mac a long, tall glass of iced heaven. "Early start?"

Mac prized his eyelids open and accepted the glass, gratefully. "5.30am delivery, then non-stop ever since." He took a mouthful of the chilled, frothy coffee and savoured the taste on his tongue. "Not great in this heat."

Isabel sat down opposite Mac and took her own glass of iced coffee. "They say it's here to stay for a while longer – the heatwave. Something to do with the jet stream."

"Great," murmured Mac, taking another sip and sighing contentedly as the coolness of the coffee mixed with a caffeine shot hit his bloodstream.

"You really do make the best coffee for miles around."

Isabel laughed, sipping her own drink. "Nice of you to say so. I put in a lot of research beforehand!" After selling her Cambridge home two years ago, Isabel had lived briefly in her late parents' house in Surrey before moving on, taking a coast to coast tour of all the best, and worst, coffee bars she could find in America. When America had shown her all it had to offer, she moved on to more refined establishments in Italy and France, before returning to England with a firm plan in place to open her own coffee house. She sold her parents' house in Surrey, which was a huge wrench and pained her in the extreme, as she had so many happy memories of growing up, but it enabled her to use the money to invest in her Kings Road project.

Isabel shifted in her seat, her eyes coming to rest on the second hand bookcase behind Mac, adorned top to toe with well-loved and well-read paperbacks, hardbacks and everything in between. On some of the shelves, in amongst the eclectic range of reading material, there rested treasured photographs in an assortment of frames, one of which always caught her eye. It was the photograph taken in the back garden at her parents' Surrey home, on her fifth birthday. 1985. A lifetime ago. She gazed at the photograph, allowing her head to be filled with memories, treasured memories that never failed to bring to life thoughts and feelings that could, and would, never be buried.

She never tired of looking into her mother's eyes, twinkling with happiness - the faint dusting of flour, or was it icing sugar, on her faintly flushed cheeks. Her father with a comforting and loving hand resting on her mother's shoulder, while Isabel beamed happily at their side, astride her brand new tricycle.

Her fifth birthday.

She could recall it as if it were yesterday.

The smell of the freshly baked birthday cake, lemon sponge in the shape of a star – with pale pink icing and little jellied sweets on top. The buttercream biscuits that were her favourites; the jellies wobbling in their little dishes. And her brand new tricycle - her most treasured present which she would ride incessantly up and down the small descent in the back garden, from her climbing tree at the far end, back down towards the house.

Isabel instinctively reached down to her right knee, letting her fingers gently circle the small scar that she knew would be beneath the fabric of her jeans. Remembering going faster and faster on her tricycle, faster and faster down the slight hill toward the house, faster and faster, unable to stop in time.

Falling.

Falling onto the soft summer grass, but scraping her knee on the pedals as she fell.

Her hot tears wiped away by a comforting and friendly hand. A strong hand. Hands that scooped her up and brought her back to the house to be comforted by buttercream biscuits and birthday cake.

Uncle Andre.

Except he wasn't her Uncle.

And he wasn't Andre.

Kreshniov.

Isabel gave a slight shudder at the name and took another sip of her coffee. Her eyes moved from the photograph of her mother and father to one directly next to it. A similar picture, almost identical. Again her mother and father in a similar stance, her father with a protective arm across the shoulder of her mother. Both smiling for the camera, both sets of eyes twinkling with happiness – yet when you looked deeply, Isabel thought there was something behind the happiness. A hollowness, a sadness that couldn't be masked no matter how large and bright the smiles were.

And the child by their side. Rosy cheeked with a beaming grin. About the same age as Isabel.

Astride a tricycle.

Yet it wasn't her tricycle.

And it wasn't her.

It was Miles.

"Do you think he knew?"

Isabel jolted from her memories at the sound of Mac's voice. She found his soft eyes catching her gaze, watching as they flickered towards the photograph of Miles on the bookcase, and then back to her.

"Do you think he knew?" Mac repeated.

"Knew?" Isabel's voice caught, sounding faint and somewhat cracked around the edges like well-worn leather.

"About you," continued Mac, softly, placing his coffee glass back on the table and leaning forwards towards Isabel. "About you being his sister." Both pairs of eyes now flickered back to the bookcase where there was a third photograph. This time, one of a broad shouldered young man, good looking with a mass of dark brown hair flopping across his forehead, a cheeky smile grinning out at them.

Miles.

Miles as Isabel had known him.

"Part of me hopes he did," she replied, clutching her coffee cup tightly on her lap. "Another part of me hopes that he didn't. I guess we will never know."

"He was a good guy. If he did know, then I'm sure he was very proud of you."

Isabel smiled weakly, and reached forwards to the plate of pastries. She nudged the plate towards Mac. "Go on, have something. You'll waste away if you're not careful, now you don't have Jack looking after you."

Mac smiled and reached for a pain au chocolat.

"And they will only go to waste," she continued. "You can take some home with you. How is Jack, anyhow?"

Mac took a bite out of his pastry and chewed thoughtfully for a moment. The rich, buttery taste mixed with velvety chocolate slid delightfully down his throat, greeted by his grumbling stomach reminding him he had not eaten since a greasy bacon sandwich at about 10 am.

"He's good," he replied, taking a sip of coffee to remove the flaky pastry from his lips. "Working hard as usual."

Isabel nodded. "And the dreams? The nightmares?" After Jack, aged just four years old, had found his mother's body hanging lifelessly from a light fitting, his adult years had been plagued by flashbacks and nightmares. Sporadic sessions with a variety of psychotherapists had had mixed results.

"Still ongoing, I think." Mac nodded, glumly staring down into the remnants of his coffee, watching the ice cubes slowly melting before his eyes. "He's started seeing a psychotherapist. Again. Well, another one. A hypnotherapist this time."

"Well, that might help."

"I guess." Mac sighed, placing the remnants of his pain au chocolat back on the plate, his appetite lost. "I hope so. I feel so guilty sometimes."

"Guilty?" Isabel frowned. "Why guilty?"

Mac raised his gaze to Isabel, where she recognised the haunted, sadness hidden behind his eyes, much like her parents in the photograph atop her bookcase.

"I don't understand."

"Neither do I, really," sighed Mac, breaking her gaze. "But sometimes, I.... I don't know.... I feel guilty that it wasn't me. That I didn't find her."

"But you were only two, Mac."

"I know, but.... Jack's had to deal with all of this on his own......finding her.....dealing with losing her.....feeling that sense of loss. I..." Mac's voice broke off, and he turned his head to look out of the window, suddenly feeling chilled in the breeze from the fan. "I don't remember it.... any of it......I don't remember her."

"But that's not your fault."

"I know, I know. I'm being stupid. I just feel so useless, sometimes. I can't share what he's feeling, because I don't feel it. I don't remember Mum; I just remember being shunted from pillar to post...people shouting... usually at me. Being made to feel a burden, like I was a problem that had to be dealt with. I felt so angry all the time."

"Angry?"

Mac nodded. "Angry. At everything. At everyone. At Mum. At Jack. I needed someone to blame why my life had gone down the toilet. I blamed Mum for leaving us. I blamed Jack for......I don't know what I blamed Jack for, but I did anyway. I was a mess."

"But you're not now. And that's all that matters." Isabel tried to catch Mac's gaze, but he continued to look out of the window. "Shit happens to us all, Mac. Sometimes you just have to face it, forget it, and then move on."

Mac turned his head away from the window and dropped his gaze to his lap. "Sorry, Isabel. You've had it tougher than any of us. Ignore me, I'm just feeling sorry for myself. It's been a crap day. I've been sweating buckets and feeling irritable all day."

Isabel smiled and reached forwards to touch Mac's knee. She gave it a small squeeze. "It's OK. You're entitled to a crap day. That's what my coffee is for. A well known prescription for a crap day."

Just then, Dominic popped his head around the door that led back down to the café.

"S... sorry to disturb, Isabel," he stammered, his eyes cast down to the floor. "I'm off now. But you have a visitor."

"Oh?" Isabel frowned and made to rise from her chair. "Who?"

Dominic hovered in the doorway, reaching into the back pocket of his jeans to retrieve his notebook and read his latest entry. "A man named... . Erik. A Mr Erik Neumann. N...E...U...M...A...two N's. And Erik with a K." Dominic looked up at Isabel. "He says he's from Hamburg. In Germany. He's interested in the advert you have in the window."

"Oh, good." Isabel quickly turned and headed across to the door. "Tell him I'll be down in a minute. And you get yourself off home now, Dominic. Lock the main door behind you."

Dominic nodded, wrote another entry in his notebook and then disappeared back down the stairs.

"I'd better go down." Isabel looked back over her shoulder at Mac, who was already rising to his feet. "You're welcome to stay up here; I shouldn't be too long."

"It's fine, I'd better be on my way too. The traffic back to Islington can be a nightmare some nights."

"Well, you drop by anytime. You know you're always welcome. And that goes for that brother of yours too."

Mac smiled. "I'll let him know. I might pop in on him now, see if he fancies a takeaway later." He grabbed his biker's jacket from the floor, together with his gloves and helmet. As he crossed the room, heading towards the door, he noticed Isabel's laptop open, resting on a sideboard. "Hey. What's this?" He nodded at the screen.

Isabel followed his gaze and then gave a small chuckle. "Ah, that's nothing. Just a bit of fun to keep me amused in the evenings."

Mac turned his attention back to the screen. It was open on a website called "London Life"; the page displaying a number of passport sized photographs of men with a short profile beneath. "Is this a *dating* website?" He looked up at Isabel, unable to mask the smile playing on his lips. "*Really?*"

Isabel's cheeks tinged pink. "It's a *friendship* site. You don't have to meet anyone if you don't want to. You can just chat. Make new friends."

Mac placed his helmet at his feet and shrugged into his heavy leather jacket, feeling his skin start to overheat immediately. "Looks like a dating site to me. Surely you don't need something like that? You meet people all day long."

"Mac, I *see* people every day. I don't actually *meet* them. I don't get to know anyone, short of how they take their coffee and whether they prefer white or brown sugar. Life can be a bit lonely at times." Isabel hovered in the doorway. "Anyway, I'm just chatting to people, nothing to get excited about. Doubt I'll even meet up with anyone. Now, come on, let's get you home."

* * *

Time: 6.45pm
    Date: Saturday 21st July 2012
    Location: Metropolitan Police HQ, London

Jack pulled the blinds tightly closed, the sun sinking lower in the sky was sending its blinding rays directly in through the open window. He left the window open, although what good it was doing with the sticky, sultry air he had no idea.

"So, where are we with the CCTV?" Jack turned and directed his gaze at DC Amanda Cassidy. Looking cool and unflustered in the searing heat, sporting a short sleeved tailored shirt over a lightweight summer skirt, she stood up from her chair and reached over to take the remote for the interactive whiteboard. Jack inwardly groaned, glancing briefly at the lost and forlorn pin board still propped up at the back of the room.

The whiteboard hummed and sprang into life, showing a road map of London.

"We're running the CCTV tapes for this area here, around location number two – the south-east corner of Hyde Park." DC Amanda Cassidy clicked the remote and a large red circle appeared on the screen, encircling the location of the discovery of Georgina Dale's body and the surrounding streets. "We've taken a good number of streets in each direction, to see what we can find. I've got a team of three PCs looking at that right now."

"OK, good work. And location number one?" Jack perched himself on the edge of the table, watching the screen intently.

DC Cassidy once again clicked the remote and a different road map appeared, with a different red circle. "The locations aren't that far apart – so some of the CCTV cameras will overlap. Patricia Gordon was found at the northern side of St James's Park, so we are checking all routes to the east and west. I've another team of three PCs on this one."

Jack nodded towards the maps. "Good work. Can we make sure they also check a good twenty-four to forty-eight hours before and after the finding of each of the bodies. Whoever this is must have been out to look for a suitable dump site prior to disposing of the bodies. If nothing unusual shows up to forty-eight hours before, increase the time frame. We know some offenders revisit the scenes of their crimes, so let's keep up an active log for the hours after the finding of the bodies too. I'm guessing we're looking for a van, or a large enough vehicle to carry a body in the boot."

DC Cassidy nodded and made a quick note in the notebook in front of her.

"Anything more from the post mortem on both victims?"

DS Cooper stood up this time and took the remote control offered to him by Amanda.

"Boss. Both victims were strangled with what looks like a ligature of some kind." DS Cooper clicked the remote and the screen was filled with the post mortem pictures of both victims. The pictures looked almost identical. The delicate skin around the neck of each victim truncated by a thin, yet violent streak of dark purple and crimson bruising.

Jack studied both photographs. "Definitely a ligature? No chance of any fingermarks?"

DS Cooper shook his head. "Dr Matthews was pretty conclusive in his report on both victims, boss. Definitely strangulation by ligature, not by hand."

Jack nodded, thoughtfully. "OK, any other similarities that we've missed?"

DS Cooper again clicked the remote control and two different photographs now filled the screen. "No, boss. No other similarities other than both seemed to have these abrasions around their ankles. Patricia Gordon's right ankle, the left ankle on Georgina Dale."

Jack nodded again, remembering reading about the abrasions in both post mortem reports. "Restraints, then. So he abducts them, keeps them restrained somewhere, before strangling and then dumping them." DS Cooper nodded and clicked off the whiteboard.

"Amanda, I'd like you to go and see both FLOs first thing tomorrow, spend some time with them. See what they've managed to come up with about both victim's lifestyles. See if they have anything even remotely in common, no matter how small." Jack paused and turned his head slightly towards DS Carmichael, who had just breezed back into the building. "And take DS Carmichael with you. Unless he has something better to do."

"Yes, boss – we'll get onto it first thing." DC Cassidy flashed a look at DS Cooper opposite, and hid her own expression behind her coffee cup.

"Are you going to involve the profiler?" DS Cooper glanced up at Jack. "I heard something."

Jack grimaced. "Good news seems to travel fast, I see. Yes, it seems we have to. Orders from above. I'm sending everything across tonight."

"And what will you be doing, Detective Inspector?" Since arriving minutes before, DS Carmichael had been sat quietly at the back of the room, coolly watching proceedings without comment. He looked down his beak-like nose at Jack, his pin-pricked beady eyes watching his every move. "You seem to have allocated jobs to everyone else, I see."

Jack felt himself bristling and clenched his teeth within his jaw. He held DS Carmichael's gaze for several seconds before replying. "DS Cooper and myself will be focusing on the shoe left at the second dumping site. Unless I'm mistaken, we have a potential victim number three out there. We need to find the owner of that shoe."

"I see," smirked DS Carmichael, rising from his chair and brushing non-existent specks of dust from the lapels of his expensively cut suit. "And after you have finished playing Cinderella?"

Jack felt his hackles rise even further, the heavy sultriness of the air in the room edging him closer to boiling point with every word emanating from DS Carmichael's thin mouth. Clenching his fists behind his back, Jack addressed the detective sergeant in a levelled tone. "We will all meet back here at four o'clock tomorrow afternoon. I want an update on the mobile phone records and the CCTV. If there is anything urgent, obviously get me on my mobile beforehand."

DS Carmichael nodded, slowly, and then moved towards the door. "If that is all, I will make a move. The landlady of the hotel I am staying in will be preparing dinner shortly." With that, he turned on his well-polished heels and left the room.

There was a few moments silence before anyone spoke.

"Cooper?" Jack stared at the closed door behind the freshly departed DS Carmichael.

"Yes, Boss?"

"Find out all you can on why our friend DS Carmichael here has been dumped on us."

"Yes, Boss. Will do."

"Discreetly, mind. See who is willing to talk back at his old station in Sussex. Coppers don't get farmed out to other areas for no reason. I want to know why they don't want him on their patch – and why he has turned up on ours."

\* \* \*

# Chapter Eleven

Time: 7.00pm
　　Date: Saturday 21st July 2012
　　Location: Isabel's Café, King's Road, London

"Hello, I'm Isabel Faraday." Isabel held out a hand to greet her visitor. A lean and elegantly dressed man, in a light coloured linen suit with open toed sandals, stood up from where he had been sitting on one of Isabel's sofas in the café. His skin had a soft, sun kissed look to it, his hair blonde with more sun kissed streaks, thick on top but cut shorter into his neck.

"Good evening," he replied, with an accent Isabel was unable to place. "My name is Erik Neumann. I saw your advert in your window. About the art studio?" He nodded towards the front window of the café and the small poster Isabel had placed there some weeks ago, inviting people to rent one of the three spare easels she had in her art studio. It was an idea that Patrick had come up with when they were sharing a late night glass of wine and trying to come up with some money-making ideas to help Isabel with the rent on the café.

"I see," beamed Isabel, "that's great. Please, come through. I'll show you what we have." Smiling warmly at her visitor, Isabel gestured for him to follow her through to the rear of the café and into the art studio.

Erik Neumann duly followed, his sandals making a soft flapping sound on the café floor tiles. Isabel drew back the concertina door that separated the café from the studio, and stepped inside. Early evening light was streaming in through the open patio doors at the back, and due to the patio being sheltered from the direct sun, the studio felt cool and airy.

The main studio table in the centre of the room was strewn with Patrick's artistic paraphernalia – a selection of rough sketchings, some charcoal pencils, tubes of acrylic paint and a couple of coffee mugs. Isabel noticed that he seemed to have started work on his latest commission for the advertising agency.

"I have a resident artist, Patrick, who generally uses the table here, plus the space behind him on the far wall there." Isabel nodded at the wall behind the table where there was an easel plus a set of rickety shelves housing all manner of paints, brushes, pencils, chalks and paper. "The spaces I have available for rent are on this side." Isabel gestured to the other side of the studio, where there were three easels set up with a trolley on wheels loaded with art materials. "The rent covers use of the easel plus any materials."

"I see, I see. It is very impressive." Erik Neumann turned on his open-toed heels and beamed, taking in all the space around him. "So much light. So much space. It is perfect."

Isabel inwardly heaved a sigh of relief. Money was a little tight due to the high rents along the Kings Road, and she had invested a lot of money into the café venture. Some extra cash flow from renting out the art studio space would be very welcome.

"Can I ask what you do for a living, Mr Neumann?" Isabel perched herself on a stool in front of one of the easels. "Are you involved in the arts?"

Erik Neumann smiled, flashing a set of brilliant white teeth, his mouth crinkling at the sides. Isabel noticed his grey-blue eyes glistened as he smiled. "Oh, I wish, Miss Faraday. I wish. As I think I told the young gentleman when I came in, I am originally from Hamburg, in Germany, yes? Have you ever been?"

Isabel shook her head. "No, no, I've never been to Germany at all, I'm afraid."

"Ah, it is the most beautiful place." Erik Neumann leant against an easel and flashed another warm smile in Isabel's direction. "You really must go if you get the opportunity. I have lived there all my life, but it is only now as I am approaching the second half of my life that I really, truly appreciate its beauty." He gave a small chuckle. "Did you know it has more bridges than Amsterdam and Venice combined?"

"Oh, really?" Isabel couldn't help but find herself returning Erik Neumann's warm smile with one of her own. "I had no idea. Is that what you are interested in? Bridges? Architecture?"

"Indeed it is, Miss Faraday. I would have brought my portfolio with me, but it was too hot today to carry it on your underground. So many people squashed into such small spaces! I have left it at the hotel I am staying in."

"How long are you planning on staying, Mr Neumann?"

"Call me Erik, please." Another warm smile. "Originally, I had planned to only stay for a few weeks, but I am falling in love with your city, Miss Faraday. I am on a, what do you call it in English? A voyage of discovery? I think I may stay for a few months, and I would really love to continue with my painting while I am here. You have so many bridges, I really need to paint them all!"

"Well, you are most welcome to rent an easel whenever you want." Isabel pushed herself up off her stool and began to head back towards the café. "We rent by the day, for as many days as you wish, Monday to Sunday. And as I said, all materials are included in the price."

"That would be perfect." Erik Neumann followed Isabel back into the café. "If it would be acceptable, I would like to rent perhaps three or four days a week? Maybe I could start tomorrow?"

"That would be perfect, Mr Neu…. Erik," beamed Isabel, reaching behind the front counter of the café to retrieve the art studio paperwork. "Let's get you booked in. I'll make you a coffee while I sort out the paperwork."

\* \* \*

Time: 7.00pm

Date: Saturday 21st July 2012
Location: Metropolitan Police HQ, London

DS Carmichael swung out of the rear car park and headed out onto the almost deserted road. If anyone had been watching, they would have noted that his chosen route was in the opposite direction to his supposed hotel lodgings.

But nobody was watching.

He pulled off the ID badge from around his neck and stowed it in the glove compartment, out of sight. Where he was going, and who he was meeting, it wouldn't be wise to announce that you were the property of the Metropolitan Police Service.

No, that wouldn't do at all.

The traffic was light for a Saturday evening, and he made good progress. He had a busy night ahead of him.

* * *

Time: 7.25pm
Date: Saturday 21st July 2012
Location: Isabel's Café, King's Road, London

Isabel closed the door to the café and smiled, contentedly. Erik Neumann. Her first artist to rent an easel. Although she wasn't charging an astronomical amount, it would certainly help towards the rent on the café and studio; help she desperately needed according to her bank balance. And with the easels sitting idle most of the time , it was the most logical and obvious idea. An idea that had come from Patrick, not long after he had arrived. She would have to thank him properly when he turned up tomorrow.

Turning away from the door, she flicked the locks and lowered the blinds. As she passed back through the café, towards the studio and stairs that led up to her flat, she straightened a few cushions on the sagging sofas and returned a couple of well-thumbed paperbacks to the shelves. Satisfied that the café looked in good order, good enough for the breakfast crowd anyway, and knowing that Dominic would have left the kitchen spotless, she headed out towards the studio.

A long, hot bath beckoned.

Despite the sultry heat of the day, Isabel craved the feeling of scalding soapy water against her skin. And maybe a glass or two of wine wouldn't go amiss either.

As she passed by the three easels, one of which was soon to belong to Erik Neumann, she wondered what type of paintings her new artist would create. He had mentioned that he liked bridges, didn't he? And architecture? Well, there were certainly enough bridges in London worthy of being brought to life on canvas. Maybe Tower Bridge? London Bridge?

Isabel's eyes flickered to the wall behind the easels, coming to rest on a medium sized canvas in the centre. The beauty of the brushstrokes never failed to stop her in her tracks, the elegance of the watercolours captivating her no matter how many times she gazed at it.

The painting was of a large oak tree, nestled in the shade at the bottom of a sweeping lawn, the summer sun glinting on the broad, green leaves. Dappled sunshine created a patchwork effect on the verdant grass beneath. Several thick branches dipped low from the roughened trunk, swinging invitingly, perfect for small arms and legs to explore. A wooden framed summerhouse peeped out from beneath one of the boughs, perfect match-box windows with red and white gingham curtains either side of a pale sky-blue door.

Isabel's heart heaved inside her chest.

As it always did.

Her tree.

Her summerhouse.

Her mother.

* * *

Time: 3.15pm
  Date: 25th August 1985
  Location: The Glade, Church Street, Albury, Surrey

Isabel peeked her head out from behind the gingham curtains.

"Peek-a-boo!" she chirped through the matchbox-sized window, then dived back inside, out of sight.

Elizabeth Faraday smiled, looking up from her easel and casting her gaze towards the summerhouse where she knew her daughter was playing hide-and-seek.

"Princess? Where are you?" Elizabeth Faraday feigned a confused look, letting her eyes wander around the garden in an apparent search for her elusive daughter. She put her paintbrush down on the palette and wiped her fingers on a well-used cloth in her lap. Faint brushstrokes of apple green and powdered blue smeared her cheeks and forehead, her pale denim dungarees spotted with dabs of orange, browns and reds. "Looks like I'll have to come and find you," she sang, rising from her stool and heading towards the shady tree. "I wonder where you could be?"

Keeping up the pretence that she knew would be causing her mischievous daughter to quiver with excitement, Elizabeth Faraday peered in amongst the branches, holding back the waxy leaves as she popped her head into the cool shade. "Princess? Are you in here?" Craning her neck skywards, she glanced up through the heavy summer foliage, searching Isabel's favourite hiding place. "Are you hiding from me, you cheeky monkey?"

Muffled giggling could be heard coming from the direction of the summerhouse. Elizabeth Faraday smiled and side-stepped slowly towards the wooden structure that nestled snugly under a sweeping branch. More twitching of the gingham curtains. More giggling.

"I'm coming to get you!" chanted Elizabeth Faraday, appearing at one of the tiny windows and peering inside. "I'm coming to get you!" Giggling turned into squeals of laughter as she pushed open the door. "Found you!" she chimed, casting her eyes around the dim interior and finding a red-cheeked, grinning face beaming out from the shadows in the far corner of the summerhouse.

Suddenly, a bundle of arms and legs rushed towards her, throwing themselves into her open arms. Elizabeth Faraday felt small arms hooking around her neck, and two legs clinging tightly to her hips. She smiled and returned the squeeze.

"You took ages to find me, Mummy!" squealed Isabel, her hot breath tickling her mother's cheek. "You're not very good at hide and seek!"

Elizabeth Faraday chuckled and backed out of the tiny summerhouse. "You are too good at hiding, that's why, Princess! I'm sure even Daddy wouldn't have found you hiding in there!"

Isabel gave more squeals of delight and wriggled out of her mother's embrace, dropping onto the soft grass. "What are you painting?" She skipped over to the easel and peered at the canvas, her small freckled nose almost touching the still wet paint. "Is it my tree?"

Elizabeth Faraday smiled and nodded, standing by her daughter's side and resting a loving hand on her shoulder. "It is your tree, yes. And your summerhouse. Look." She pointed towards the beginnings of the tiny wooden house poking out from underneath some chocolate coloured branches. "And I may even paint you in one of the windows," she laughed, bending down to pick up her paintbrushes. "Come on, let's go inside for some lemonade."

Isabel yelped with delight and started to run back towards the house, cartwheeling as she went.

\* \* \*


Time: 7.35pm
    Date: Saturday 21st July 2012

Location: Isabel's Café, King's Road, London

Isabel gazed at the canvas, her eyes drawn as they always were to the tiny matchbox windows on either side of the door. The faint outline of a face could be seen in the shadows behind the red and white gingham curtains.

Isabel.

Her mother had painted her at the window.

Just as she said she would.

In the corner of the painting, Isabel saw the small, neat handwriting that belonged to her mother. '*E. Faraday (August* 1985)'. Reaching out, she ran her fingertips lightly over the words, feeling the slightly raised brushstrokes under her skin. Isabel would often touch her mother's last painting, running her fingers over the gnarled-looking bark, the soft sheen of sunlight on the leaves, the coolness of the shady summerhouse. Each time she did, she was transported back to that day. The memory was so vivid it was as though she was almost there again, back in her garden, back in her summerhouse, back in her mother's arms. It was almost as though by touching her words, touching her paint strokes, she could feel her mother's soft skin, her soft caresses, her warm embraces.

Isabel could feel tears beginning to prick at the corners of her eyes. With a final touch of "E.Faraday" she dragged her gaze away from the dappled sunlight, away from the chocolate-box summerhouse, and away from her memories.

* * *

Time: 7.35pm
Date: Saturday 21<sup>st</sup> July 2012
Location: King's Road, London

Erik Neumann leant against the low-rising wall and took a long drag on the hand-rolled cigarette dangling from the corner of his mouth. He cocked his head to one side as he stared across the road towards Isabel's café.

"Perfect," he murmured to himself, taking another deep lung-full of tobacco. "Absolutely perfect." He pushed himself off the wall and lightly brushed his linen suit with his other hand. He smiled, warmly, at an approaching elderly lady, out walking with her rat-like dog in the cooling summer evening air. The tiny, yapping bundle of energy strained on its leash, and made a beeline for Erik's feet – sniffing and snorting at his open-toed sandals. Erik recoiled slightly, fighting back the urge to give the snapping dog a swift kick as he felt its drooling tongue lapping at his toes. Instead he maintained his plastic smile and inclined his head towards the elderly lady, who was trying her best to shoo the dog along, her arthritic limbs protesting wildly.

"Good evening," greeted Erik, through gritted teeth, as the woman tottered towards him. Her upper back was hunched forwards at such an angle that it made her appear a good foot shorter than she actually was. He could smell her lavender scent already, and the hairspray that caked her blue-rinse hairstyle into its rock hard shape. Two patches of inexpertly applied blusher and a smear of pink lipstick completed the look.

"Come on, Bertie," she croaked, the opening of her mouth causing crater-like wrinkles to appear either side. "Leave that poor gentleman's feet alone. I'm very sorry." She looked up from her hunched frame and gave Erik a smile through cracked lips.

"No problem," he replied, stepping to the side to escape the attention of the four-legged saliva machine below. "He's very sweet," he added, not meaning a word of it.

Bertie was eventually dragged away to continue his evening walk, and Erik turned to head back towards Sloane Square Underground station.

Bridges, he muttered to himself. I must find some bridges.

\* \* \*

100

# Chapter Twelve

Time: 9.20pm
    Date: Saturday 21st July 2012
    Location: Kettle's Yard Mews, London

Jack left the living room curtains open to allow the faint evening breeze to waft through the open window. At least it was cooling down now that the roasting sun had slipped behind the horizon, turning the skies into a mesmerising streaked light show of vivid pinks, purples and dusky oranges. The window had been open all day; Jack thought that if a determined burglar really wanted to get inside then he would have to scale a two storey building in full view of the whole street. Policeman or no policeman, Jack couldn't face another sticky, humid night.

"Tea?" Mac snapped on the small recessed lights that shone above the kitchen sink. He placed the Chinese takeaway they had picked up from around the corner onto the countertop while reaching for the kettle.

Jack nodded and collapsed into the comfort of the sofa. "You might need to check if there's milk in the fridge though."

Mac pulled the door of the fridge open, bathing the rest of the kitchen area in bright light. He rummaged inside the sparsely filled shelves. "Hmmmm, no milk, brother."

"I had a feeling I might have used the last of it this morning," mused Jack, loosening his tie and putting his feet up on the small table in front of him. "Sorry. You'll have to take it black"

Mac grimaced. "Beer?" He raised a questioning eyebrow at Jack, whilst eyeing the row of beer bottles in amongst a solitary egg and slab of cheese.

"Beer," agreed Jack.

Mac pulled out two bottles of Budweiser from the fridge, snapping the lids off with the bottle opener he spied lying conveniently by the side of the kettle. He brought the bottles over to the table along with the cartons of Chinese takeaway. It had been his idea to grab a takeaway after he had left Isabel's earlier. Not fancying the journey back to Islington until the heat had died down, he took a detour to Jack's office and suggested a Chinese on the way home. He had had to wait around while they wrapped up whatever it was that they were doing, but eventually Jack had signalled that it was time to go.

Passing Jack a bottle of beer, Mac sat down opposite and took a long gulp from his own bottle. He felt the ice cold liquid slip down his throat, quenching the thirst that had built up through the long, hot, humid day.

"You know you can buy milk in shops these days, Jack. Along with your shopping." Mac glanced at his brother out of the corner of his eye.

Jack gave a smile and pressed the cold bottle against his forehead for a second. He took a long draught of his beer before replying. "I know, Stu. I know."

"And that way you might not run out quite so often. You can even buy that UHT stuff and keep it in your cupboards."

Jack made a face and took another gulp of beer, closing his eyes as the liquid quenched his dry throat. "I like getting my milk from the milkman, Stu. You know that. End of discussion."

* * *

Time: 10.01pm
Date: 5th April 1971
Location: Old Mill Road, Christchurch

Jack felt the hardwood floor painfully beneath his bare knees, rough wooden splinters pricking at his skin as he knelt down and looked up.

She was swinging, slightly, as if rocking in a gentle summer's breeze.

And Jack didn't know what to do.

"Mummy?" he whispered, gazing up at the lifeless body still swaying in front of him. "Mummy?" He noticed that her feet were bare but her toenails were painted a bright red. Blood red. She was wearing a silky nightdress that rippled as she swayed.

Jack reached out with a tiny, quivering hand and touched one of his mother's bare feet. It was cold. Ice cold. He pushed and prodded at her toes, making her leg swing back and forth. "Mummy?"

The sound of the thunderstorm raging outside crashed against the kitchen window, filling Jack's ears with noise. Placing his tiny hands over his ears, he began to cry. "Mummy?" A crack of lightning bathed the room with light, causing the ceiling lights to flicker and hiss, threatening to plunge the room into darkness.

Jack crawled away from the swinging body, his knees scraping on the rough floorboards until he reached the hallway. He pulled himself to his feet and rubbed his knees, small pinpricks of blood smearing his skin from the jagged wooden splinters. He rubbed his eyes with the back of his hands, salty tears mixing with the blood on his hands.

He didn't know what to do.

What should I do, Mummy?

He looked towards the bedroom door where he knew his brother, Stuart, would be sleeping, tucked up in the bottom bunk. Jack started walking down the hallway, padding past the bedroom and heading towards the front door.

"Never go outside the front door, Jack. Never." His mother's words sang out through the darkened shadows, echoing around his head. "Promise me. Never open the front door."

She would repeat those words every night before she went out to work, giving Jack a tight hug and ruffling his hair with her delicate hand, and kissing him on the top of his head. Jack could feel her warm body pulling him close, the scent of her perfume filling his nostrils.

And Jack had never opened the front door before.

Never.

Until now.

Jack reached out and pulled the heavy door towards him, but it wouldn't budge. He tried again, his tiny frame pulling with all his might. But still it refused to move. Wide-eyed with an ever-growing panic, Jack's gaze rested on the wrought iron key poking out of the lock. He remembered seeing his mother turn the key sometimes, causing it to make a heavy click echo down the draughty hall.

Jack placed his tiny fingers around the key, feeling the cold metal against his skin, as cold as his mother's foot. He gave it a twist. Nothing. He tried again. Still nothing. With a glance over his shoulder towards the door, his lower lip began to tremble and fresh tears ran down his already tear-streaked cheeks. He twisted the key the other way. This time there was a satisfying muffled click.

Pulling at the door once again, Jack found that it creaked open. The sound of the thunder magnified as he peered out into the communal landing and down the spiral stairs that led to the front door.

I don't know what to do, Mummy, Jack cried inside his head.

I don't know what to do.

Another bolt of lightning made Jack flinch, the landing momentarily bathed in bright, white light from the windows above. He saw several other doors, but didn't know who lived behind them, and was too frightened to knock and find out.

Jack only knew one other person.

George.

He would wait for George.

George would know what to do.

* * *

Time: 5.12am
  Date: 6<sup>th</sup> April 1971
  Location: Old Mill Road, Christchurch

"Hello, sonny. What're you doing sitting out here on the stairs?"

George Robertson gently lowered the wire basket housing twelve thick glass milk bottles down on the stairs, and knelt down beside Jack. He placed a liver-spotted hand on top of Jack's small head, and patted him comfortingly. The boy looked frozen solid, George mused, kneeling down as low as his ageing back would allow. Fifty years he had been doing this job, starting not much older than the poor slip of a boy in front of him, helping his father on his rounds, and his joints were now protesting violently. He took his white, peaked cap off his head, displaying a shiny bald crown with ice-white tufts above each ear.

George touched the boy's cheek with the back of his hand. Ice cold to the touch. He took in the boy's trembling limbs, seeing his bruised and scratched knees shivering and knocking together as he hugged them close to his body with his thin, bony arms.

"Jack, son. You're freezing. Why are you sitting out here, all alone?" George looked up to see the front door to the MacIntosh flat was ajar. "Is your mother at home?"

Jack looked up, mournfully, with wide eyes that were red-rimmed, dirty cheeks stained with tears. "Mum…. Mummy," he croaked, his body still shivering uncontrollably. "I…. I don't know what to do."

George patted him on the head again, flattening down his tousled, matted hair. "It's OK, sonny. Let's go inside and warm you up, shall we?" He gently pulled Jack to his feet. "And find your Mummy."

So, George took Jack inside.

And they found his Mummy.

\* \* \*

Time: 9.25pm
Date: Saturday 21ˢᵗ July 2012
Location: Kettle's Yard Mews, London

"I like getting my milk from the milkman," repeated Jack, taking another swig from his beer bottle. "You know that."

Mac nodded, draining his own bottle. "Fair enough." He knew Jack placed a great deal of gratitude on their old milkman, George. Mac wasn't sure that he really remembered George, or even that they had had a milkman – but Jack had never forgotten how George had saved their lives. That was how he put it. George had saved our lives. No one else would have come to see us, Stu, Jack would tell him. No one else would have bothered to ask why a little boy was sitting on the stairs outside his flat. No one else. No one else but George.

So Mac could see the logic; that Jack felt the need to keep a milkman in his life, as a testament of thanks to George. George himself had passed many years ago; Jack attending his funeral and laying his own message of thanks to the kindly, liver-spotted, bald-headed milkman who had saved their lives without ever realising it.

And it had been hard to find a milkman in London. No one seemed to use them anymore, preferring to buy their milk more cheaply and conveniently at a supermarket or online shop. Or the garage. Milkmen like George were a dying breed.

But Jack needed a George in his life.

\* \* \*

Time: 9.30pm
Date: Saturday 21ˢᵗ July 2012
Location: A cellar in London

Hannah watched, curiously, as the woman was dragged across the stone floor of the cellar to the bare mattress opposite, her body as limp as a child's ragdoll. She didn't make a sound, or even dare to breathe, watching him fasten the chain around the woman's ankle.

She tried to think back to when she had first arrived. How long ago was it now? One day? Two days? More? The eternal darkness and silence made each minute seem to last a lifetime. No day. No night. Minutes, hours, days just drifting in and out of her consciousness, merging into one.

But when Hannah had arrived, she had not been alone.

There had been someone else in the cellar as she took her own first drugged, stumbling steps across the cold, damp floor. She remembered squinting through the darkness to find a pair of wide, doleful eyes peering back out at her through the gloom. At first, Hannah wasn't sure who or what the eyes belonged to. Was it even human? Was it an animal? The owner of the eyes didn't make a move or utter a sound, and Hannah began to wonder if she were hallucinating, seeing things that weren't there. He had drugged her; she knew that much. Her body felt strangely limp, her brain fogged and cluttered.

But then the eyes had spoken. Hesitant at first, and with a voice so quiet it was barely above a faint whisper. "Georgie," the voice had murmured. "My name is Georgie."

But Georgie had gone. Just like that, she had been released from her chained restraints and taken from the room.

And Georgie had not returned.

Hannah continued to watch as he placed a fresh bottle of water by the woman's side. As he did so, he muttered something under his breath, in such a hushed tone Hannah couldn't make out the words. As he turned towards her, she averted her gaze, not wanting to look into those eyes.

Leaving the woman's limp form on the bare mattress, he padded silently across the stone floor towards Hannah. She shrank further underneath her blanket and closed her eyes, holding her breath and pretending to be asleep. It was always better if she pretended to be asleep.

"There, there," he whispered, bending down by her side. "You sleep tight." Hannah heard the sound of water being trickled into the empty bottle by her mattress, but firmly kept her eyes clamped shut. After several seconds of keeping the air within her lungs, she heard the cellar door being pulled shut and the key turned in the lock. She exhaled gratefully, pulled the blanket further around her body and let a silent tear slide down her cheek.

\* \* \*

# Chapter Thirteen

Time: 9.30pm
    Date: Saturday 21st July 2012
    Location: Kettle's Yard Mews, London

"Have you seen Isabel lately? I popped in yesterday with Cooper." Jack handed Mac a black coffee and watched the grimace crossing his brother's face as he accepted the mug.

After taking a sip and wincing at the lack of milk, he nodded. "I stopped by earlier today as I was delivering nearby."

"You think she's doing OK?" It was Jack's turn to make a face as he sipped his milk-less coffee. "After everything?"

Mac hesitated, thought about taking another sip of the scalding coffee then decided against it, putting the mug back down on the coffee table. "I guess." He tried to disguise the wavering of his voice, but Jack picked up on the worried tone.

"What are you not telling me?" Jack leant forwards and tried to catch his brother's eye. "Stuart MacIntosh. I can read you like a book. What have I missed?"

Mac let the question hang in the still, lifeless air. He glanced over at the open window, willing a breeze to wash over them and diffuse the rapidly increasing tension. Knowing he couldn't put it off any longer, he took a deep breath and turned to face Jack's inquisitive face. "I took her to the cemetery. In Surrey."

"The cemetery? Her parents' graves?" Jack shrugged. "Well, that's a good thing. Isn't it?"

"Yes." Mac felt his skin prickle and began to shift uncomfortably in his seat. "And no."

"What do you mean, yes and no?" Jack felt an unease creep into the pit of his stomach. "Stu, what have you done?"

Mac gave a small, throaty chuckle and shook his head. "Jesus, Jack, why do you always think I've done something?"

"History, Stu, history." Jack fought the exasperation out of his voice. "So, what happened then?"

"Promise you won't kick off?"

The sense of trepidation in Jack's stomach began to deepen. "When do I ever 'kick off'?" He ignored the look that Mac flashed in his direction. "OK, just tell me."

\* \* \*

Time: 12.30pm

Date: Sunday 8<sup>th</sup> July 2012

Location: Albury Churchyard, Surrey

Isabel leant back, turning her face upwards to feel the warmth of the sun's rays caressing her cheeks. She could feel the wispy grass tickling her feet through her open-toed sandals. Birds chirped in the nearby yew trees, the sound of their song lightening her heart. For a moment, she could forget about everything. Forget about the café, forget about the bills, forget about the coffee machine that needed a service. For a moment, she could be free. She loved it here, just sitting in the shade of the trees, letting her worries melt away. And closing the café for the day had been just the tonic she needed.

"Why do they always plant yew trees in cemeteries and graveyards?"

Isabel opened her eyes and looked at Mac, who was kneeling down at the side of her parents' graves tidying away the weeds that were crawling up the sides of the headstones.

"Sorry?" she replied, pushing herself up onto her knees and shielding her eyes from the sun. "Yew trees?"

"Yes, yew trees." Mac nodded at the huge branches reaching out above them. "That's what they are, isn't it? Always seem to see them in churchyards and cemeteries. I just wondered why."

"I'm not sure anyone really knows. Some call it the tree of death – that its roots feed on the dead within the ground. Others say it is a sign of new life and resurrection." Isabel gave a shrug and gazed skywards. "They can be really poisonous, you know. Their bark is used in chemotherapy drugs."

"How do you know things like that?" Mac threw the weeds he had collected into the plastic tub they had brought with them.

"There's a lot about me you don't yet know, Stuart MacIntosh," teased Isabel, flashing him a grin. "Behave yourself and you might find out one day."

Mac felt a smile tickle his lips as he returned to the gravestone of Elizabeth Faraday. He brushed aside the grass cuttings from the base of the headstone and picked up the random twigs that had fallen from the boughs of the overhead trees.

And it was then that he saw it.

\* \* \*

Time: 9.35pm
Date: Saturday 21st July 2012
Location: Kettle's Yard Mews, London

"It was a prism." Mac's words hung in the sultry air like a hangman's noose, mirroring the noose-like knot that had been forming in Jack's stomach, and which was tightening further.

"A prism?" Although he asked the question, Jack wondered if he really wanted to know the answer. "Where?"

"There was a single rose in one of the plant stands – at the side of the headstone. I didn't think anything of it. I thought maybe a friend or neighbour had brought it. Isabel didn't bring any flowers; they wouldn't last five minutes in this heat."

"The prism?" reminded Jack. "You said there was a prism."

Mac nodded, the strain evident on his face as he cast his mind back. "There was a small card attached on a ribbon, around the stem. So small you could have missed it." Mac paused and locked eyes with Jack. "The card had a prism on it. Nothing else. Just a prism." Mac reached into the back pocket of his jeans and brought out a small two inches by three inches piece of card. "I managed to get it without Isabel noticing." He placed the card down on the coffee table in front of Jack.

Jack stared at the small card, now battered around the edges and creased from Mac's pocket. Plain white, greying now around the sides. A prism drawn in black ink in the centre. Great. Forensics would be impossible now. "What did Isabel say? Did she notice it at all?"

Mac shrugged. "She saw the rose. I made an excuse that it must have been a neighbour who left it." He paused and let his eyes focus on the card. "I didn't want her to worry."

"You like her, don't you?" Jack smiled as he saw the concern etched onto his brother's face.

"Sorry, who?" Mac picked up his abandoned coffee and took another sip, fighting a grimace at the now lukewarm, acrid taste.

"You know who," replied Jack, softly. "Isabel. You like her."

"We all like Isabel, Jack. She's a nice person." Mac drained his coffee cup and looked at his watch. "I need to go." He rose to his feet and turned away to hide the pink tinge flooding his cheeks. "I've got an early start in the morning."

Jack nodded and watched as Mac wrestled back into his bike leathers.

"Don't tell her about the card, Stu. Next time you see her, don't say anything."

Mac paused, reaching down to pick up his bike helmet. "It's him, isn't it? Kreshniov." Jack felt his stomach tighten at the name. "He's back, isn't he? All those months you spent looking for him – and he's just showed up right on our doorstep."

Jack hesitated before nodding, slowly, his gaze still lingering on the card. "Maybe. Maybe not."

"Why come back now?" Mac began heading towards the door. "What does he want with her?"

"I'm not sure," replied Jack.

But I'm going to find out.

As he shut the door on his departing brother, he found his mind casting itself back to the last time he went in search of the elusive Russian.

* * *

Time: 12.00pm

Date: 19<sup>th</sup> November 2008

Location: Liberec, Czech Republic

Boris Kreshniov quietly surveyed the town square before him. It was a shame he had to leave. He had become quite attached to the place. Its sedentary way of life, its early morning coffees and late afternoon trdelnik. The lazy, tranquil evenings filled with wine and good food.

But leave he must.

He snapped the clasps shut on his briefcase and swung the small knapsack high up onto his shoulders. His taxi was picking him up from outside the Town Hall in precisely ten minutes. He adjusted his sunglasses and glanced down at his watch.

Come on, Detective.

Where are you?

Kreshniov smiled to himself as he watched the Czechs go about their daily business across the square. The waiters and waitresses at his favourite bistro were busily taking orders for cappuccinos, strudels and medovnik, and barely noticed the watchful gaze of the lone stranger loitering in the shadows. He longed to have seen the expression on Detective Inspector Jack MacIntosh's face when the mobile phone mast at Liberec had revealed his location. The mobile phone Kreshniov had purposefully left on in order to taunt the overworked detective and lure him into this cat and mouse game.

The mobile phone in question now lay buried somewhere in a landfill site east of the town.

And Boris Kreshniov was, once again, no more.

Dr Samuel Winterburn now resided in his place.

The sun was creeping high in the sky, casting its weak rays down onto the square. The recent snowfall was beginning to melt, but the inhabitants of this small Czech town knew it was only a brief respite; the grip of winter wasn't far away. Kreshniov moved further into the shadows of a nearby bakery, the early morning shoppers having already descended to fill their baskets of freshly baked breads and pastries. He looked at his watch again.

He had nine minutes.

Nine minutes until his taxi arrived.

Nine minutes until he needed to leave.

Nine minutes for Detective Inspector Jack MacIntosh to show his face.

A movement out of the corner of his eye momentarily lifted his spirits, but it was just a hungry pigeon strutting across the pavement in-between the tables of an outside café, pecking at the crumbs left by its recent occupants.

Eight minutes.

Kreshniov slunk back, further out of sight, glancing again at his watch. He blinked behind his wraparound sunglasses which housed the pale green contact lenses he had inserted into his eyes earlier.

Come on, Detective. Don't let me down now.

We've been playing so nicely together.

As if in answer to his prayers, another movement across the square caught his attention. It was not a pigeon this time. Kreshniov couldn't help but let a smile slide across his lips as he saw the unmistakable figure of Detective Inspector Jack MacIntosh hurrying towards him.

Kreshniov shrank back further into the welcome shadows of the bakery, his heartbeat racing faster and faster as the Detective moved closer.

Just a little bit further, Detective Inspector MacIntosh; just a little bit further.

\* \* \*

Time: 12.05pm
 Date: 19<sup>th</sup> November 2008
 Location: Liberec, Czech Republic

Jack reached the outside tables of Café Letka and scanned the tables. He knew it was a long shot, but Kreshniov's mobile phone had pinged at this exact spot some forty-eight hours ago. With the fallout from the Phoenix Project still reverberating around Metropolitan Police headquarters, no one had batted an eyelid at Jack's request for a few days leave.

The tables were almost deserted; only two were occupied. At one table there was a middle aged woman, sitting alone reading a newspaper. At the other, a young couple held hands over cooling matching cappuccinos.

Jack sighed and moved towards the row of shops behind the café. Maybe if he showed a photograph of Kreshniov to the shopkeepers, the waiters and waitresses, just maybe someone may recognise him.

It was a long shot; Jack knew that.

But a long shot was all he had.

And he owed it to Isabel to try.

\* \* \*

Time: 12.05pm
Date: 19<sup>th</sup> November 2008
Location: Liberec, Czech Republic

Four minutes.

Four minutes to go.

Kreshniov was loathed to leave so soon, not now that the Detective Inspector had finally arrived, but he had a plane to catch.

Correction.

Dr Samuel Winterburn had a plane to catch.

Kreshniov stepped out from the shadows of the bakery and into the hazy sunshine, letting the weak rays warm his skin. He stepped around the tables and chairs of the café next door and started heading towards the Town Hall and his waiting taxi.

Three minutes.

Kreshniov could see the Detective Inspector only a few metres in front of him, heading towards the small butcher's shop and delicatessen next to the bakery. He smiled as he saw the small piece of rectangular card in Jack's hand. A photograph. The detective had brought a photograph with him. Kreshniov suppressed the urge to chuckle.

Show my photograph to as many people as you want, Detective Inspector. You still won't find me.

Boris Kreshniov has never been to Liberec.

But with blonde hair, false teeth, cheek contouring and lip fillers, green contact lenses and inserts in his shoes, Dr Samuel Winterburn, a leading cosmetic surgeon from Harley Street in London, most definitely had.

Two minutes.

Dr Samuel Winterburn continued heading away from the town square in the direction of the Town Hall. He allowed himself a small smile as he passed the tired detective, so close he could have reached out and touched his shoulder, but instead he merely nodded his head in passing and carried on to his waiting taxi.

* * *

Time: 9.40pm
    Date: Saturday 21<sup>st</sup> July 2012
    Location: Kettle's Yard Mews, London

Jack leant against the window frame and watched Mac pull away from the side of the road through the open curtains. The throaty sound of the motorbike engine carried effortlessly through the still night air. Watching his brother disappearing out of sight, on two wheels, gave him a familiar and unwelcome wrench in the pit of his stomach.

* * *

Time: 1.35pm
    Date: 10<sup>th</sup> May 1982
    Location: West Road Comprehensive School, Christchurch

"Don't be so stupid, Stu. Put that down and come back in with me." Jack nodded towards the motorbike helmet in Stuart MacIntosh's hand. "Lunch break ended five minutes ago, we'll be late." Jack pushed himself off the low wall he had been sitting on and headed back to the entrance of West Road Comprehensive School, swinging his rucksack high up onto his shoulder. "If we run down the side of the gym we might not be seen."

Jack paused just inside the school gates and turned to look back over his shoulder, noticing how his brother had not moved an inch. Stuart MacIntosh stood next to the bike, one hand resting on the worn leather seat, the other one swinging the battered helmet by his side. A smirk crossed his face, his hot eyes full of defiance.

"You can't make me, Jack." Stuart MacIntosh thrust his thirteen-year-old chin out and fixed his older brother with a hard stare. "You can't make me do anything." His tired-looking school jumper was tied around his waist, revealing a stained and creased once-white shirt beneath. His tie was undone and hanging, loosely, around his neck.

Jack sighed and looked at his watch. He would get a detention for being late to Mr Buckley's chemistry lesson, his third this month already. And always because of Stu. They had only recently been placed in the same school, Stuart having been kicked out of every one he had attended before. This was his last chance; placing him with his older brother was seen as a last ditch attempt to curb his unruly ways.

It wasn't working.

"Stu, come on. Don't be daft. Stop hanging around with that lot, they're bad news." Jack gave a discreet nod towards a gang of teenagers congregating at the side of the road, circling like vultures around three more motorbikes. Three broad-shouldered youths, dressed in a uniform of black jeans and hoodies, stared out at Jack with their hollow, menacing eyes. None of them were pupils at West Road Comprehensive School. Jack suspected they weren't pupils at any school - most likely suspended or expelled from any institution they had been enrolled in, and then allowed to melt away from the education system into insignificance. They clustered together like wolves in a pack, passing skinny hand-rolled cigarettes around with dirty, nail-bitten fingers.

Jack didn't know where Stuart had met them, but anything was possible at the foster home Stuart had been placed with for the last five years. On the other side of Christchurch, out in the rural stretches towards Hinton and the New Forest beyond, Jack barely saw his brother, other than at school. When Stuart could be bothered to attend. Separated when Jack was six, Jack had been lucky and taken in by a loving foster family for the first five years. When he was nine, he moved to another family, who provided an equally loving environment for him to settle and grow. Stuart hadn't been quite so lucky. A series of short term foster placements followed; each family finding it harder and harder to manage his temper and wayward tendencies. So much so that for the last five years, Stuart had been living at the St

Bartholomew's Home for Boys, an imposing building on the outskirts of Christchurch, housing a disturbingly growing number of boys that society had abandoned.

"They're my friends," retorted Stuart, his breath coming out hot and thick.

"They're not your friends, Stu," replied Jack, eyeing his watch again. "They're using you. They'll get you into all sorts of trouble – and you've been caught enough times by the police recently. You know that the next time you get caught, they'll take you away. You'll end up in Borstal."

Stuart laughed and kicked the side of the kerb with a dirty boot. "I don't care, Jack. No one cares about me, so I don't care about them. Just go, Jack. Leave me alone." With that, Stuart MacIntosh pulled the motorbike helmet onto his head and swung his leg up over the seat. Grabbing hold of the waist of the equally defiant teenager at the front, and before Jack could say anything more, Stuart sped off down the street, the high pitched whining of the motorbike engine filling the air.

* * *

Time: 9.45pm
   Date: Saturday 21st July 2012
   Location: Kettle's Yard Mews, London

Jack listened to the last echoes of the motorbike engine filtering through the sultry evening air, before pulling the curtains closed and collapsing onto the sofa. That ride on the motorbike had been Stuart's last...for a while. Later that day, he was arrested with the rest of the gang for a violent robbery at a corner shop; the terrified shop owner subjected to the teenage mob brandishing baseball bats and knives - all for the sake of a few packets of cigarettes and cans of cheap lager. The father of five later died of a heart attack brought on by the ordeal. Stuart spent the next three years in an approved school, followed by several more in youth detention, and then disappeared from Jack's life.

Jack shuddered, even though the evening air was still sticky and warm.

Reaching for the bottle of single malt still sitting by the side of the coffee table, he sat and poured two inches of amber liquid into a glass, swirling it briefly before gulping the entire lot down in one. He grimaced at the fiery back burn in his throat, but welcomed the warmth as it slid down towards his stomach. Placing the empty glass back down on the coffee table, he sighed and closed his eyes, rubbing at the faint throbbing headache threatening his temples.

He leant forwards and picked up the bottle again, pouring another two inches into the bottom of the glass. As he replaced the bottle, his eyes came to rest on the leaflet sitting by the side of the pile of as-yet unopened post.

PTSD – The Facts.

Jack hesitated. He swung the glass back up to his lips and drained the whisky in one again, wincing as the alcohol made his eyes water. As he replaced the glass, he picked up the leaflet and stared at it.

Post-Traumatic Stress Disorder.

This was what his psychotherapist said he had.

Apparently.

It had a name.

Apparently.

Jack held the leaflet in his hand and continued to study the front cover. There was a picture of a brain in the centre – a normal looking brain with various speech bubbles surrounding it, each containing the description of a particular trauma.

I bet they don't have 'finding your mother's dead body hanging from a light fitting', mused Jack, the neat whisky now penetrating his bloodstream. He could feel the light-headedness beginning, his muscles starting to relax, his mind beginning to wander. He took a swig directly from the bottle, bypassing the glass this time.

Post-Traumatic Stress Disorder.

A label.

Not a label he particularly liked; but then again, Jack didn't particularly like any labels.

Jack flipped the leaflet over in his hands, his eyes scanning the back where it gave a list of websites and telephone numbers for accessing emotional and wellbeing support. He flipped the leaflet back to the front again and then tossed it onto the coffee table, picking up the bottle of single malt once more.

Emotional and wellbeing support.

I'm forty-five years of age, thought Jack.

I think that ship has sailed.

Jack felt the alcohol swirling through his bloodstream, his mind now flooding with thoughts and images in an uncontrollable whirl.

Emotional and wellbeing support from the bottom of a bottle of whisky.

That was unlikely to be printed on any leaflet, he was sure of that.

His gaze came to rest, as it often did, on the battered and tatty teddy bear that was tucked behind a cushion on the chair opposite. Unable to explain why, Jack had always kept the bear with him – never having the heart to shove it away into storage or pack it off to a charity shop or jumble sale, even after all this time.

The bear seemed to sense that its mere presence was a link to the past – following Jack around the room with its beady black stare. Whenever Jack looked at it, all he could see was Stuart. When they were small, the pair of them were inseparable; Stuart and his bear. Until that day. Until that fateful day. The day that Jack would always remember as the day he lost his brother.

When Stuart had been removed from their foster family, and taken away, Jack had wanted to take the bear to him. He'll be missing his teddy bear, he would tell his foster mother. Can't we take it to him?

The young six-year-old Jack had been reassured that Stuart was fine, happy with his new family and wasn't missing his teddy bear at all. But maybe Jack would just look after it for him, as the kind big brother that he was.

So that was what Jack had done.

Big brother Jack.

Jack knew that the collapse of Stuart's world, and the slide into adolescent crime and delinquency, was not because he didn't have his favourite teddy bear with him. But it was a reminder to Jack of how different their lives had been. Just looking at the battered teddy bear reminded him of how life had been before – before their world had turned upside down.

Before he had lost his brother.

Although Stuart was now back in his life, Jack couldn't help but wonder if he was truly back. Physically yes, he was here. But what about beneath the physical appearance? Was the brother he knew really back? Would he ever be?

Jack shook his head, vigorously, to dislodge the thoughts now flooding his brain. He needed to stop drinking whisky - whisky always did this to him. He pushed himself up off the sofa and padded through to the bedroom. He needed sleep more than anything. The new investigation needed his attention; and his brain needed to rid itself of the unwanted memories clogging its wheels.

* * *

Time: 10.00pm
Date: Saturday 21st July 2012
Location: A cellar in London

"He calls me Carol." Her voice shook, quivering at the edges just like the tremor she was feeling in her limbs. "He calls me Carol."

Hannah found herself nodding, even though the cellar was too dark to see. "I know. I heard him." She paused, searching through the gloom to try and make out the form of her new companion, but all she could see was a dark mound on the mattress opposite. "He calls me Jess."

Hannah saw the mound shifting in the murky shadows, and then the glimpse of white flesh as two legs appeared from underneath the blanket.

"I'm Zoe," the woman added, uncurling herself so that Hannah could see the rest of her.

Hannah pushed herself off her mattress and shuffled, tentatively, across the stone floor, the sound of the cumbersome metal chain being dragged in her wake scraping over the concrete. She stopped by the side of Zoe's mattress, the chain now taut and preventing her from moving any closer. She could now see Zoe much more clearly, dressed in a close-fitting business suit with her dark hair scraped back off her face and tied into a loose plait behind her. Loose wisps of hair had worked themselves free and framed her pale face. Her skin was wan and blotchy, her eyes red raw with painfully shed tears. Her smooth, slim legs were tucked at her side, encased in thin, sheer tights that now sported gaping holes ripped through them.

And she only wore one shoe.

As did Hannah.

Hannah looked down at her feet, and the solitary black stiletto she still wore. Somehow she hadn't wanted to take it off.

"I'm Hannah." She introduced herself, giving the closest thing to a warm and welcoming smile that she could muster.

"How...how long...?" Zoe's voice cracked, her head dropping down so her chin rested on her chest. Her shoulders heaved in time with the rhythm of the tears cascading down her cheeks.

"I'm not sure," replied Hannah, truthfully. "A day? A couple of days? Longer? It's impossible to tell in the darkness."

"How...how do we...?" Again Zoe's voice broke off as she rocked slowly from side to side. Hannah noticed the dark, wet stain underneath Zoe's skirt, spreading out onto the mattress beneath.

"It's OK. There's a bucket. Over there." Hannah nodded to a corner of the cellar between the two mattresses, where a solitary metal bucket sat amongst the cobwebs. "The chain just about stretches far enough."

Hannah glanced behind her, back to her own mattress, seeing the stains she knew were there, only visible to her own eyes. "But it doesn't matter if you don't make it in time."

Zoe raised her head and stared out from beneath long, luscious eyelashes, rapidly blinking away the fresh, hot tears. "We are going to get out of here, aren't we?" She looked, pleadingly, at Hannah, her lips trembling. "There has to be a way out, right?"

Hannah glanced around the windowless, coffin-like cellar. If they looked closely, they would be able to see the scratches around the heavy oak doorframe – evidence of desperate fingernails trying to gnaw and scrape their way out of their hell-like prison. Had they been Georgie's fingernails? Someone else's? Hannah shuddered and pushed the thought from her mind. Instead she knelt down at Zoe's side and reached out to grab her hand, squeezing it as if it were their only lifeline.

"I hope so."

* * *

# Chapter Fourteen

Time: 9.30am

Date: Sunday 22$^{nd}$ July 2012

Location: St George's Road, Lambeth, London

DC Amanda Cassidy placed the tray of tea down on the coffee table in the living room. Tea that nobody had asked for, nobody wanted and nobody would drink.

The sound of deep, impenetrable silence hung heavily around them.

The sound of bereavement.

So quiet it was deafening.

The first time DC Cassidy had visited a bereaved family as a fresh faced, wet behind the ears PC, she had not appreciated how bereavement could be so tangible. You could hear it. You could feel it. You could touch it, and even smell it. It was there, touching everything, clinging to every surface, seeping into every pore.

DC Rachel McBride, the Family Liaison Officer assigned to the family of Georgina Dale, nodded gratefully at DC Cassidy as she began to pour the tea from the teapot. Sitting together on a two-seater floral sofa underneath the window opposite the coffee table, were Mr and Mrs Dale, Georgina's parents. Clutching each other's hands, their faces raw with grief, DC Cassidy could tell neither had slept since being given the terrible news less than twenty-four hours ago.

The dull tick-tock, tick-tock from the mantelpiece clock sounded muffled in the heavy air. Death had that effect. It made everything heavier. The air around you took on the consistency of treacle, words sounded muffled, time seemed to stand still.

DC Cassidy handed a cup and saucer to Mrs Dale first, noticing how her hand shook as she took hold of the dainty china. The teaspoon rattled in the saucer. DC Cassidy wondered if mugs might have been a better choice. Mrs Dale looked up briefly and caught Amanda's eye, a faint glimmer of thanks and appreciation hovered behind the glassiness of grief which otherwise washed over her. Her face had that translucent look, of someone almost ghostlike and not of this world; feeling as though this were some macabre dream, a horrific nightmare from which she would awaken.

But it was no dream.

It was no nightmare.

Except a living one.

Sitting next to her, Georgina's father had an equally ashen complexion, the laughter lines around his mouth devoid of mirth. Both in their fifties, DC Cassidy saw the grim realisation of bereavement add twenty years to them overnight.

DC Rachel McBride accepted a cup of tea from Amanda, and then began filling her and DS Carmichael in on the developments so far.

"As you know, Georgina didn't live at home while she was studying at university, so a search of her room here hasn't revealed anything substantial. Her room at the halls of residence has been cordoned off and is currently being processed."

DC Cassidy made a note in her notebook to check what, if anything, had come of the forensic search of Georgina's university room.

"Mr and Mrs Dale," DC Cassidy began, her voice quiet and calm, almost smothered by the curtain of grief hanging before them. "I know how terrible this must be for you, and how talking about Georgina must be deeply distressing at this time, but anything you can tell us at this point could be invaluable in our investigation. Is there anything out of the ordinary that you can recall, over the last few weeks? When did you last see or speak to Georgina?"

126

Mr and Mrs Dale looked at each other, exchanging mirror imaged expressions of haunted sadness. It was Georgina's father who eventually broke the silence.

"Georgie was a beautiful girl. A beautiful daughter. She had her issues.... before. But she had turned herself around.... she..." He broke off suddenly and gulped back a sob. "She had left all that behind her. She was moving on with her life."

"Georgina had been involved with some minor drug use in her late teens," explained DC McBride, catching DC Cassidy's frown. "A caution for possession." DC Cassidy nodded, remembering how her DNA had been flagged up on the system, and flashed a sympathetic look at Mr and Mrs Dale while she wrote the details in her notebook.

"She got in with the wrong crowd at college," explained Mrs Dale, leaning forward and placing her cup and saucer back down on the coffee table to stop it rattling in her frail grip; the tea, predictably, untouched. "We know she went off the rails for a while, but.... she.... we had got her straight again. She had got her place at University, and was doing so well."

DC Cassidy nodded again. "Well, there is nothing at this stage to suggest that drugs had anything to do with what happened. Do you know if she still kept in touch with anyone from her past?"

Mrs Dale shook her head. "She didn't. I know that for a fact. She had completely cut herself off from them, wanting a clean break."

DC Cassidy made a few more notes in her notebook. "And she was doing well at University? Enjoying it?"

Mr Dale gave a wan smile and nodded. "She loved it. She had really found her element, I think. She was completely transformed. And living in halls, although it was more expensive for us than if she had lived at home, it was what she wanted to do. To experience the full University life. She was thriving."

"And she was studying English?"

Mrs Dale nodded, continuing to wring her hands together as if they were a dishcloth. "English language and literature. She loved it. She wanted to go travelling next summer, learn as much as she could about other countries."

Her voice caught and fresh tears slid down her already saturated cheeks.

"And when was the last time you saw her, or spoke to her?" DC Cassidy watched both Mr and Mrs Dale's faces visibly sagging even further under the weight of their grief; if that were possible. It was Mr Dale who finally found a voice.

"That would have been about a month ago. She came here for my birthday – we had lunch." Mr Dale broke off as the words became stuck in his throat, several fat tears trickling down his cheeks to match his wife's. "That was the last time we saw her."

DC Cassidy nodded, added the information to her notebook and then slipped it into the breast pocket of her jacket. "I think that is all we need for now, Mr and Mrs Dale. We will leave you in peace." She nodded at DC McBride and rose from her seat, heading towards the door to the hallway.

DS Carmichael, who had been sitting silently in the corner of the room, nodded and rose also, following DC Cassidy towards the door. Once outside he turned to her and with a smirk said, "Well done, Detective Constable. You handled yourself well in there. Almost as if you were a proper detective. Not a bad cup of tea, either."

DC Cassidy stopped in her tracks, momentarily speechless. She itched to pick up her mobile phone and call Jack, tell him she needed to come back to the station, anything to get out of the company of the pompous, holier than thou DS Carmichael.

But she knew that she wouldn't.

DC Cassidy was stronger than that.

DS Carmichael led the way back to the car. "Chop chop, Detective. We have places to be. Next stop – Patricia Gordon's son."

* * *

Time: 9.45am
Date: Sunday 22nd July 2012

Location: Metropolitan Police HQ, London

"It's no use, Boss." DS Cooper sat back in his chair, shaking his head. "It's like looking for a needle in the proverbial haystack." Blown up photographs of the black stiletto shoe found at the second murder scene were strewn over the investigation table. "I've looked online – there are literally hundreds of places this shoe could have come from – pretty much every high street shop you can think of."

Jack sighed and rubbed his forehead. The shoe was a dead end. There was no way they would be able to trace all those who had bought a similar shoe, the pool would be far too vast. They needed to change their focus.

"Missing persons?" said Jack, looking away from the photograph of the shoe. "Any joy there?"

DS Cooper shook his head. "We've got the unit on high alert – but they don't have anything that sets off any alarm bells at the moment."

Of course not, thought Jack. No missing person's report that he had ever seen would record someone's shoe size. "We need to work with what we've got." Jack rose to his feet and nodded at DS Cooper to follow him. "While Amanda and Carmichael are covering the family liaison angle, we'll go over to Patricia Gordon's workplace; the last place we have a positive sighting of her."

DS Cooper got to his feet and grabbed the jacket he wouldn't need to wear. "Shall we take my car? It's got air con."

\* \* \*

Time: 10.30am
Date: Sunday 22nd July 2012
Location: Isabel's Café, King's Road, London

Isabel threw the dishcloth into the sink and gave a sigh of relief. The morning rush was subsiding. They had been rushed off their feet since opening, and Isabel had been glad to have Sacha's help as an extra pair of hands. With Dominic working three days a week, his mother often helped out on the other days, and the arrangement was a lifeline for Isabel. Sacha Greene was an excellent baker and kept the café supplied with plenty of mouth-watering home-baked goods to tempt their customers, bringing more supplies in with her earlier this morning.

Isabel smiled at Sacha, busy loading the dishwasher with the last of the morning's baking trays. "Coffee?"

"An iced tea would be fantastic," she replied, closing the door of the dishwasher and starting to wipe down the surfaces next to the double oven. She ran a hand across her forehead, her cheeks tinged pink with the heat. "It's been a warm one this morning!"

"Coming right up." Isabel busied herself preparing their drinks while Sacha lined up the next batch of tantalising delicacies ready to bake for the lunchtime crowd. With drinks in hand, Isabel took them through to an empty sofa at the front of the café, placing the cups down on the second-hand coffee table. She moved a pile of magazines and some well-thumbed paperbacks, then flopped down in amongst the cushions. This was one of her favourite times of the day. In between the morning rush and the lunchtime scrabble, there was a delicious moment of calm.

Sacha deposited herself next to Isabel and mirrored her sigh of relief. "That was a busy one!" Reaching forwards, she took hold of her iced tea, cradling the coolness of the cup in her hot hands. "How on earth will we cope when the Olympics are on?!"

Isabel laughed, and took a sip of her own iced tea. "Well, your cakes and pastries are too delicious, that's the problem!" She tucked a few stray strands of hair behind her ear and adjusted her ponytail. "And as for the Olympics..." Isabel paused and then shrugged. "You will just have to bake twice as fast!"

"So, what's this?" Sacha nodded at the laptop Isabel had brought over to the coffee table. It was open on the home page of "London Life."

"Ah, nothing really." Isabel went to close the laptop, but Sacha was too quick for her and grabbed hold of her arm.

"Not so fast," she grinned, taking the laptop from Isabel and balancing it on her knees. "London Life." She looked, quizzically, at the home page, and then up at Isabel. "Looks like a dating website to me. Since when??"

Isabel smiled, sheepishly, trying to tuck another non-existent hair behind her ear and avoid her friend's gaze. "It's nothing, like I said. Just a bit of fun. I'm not going to *meet* anyone."

Sacha gave Isabel a knowing smile and nodded, handing the laptop back. "If you say so."

"I'm not, honestly! I'm just chatting with a few people, that's all. I'm too busy to meet anyone, anyway." Isabel raised her cup to her lips to hide her cheeks.

"The lady doth protest too much, methinks," smiled Sacha, taking a long sip of her cooling ice tea, enjoying seeing her best friend squirm. "Just you be careful," she added, a serious tone entering her voice.

"Really, it's just chatting," replied Isabel, finding her already hot cheeks turning even pinker. "Sometimes I feel like I want a chat. It can get a bit lonely upstairs on my own, with just a cat for company. That's all."

Sacha smiled and nodded again, giving her friend a playful squeeze on the knee. "Just be careful," she repeated. "There are some weird people out there. Just stay safe."

Isabel nodded. "I will, of course I will. Like I said, I'm not planning to actually meet anyone." Just at that moment, Patrick popped his sandy head out from the art studio at the rear of the café. "Any chance of a cuppa, Isabel?" His pale green eyes glinted mischievously from beneath the fringe that flopped across his forehead. "Now the rush has died down?"

"Coming right up, Patrick." Isabel pushed herself up from the sofa and snapped the laptop shut, catching Sacha's gaze as she did so. "Sacha would love to make you both a coffee."

"And you should come through and see what your new artist is producing. It's pretty good." Patrick disappeared back inside the studio. "He's putting me to shame out here."

Isabel headed back towards Patrick and the art studio, while Sacha quickly filled two mugs with freshly brewed coffee. Upon entering the studio, Isabel went and stood behind the easel that Erik Neumann was staring intently at, brandishing his paintbrush in slow, controlled flourishes.

"Wow, Erik, that's amazing." Isabel peered over his shoulder at the canvas and saw the most intricately drawn picture of Tower Bridge, overlaid with the most wondrous choice of watercolours. The canvas came alive with every brush stroke. "I had no idea you were such a talented artist."

Erik Neumann stopped mid brush stroke and fixed the canvas with a pair of critical eyes. He leant closer towards it, his nose almost touching the wet paint. "I'm not so sure," he murmured. "I'm not sure I have the lighting right. The sky…it looks too……how do you say it in English? With menace?"

"Menacing?" frowned Isabel, shaking her head while still taking in the glorious watercolour scene. "No, no, it's absolutely perfect, Erik. It's stunning. You capture the feeling that the skies are about to darken with an oncoming storm, but the picture itself is light and fresh. The colours you have on the water are amazing. It's so lifelike. Where did you learn to paint like this?"

Erik Neumann put his paintbrush down on the rack next to his easel and turned towards Isabel. "I learnt from my mother. She was a great artist and she loved to paint. I must have inherited her talent. We learn so much from our parents, don't we?"

Isabel found herself nodding while her eyes flickered towards the canvas on the wall above Erik's easel – her mother's watercolour. Her eyes once again swept over the painting of her childhood home, seeing her own mother's talent encased in each sweep of the brush. The familiar flutter inside the pit of her stomach made Isabel shiver. She had often wondered if any of her mother's talent as an artist had travelled down through the genes to herself – but she had never had the courage to find out.

"Patrick, how is your commission coming along?" Sacha entered the studio with the two mugs of coffee and a tea towel draped over her arm. "Isabel tells me you're working for an advertising agency?"

Patrick was sitting at the large artist's table in the centre of the studio. He merely sighed and nodded towards the array of ad hoc, hastily drawn sketches that covered most the table's surface. "It's going painfully slowly, my dear. Painfully slowly." He gestured towards the piles of paper, adorned with charcoal, chalk and acrylic paint. "I appear to have a crisis of confidence. A block in my flow of artistic genius." He looked up at Sacha and shrugged, gratefully accepting the offered mug of coffee. "Any ideas?"

Sacha laughed and held a hand up in mock surrender. "Oh good God, don't ask me. I can't draw a straight line. Isabel is far more artistic than me. Or even my Dominic, for that matter."

"Yes, where is young Dominic today?" enquired Patrick, picking up a charcoal pencil and adding more strokes to a half-finished, or half-started, sketch. "We were having a good old chat yesterday. He's really into languages, isn't he?"

"He's into just about everything, Patrick," grinned Sacha, passing the second mug of coffee over to Erik, who had stopped staring intently at the clouds billowing above Tower Bridge. "He exhausts me just trying to keep up with him. But yes, he's always been into languages – says he wants to learn every language in the world."

"Yes, so he told me. Seems like I may have offered to give him a helping hand." Patrick raised his eyebrows above emerald green glinting eyes. "Does he always manage to do that?"

"Oh yes," smiled Sacha, ruefully. "He always manages to do that. I'm sorry!"

Patrick held up a hand and shook his head. "No problem, no problem at all. I have a smattering of some languages, happy to feed the knowledge-hungry young Dominic – we've started already as it goes. He has a brain like a sponge, doesn't he?"

"Well, thank you." Sacha gave a nod of thanks towards Patrick. "It means a lot. Someone taking the time to be with him. To interact with him. I appreciate it. We *both* appreciate it."

Patrick waved away the compliments and took several deep mouthfuls of his coffee. "He's a pleasure to be with. He really is." After several more gulps, he pushed himself off his stool and headed for his small knapsack hanging on one of the easels behind him. He glanced at his watch.

"Well, I need to be on my way. Time to go and get some inspiration from somewhere." He cast his eyes back down to the charcoal scribbles in front of him. "Anywhere."

He swung the knapsack onto his shoulder, slipping a small sketchpad and some pencils inside. "Tell young Dominic I will be around later tonight if he fancies some more linguistics."

Both Sacha and Isabel raised a hand at the departing Patrick, and then turned their attention to Erik, who was still staring at his painting with a frown on his face.

"I'm still not sure about these clouds." Erik peered closely once again at the canvas, wrinkling his nose in apparent distaste. "They feel..." He gave a little shiver. "Depressing."

Isabel stepped behind him, letting her eyes rake over the drying canvas. She shook her head. "No, no...I still think it feels...atmospheric. It doesn't feel depressing at all. The opposite, in fact." She touched him, lightly, on the shoulder. "Don't you dare change it. And you should paint some more. Plenty of bridges in London!"

Erik quietly nodded his head and placed the paintbrush he had been brandishing once again back onto the art trolley. "Maybe you are right," he murmured, nodding once again. He drank, thirstily, from his coffee mug before getting to his feet. "I feel I need to roam around your wonderful city some more – and see if I can spot a bridge to paint that would put Hamburg to shame!" He bent down to pick up a well-worn, battered leather satchel. "Where do you ladies suggest I go?" He picked up some loose paper and sketching pencils. "I have a travel card and can go anywhere!"

Isabel and Sacha exchanged raised eyebrows. "Gosh, I'm not sure I can think of any bridges off the top of my head," laughed Sacha. "I'm usually too busy rushing from one place to another to notice if I'm even on a bridge! I could be in a tunnel and not know about it some days!"

Isabel smiled. "Well, you must go and see the Millennium Bridge – near St Pauls. And maybe Westminster Bridge, if you want something older. It's pretty old – close to the Houses of Parliament and Big Ben, if you're interested in other London landmarks and architecture. Or even Vauxhall

Bridge – a bit further away. That's got some colourful bits if I remember rightly."

"How come you know so much about bridges?" enquired Sacha, a grin stretching across her face. "You dark horse, you! I never knew you were so knowledgeable!"

Isabel's cheeks coloured slightly. She grabbed the tea towel that Sacha had left on the table and playfully threw it across to land on her friend's shoulder. "You know I like Harry Potter! The death eaters destroy the Millennium Bridge at the beginning of the Half Blood Prince!"

Erik ran a hand through his thick blonde hair and shook his head. "I don't know what you ladies are talking about, so I will be on my way. I've never even seen one Harry Potter movie." He gave a little bow and made his exit from the studio, calling back over his shoulder, "I will see you again tomorrow," before closing the door behind him.

Isabel and Sacha returned to the café, ready for the influx of Sunday strollers who would be in desperate need of her chilled iced tea, or the cool and refreshing frappes, as they sought to escape the heat of the day. Isabel had seen the sales of the cooler drinks, such as milkshakes and smoothies, far outstrip her usual hot offerings over the last few weeks due to the heatwave. People had been known to even just ask for iced water.

Even Livi was finding the heat too much and had padded back inside to find a cool corner to curl up in. Isabel refilled the saucer of cool water by the back door, and watched as Livi's pale pink tongue lapped at it, thirstily. Smiling to herself, Isabel turned around as the bell jangled to announce another customer seeking respite from the heat.

* * *

# Chapter Fifteen

Time: 10.45am

Date: Sunday 22$^{nd}$ July 2012

Location: The Briars Residential Care Home

DS Cooper pulled up outside the entrance to The Briars Residential Care Home. In the passenger seat, Jack peered out of the window to see a rather imposing, Victorian façade greet him. All it needed, mused Jack, were some metal bars on the windows and you would have yourself a Victorian lunatic asylum or workhouse.

The red bricked building rose up three storeys high, with a large wooden double-fronted door set above five concrete steps, with a huge brass knocker in the centre. Each level had eight arched windows looking out onto the narrow gravel driveway. As Jack got out of the car, he found himself looking up at each window, checking for any sign of life. Even in this heat, he noticed none of the windows were open.

The sound of DS Cooper slamming the driver's door jolted Jack's gaze away from the windows, and away from searching for any of the lost souls within, and he followed his partner up the five steps to the imposing front door. Three knocks from the brass knocker echoed loudly in the breathless air.

Before the last echo had subsided, the door creaked open. Greeting Jack and DS Cooper was a middle-aged woman dressed in a black matron-style dress-uniform, belted at the waist, with a silver fob watch attached to her ample breast. Her greying hair was scraped back into a harsh-looking bun atop a round head, her legs encased in thick black tights and sensible black shoes. Despite her rather austere attire, she greeted both Jack and DS Cooper with a warm smile that reached her eyes, causing them to twinkle.

"Police?" she enquired, her voice as warm and comforting as her smile. She held out a hand towards Jack, which he found himself taking in his own, noting her soft, pliable skin and reassuring squeeze.

"Indeed. Detective Inspector Jack MacIntosh," introduced Jack, trying to return the warm smile as best he could. "Metropolitan Police. And this is DS Cooper. Thank you for seeing us."

"No problem at all, gentlemen. Please come in. I'm Marion Masters, matron here at The Briars." Mrs Masters stepped sideways to allow Jack and DS Cooper to enter the building.

Once inside, Jack felt the temperature drop a rather comfortable ten degrees or so, the thick Victorian brickwork doing its job in keeping the unseasonable hot summer heatwave at bay. They stepped into a large entrance hall, the high ceiling stretching up above them with ornate Victorian-style cornice plaster work. At their feet was an expanse of original Victorian parquet flooring, buffed to a healthy shine, which echoed under their footfall. To the side, an imposing mirror covering one wall gave the hall an empty, cavernous feel. Jack gave an involuntary shiver, not just because of the temperature drop. The hall greeted its visitors with a stark coldness, conjuring up images of harsh treatment, ragged clothing, starving Victorian workhouse children pleading for more thin gruel-like soup. Jack's mind flipped back to the unopened windows outside, wondering how many of its current residents were desperate to escape its confines.

"If you would like to follow me." Mrs Masters' voice dragged Jack's attention back to the present. She turned on her comfortable heels and began walking towards the rear of the entrance hall where there was another Victorian-style heavy oak door. Jack and DS Cooper did as they were bidden and dutifully followed the matron through the door, where they were greeted by an altogether unexpected transformation.

Gone was the austere frostiness of the vast entrance hall. Similarly gone from Jack's imagination were the rows of hungry, ragged children, clamouring at the windows desperate for a better life. Instead, they moved into a newly carpeted foyer, complete with modern lighting, smooth plastered walls painted in invitingly-warm tones, a range of indoor plants and comfortable-looking furniture giving the space a lived-in, homely feel.

"We have four wings to the building," explained Mrs Masters, gesturing to the four corridors fanning off from the foyer. "The residents' rooms are all accessed via these corridors. We have three floors – the most bedridden and least mobile are given rooms on the first and second floors. Our most mobile residents have rooms on the ground floor, so that they can access the outside space more easily." Mrs Masters turned to face Jack and DS Cooper. "Shall I take you through to the office?"

Jack nodded and followed the Matron a short way down one corridor, noticing how the soft, grey pile of the carpet underfoot no longer emitted the harsh squeaking from her comfortable shoes. Jack and DS Cooper were shown into a compact open-plan office space, housing several desks.

"Please take a seat." Mrs Masters nodded towards some visitor chairs opposite a desk which was overladen with paperwork. Jack and DS Cooper dutifully slipped into the seats, while Mrs Masters moved a pile of papers out of the way, tutting to herself as she did so. Tucking herself behind the desk, she squeezed her ample frame into the small swivel chair. "So, how can we be of help, Inspector? I was so shocked when I heard the news about poor Patricia. I don't think any of us here can really quite believe it yet."

Jack gave a small nod and what he hoped was a sympathetic smile. "Indeed, Mrs Masters. It must have been, and still will be, a huge shock for you all."

"We're all like one big happy family here, you see, Inspector." Mrs Masters' eyes clouded over, and Jack thought he could see the beginnings of watery tears forming at the edges.

"Yes, well, we won't keep you any longer than we have to, Mrs Masters," replied Jack, nodding at DS Cooper to get his notebook out. "We just need to get a few more background details on Mrs Gordon - her usual routines, her usual contacts, anything anyone can remember about the last time she was seen here."

Mrs Masters nodded, a slight tremble playing on her lips.

"I know you have already spoken at some length to one of our liaison officers," continued Jack. "But I just wanted to come and visit myself, see if there was anything else you could tell us."

Again Mrs Masters nodded, the tremble on her lips intensifying. She reached into a side pocket of her starched uniform and pulled out a neatly folded handkerchief. She dabbed at the corners of her eyes. "Of course. Anything to help."

Jack nodded. "We've been told that the last time anyone saw Mrs Gordon was here at about four o'clock in the afternoon on Friday 6th July. Is that correct?"

Mrs Masters finished dabbing her eyes and nodded, returning the hand-kerchief to her lap, wringing it in between her hands. "Yes, yes. Her shift usually finished at 2pm - she does an early shift you see – but on occasions she would stay on a bit longer, to help out. She was like that, you see. Always willing to help." Mrs Masters paused, her voice cracking. "She left at about four o'clock, or just after, that day. I know because The Chase had just started on television in one of the resident's rooms when she popped her head in to say that she was off."

Jack nodded. He remembered reading this from the notes from the family liaison officer. "And she didn't turn up for work the next morning?"

Mrs Masters shook her head, sadly. "She wasn't due in the next day. She had booked a week's leave, so we weren't expecting her. If she had been due to come in, we would have known that something was wrong. She was never late for work, you see. Never ill. Didn't even take the paid holiday she was entitled to sometimes."

"And how long had she been working for you?"

"About four years." Mrs Master returned the handkerchief to her eyes, dabbing away the newly erupting tears. "She had recently separated from her husband, needed a full time job I think. She came to us with exceptional references from working in the hotel industry. To be honest, she was more than a bit overqualified for a simple housekeeping job, but she was so enthusiastic and really wanted the job. We are so lucky to have her." Mrs Masters words caught in her throat. "We *were* lucky to have her." She let a lone tear slide down her cheek, the handkerchief staying in her lap.

"Her husband," enquired Jack. "Have you met him?"

"Frank? Oh yes," nodded Mrs Masters. "He's a lovely man. Very caring. Used to give Patricia a lift to work when the weather was bad, pick her up again too."

"Really?" Jack frowned slightly, and nodded to DS Cooper to make a note. "That sounds rather strange, for an ex-husband?"

"Oh, not really," continued Mrs Masters, wiping another stray tear away from her cheek before it dripped from her chin. "They were still very amicable with each other. Stayed good friends. Just better off apart, I think that's what they said. They never actually divorced, just separated. Nothing acrimonious, I don't think."

"Hmmmmm," mused Jack, mentally making a note to check out Mr Gordon. Amicable or not, marriages usually didn't disintegrate without a little disharmony. "And did you see him at all on that Friday – the 6th July? The last time you saw Mrs Gordon? Did he come to pick her up?"

Mrs Masters shook her head. "No, I haven't seen him in a while. As I said, it was usually when the weather was bad. In nice weather like this," Mrs Masters gestured towards the window at the side of the office, "she liked to walk. She would hop on a bus and then walk through the parks."

Jack nodded; their next call was going to be Mrs Gordon's home address. Plus, Mr Gordon not long afterwards. "Is there anything else you think you can tell us, Mrs Masters? Anything at all? Anything out of the ordinary that happened in the last few weeks or months? She didn't mention anyone new in her life? Any new places she had been to? Anything different to her usual routine?"

Mrs Masters shook her head. "No, not that I can think of. She didn't have that much spare time. Always working. Such a hard worker, she is. Sorry, was." Mrs Masters took a deep breath in, fighting back more tears. "Determined to keep a roof over her head and have nice things, without claiming a single penny in support. I've never met anyone who worked so hard."

Jack nodded and indicated to DS Cooper that they were finished and he could close his notebook. "Well, thank you very much for your time, Mrs Masters. You've been most helpful. If there is anything else you think of in the next few days or so, no matter how small, you just let me know." Jack reached into his jacket pocket and handed over a small business card. "All my contact details are on there."

"Is it true?" Mrs Masters looked at the business card before slipping it into her breast pocket, next to her fob watch.

"Is what true, Mrs Masters?" replied Jack, as he got to his feet.

"What they're saying in the papers, this morning?" Mrs Masters paused, before raising her watery gaze to meet Jack's. "That it's a serial killer?"

Jack hesitated before responding, noticing the frightened and distressed look on the Matron's face. "It would appear so, Mrs Masters. But please don't be alarmed. We are doing all we can to apprehend the person responsible."

"You will catch him, won't you?"

"Yes, Mrs Masters. We will."

* * *

Time: 11.45am
  Date: Sunday 22nd July 2012
  Location: St Pauls Cathedral, London.

The vast stone sides of St Pauls Cathedral stretched skywards, the shadows cast by the thick columns creating a much sought after shade and respite from the midday sun. Several straw-hatted tourists, with cameras slung around their perspiring necks, hovered in the shade while sipping thirstily from bottles of water.

Erik Neumann casually sauntered past, slowing his pace and gazing upwards to absorb the beauty of the domed structure towering above. It was a truly magnificent structure; there was no denying it. But he wasn't interested in St Paul's Cathedral. Not in an artistic sense. Isabel had mentioned the Millennium Bridge; and so that was where he needed to be.

He continued past the cathedral and crossed the road, taking the short walk along Peters Hill that led down to the beginnings of the bridge. He smiled at the ice-cream seller who was, himself, melting in the sun as if he were one of his own creations. A line of withering people snaked across the pavement, patiently queuing for the iced delights that they hoped would last long enough to eat before disintegrating into a stream of milky stickiness trickling down their arms. Erik didn't hold out much hope judging by the number of tissues being rubbed on forearms, and dabbed at the front of t-shirts, from previous customers.

He skirted around the queue and headed for the bridge. He did know about Harry Potter, and the film that the bridge had appeared in. He had seen them all, more than once; who hadn't? Why had he lied to Isabel about something so seemingly unimportant? He frowned. He wasn't sure. It had just seemed like the right thing to do at the time.

Shaking the thought from his mind, Erik stepped onto the bridge and gazed across to the far side, towards the South Bank and the Tate Modern art gallery. The bridge itself glistened in the sunshine, reflecting the sun's hot rays and dazzling passers-by as they squinted against the brightness. Erik adjusted his sunglasses, peering over the side of the bridge to see the usually slate-grey swirling Thames river water almost taking on a hint of a summer blue, ocean-like lustre. Almost. It was amazing what a bit of blue sky and sunshine could do. He thought back to his painting of Tower Bridge and the cluster of greys and browns he had used to convey the choppy waters beneath.

This picture was going to be different, he thought to himself, already churning over in his head the watercolour choices he would make. It would be lighter. Cleaner. Fresher. No dark greys or smoky browns. The Thames in this picture was going to look so inviting you would want to dip your toe in right away.

He paused a quarter of the way across the bridge and settled his leather satchel down on the ground. Taking a few sheets of paper out of the satchel, and a small board to rest them on, he leant against the railings and began to sketch.

\* \* \*

# Chapter Sixteen

Time: 12.45pm

Date: Sunday 22<sup>nd</sup> July 2012

Location: St James's University, London

Dr Rachel Hunter's office was light and airy, the floor to ceiling blinds covering the main window, blocking out the heat of the morning sun. Jack could feel the welcome ripple of air conditioning as he lowered himself into one of the soft leather armchairs facing a low glass-topped coffee table.

"Coffee?" Dr Hunter gestured towards a complicated looking coffee machine nestled in the corner, but Jack shook his head.

"No thanks, I'm fine." Jack felt himself sinking further into the plush leather of the armchair – reminiscent of his visit to Dr Riches yesterday. He glanced around the office, noting the similarities to Dr Riches' own rooms on the other side of the campus. "Thank you for seeing me at such short notice, and on a Sunday."

Dr Hunter, the Metropolitan Police criminal profiler, settled herself into the other leather armchair opposite Jack, smoothing out her skirt and tucking her shapely legs to one side as she did so. Her light grey suit fitted her slim figure neatly, a cool, crisp white blouse contrasting with the light sun-kissed tan that glowed from her skin.

Jack glanced down at his creased shirt and trousers, possibly still yester-days, and ran a hand over the several days' worth of stubble hugging his chin. He crossed one leg over the other to hide the worst of the creases.

Psychologists.

They made him nervous.

Jack felt the familiar feeling of inadequacy begin to wash over him.

Even her office was tidier than his.

Although, sharing an office with DS Cooper, that was not hard to achieve.

"So, your killer," began Dr Hunter, nudging her wire-rimmed glasses with a well-manicured finger. She tucked a strand of light, auburn hair back behind her ear, the rest piled high on top of her head in a strategically messy bun. "Would you like to hear what I've got for you?" Her light green eyes twinkled from behind the lenses of her spectacles.

Jack raised his eyebrows, giving a faint shrug of the shoulders and a nod at the same time. "Sure."

Dr Hunter reached forwards, selecting a thin, manila folder from the coffee table. Upon opening it, she slid out two pieces of paper, passing one across to Jack.

"I would say your perpetrator is aged between thirty and fifty-five," began Dr Hunter, inclining her head towards the piece of paper.

Jack lowered his eyes and saw a list of typed bullet-points. "Thirty to fifty-five? That's quite specific?"

"I don't believe your killer is a young man, Detective Inspector. The details of the two crimes you sent over to me to analyse show me a more mature killer. His crimes are well thought out."

Jack shrugged and returned his gaze to the list.

"Capable of intimate relationships, with some difficulties." Dr Hunter read out the second characteristic. "Possibly divorced or separated."

"So single, then?" suggested Jack.

"Not necessarily," replied Dr Hunter, giving a slow shake of her head. "He could be in a relationship, but any relationship is likely to have its difficulties."

Jack suppressed a sigh. This was exactly the reason why he didn't like using profilers. He might be single. He might be married. He might be divorced. He might find relationships difficult. Who didn't, thought Jack.

"There is something I should add, which isn't yet in my report." Dr Hunter nodded at the list. "He is likely to be well presented, attractive. Charming, even."

"Charming?" Jack frowned. "What makes you say that?"

"These women trusted him. As far as I can tell, there were no defensive marks on them, other than the abrasions around the ankles, from the restraints. No witnesses to a forced abduction. No indication they were taken forcibly from their homes. Whoever he is, they went with him willingly. They trusted him." Dr Hunter paused. "Initially, at least."

"You say "he"," continued Jack, glancing up from the list. "So we are definitely looking for a male killer?"

Dr Hunter met Jack's gaze, her pale green eyes continuing to twinkle behind her glasses. She knew how mistrustful Jack MacIntosh was of her profession. His loathing of profilers was legendary within the department and beyond. "I think both you and I know the chances of a serial killer being female are pretty remote. I would be most surprised if your killer was a woman."

Jack nodded, breaking Dr Hunter's gaze, and cast his eyes back down to the list. Characteristic number three. "Educated. Intellectual. Intelligent. White collar worker."

"Indeed," confirmed Dr Hunter, nodding slowly. "Neither crime was impulsive. Both were meticulously carried out, to precision. Your killer is highly intelligent. Certainly not a manual labourer."

"Can't manual labourers be intelligent?" questioned Jack. "That doesn't seem very politically correct."

Dr Hunter smiled in Jack's direction, a perfect row of sparkling white teeth set against a pair of pale, pink lips. "You know what I mean, Detective Inspector. This killer is clever. I would put him in a job that equated to his high intelligence level."

Jack shrugged and moved on to the next characteristic, the contents intriguing him the moment he read it. "Doesn't kill for pleasure." He once again sought out Dr Hunter's gaze. "What makes you say that?"

"The method of killing is very clinical. I've studied both post mortem reports that you kindly sent through. Both victims died as a result of strangulation via a ligature around the neck. This is a very cold method of killing someone, Detective Inspector. The killer doesn't want to look into their victim's eyes at the time of death, positioning himself behind while he chokes the life out of them."

Dr Hunter paused and Jack noticed a cloud crossing her emerald green eyes, extinguishing the sparkle that had been there before. "He has some other motivation for killing these women. It is not done for pleasure. If he gained pleasure or excitement from his acts, he would want to be facing them, to see the fear and horror in their eyes as he ended their lives. He would strangle them manually, with his hands, facing them at the point of death." Dr Hunter caught Jack's gaze. "Your killer uses a colder and more clinical method. He is distancing himself from the actual act of killing. There is a degree of emotional detachment there. I don't believe he gets pleasure from it – at least not in the traditional sense."

Jack conceded the issue. She had a point. He reminded himself of a conversation with Dr Philip Matthews not long after receiving his first post mortem report on Patricia Gordon. "It's a cold act, Jack. Very clinical, using a ligature like that. You've got a cold-hearted killer on your hands here."

"You haven't mentioned the shoes." Jack nodded at the list in his hand. "The shoes found at the scene."

Dr Hunter gave a slow, methodical nod, and let her eyes catch Jack's. A faint frown teased at her temples, causing her flawless complexion to succumb to a hint of a worry line. "Yes, the shoes." She paused, the silence hanging palpably in the air between. Jack tried to catch her gaze again, but she had lowered her eyes and the frown on her forehead deepened.

"And?" Jack nodded once more towards the list.

"The shoes worry me." Dr Hunter glanced back up and gave a nondescript shrug of her narrow shoulders. "I haven't commented on it in my report because I just don't know."

"Isn't it some sort of fetish?" Jack had already Googled shoe fetishes, and had been quite intrigued. "Retifism, isn't it called? Sounds the most likely, to me."

Dr Hunter nodded. "Yes, it can be known as retifism. But I don't believe that is what we have here."

"You don't?" It was Jack's turn to embrace a frown. "Why not?"

"As I mentioned before, this man kills for some other reason than pleasure. He is an emotional void at the time of the killing. I don't believe he is using the shoe as some form of sexual gratification."

"So.... why leave it at the scene? Are we looking at a trophy killer?"

Dr Hunter shook her head again, a stray lock of her auburn hair brushing her jawline. She tucked it behind her ear before replying. "Not in the traditional sense, no. He isn't taking the shoes as a trophy, at least not in the strictest sense. You said it yourself, Detective. He left the shoe of the next victim at the scene. He isn't keeping them."

"So why do it? There must be a reason for it, surely?" Jack felt a hint of irritation seeping into his tone. "I need to get into this man's head."

"I can assure you, Detective Inspector, that is the last place you want to be." Dr Hunter shifted in her seat. "It isn't a fetish. And it isn't a trophy." She looked up and locked Jack in her gaze. "I think he is leaving them as clues."

"Clues?" The irritation in Jack's voice deepened.

"Yes, clues." Dr Hunter paused. "I believe he wants to be found, Detective. He is teasing you; playing games with you. He wants you to find him."

"A killer that wants to be caught?" The irritation had now morphed into more of an exasperated tone. "Why would he want to be caught? It makes no sense. I thought you said he was intelligent?"

"Your killer is a complex character." Dr Hunter looked back down at the list of characteristics she still held in her hand. "We've already established that he is educated, intelligent. And he kills for some other reason than pleasure. It wouldn't surprise me if he is testing your powers of detection."

Jack sighed.

A complex character.

Great.

"Number five," he continued, nodding back down at the list. "Location –

living in or having a good knowledge of London." He paused, trying to stop frustration creeping into his voice. "That goes without saying, surely?"

"Indeed it does. Your killer certainly knows his way around London. I understand you haven't had many leads from the CCTV images?"

Jack had to concede that they hadn't. DC Cassidy had organised a team to work through the night analysing hours and hours of footage. As yet, nothing had shown up. "Not as yet, no. We're widening the search."

"So, your killer is either very lucky and has avoided the CCTV cameras or......" Dr Hunter let the question hang in the air.

"Or he knows where they are," finished Jack, nodding. "I get the picture, Dr."

"Which takes us back to my third point," continued Dr Hunter. "He is an extremely clever man. These are not random or opportunistic killings. They are well thought through, even to the point of when and where to dump the bodies."

Jack sighed again.

A clever killer.

Even better.

He let his eyes wander back down to the next characteristic and instantly felt a shiver course through his blood, not caused by the deliciously cool waft of air circulating the warm room. Two words which would always make any detective's blood run cold.

Forensically aware.

Dr Hunter noticed the expression that had crossed Jack's face. "Yes, Detective Inspector. Your killer is very forensically aware. Again tying in with the belief he is an extremely intelligent and clever individual. The post mortem reports both confirm there is no trace of any DNA or any other evidence on either body. Nothing to connect the victims with any other person or location. I strongly believe your killer has an in-depth knowledge of forensics and has taken special precautions to ensure no traces of himself, or where he kills his victims, are found."

Further conversations with police pathologist, Dr Philip Matthews, filled Jack's head.

"This is either one very clever chap, Jack, or he is extremely fortunate. I cannot find any trace of DNA or other fibres on either body. It is as though both victims were cleansed before they were dumped. No DNA from the killer. Nothing from the car. No fibres from wherever they had been kept beforehand. They are clean. Forensically sterile."

Cleansed.

Sterile.

Clever.

Jack knew from experience the problem "forensically aware" posed. And it worried him. Like it worried every detective. Even with the growth of the various CSI programmes available on TV these days, crime scenes would almost always give up some evidence, no matter how small, to tie the victim to the killer, or at least to the location they were killed. But a sterile forensic scene? Bodies being cleansed?

That worried Jack.

That worried Jack a lot.

The next characteristic on the list didn't lift Jack's mood much either.

"No criminal record." Dr Hunter read out the last of her conclusions. "I doubt he has ever come onto your radar before, Detective Inspector. I feel he is far too clever for that."

Jack sighed and folded the piece of paper in half, tucking it into his shirt pocket. He wasn't sure any of this had brought them any further forwards, and the expression on his face showed it.

"I know you don't think much of profiling, Detective Inspector." Dr Hunter slipped her copy of the profile report back inside the manila folder.

"Why do you say that?" Jack met her gaze, noticing the softening of her eyes and the mischievous sparkle returning.

"Your reputation goes before you," Dr Hunter smiled. She paused before continuing. "I'm not going to give you the name and address of your killer, Jack. That's a job for you and your team."

The use of his christian name caused Jack's gaze to linger, feeling the psychologist's eyes tunnelling into his from behind the protective lenses of her glasses. A twitch at the corner of her lips, which parted slightly to reveal her tongue dancing briefly across her perfect white teeth.

Was she flirting with him?

Jack felt instantly uneasy.

Women never flirted with him.

Did they?

Dr Hunter continued. "All I can do is possibly help to narrow down the pool of suspects." She paused again and inclined her head towards the door, indicating that Jack was free to leave. "It's up to you to catch him, Jack."

* * *

Time: 1.00pm
Date: Sunday 22ⁿᵈ July 2012
Location: A cellar in London

Zoe stretched out from underneath the scratchy blanket. Where she had lain with her legs curled up beneath her, she now felt a numbness spreading down her calves and into her ankles. She flexed her feet and shuddered.

She had no idea how long she had slept for. The last thing she remembered was drinking the bottle of water that had appeared earlier that day – or was it yesterday? She had no idea what time it was, or what day it was. The remnants of what looked like breakfast still sat next to her mattress. Cold toast, now stiff and stale. A banana she appears to have nibbled at. She yawned and rubbed her eyes. She still felt groggy.

Her eyes rested on the water bottle. Was he drugging them? Was that why she felt so tired? She glanced over towards the other side of the cellar, where she presumed Hannah was curled up under the faint mound of blankets that she could see by the far wall. Had Hannah been drugged too?

Zoe shuddered again, and not just because of the cool, damp air that clung to her. All she could see in her mind was him – bending down over her, that sickening smile he plastered over his face. His cold touch against her skin.

Another shudder wracked her body, and she pulled the blanket back over her legs.

What were you meant to do in situations like this? Were you meant to comply? Were you meant to fight, scream and shout? Zoe's usual confidence and composure had left her the minute she had been overcome – the minute she had been swiftly subdued and brought to this place. This prison.

Her mind scrabbled for clarity. What should she do? Escape seemed impossible – there were no windows, and only one door that was locked. And then there was the chain. She moved her left leg and heard the metal clunk against the stone floor. Her mind continued to race, and it took her a while to acknowledge the voice that floated through the still air.

"Zoe? I'm scared."

* * *

# Chapter Seventeen

Time: 2.00pm

Date: Sunday 22$^{nd}$ July 2012

Location: St John's Wood, London

Clean.

Neat.

Tidy.

Orderly.

Everything in Patricia Gordon's flat was in its rightful place. Jack and DS Cooper carefully wiped their feet on the mat as they entered, even though the owner was no longer here to see. Visiting the homes of murder victims was always difficult; the warm, homely feel of a well-loved and well cared for home was always tinged with a cold emptiness, as if the very walls could sense the loss.

The scene of crime team had already been and gone. Nothing had been found to suggest she met her killer within these four walls, and nothing had been found to assist the investigation. Her laptop and mobile phone had been taken away to be analysed by the tech team, but everything else had been left in situ; frozen in time.

"Nice place," commented DS Cooper, peering through the venetian blinds that gave a view out onto a tidy courtyard area at the rear of the flat.

"Indeed," agreed Jack, noting the high-end, wide-screen TV and cinema sound system, iPod docking station and satellite set-top box. The low-rise, soft leather cream sofa stretched along one wall, with a plush terracotta coloured rug at its feet. A floor to ceiling bookcase hugged the opposite wall, housing shelves full of well-known paperback bestsellers, a series of Encyclopaedia Britannica and a small collection of CDs. "This is what we had before Google, Cooper," mused Jack, bending down to take a closer look at the impressive row of thirty-two hard-back volumes of the encyclopaedias. He pulled one out; volume six.

DS Cooper looked over his shoulder in the direction of the bookcase and frowned. "Encyclopaedias? They could be worth a pretty penny."

Jack returned the volume and continued his search of the bookshelves, not entirely sure what he was looking for. A feeling, an instinct, a gut reaction that would provide him with a clue as to why a seemingly ordinary middle-aged care home worker crossed the deadly path of a serial killer. He noted the framed photographs of Mrs Gordon and a similarly aged man; a man that Jack guessed would be her ex-husband. A couple more photographs showing a young boy in various locations; beaches, forests, Christmas dinner tables – a son, Jack mused. He wondered how they were coping with the news.

Jack's eyes swept the rest of the room.

Everything looked normal.

Ordinary.

But nothing ordinary had happened to Patricia Gordon.

The only bedroom in the flat was equally well-kept. Bed newly-made, nightclothes folded up and placed neatly under the pillow, never to be worn again. A dressing table housed the usual mundane items – hairspray, deodorant, perfume bottles, various pots of face cream that claimed to make you wrinkle free.

Jack sighed with hidden annoyance. Nothing was standing out. Nothing that was going to help them flush out the killer. He returned to the living room where DS Cooper was rifling through some paperwork on a small bureau next to the sofa. The usual stack of bills, invoices and junk mail. From what he could see, Mrs Gordon was in credit with her gas and electricity provider and her credit card balance was zero.

Jack joined DS Cooper at the bureau and picked up the credit card statement. The balance was, indeed, zero – the previous balance of £1,550 had been paid off in full. To Jack it looked like the balance for a holiday – paid to SunSeekers Ltd.

A holiday that she would never take.

"Let's go, Cooper. I don't think there is anything here to help us. Take some photos, then we'll go and see the husband." Jack slipped the credit card statement back into the pile and headed towards the door. DS Cooper dutifully snapped a few shots of the living room lay- out, the bureau and paperwork, then joined Jack in jogging down the communal steps to the front door.

\* \* \*

Time: 2.10pm

Date: Sunday 22<sup>nd</sup> July 2012

Location: White Horse Road, Southwark, London

DS Carmichael held the passenger side door open while shielding his eyes from the baking sun overhead. DC Cassidy slipped into the passenger seat, giving him an odd sideways glance while she did so.

Who held doors open for women these days? she mused, watching as DS Carmichael slammed the door shut after she had tucked her legs inside. It was either oddly charismatic or just plain odd. She couldn't decide, and the feeling unnerved her.

He had been very quiet during the interview with Patricia Gordon's son, letting her do all the talking. And on the drive over he had seemed unusually distracted. Several times he would brake at the last minute, or drift over the white line into the opposite lane, his mind clearly elsewhere. She had tried to make conversation during the journey from the Dale's family home, but most of her questions went unanswered or elicited a monosyllabic yes or no response. She had tried to ask about his family, where they came from, where they lived, but that in itself seemed to make him clam up even more. Whenever she caught his eye, those beady bird-like pupils gave nothing away.

Determined not to have another silent journey back to the station, DC Cassidy pulled out her notebook.

"James seems to have built a good rapport with the son," she commented, flipping over the pages. James Anderson, the FLO assigned to the Gordon family, was someone Amanda knew fairly well. They had started their careers and completed their initial training together at Hendon, followed by periods of working alongside each other on investigative teams. She knew him to be a thorough and reliable officer; if there was anything worth knowing about the Gordons, James Anderson would find out.

DS Carmichael appeared to grunt a reply, turning his head away from DC Cassidy while he tried to pull out across the two lane carriageway.

DC Cassidy continued. "The son seemed to be quite close to Patricia, his mother, but I detected a bit of hostility towards the father. Did you sense that too?" She looked up from her notebook, trying to catch Carmichael's eye and urge him to respond. "Well, did you?"

DS Carmichael flashed a sideways look and merely shrugged. "I guess."

"Maybe there's more to the separation than we thought?" DC Cassidy made a note to herself at the back of her notebook. "Maybe it wasn't as amicable as the husband wants us to believe?"

Again DS Carmichael gave a non-committal shrug of the shoulders in response.

"Could be a motive?" continued DC Cassidy, refusing to give up.

"I wouldn't read too much into it," replied DS Carmichael, finally engaging in conversation as he pulled into a steady flow of traffic heading towards Waterloo station. "Families can be complex structures. Not everyone comes from the perfect home."

"No, but…"

"Some people get dealt a raw deal by the families they happen to be born into; some parents aren't exactly the best role models for their offspring. But it doesn't necessarily mean they're monsters."

"I still think it's a line of enquiry," persisted DC Cassidy. "There was definitely something off between the son and his dad."

DS Carmichael conceded the point with a nod of the head and turned his attention back to driving. "Well I'm sure you'll raise it with Jack when we get back."

DC Cassidy already knew that she would, and turned her attention back to her notebook in her lap. James Anderson had done a thorough job, obtaining all the relevant background on the family. Other than the strained relationship with his father, the son, David, didn't reveal any other potential lines of enquiry. As far as he knew, his mother had no known enemies, hadn't befriended anyone in recent weeks, and pretty much kept herself to herself. The likelihood that the killer was someone that the family knew was looking less likely by the second. After the usual platitudes and routine tea-making, and promising they would keep the family informed of any developments, DC Cassidy had led DS Carmichael out of David Gordon's well-kept three-bedroomed semi, and made their retreat.

"So, what made you become a police officer, detective?" The question came out of the blue, just as DC Cassidy was resigning herself to another lengthy drive in silence. She turned her head away from the passenger side window where she had been watching a young family washing their car on their front drive, the father turning the hosepipe onto two small children, to their animated shrieks of delight.

"I'm sorry?" she frowned.

"The police," repeated DS Carmichael, flipping the car's visor down to block out the searing sun's rays as they turned off the main road. "What made you join up?"

"Um...it was just something I always wanted to do as a kid. I don't know really. There was never any doubt that it was what I would end up doing. Maybe there were too many Miss Marple books around the house when I was growing up." DC Cassidy smiled at the memory. "And my Mum was always watching Juliet Bravo - although I was too young to watch it and would get sent to my bed. But I can still remember the theme tune though." She paused and turned to DS Carmichael. "So, what about you?"

She had asked this question on the journey over and had received nothing in response; but it was worth another shot. "What made you want to be in the police?"

The question hung in the air as DS Carmichael followed the Sunday afternoon traffic across Westminster Bridge. He pulled up at a set of traffic lights and stared directly ahead, chewing at his bottom lip whilst fixing his eyes on the red light in front of them. Eyes that DC Cassidy could see softening around their hard exterior.

"Were your family in the force?" DC Cassidy continued, cautiously, feeling that now she had him talking she needed to keep up the pressure. "Your parents?"

The lights turned green and DS Carmichael stepped heavily on the accelerator, lurching the car forwards. He glanced in his rear-view mirror and quickly pulled over to the side of the road.

"I've just remembered that I need to be somewhere." DS Carmichael nodded at the passenger side door. "The station is only a ten-minute walk from here. Do you mind hopping out?"

As he glanced over at her, DC Cassidy noticed that the hardness had returned to his eyes, replacing whatever softness she had thought she had seen. He raised his eyebrows and nodded once again at the door. "Please?"

DC Cassidy mumbled a reply and scrambled to get out. Before slamming the door behind her, she bent down and poked her head back inside the car. "Don't forget we have a briefing at four."

Without replying, DS Carmichael sped off as soon as the door was shut.

\* \* \*

Time: 3.15pm
Date: Sunday 22<sup>nd</sup> July 2012
Location: Kennington, London

"I still can't believe it." Frank Gordon sat on the edge of the stiff leather sofa, his hands knotted together on his knees. His face had a translucent, ashen hue, his eyes red-rimmed, as if sleep had evaded him for days.

"I still can't believe it," he repeated, his voice hoarse and grating. "I really can't." His thinning hair had been closely cropped, but his face looked as though it had been days since its last contact with a razor. Jack instinctively rubbed a hand over his own prickling chin.

Leaning up against the wall opposite, Jack noticed the same well-ordered, well-presented house, almost a mirror image of the one they had just left. "We're very sorry for your loss, Mr Gordon," Jack replied, spouting the text book phrase all rookie policemen were taught during their training. Jack had long since forgotten how many times he had had to say it. "We're doing all we can to find the person responsible."

"Is it true?" Frank Gordon looked up at Jack, fresh tears brimming at the corner of his raw eyes. "What they said in the papers?"

"The papers?" A frown teased Jack's forehead as he raised his eyebrows, quizzically. He knew what Mr Gordon was referring to, but feigned ignorance, and ignored the folded copy of the Mail on Sunday sitting on the coffee table between them.

"About Patricia. And the other girl." Mr Gordon hesitated, swallowing past the invisible lump that had settled in his throat. "They say there's a serial killer on the loose." His voice cracked, painfully, as he spoke.

Jack lowered his gaze to the floor, studying his less than polished shoes, comparing them with the gleam that shone from DS Cooper's. "I will be honest with you, Mr Gordon," replied Jack, raising his eyes to meet the tear-stained face opposite. "We are looking for one person; the same person responsible for both crimes."

Frank Gordon nodded miserably, silent tears sliding down his unshaven cheeks.

"We won't take up too much of your time, Mr Gordon, but there are a few questions we need to ask you." Jack pushed himself off the wall and sat himself down into the spare section of the sofa. He nodded at DS Cooper to get his notebook ready. "I appreciate you have already spoken to officers recently; the family liaison officer DC Anderson has been round? And I believe he is currently with your son and his family?"

Frank Gordon nodded.

"There are just a few additional questions that might help us." He paused and waited for Frank Gordon to gently nod, noting he continued to wring his hands in his lap, the nails bitten down to the quick. "When did you last see your wife.... ex-wife?"

Frank Gordon paused, his eyes misting over as he cast his mind back to a time before the nightmare began. Opening his mouth to speak, his tone so soft it was hard to discern what he was saying. Both Jack and DS Cooper inched closer, inclining their heads to catch the hushed words. "The day before.... the day before she......" He broke off and lowered his gaze once again to his lap. "I went round to her flat to help her set up her new TV."

Jack nodded, remembering the state of the art TV and cinema surround sound system sitting in the corner of the flat.

"I don't know why she's bought herself a new one – her old one was just as good. Waste of money if you ask me, but Patricia always likes the good things in life. Sorry...." Frank Gordon broke off, his voice cracking once again. "*Liked* the good things in life. Sorry, I just can't believe she's gone."

"That's OK, Mr Gordon, you have nothing to apologise for." Jack nodded at DS Cooper to continue the line of questioning that they had agreed in advance, while he slipped out, seemingly unnoticed, to look around the rest of the house.

With the sound of DS Cooper's voice in the background, Jack quickly jogged up the stairs. Three bedrooms opened off the landing, only one clearly in use, one a guest room and one a junk room. Jack popped his head into all three. Nothing seemed out of place. All tidy. All orderly. Jack headed to the far end of the landing where he found an equally spotless bathroom.

Jack stepped in and sniffed. The bath had recently been cleaned, the smell of detergent heavy in the air. Leaning closer over the bath itself, Jack sensed the aroma of bleach was even stronger. Raising his gaze, he noticed the mirror-fronted cabinet over an equally clean and gleaming sink. No splash marks, no smudged fingerprints around the edges.

Opening the cupboard, Jack noted the usual array of toiletries, painkillers, plasters and razors. Again, nothing out of the ordinary. Nothing out of place.

Ordinary.

And clean.

Very clean.

* * *

Time: 4.10pm

    Date: Sunday 22nd July 2012

    Location: Isabel's Café, King's Road, London

The hint of a teasing, welcoming breeze rippled in through the open patio doors, starting to gently wash away the heat and stifling humidity of the day. Isabel smiled as she leant against the door frame, watching Livi curled up fast asleep underneath the shadow of the ornamental grass nestled in the corner of the walled garden.

It was moments like this that Isabel treasured. She closed up early on a Sunday, to make up for all the early starts. She loved the peace and quiet after closing time, with no sound other than the thoughts churning in her head. Pushing herself off the doorframe, she turned back inside the studio where Patrick was packing up his work for the day, washing his paintbrushes at the small, porcelain sink.

"Do you think I should stay open later?" she asked. "Once the Olympics start?"

Patrick raised his head, shaking the brushes dry and stacking them in a jam jar. "Do you want to?"

Isabel shrugged and slipped onto one of the stools tucked under the table which was still littered with Patrick's sketches. "I'm not sure. I know we aren't on the doorstep of the Olympic Park, but there will be more visitors to London over the next few weeks, more customers. And there are some other venues that are a bit closer to us." Isabel paused, reaching forwards to start gathering up some abandoned charcoal pencils. "I probably should have thought about it sooner; the games start on Friday."

"Do you need to?" Patrick leant on the table and gave Isabel an enquiring look. "Open later, I mean? How's business?"

"Oh, you know. Up and down. It has its moments." Isabel began straightening some of the sketches, avoiding Patrick's gaze.

"Really? "Patrick eased himself into the stool opposite. "I know the rent along this road isn't cheap."

Isabel nodded, still managing to avoid Patrick's penetrating gaze. "I'm doing OK. And now Erik has joined us, that'll be a big help. And Dominic and Sacha are a godsend; they refuse to let me pay them what they would get elsewhere. I'm not sure what I would do without them."

"You could always increase my rent?" Patrick let the question hover in the air while he joined Isabel in collecting up the pencils and chalks scattered across the table in front of them. "You don't charge half as much as other art studios would. And we are in Chelsea."

"Oh, good God no." Isabel reached forwards for a stray pencil and lightly tapped Patrick on the wrist with it before popping it into the tray with all the others. "Don't you even think about it. Your rent is fair. You're not here all the time. I'm doing fine, honestly." She looked up and this time held Patrick's gaze firmly in her own, giving him what she hoped was a warming smile. "Truly."

"Well, OK. If you're sure." Patrick made a move to gather up his jacket from where it was draped over a stool. "You don't owe me any favours, Isabel. You know that."

"I know." Isabel smiled once again, and reached across to pick up Patrick's wallet and keys which were next to her. As she went to hand them across the table, the wallet fell open, spilling its contents. "Oh, sorry. Butterfingers." Isabel gathered up the loose bank cards and receipts, when her gaze fell upon a small two-inch by two-inch photograph. Picking it up, she noted its roughened edges curled at the corners, indicating it had been well loved. The photograph pictured a woman with strawberry-blonde shoulder length hair, laughing and smiling, her bright eyes shining for the camera. She hugged a younger girl with the same strawberry blonde hair pulled back into a neat pony tail close to her chest, her arms wrapped around her, both grinning with delight at the picture taker.

"That's a nice photo," commented Isabel as she handed the picture over the table towards Patrick, along with his wallet and keys. "Family?"

Isabel realised that she didn't really know much about Patrick's private life. She assumed he wasn't married or with anyone, as he never seemed to mention anybody special. But maybe he was. Maybe he just kept his private life exactly that. Private.

Patrick took the photograph along with his wallet, but didn't reply. Isabel noticed the way he handled the worn picture, carefully smoothing out the edges before slipping it back inside his wallet. Such love. Such care. She also noticed how he continued to avoid her gaze.

"I'm sorry," continued Isabel, realising she might have stumbled across something she wasn't meant to. "I didn't mean to pry."

Patrick shook his head, slowly, returning his wallet to his pocket. With an awkward sigh, he looked up and found Isabel's worried gaze. He managed a weak smile. "It's fine. Don't worry."

Now that Isabel could see into his eyes, she noticed the haunted, hollow look that had clouded his features. It was as if a dark storm cloud had blocked out the sun, taking away all the warmth and happiness from his eyes. Instead, a deep sadness descended. The usual lightness of his emerald green eyes had faded, their brightness instantly dimmed. The laughter lines that usually crinkled around his eyes were empty.

Isabel knew that look.

It was one of pain.

Pain and overwhelmingly sadness.

"I'll get us a coffee." Isabel quickly slipped back out into the café and returned with two steaming mugs of thick coffee, the freshly brewed aroma permeating through the sombre air. Patrick accepted the cup, gratefully, nodding his thanks and affording Isabel another weak smile. They sipped their drinks in comfortable silence before Patrick began to speak.

"I miss them every day, you know? Not a day goes by when I don't think about them." Reaching back into his pocket, he drew out the battered photograph from his wallet. Holding the picture gently in-between his fingers, he ran a fingertip across their faces, feeling the roughened paper beneath his touch. "This is all I have left."

Isabel felt her stomach clench as she saw the visible grief still so raw upon Patrick's face. "It's a beautiful photograph," she replied, thinking of her own photographs upstairs that held long-lost treasured memories bound together in grief and heartache.

Patrick looked up and saw the exact same grief in Isabel's eyes, reflected back to his own. It was like looking into a mirror. The connection between them was palpable.

"It was a while ago now." Patrick's eyes began to glisten at the edges, his voice cracking like old leather. "One minute they were there...the next... they were gone."

"Your wife?" Isabel nodded towards the photograph still being held between Patrick's fingers. "And....?"

"My wife, yes. And my daughter, Eleanor." Patrick stared at the smiling images before him, breathing in deeply as if to suppress a sob. He took a sip of coffee before continuing. "It was a house fire. And it was all my fault. I only popped out to put some petrol in the car. By the time I got back...."

Isabel felt her breath catch, a feeling of overwhelming sadness engulfing her as she slipped off her stool and rounded the table to take the seat next to Patrick. Without speaking, as words were unnecessary between two souls joined by grief, she wrapped her arm around his shoulders and pulled him close. She felt his body shudder underneath her touch.

A fire.

They stayed like this for a while, two kindred spirits lost in sadness. Time had no meaning for either of them. Patrick's head rested against her shoulder, her comforting squeeze letting him know that she understood his pain.

She understood his sadness.

She understood his loss.

She knew.

"I lost my parents in a fire." Isabel's voice was quiet as she thought back to the treasured photographs sitting upstairs on her bookcase. "And I lost my brother too." She felt her heart leap inside her chest as images of Miles and her parents filled her consciousness. "Nothing can prepare you for losing the ones you love. Nothing. And nothing compares with the grief you feel at their loss; the space that they leave behind. Nothing." She gave Patrick's shoulder another squeeze. "But it wasn't your fault."

Patrick lifted his head from Isabel's shoulder and turned to catch her haunted expression. Instantly he could see his own pain, his own heartache, his own anger, reflected right back at him from within her own eyes. He gave a small shrug.

"Maybe. Maybe not. But maybe things could have turned out differently."

"True. Maybe they could have. Maybe they couldn't." Isabel squeezed Patrick's arm again and nodded her understanding. "But it still wasn't your fault. How could it be?" She instinctively reached for the silver chain around her neck, letting her fingers grasp the prism that hung there. "Things happen that are beyond our control. Awful things. Dreadful things. And it is a test of our own courage as to how we carry on afterwards. We shouldn't spend our time blaming ourselves, or blaming others." An image of Kreshniov's face flickered into her headspace. "We need to spend this time showing our loved ones how strong we are, how courageous we are, and why we loved them so much. Blame only taints their memory."

Patrick gave a small nod. "Have you ever heard of the expression 'crying at the moon'?"

Isabel frowned, quizzically. "No, I haven't. Sounds like something to do with werewolves."

Patrick smiled, but Isabel noticed that it didn't quite reach his eyes. "It means asking for what is impossible."

"And what are you asking for that is so impossible?"

"Peace. Forgiveness."

"And you think that's impossible?"

Patrick shrugged and looked away. "At the moment, yes. No matter what I do, I can't find it."

Isabel felt her heart ache inside, wishing she could say something that would bring Patrick what he so desperately searched for. But she knew from her own bitter experience that peace only came when it was ready. It could never be hurried. Instead she nodded at the cup of coffee sitting on the table in front of him. "Now, drink your coffee and get yourself home. I want to see you bright and early tomorrow with some more ideas for your commission." Isabel gestured towards the random sketches still littering the centre of the table. "I don't think Dominic will be coming back for any more lessons today."

Patrick managed a small smile. Although his eyes remained empty and hollow, devoid of humour, Isabel saw a fleeting brightness creeping in. "Thanks, Isabel. I'll see you tomorrow." With that, he gulped down the remaining coffee and shrugged himself into his jacket. With a last look at the photograph in his wallet, he turned and made his way to the front door.

Isabel followed him to the door, and waved him goodbye. Making sure that the sign was turned to 'closed', she secured the bolts and turned the heavy key in the lock, watching Patrick's sombre frame disappearing along the pavement towards the tube.

After disturbing Livi from her peaceful slumber underneath the shade of the ornamental grass and shooing her inside, Isabel secured the patio doors and climbed the stairs up to the flat.

\* \* \*

Time: 4.35pm
Date: Sunday 22$^{nd}$ July 2012
Location: Metropolitan Police HQ, London

Jack pulled the blinds down over the window and switched on the fans. "I guess we won't wait any longer for DS Carmichael to grace us with his presence; let's get started."

DS Cooper sat down at the table, while DC Cassidy stood by the open window to try and get the illusion of a breeze where none truly existed.

"Amanda, tell us about the Dales."

DC Cassidy brought out her notebook and began to update Jack and DS Cooper on the meeting at the Dale's family home earlier that morning. "Not much that we didn't already know, to be honest. She doesn't live at home; had a pretty chequered past until a couple of years ago. Some minor dabbling in the drug scene. Seemed to have sorted herself out. Parents are adamant she was not back on the drugs or even in contact with anyone from her shadier days." DC Cassidy paused as she flicked over a few pages in the notebook. "Studying English. Parents last saw her about a month ago. No contact since, but that wasn't unusual.

"Now, we know she was last seen on Thursday 12th July, a week or so before she was found, at her halls of residence. Failed to turn up for lectures the following Monday – although the academic year had finished, she had signed up for some summer classes. No real alarm was raised when she failed to show up; she could be a little sporadic in her attendance at times."

Jack nodded. "Anything else?"

"Nothing as yet, no. Rachel is doing a great job – the family are, understandably, devastated."

"OK, so what about the Gordons?"

DC Cassidy flicked over another page in her notebook. "We went to see David Gordon – Patricia's son. Again, understandably distressed at the loss of his mother."

"But...?" Jack cut in. "I can sense there's a but coming."

DC Cassidy nodded. "I sensed there was a tension between him and Mr Gordon – the husband. Nothing was actually said, but I could just feel that the son didn't get on well with his dad. For whatever reason. I'm not sure that the split was as amicable as we were maybe being led to believe."

Jack rubbed his chin and crossed the room to where DS Cooper was sitting. "What did we get from the husband? Did he mention his son at all?"

DS Cooper flicked open his own notebook. "I'm pretty sure he didn't mention him at all, boss."

"Hmmmm, interesting," pondered Jack. "You would have thought he would be concerned about how his son was coping. Would you not?"

"Did you get anything else from him? The husband?" asked DC Cassidy, now standing in front of the fan.

"Upset," answered DS Cooper. "Very upset. Very weepy. Which is as expected if they were as close as we were told they were. *If* they were."

"And a very clean home," added Jack, remembering the smell of bleach.

"Boss?" frowned DS Cooper.

"A clean house," repeated Jack. "That bothers me a little. We know our killer is forensically aware and leaves his crime scenes impeccably clean. Mr Gordon's home wasn't just tidy. It was *clean*. His bathroom was *sterile*."

"Some people are like that," commented DC Cassidy, fanning herself with her notebook. "Especially when they live on their own."

I live on my own, thought Jack. He let his mind recall the stacks of washing up in his kitchen, the overflowing washing bin and the less than sterile bathroom. "Indeed. Indeed. Let's just bear it in mind, though." He joined DC Cassidy by the window in search of fresh air. "So, where are we on the CCTV and phone records. Any updates?"

"Phone records not showing anything up yet, boss." DS Cooper clicked the mouse and the whiteboard flickered into life. "Latest updates confirm Patricia Gordon's phone was left in her flat – forensics will work through downloading her recent messaging and call history. They should have that sometime tomorrow, hopefully. Georgina Dale's phone is missing. It wasn't in her room at the University, and wasn't found with her body. But last activity was at her halls of residence on the day she disappeared. Either switched off or ran out of battery. Again, forensics will see what they can pull out of her messaging and call history."

"OK, CCTV?"

"Still playing through," said DC Cassidy. "The team are compiling lists of vehicles seen in each location and vehicle registration checks are being carried out as we speak. We'll know more tomorrow."

"I want to know the minute anything suspicious turns up."

"Have you thought about making the black stiletto shoe public?" DS Cooper nodded at the photograph of the shoe found close to Georgina Dale's body. "Asking if anybody recognises it?"

"I had considered it, Cooper, but I think it would be a one-way ticket to mass hysteria. And not necessarily helpful. We've already established that it is a very common shoe – so all we will do is attract several thousand calls identifying everyone's wife, sister, mother and lover as having owned a pair." Jack paused. "I don't think our system can cope with that."

"And keeping the shoes out of the press is our one way of excluding prank callers," added DC Cassidy. "Only the killer knows he leaves a shoe at the scene."

"Exactly," confirmed Jack, moving away from the window. "Let's wrap this up until tomorrow. Can you both make sure your notes are uploaded onto the system before you leave tonight?"

Both DS Cooper and DC Cassidy nodded.

"Briefing at 9am then." Jack paused and glanced at his mobile phone. "I'll have to text DS Carmichael later in case he wishes to join us." The sarcasm in his voice wasn't lost. "Do we even know where he is?"

DC Cassidy shook her head. "He just let me out at a set of traffic lights and said he needed to be somewhere."

"The place he needed to be was here." Jack sighed and waved at the door. "Get the notes uploaded onto the system and get yourselves off home. It's been a long day."

\* \* \*

# Chapter Eighteen

Time: 5.35pm

Date: Sunday 22<sup>nd</sup> July 2012

Location: Kettle's Yard Mews, London

Jack headed towards the small bathroom, shrugging off his shirt and unbuckling his trousers as he went. His shirt had almost welded itself to his back during the course of the day, and peeling it off was like shedding another layer of skin. He had listened to the radio in the car on the way home; the weather report predicting yet another week of record breaking temperatures. Officially the hottest July on record – beating even the summer of 1976. Not a millimetre of rain had fallen since May. The water companies were about to issue severe drought orders and impose a swathe of hosepipe bans across much of the country, and everyone was being urged to conserve water wherever possible.

No baths. No car washing. Save your washing up for one big wash at the end of the day. Only use your washing machine with a full load, and only on an energy and water saving programme. Jack glanced back towards the kitchen and noticed the full sink of dirty dishes. And then the washing bin full to overflowing of clothes that had yet to be anywhere near the washing machine.

Just doing my bit to conserve water, thought Jack, as he stepped into the shower. He hit the button and sent a deluge of water cascading down onto the top of his head. He remained there for fifteen minutes, just letting the cool water pulsate against the back of his neck and upper back.

An illegal power shower.

But at least he wasn't doing the dishes.

Half an hour later, Jack had rinsed the shower and dried himself, pulling out an old pair of Hawaiian shorts from his wardrobe that had not seen the light of day for many a year. He pulled on a short sleeved t-shirt and sunk down onto the sofa, already starting to feel hot again. He hadn't quite been quick enough to buy a fan from any of the local shops, and everything was sold out online. He opened his main window as far as it would go, hoping for at least some sort of breeze as the sun went down.

At least his fridge was full of ice-cold beer.

That was something the shops didn't seem to be running out of.

He closed his eyes and leant back against the sofa. As he settled, he felt something buried underneath one of the cushions behind his back. Wriggling to the side, he managed to reach behind and pull it out.

Stu's teddy bear was still where he had left it last night.

Stuart hadn't wanted to take it home with him, once he had moved out of Jack's flat and set himself up in Islington. He had said something about wanting to keep the past in the past.

But Jack couldn't keep the past in the past, no matter how hard he had tried. The past had a way of invading his thoughts and memories, penetrating his dreams when least expected - and casting aside mementoes from the past would not change that. He could get rid of the teddy bear – donate it to a charity shop or local hospital, or put it in the recycling bin. But the past would still be there.

The past would still continue to haunt him.

None of his previous therapists had concluded that getting rid of the teddy bear would solve the problems of his nightmares.

So the teddy bear had stayed.

Jack actually liked to think back to the days of Stuart and his teddy bear; the days before the nightmares began. The days when they were happy and carefree little boys.

And they had been happy – Jack, Stuart and Mum. They may not have had much, growing up, not by today's standards anyway, but they had had fun, hadn't they? He could remember Mum making toy cars out of old cardboard boxes that she would find discarded by the communal bins outside. She would cut spaces for their legs and they would run around the flat pretending to be racing cars; or police cars in Jack's case.

Or she would find the biggest box she could, and sit them both inside – then she would drag them around the flat to the sound of their screams of delight. Stuart would sometimes make a racing car just for his teddy bear too, decorating the sides with multi-coloured scribblings. He would even leave his teddy bear inside the car at bedtime – telling Jack that teddy liked his racing car so much that he wanted to sleep in it.

* * *

Time: 10.00pm
Date: 5<sup>th</sup> April 1971
Location: Old Mill Road, Christchurch

Teddy's eyes reflected the light from the moon outside, shining brightly from the end of Stuart's bed. Jack sat up, unable to sleep because of the howling gale blowing outside. Thick, black clouds scurried across the stormy sky, pushed along by ferocious winds – the moon appearing and then disappearing, appearing then disappearing.

Jack rubbed his eyes. He was tired but he knew that he wouldn't be able to sleep while the storm continued. He looked at the rickety bedside table next to the bunk bed and saw that his glass tumbler of water was almost empty. He swung his legs over the edge of the top bunk and began to climb down the wooden ladder towards the ice-cold floor.

He glanced at Stuart in the bottom bunk, seeing that he was still sleeping peacefully, his thumb in his mouth, his shoulders rising and falling rhythmically with each breath. The storm wouldn't wake Stuart. Stuart could sleep through anything.

But not Jack.

Jack picked up his tumbler and padded across the floor towards the door that had been pulled shut. He shivered in his shorts and t-shirt pyjamas, and hopped from one foot to the other to keep warm. He carefully pulled the door open and peered out onto the landing outside. He hadn't heard their mother coming back, but then again he normally didn't. Usually he would be curled up fast asleep, slumbering peacefully while she was gone.

Various important people had been round to the flat. "The Social", he had heard their mother call them. "The Social" weren't very happy at Jack and Stuart being left alone in the flat at night. Various complaints had been received from other residents in their block at the comings and goings from the MacIntosh's flat. So their mother had promised them that she wouldn't leave them alone again.

But she did.

Mummy had lied to "The Social" and Jack wasn't sure if that was a good thing or not.

He quietly padded down the landing towards the kitchen. He passed their mother's bedroom but didn't peek inside. If she was there, he didn't want to wake her, and he didn't want her to know that he was up so late at night.

"The Social" might come round again if they knew that.

Jack continued past his mother's bedroom door and then pushed open the door to the kitchen. The next thing he heard was the sound of splintering glass as the tumbler fell from his hand and crashed to the floor.

* * *

Time: 7.15pm

Date: Sunday 22nd July 2012

Location: Kettle's Yard Mews, London

Jack woke with a start, unaware that he had even been asleep. He hastily glanced around him while his brain played catch-up. He must have dozed off. He looked at his watch. It was a little after seven o'clock. He noticed one of the dinner plates he had stacked up in the kitchen sink had somehow slid off the pile and crashed to the floor; shards of shattered china decorated the kitchen tiles.

The sound of splintering china.

The sound of splintering glass.

He pushed himself up from the sofa, still clutching the soft brown teddy bear that had been lying on his lap. Still bleary eyed, he headed towards the kitchen and began shovelling fractured china pieces into the kitchen bin. As he did so, he noticed the crumpled leaflet sitting on top of the empty pizza boxes and beer cans.

PTSD – The Facts.

Smoothing out the creases, he pulled the scrunched up leaflet out and slipped it into the pocket of his shorts.

Label or no label, maybe it was time Jack stopped ignoring what was staring him in the face.

\* \* \*

Time: 10.15pm

Date: Sunday 22$^{nd}$ July 2012

Location: A cellar in London

He paused at the top of the stone steps, listening to his own quickening breath. It was always the same; whenever it was "time". He felt his heart-beat thumping rhythmically at the side of his neck, the sound amplified inside his head.

Throb.

Throb.

Throb.

He could almost feel his temples pulsating in time with the rhythm.

The rhythm of life.

Or death.

He began to descend the steps, holding onto the bannister at the side to steady himself. His knees felt weak at the thought of what was to come.

But it had to be done.

There was no question.

There was no choice.

Jess needed to go to a better place.

He turned the heavy wrought iron key in the lock, the sound seeming more amplified than usual. Placing one shoulder against the oak door, he shoved hard and pushed it open into the cellar. The darkness and dampness enveloped him as he stepped inside. As he sniffed, he could sense that the air was tinged with the sweet smell of perspiration, masked by an overpowering stench coming from the metal bucket in the corner at the far side of the cellar. He wrinkled his nose.

Maybe he was keeping them too long.

Neither Jess nor Carol were making a sound. Through the dense blackness it was hard to even make out their forms, but he knew they would be huddled underneath their blankets, shutting out the world. He followed the outline of the metal chains from the radiator – one chain to his left, the other to his right.

Walking towards the chain on the right, he edged his way towards the threadbare mattress. As he approached, he heard sobbing sounds coming from underneath the thin blanket that was draped over Jess's crumpled form. He watched closely as the blanket shuddered up and down with each tear-ridden cry.

Next to the shrouded figure were the remnants of the Sunday lunch he had brought them both. Jess had mostly eaten hers – a chicken and sweetcorn sandwich – with only the crusts remaining. He glanced over his shoulder towards Carol's mattress – noting the untouched sandwich and drink by her side, on the floor.

"Ssssh now, Jess. Everything's all right." He turned back towards Jess's mattress and knelt down by her side, gently pulling the blanket away from the trembling figure beneath. The paleness of her skin, and the whites of her eyes, stood out in the darkness around them. "Ssssh Jess. Daddy's here."

Taking another key from his pocket, he reached forwards and took hold of Jess's slim ankle. If she had had any strength left then she would've kicked out violently, and maybe started screaming and yelling.

But Jess had no energy to do anything.

All Jess could do was trust in her Daddy.

Hannah watched, silently, as he unlocked her ankle restraint and placed the heavy chain to one side. She was surprised at the strength of his grip, feeling his bony fingers clasped around her wrists. She lay still, not moving, not intending to get to her feet, but he dragged her up with surprising ease. With a wiry arm encased around her neck, he began dragging her across the stone floor towards the door.

She saw a light at the top of the stairs. Light and fresh air that she could feel on her skin as they slowly ascended the steps. Hannah's own heartbeat was quickening in her chest, and panic was rising like bile in her throat. Looking back over her shoulder, as she was dragged further and further away from her prison cell, she all of a sudden craved the darkness, the dampness, the smell of sweat and fear. She longed for the hard, cold ground and sense of hopelessness.

She would rather have all that than this.

Whatever *this* was.

\* \* \*

# Chapter Nineteen

Time: 6.15am
   Date: Monday 23$^{rd}$ July 2012
   Location: Green Park, London

The fluttering blue and white police tape had been wound around two conveniently placed tree trunks and stretched lengthways along a section of the quietest part of Green Park. Jack nodded at the police officer standing guard at the outer cordon of the crime scene, ducking under the tape once he had signed his details onto the police log and donned his protective suit.

His heart sank as he stepped, cautiously, along the improvised walkway, snapping the elasticated hood over the top of his head. He could tell from the white-clad bodies in the distance that the crime scene manager and forensics team had already been called – and he had every expectation of seeing the bald-headed Dr Matthews appear at any moment.

Number three.

It had to be.

Jack had hoped with all his heart that he would be proved wrong, but his head was telling him otherwise. And his head usually won.

True enough, the closer he got to the inner cordon, and the white tent that had already been erected over the scene, the flaps to the entrance of the tent parted and Dr Matthews made his exit. It wasn't long before the well-dressed pathologist caught Jack's eye.

"Jack." Dr Matthews nodded in greeting, shrugging off his protective suit and brushing away the invisible fibres from his three-piece tweed suit. He motioned for Jack to step to the side, away from the quiet hustle and bustle of the forensic tent.

"Doc," replied Jack, shuffling across in his blue plastic overshoes. "I'm guessing we have our number three."

Dr Matthews nodded, grimly, the ghost of a haunted expression crossing his cleanly-shaven face. Jack couldn't begin to imagine how many shocking scenes this seemingly unassuming and placid man had had to witness. His demeanour was always one of cool professionalism, appearing to Jack to be able to detach himself from the horrors he witnessed up close; to be able to compartmentalise the violence and evil that cruelly ended the lives of the bodies he examined. But Jack was now seeing a layer of humility and sadness that he had never quite detected before in the ageing pathologist. Maybe it had always been there, and Jack had just not been looking quite hard enough.

"We have a female; age approximately seventeen to twenty-two years. Slightly built." Dr Matthews spoke in a hushed, respectful tone, while Jack gazed over his shoulder at the shrouded tent.

"Cause of death?"

"Preliminary – *very* preliminary - strangulation by ligature. You will have to wait for my full report to confirm."

Jack nodded. "Of course."

"And yes," confirmed Dr Matthews, anticipating Jack's next question. "Wearing just the one shoe. A black stiletto."

Jack nodded. A black stiletto shoe that no doubt matched the one found alongside Georgina Dale's body only three days before, and was currently in an evidence bag back in the investigation room.

"If we can get her away from here soon, I will ensure that I schedule the post mortem examination for later on this afternoon." Dr Matthews turned to go, heading back towards the cordoned off section of road where he had parked his trusty Volvo. "You may want to send someone along this time, Jack. Now we are getting a pattern."

Jack raised a hand in acknowledgment as the pathologist backed away and headed towards the sanctity of his car. Breathing in deeply, Jack turned towards the white tent and the sombre dance being played out before him; white bodies moving in synchronised sequence to the inaudible tune of death. As he approached the tent, he noticed DS Cooper waving at him from a deserted corner of the park.

Keeping to the walkway, Jack headed in DS Cooper's direction, his already heavy heart sinking further as he noticed the pensive expression on the sergeant's face as he approached. DS Cooper nodded his head towards the longer grass at the edge of the park – no words were necessary. The look on his face told Jack everything he needed to know.

Nestling in amongst the sun-baked grass, was a solitary shoe. Jack knelt down, careful not to disturb the surrounding area. Snapping on a pair of latex gloves, he gently parted the wispy strands to reveal a patent black court shoe with a low heel.

"Number four?" DS Cooper stepped back as one of the forensic officers appeared, snapping several photographs of the shoe in-situ, before lifting it gently into a waiting plastic evidence bag.

Jack nodded. "Number four."

* * *

Time: 6.45am
Date: Monday 23rd July 2012
Location: A cellar in London

Zoe had pretended to be asleep when he had opened the door earlier, listening to him shuffling across to her mattress and kneel down by her side. She held her breath and waited for the touch of his cold fingers on her bare skin, recoiling underneath her blanket at the very thought. But although she knew he was there, he didn't touch her. Not this time. Instead, she heard him shuffle backwards and close the door on her once again.

She had lain frozen in time beneath the blanket for what seemed like hours afterwards; not daring to move or breathe in case he was still there, playing some kind of warped game. How long it had been she could only guess, but eventually she found the courage to peek out from beneath her cocoon to only be confronted with darkness.

He had replaced her water bottle, but everything else remained the same.

But she was alone.

Completely alone.

\* \* \*

Time: 7.35am
Date: Monday 23rd July 2012
Location: Green Park, London

"You head on back to the station." Jack walked beside DS Cooper as they headed back towards their cars. "Get yourself some breakfast and freshened up." Taking a brief look over his shoulder, he knew that there was no point in them hanging around any longer. The crime scene manager was in charge now, and two detectives would just get in the way. The scene would now be expertly processed, evidence bagged and logged – and the body removed in a nondescript black private ambulance and taken to the mortuary where, no doubt, Dr Matthews would be waiting. "I'll meet you there. Get a briefing together – make sure Amanda and Carmichael are there."

DS Cooper nodded and headed towards his small silver Golf. Jack watched as the young detective reversed out into the early morning traffic, before heading towards his own car.

Another shoe.

Another shoe meant another victim.

Pulling open the driver's door, he glanced at his watch. It was still early – he would swing by his flat and have a shower and change of clothes; both of which were needed after death had roused them all so brutally in time for the dawn chorus.

$$* * *$$

Time: 9.05am
  Date: Monday 23rd July 2012
  Location: Hammersmith Magistrates Court, London

Anthony Saunders jogged down the steps of Hammersmith Magistrates Court and glanced at his watch. His case had been adjourned for the third time, and he still had some time to kill before he was needed back. Although it was still early, he had been up for hours already; the early start beginning to make itself known by the dull, throbbing headache pounding at his temples. Turning right, he began walking aimlessly along the street, not really thinking about where he was heading. The day was already hot and sticky and he didn't fancy being cooped up in his stuffy office for any longer than necessary. As far as his secretary was aware, he was meant to be in Court all day – and he wasn't about to put her straight.

He continued walking, keeping in the shade as much as possible, and before he knew it he was walking through the entrance to Brompton Cemetery. The cemetery was a place his father had often brought him to as a child – and whereas, as a six-year-old, the headstones and burial plots had frightened him, now they instilled in him a sense of peace. He could easily fritter away several hours strolling around the cemetery and gardens, lost in his own world, reading the memorials dedicated to the artists, actors, soldiers and scientists buried within its grounds. From Emmeline Pankhurst to Brian Glover.

He thought about getting a takeaway coffee and strolling around the headstones once again, but decided instead to keep on walking. Out the other side, he thought about heading in the direction of Battersea Park;

maybe he could while away an hour or so, people watching. No one at the office would be missing him. Taking a glance at his watch, he knew that by now all of the benches underneath the shady trees would be taken and he would have to sit in the blazing sun and cook.

Instead of crossing the water in the direction of Battersea Park, he headed towards the Kings Road. Still ambling aimlessly, without any true purpose, his nose took him in the direction of Sloane Square and a coffee shop he hadn't noticed before. Shops popped up all the time along this stretch of road, and many didn't last. The Chelsea price tag placing a huge financial burden around their necks, slowly dragging them down and eventually forcing them under when the rent exceeded their income.

Shouldering his laptop bag, Anthony Saunders pushed open the door to Isabel's coffee shop.

* * *

Time: 9.30am
Date: Monday 23rd July 2012
Location: Kettle's Yard Mews, London

Jack finally stepped out of the shower. Twenty minutes under the pulsing jets had done little to wash away the aura of death that had clung to him the minute he had stepped into that little white tent. She had been carefully positioned on the grass, arms by her sides, legs tucked up beneath her. One black stiletto shoe on one foot. She had looked peaceful. Almost serene.

Yet Jack knew that the end to her life had been anything but peaceful and serene. He had seen the markings around her delicate neck becoming more visible as time progressed. But other than that, she appeared to be untouched. Her eyes stared lifelessly skywards; her face pale and empty.

Jack shook his head to try and rid himself of the image. He pulled out a fresh shirt and pair of trousers from his wardrobe, and encased himself in a liberal dose of 48-hour antiperspirant. With a quick look out of the window as he dressed, he once again noticed the searing hot sun sitting in a cloudless sky. Slipping on his socks and shoes, he wondered if the antiperspirant would live up to its name.

He glanced again at the sink full of dirty dishes, adding his coffee mug to the top.

Later. He would deal with that later.

Grabbing his keys and phone, he headed for the door.

* * *

Time: 10.15am

Date: Monday 23$^{rd}$ July 2012

Location: Isabel's Café, King's Road. London

A comforting draught greeted him as he stepped over the threshold. A mixture of the heavy, rich scent of coffee, cake and pastries hand in hand with a faint aroma of sweet cinnamon made his stomach begin to give a low rumble. The walk from court had awakened his appetite.

He was then greeted by an even warmer, richer smile.

"Morning!" The smile belonged to an attractive woman he guessed to be in her early thirties, dressed in a pair of dark-blue denim dungarees, with a white t-shirt underneath; everything wrapped up in a red and white checked apron. Her light, sun-kissed hair was scraped away from her face into a high pony tail, her cheeks glowing rosily from the heat of the coffee machine steaming behind her. "Coffee?"

Anthony Saunders found himself returning the smile and nodding. "Yes, th.... thanks. That would be great."

"Anything in particular? We do a great Americano, or if you fancy something frothy, a cinnamon latte?" Isabel wiped her hands on a nearby tea towel and smiled once again at her new customer. Her new, very handsome customer. "Or iced? If you need cooling down?"

Swinging his laptop bag off his shoulder and placing it on one of the comfortable looking sofas, the defence lawyer gazed up at the blackboard behind the counter which listed the various beverages on offer. "Um, a latte would be great. Sounds good." He paused while he cast his eyes around the rest of the coffee shop, noting he was the only customer. "Do you mind if I just sit here and do some paperwork? I don't fancy going back to the office just yet."

Isabel smiled and nodded, gesturing towards the empty sofas. "Be my guest. I'm Isabel by the way. You've not been here before?"

"Me? No. I've not been out this way for a while." Anthony Saunders slipped off his jacket and folded it over the back of one of the sofas, seating himself amongst the soft cushions. He looked up and took in the homely looking armchairs, and the bookcases rammed full of paperbacks, hardbacks and magazines. "This place is amazing."

Isabel's rosy cheeks flushed a little darker. She turned towards the coffee machine, a jet of hot steam exploding from the spout and filling the room with the rumble of hot milk being steamed to its frothiest. Once the steam subsided, the aroma of sweet cinnamon floated through the air.

Bringing the coffee over to where Anthony Saunders was sitting, Isabel noticed his laptop was already open and a pile of paperwork sat next to it. Careful not to spill any of the coffee onto what looked like very important papers, Isabel set the tall glass down on a hessian coaster. Straightening herself up, she tried to imagine what this tall, dark, handsome stranger was doing.

Writer?

Journalist?

Film critic?

"Thanks." Anthony Saunders nodded towards the coffee, taking a deep breath and inhaling the heady scent of cinnamon. "It smells lovely."

Isabel stepped back about to turn away, when she spied the man's mobile phone on the arm of the sofa. It was open at a mobile app that she recognised.

London Life.

Isabel hesitated. London Life. Did that mean he was single? She considered things for a moment, her gaze falling on his ring-less left hand. Just at that moment her jumbled thoughts were interrupted by Dominic appearing from the archway that led through to the kitchen.

"I've put fourteen pastries into the second oven," he informed her, already carefully recording the information in his notebook. "They will be ready in exactly nineteen minutes."

Isabel smiled and returned to the counter. "Thanks, Dominic." She glanced at her watch. There would be a lull now until the pre-lunchtime rush started. She looked back over her shoulder at their only customer, noting the strange fluttering sensation in her stomach that she hadn't experienced in a long time. So long that she wasn't exactly sure what it heralded. "How about you take a break for a while? It's quiet in here at the moment. I know Livi is upstairs and would probably like some fussing."

Dominic raised his head from his notebook, noticing their lone customer for the first time. He took in the stranger's appearance – medium build, dark-coloured neatly cropped hair, dark brown eyes, smart suit - a jacket laying across the back of the sofa displaying the Gieves and Hawkes, Savile Row, label. Working from an HP laptop; an iPhone 4s on the arm of the sofa. Freshly made cinnamon latte on the table. Dominic made the appropriate entries into his notebook and then, satisfied, he left in search of Livi.

Isabel smiled at the departing Dominic. She loved that boy with all her heart. He reminded her so much of Miles. Feeling her heart start to sink heavily inside her chest, Isabel turned back to the counter and began to straighten the napkin holder and cutlery tray.

"Are you sure you don't mind me sitting here and working?" The voice jolted Isabel back to the present, away from her thoughts of Miles and Dominic. She turned her attention back to her customer, who was looking across at her with what she could now see were large, milk-chocolate warm eyes. There were slight crinkles around the edges, suggesting a face that was used to smiling, used to happiness. Isabel instinctively reached up and touched her own face, wondering if happiness and laughter would one day re-enter her life and etch themselves onto her skin.

"Of course not," she replied, walking out from behind the counter and perching herself on the arm of the chair opposite him. "As you can see, we're not busy. You have at least another hour before the pre-lunchtime rush begins. Stay as long as you want. I can give you the Wi-Fi password if you need it?"

Anthony Saunders looked up and his gaze met Isabel's. He noted her eyes glinting back out at him were tinged with something – what was it? A sadness? A sorrow? A melancholy that dulled their brightness. Before he knew it, he was introducing himself.

"I'm Anthony Saunders." He held out his hand. "Pleased to meet you."

"Isabel." Isabel leant forwards and found herself taking his warm hand in her own, and then laughed. "Sorry, I've already told you that."

Anthony smiled, letting his eyes rest on hers. Had he really never seen this coffee shop before? He must have passed by a few times at least, and each time he hadn't realised what beauty lay within. "How long have you been here?" he asked, clearing his throat and reaching for his coffee. He lowered the lid of his laptop, suddenly the lure of paperwork wasn't so strong.

"Oh, must be about three or so months now," replied Isabel, feeling the blush still tingling at her cheeks. "I have a small art studio out the back too." Isabel nodded towards the rear of the café. "I have a couple of artists who rent space from me, but neither of them are here at the moment."

"And you live above?" Anthony nodded towards the ceiling and the flat above.

Isabel nodded. "Yes, it's only small but it's big enough for us. It's just me...and my cat." Isabel felt a fresh wave of heat cross her cheeks. Why had she just told him, a perfect stranger, where she lived, and that she lived alone? With a cat. Before she knew it, she felt herself ask the next question. "You?"

"Me? Oh. I live along The Embankment. Alone. Just me. No cat." Anthony smiled, his chocolate eyes twinkling.

Isabel couldn't help herself. "I couldn't help but notice the app.... on your phone. London Life. Do you use it?" She nodded at Anthony's mobile phone still sitting on the arm of the sofa, still open on the London Life home page.

Anthony's gaze flickered towards his phone. Putting his coffee cup down, he swept the phone up and closed the app down, slipping the phone into his trouser pocket. He looked up and caught Isabel's enquiring gaze and gave a slow nod.

"I do. And I don't. It's a little embarrassing." He gave a short chuckle and reached for his coffee cup again. "A dating app at my age. If anyone knew at work, I'd be a laughing stock."

"Me too," blurted out Isabel, a little louder than she had anticipated. "I mean; I use it sometimes. And it makes me feel a little like that too. I daren't tell anyone!"

"Really?" Anthony looked up and raised an eyebrow. "That makes me feel a whole lot better! I just find my job keeps me so busy, I don't have time for meeting anyone. I'm divorced. Live on my own. I don't usually have much luck at relationships. And London is so... well, it can be a quite unfriendly place sometimes."

Isabel felt herself relax. "I feel exactly the same. I work here seven days a week, often until quite late. I never really get time to meet anyone either."

"Well, today you've met me." Once again Anthony held out his hand towards Isabel and grinned, his smile reaching his chocolate brown eyes and making them sparkle. Isabel laughed and shook his hand once again.

For the next ten minutes, Isabel had something she hadn't experienced for a long time. A conversation. With a man. And an attractive one at that. She quickly found out that he had been married just the once, now divorced, lived alone in a flat near the Embankment, originally came from Oxford, but moved to London when he got a job as a solicitor. No pets. Likes pasta and Indian takeaways. Not keen on Chinese. Has a gym membership but rarely goes. Doesn't smoke. Tried weed at college once. And can't swim.

Suddenly, the bell on the coffee shop door jangled, jolting Isabel back into the present.

"Jack! Good to see you again," greeted Isabel, pushing herself off the armchair and returning to the counter. "Twice in one week. What brings you out this way?"

"Just a flying visit," replied Jack, closing the door behind him and inhaling deeply, letting the enticing aroma of freshly baked pastries and coffee fill his nostrils. The low rumble in his stomach reminded him that he hadn't eaten yet today. The combination of the early start and the partially clothed dead body in Green Park had dampened his appetite. "Just in the vicinity. Thought I'd treat the team to a proper coffee rather than the muck from the canteen."

As Jack stepped towards the counter he noticed they were not alone. Glancing over to the sofa, he nodded in recognition at the defence lawyer, noting the pile of paperwork and laptop. "Saunders."

"Detective." Anthony Saunders returned the recognition with a short, curt nod of his own.

"DC Cassidy tells me you got everything you needed from the unused material in the McArthur case." Jack pulled out his wallet and handed a twenty-pound note across the counter towards Isabel's outstretched hand. "Give me four coffees – whatever you recommend. I have no idea what any of this means." Jack nodded at the coffee menu behind Isabel.

"Indeed we did," replied Anthony, draining the last of his now-cooled latte. "We're good to go."

Isabel busied herself behind the counter, placing four recyclable takeaway coffee cups into a cardboard tray. "The skinny latte is for Amanda." She tapped on top of one of the lids. "I've given you and Chris a cinnamon latte each. And then a mocha."

Jack nodded, lifting the tray from the counter. "Keep the change. Put it in your charity box." He pointed at the Marie Curie Cancer Care money box sitting by the cutlery tray. "I'd better get back before these get too cold."

With a brief smile at Isabel, Jack turned away and headed for the door.

"Cheerio, Inspector." Anthony Saunders didn't lift his eyes from his laptop. "See you in court."

\* \* \*

# Chapter Twenty

Time: 10.50am

Date: Monday 23rd July 2012

Location: Metropolitan Police HQ, London

"But why would he kill his wife?" DC Amanda Cassidy frowned towards the whiteboard where Frank Gordon's face had been added to the investigation thread.

"*Ex*-wife," corrected Jack, walking around the table handing out the coffees he had collected from Isabel's. Hopefully they would still be warm.

"Ex-wife," conceded DC Cassidy, taking her skinny latte and inclining her head towards the screen. "Although they were technically still married. But what's his motive? I still don't see it."

"You know the stats," replied Jack, sipping from his coffee. "It's usually someone they know. An ex-husband will always be a prime suspect until proven otherwise. And you said yourself in your reports from yesterday; his split from Patricia might not have been as amicable as he had wanted people to believe."

"I agree." DS Carmichael, sitting at the far end of the investigation room, nodded his head towards Jack. "Statistically, murders are solved from within the close family unit."

"Single murders maybe, but not for serial killers," continued DC Cassidy, still shaking her head. "The son was off with him, but that doesn't prove anything. Let's say he did kill his ex-wife; why on earth would he kill

Georgina as well? He has no connection to her; it makes no sense. And now we have a third."

"He's only up there as a suspect." Jack drained his coffee and tossed the empty carton into the bin behind him. "Nothing more. And he stays there until he can be eliminated." Jack paused and caught DC Cassidy's gaze. "He fits some of the psychological profile characteristics."

In reality, Jack's gut feeling matched that of DC Cassidy's. Frank Gordon was an unlikely serial killer. If he had a falling out with his son, then it was likely to be unconnected. Most families had some kind of splintered fractiousness underneath the surface if you scratched hard enough. But the list of profile characteristics given to him by Dr Hunter was burning a hole in his shirt pocket.

Frank Gordon fit the age range.

He was divorced, or as good as.

He was an educated man.

But there was one other thing that really alerted Jack's detective instincts.

The cleanliness of the house.

And the smell of bleach.

"What else do we have?" Jack shook the thoughts clouding his mind and looked from DC Cassidy to DS Carmichael. "As yet we don't have an ID on the body found this morning – make a note to put a call in to Missing Persons when we're done here. So, for now, we will have to concentrate our efforts on Patricia and Georgina. How are we getting on with the CCTV?"

"We still have two teams trawling through the images." DC Cassidy sipped her skinny latte. "A list of vehicles seen at each vicinity in the hours before the bodies were discovered are now being followed up, the owners being traced. They will be spoken to and ruled in or out as appropriate. I'm expecting an update later this afternoon, but so far we haven't been able to find a vehicle that shows up at both sites."

Jack nodded. It was as he had expected. The road traffic division had informed him that roadworks around the capital had meant that traffic was being diverted away from its usual course, and many CCTV cameras were out of action. "Let's add the third murder scene to the CCTV. And widen the location; search more streets in and around each dump site. He has to have got the bodies to the sites in some way, seemingly undetected. He needs a vehicle. Let's focus on vans or large estates."

DC Cassidy nodded and made a note in her notebook. "Myself and DS Carmichael will go through it again when we're finished here."

"Anything more from the mobile phone companies?" continued Jack, turning his head towards DS Cooper. "Anything to track their movements?"

"Full phone records are now in," nodded DS Cooper. "Not immediately helpful location-wise for Patricia Gordon as she had left her phone at home. And Georgina Dale had switched hers off on the day she disappeared – last mobile phone mast places her location at the University. Digital forensics are still trawling through the message and call history on both phone numbers to see if it comes up with anything."

But don't hold your breath, thought Jack, sighing inwardly. "OK, every-one. Amanda, if you and DS Carmichael focus on the CCTV, and touch base with Missing Persons. And don't forget I need you both at the mortuary later this afternoon – Dr Matthews has confirmed the post mortem will be happening around three o'clock." Jack watched as DC Cassidy gave a slow nod, her cheeks slightly colouring, and DS Carmichael raised his eyebrows. "And Cooper – you and I are going to visit Georgina Dale's halls of residence. Get yourself ready to go."

"And the shoe found this morning, boss?" DS Cooper got to his feet, depositing his empty coffee cup in the waste paper bin.

Jack was aware of the three pairs of eyes trained on him. "The shoe found at the scene in Green Park this morning has been bagged up and is now with forensics."

"So he has another." DS Cooper's voice was sombre as the realisation hit them all.

"Yes," replied Jack. "So it would seem."

"And the body found this morning?" DS Cooper let the question hang in the air.

"Was wearing only the one shoe." Jack let his eyes rest on the matching stiletto on the table in front of them. "A black stiletto with a diamante buckle.”

* * *

Time: 12.00pm
  Date: Monday 23<sup>rd</sup> July 2012
  Location: Isabel's Café, King's Road, London

The café was almost full, and the aroma of rich coffee and baking pastries filled the air. Isabel was steadily working her way through the orders at the counter; two macchiatos with hot sausage rolls, one cinnamon cappuccino with a Danish pastry, and two caramel lattes with hazelnut and chocolate chip cookies. She wiped her brow with the back of one hand, pushing away the wisps of hair that had worked themselves loose from her pony tail.

But Isabel loved the café when it was busy.  She loved the buzz and electricity that she felt from moving between the steaming coffee machine and the heat of the kitchen beyond.

“Two more trays of sausage rolls, Dom,” she called out over her shoulder. “We're getting a bit low, and the school runs will hit us soon.” It was the last day of school and college for some of the children in the borough, others finishing up tomorrow, meaning that scores of hungry teenagers would descend on the café on their way home, usually snapping up her hot, buttery sausage rolls as if they hadn't eaten all day.  Which maybe they hadn't – they were teenagers after all. Their body clocks were all over the place.

Sacha had come in to help with the lunchtime rush - working the café floor, clearing away empty plates and cups and wiping down the tables. Dominic was hard at work in the kitchen, keeping the ovens ticking over with trays of baked goods.

Despite the frenetic activity of the kitchen and coffee machine, the café had a relaxed, almost serene, feel to it. Customers were settled into their comfy sofas and armchairs, nestling in amongst the cushions with a paperback taken from the groaning bookcase. Some opted for a magazine or newspaper from the racks by the door, others merely stared out of the window and watched the world go by.

People sighed as they sipped their rich and frothy cappuccinos, momentarily slipping away from the hustle and bustle of modern life, taking a few stolen minutes to themselves. Eyes closed. Smiles flickered onto lips. Shoulders rose and fell with contented sighs.

Stepping inside Isabel's café was like stepping inside a time vacuum. Time stopped for as long as you wanted it to; the world outside could wait.

Both Erik and Patrick were in attendance in the art studio. They could hear the hiss and splutter of the coffee machine, the clinking of the coffee cups and the scraping of plates, but the sound was muted and hushed. They had opened the rear patio doors to let a gentle breeze waft in from the courtyard, occasionally enough to ripple the papers that lay strewn over the table.

Patrick had a concentrated frown across his brow and a charcoal pencil in his mouth, while he stared intently at the rough sketches in front of him. He was almost there; he could feel it. Inspiration was around the corner.

Erik was quietly humming to himself as he casually dipped his paintbrush into the sea of watercolours by his side. He tapped his feet, still clad in their open-toed sandals, in time with the imaginary music floating inside his head.

Dominic slid into the studio carrying two iced waters, the cubes of ice clinking against the sides of the glass. He put them down on the table.

"Thank you, young Dominic," acknowledged Patrick, not taking his eyes from the sketch in front of him, the charcoal pencil now dancing across the paper with a flourish. "Just what we needed."

Dominic turned to go, but as he did so he glanced at the easel where Erik was sitting and hovered on the spot. "The Millennium Bridge," he said. "Three hundred and twenty-five metres long, four metres wide. Opened in June 2000 but needed to close soon afterwards due to movement vibrations. Designed to allow five thousand people to cross at any one time."

Erik rested his paintbrush along the easel edge and looked across at

Dominic, still hopping slowly from foot to foot. "That's remarkable. You are a very clever and observant young man, Dominic." Erik smiled, flashing a set of perfectly white teeth. "It is indeed the bridge that you call the Millennium Bridge. I found it one of the most interesting structures that I have ever seen. Even in Hamburg we do not have anything quite this unique."

"It's appeared in many films," continued Dominic, nudging his round-rimmed spectacles higher up on the bridge of his nose.

"Yes – a Harry Potter film, so I have been told," replied Erik, casting a glance towards the café. "Something to do with a King?"

"The Half-Blood Prince – Harry Potter and the Half-Blood Prince," answered Dominic, taking a step closer to the easel. "The Death Eaters destroy the bridge in the opening scene."

"Do they really?" Erik picked up his paintbrush again, dipping it into the watercolours. "I really must watch it for myself some time."

Dominic nodded and then turned to go back towards the café, aware that he only had three minutes until the sausage rolls would be ready.

"Adeus, Dominic." Patrick raised his charcoal pencil in the air. "Obri-gado."

"De nada," replied Dominic, beaming from ear to ear, as he disappeared back through the archway and into the café.

"A little Portuguese," explained Patrick, catching Erik's inquisitive eye across the table. "He's the perfect pupil."

"Well, we all have our little secrets," replied Erik, casting his eye back to his easel and resuming his careful brushstrokes across the canvas. "Some of us are just a little better at hiding them."

\* \* \*

Time: 12.30pm
  Date: Monday 23rd July 2012

Location: St James's University, London

The room looked like any typical student digs – or as typical as Jack assumed they would look. There was a single bed tucked away in a corner with a small bedside table. A single wardrobe opposite, a desk nestling beside it. Standard cheap flat-pack furniture Jack mused as he turned around and noted the compact shower room and ensuite completing the lay out.

Georgina Dale's room had already been processed by the forensic team, the bedding bagged and taken away for analysis, along with her laptop and other possible items of evidence. So far, nothing had come back from the labs as showing up anything suspicious – no unusual fibres or DNA other than the victim's herself. The crime scene manager was re-processing some items to be doubly sure, but Jack didn't hold out much hope.

He walked over to the small window that looked out onto a patchy triangle of grass, scorched almost white by the sun's intense rays. A handful of students were lazing beneath the trees, dozing between lectures or trying to catch up on coursework. Jack looked across the grass to the building opposite, to where both Dr Hunter and Dr Riches both had rooms.

Turning away, he glanced around the room once more, his eyes combing it for any signs of something that looked out of place. Anything that might lead them to know how Georgina met her fate.

But there appeared to be nothing.

Text books were stacked up neatly on the desk, next to a half-finished essay on A4 lined paper. Jack leant in closer. An essay on Daniel Defoe's Journal of the Plague Year. Never to be finished.

"Anything, boss?" DS Cooper stepped over to join Jack at the desk.

After one last sweep of the room, Jack shook his head. "No. Just do the usual photos, then let's get out of here."

\* \* \*

Time: 3.05pm
Date: Monday 23<sup>rd</sup> July 2012
Location: Westminster mortuary, London

The bitingly chilly air caused DC Amanda Cassidy's arms to prickle with goose bumps. She shivered and wished she had brought a jacket with her; the flimsy blouse she was wearing did nothing to protect her from the fridge-like air of the Westminster Mortuary.

Maybe I should be thankful, she mused, as she slipped on a pair of rubber overshoes. The temperature was soaring once again outside.

But then again.

This was a mortuary.

Nothing to be thankful for here.

Other than not being the one on the frozen slab.

She pushed open the door that led from the female changing room out into the corridor where DS Carmichael was waiting for her.

"What took you so long?" he frowned, letting his beady eyes roam up and down her body that was now encased in a protective rubber apron. "Nice outfit."

DC Cassidy made a face and ignored the remark, pushing past him and heading towards the main post mortem room doors. "I could say the same to you. Let's just get this over with."

DS Carmichael fell into step behind her, following through the heavy swing doors that led to the examination room. "Something tells me you're not that thrilled to be here, Constable. This your first time?"

DC Cassidy swung round mid-step, almost causing DS Carmichael to collide with her. He quickly side-stepped, holding his hands up in mock defence. "Careful now! Looks like I touched a nerve...."

DC Cassidy opened her mouth to reply, but found the words catching in the back of her throat as the smell of antiseptic mixed with death filled her nostrils. She could almost physically feel the colour draining from her face. She swallowed and tried to clear her throat.

"No, this is not my first time, thank you very much. And even if it was, it's none of your business."

It was true.

It wasn't her first time.

But her first time was not something DC Cassidy wished to dwell upon.

It hadn't been her greatest moment – having to be carried out of the examination room mid post-mortem by two mortuary assistants wasn't something you normally wished to remember.

She swallowed past the constriction that continued to form in her throat, raising a hand to cover her nose and at least attempt to shield her senses from the smell.

That mortuary smell.

A smell like no other.

During her training, the supervising officers had described it as the smell of decay. But it was worse than that. More intense than that. Putrid. Fetid. There weren't enough words to encompass the unique aroma of a mortuary room.

DC Cassidy felt her stomach give a familiar lurch, regretting the large latte and hot sausage roll she had consumed on her way into the station earlier that morning.

"Just asking." DS Carmichael shrugged and turned away, striding across to the far end of the post mortem room where Dr Matthews was hovering next to a stainless steel bench.

DC Cassidy inhaled a deep breath, recoiling at the taste of death invading her airways and followed on behind.

"Ah, Detective Constable Cassidy, nice to see you again." Dr Matthews gave a slow nod of his head and smiled warmly. His brow crinkled beneath the tight surgeon's protective cap covering his head.

He remembers, thought DC Cassidy, feeling her cheeks glow under a warming blush. Although she doubted that there was actually any change in skin colour, her cheeks having taken on a pallid tone the second she had walked in.

He remembers what I did last time.

"And who have we here?" Dr Matthews turned his attention to DS

Carmichael who was leaning, lazily, up against the stainless steel bench. He raised his eyebrows and let his eyes twinkle. "A stand-in for DI MacIntosh, are we?"

DS Carmichael held out his hand. "DS Robert Carmichael, Doctor. Here to supervise." He gave a small, sideways glance at the green-tinged complexion of DC Cassidy standing next to him. DC Cassidy baulked at his tone, her pulse rate quickening at the clearly intended jibe.

As if I need supervising, she grimaced. Looking after like a child. If she hadn't felt so queasy she would have retorted with a clever quip of her own, but knew full well that opening her mouth right now might give her stomach contents an excuse to make their exit.

Dr Matthews waved away DS Carmichael's proffered hand. "Time to crack on." He turned towards the stainless steel table that housed the shrouded body of Hannah Fuller.

\* \* \*

Time: 3.15pm
  Date: Monday 23$^{rd}$ July 2012
  Location: Metropolitan Police HQ, London

DS Cooper thrust open the door to the office he shared with Jack, relieved to see Jack sitting at his desk.

"The body from this morning, guv? We've now got a positive ID."

Jack raised his gaze from his desk, glad to look at something other than the ever-growing mountain of paperwork in front of him. "An ID? Already?"

DS Cooper nodded and joined Jack at his desk. "Well, it's a potential ID – nothing confirmed as yet because they haven't been in touch with the next of kin. But Amanda spoke with Missing Persons this morning and they've got a potential match."

Jack held his hand out for the folded piece of paper DS Cooper was flapping in his hand. He flicked it open to reveal a passport-sized photograph and list of brief details.

"Hannah Fuller," read Jack. "Reported missing by her social worker last Thursday after failing to pick her daughter up from nursery."

"You think it's her?" DS Cooper nodded at the photograph.

Jack let his eyes rest on the passport picture. It showed a young woman's face, almost child-like – certainly no more than a teenager. Pale and gaunt looking, with blonde hair scraped away from her face. A faint scowl hovered around her complexion. Jack thought back to the white tent from earlier that morning.

The face staring lifelessly towards the sky.

The pale face.

The hollow eyes.

The wispy blonde hair.

Jack slowly nodded. "It's her. I'm sure. Next of kin?"

DS Cooper shook his head. "There's nothing on record. Missing Persons are in touch with social services to see if they can trace anyone. From the brief notes they have, she lived in a mother and baby unit out in Camden. No family support."

"OK, keep in touch with them. Upload what you have onto the system."

"Yes, Boss." DS Cooper headed for his desk. "You thought any more about DS Carmichael?"

"Carmichael?" Jack frowned, moving a pile of paperwork from one side of his desk to the other. "In what sense?"

"Finding out why he's here. And where he really came from?" DS Cooper picked up the remnants of what looked like a bacon sandwich from his own cluttered desk, giving it a tentative sniff before taking a bite. "You still want me to do some digging?"

Jack sighed. "Something isn't right about him, but I guess we have bigger and better things to worry ourselves about right now."

"You wouldn't mention it to the Chief Super?"

Jack paused, watching DS Cooper demolish the rest of the sandwich and wash it down with a cold cup of coffee. He imagined turning up at

Chief Superintendent King's office, raising his suspicions about their new member of the team. And imagined the response he would receive.

"No, I don't think so, Cooper. Do some digging, see what you can find out. But we'll keep it between ourselves for now – concentrate on catching this killer."

But Jack wasn't going to forget about DS Carmichael.

Killer or no killer.

\* \* \*

# Chapter Twenty One

Time: 3.15pm
    Date: Monday 23$^{rd}$ July 2012
    Location: Westminster Mortuary, London

Dr Matthews reached up and angled the overhead light in order to take a closer look at the deep ligature marks to Hannah Fuller's neck.

"We have a Caucasian female, well nourished, 165cms tall, weight of 60kgs." He spoke into a dictation machine that was suspended on a thin wire above his head.

DS Carmichael leaned closer, a look of morbid fascination on his sharp features. DC Cassidy hung back, averting her eyes from the pale skinned, naked body lying before her, fixing her gaze instead on a bright red plastic bucket beneath the table.

"Clear ligature marks to the neck, compressing the trachea. X-rays taken prior to the examination show a hairline fracture to C1. The skin is broken, indicating extreme force. Classic haemorrhaging spreading from the site of compression." Dr Matthews cleared his throat and glanced up at DC Cassidy. "Everything all right there, Constable?" His kind eyes found her gaze. "Let me know if you need to step outside for a breather."

DC Cassidy responded with a shake of her head and a faint smile shadowed her blue-tinged lips.

"In that case," nodded Dr Matthews, "I will continue with the upper body dissection."

Dr Matthews reached for a slim, silver scalpel from the instrument trolley by his side, and made a long, slow incision from Hannah's throat down to her pubic bone. The chilled air in the post mortem room was still and quiet, the incision into the lifeless skin making no sound. The faint hum of the refrigeration units next door gave off a gentle, calming vibration.

DC Cassidy felt her eyes unwittingly drawn to the macabre showcase in front of her. She bit her lip and willed herself to break the gaze, to go back to studying the red plastic bucket beneath, but her eyes remained locked in their focus on the skin of Hannah's chest and abdomen being peeled back like the rind of a ripe orange.

After he had finished dissecting and exposing Hannah's skin and sub-cutaneous tissue, Dr Matthew's soft tones once again filled the vacant air. "Normal sized chest cavity, ribs and sternum intact. Diaphragm, liver and spleen, no abnormalities detected. Kidneys and bladder undamaged."

DC Cassidy watched as Dr Matthews reached inside Hannah's abdomen, her ears unable to block out the unmistakable squelching sound as he rummaged unceremoniously amongst the organs inside. "Bringing out the colon now." Dr Matthews slowly withdrew his hand from the cavity, bringing with it a length of sausage-like organs, folded and intertwined. The organs slipped through his gloved hands, blood and mucous staining them a russet red. DC Cassidy felt her own intestines clench involuntarily, and she fought the overwhelming urge to retch.

"What about the stomach contents?" DS Carmichael had stepped even closer, his inquisitive eyes following each and every move and sweep of the pathologist's hands.

"You're ahead of me, Sergeant," commented Dr Matthew's, his attention still firmly locked on the length of colon in his hands. "Large intestines intact, no abnormalities detected." He paused and flashed his new spectator an inquisitive, yet appreciative gaze. It was unusual for a member of the police force to be so interested in his work. Usually they would stand at the back of the room, on the fringes of the examination, and leave at the earliest opportunity to await the formal post mortem report rather than asking any questions.

But DS Carmichael was different. Dr Matthews could see that. And different could be both good and bad. "Coming to the stomach now," he continued, replacing Hannah's colon back inside her abdominal cavity.

Once again, the scalpel quietly and soundlessly sliced through the tissue. Reaching inside the cavity, Dr Matthews brought out a surprisingly large J shaped organ encased in strands of bloody mucous. "Weight, please." He passed the organ to a mortuary assistant standing by his side who placed it into a metal bowl and quickly took it to the stainless steel work station behind them.

"1406 grams," came the reply, and the metal bowl returned to Dr Matthews' outstretched hand.

Placing the bowl in front of him, Dr Matthews carefully made an incision with the scalpel, slitting open the organ and allowing the stomach contents to run out into the base of the bowl. He peered closer, reaching for the overhead light, and using a stainless steel spatula began to move and inspect the contents.

"Some undigested food contents are present." Probing with the spatula once more, he continued. "What looks like meat – possibly chicken – and some corns. Sweetcorn most likely. Some starch-like substance, most probably bread."

"A chicken and sweetcorn sandwich," murmured DS Carmichael, edging closer to the bowl so he could see the full contents for himself.

"Indeed," replied Dr Matthews, tipping the bowl at an angle for his avid viewer.

"Are we talking M&S or a homemade variety?" DS Carmichael continued to peer ever closer.

Dr Matthews let a faint frown cross his brow. "Whichever it was, Sergeant, it was the last meal this poor unfortunate lass was to eat."

DC Cassidy brought a hand up to cover her mouth, trying to force the bile back down into her own stomach. She tried her hardest not to breathe in, the smell of undigested food and stomach acid mixing in with the stale odour of death that already hung in the air. She forced her eyes to look away, anywhere but the body on the table before her.

The red bucket.

She focused once again on the red plastic bucket.

But the red bucket was no longer a welcome source of distraction. DC Cassidy watched helplessly as the blood and body fluids released from Hannah's body flowed slowly along a deep rutted channel on the examination table, and then dripped down into the bucket.

Drip.

Drip.

Drip.

DC Cassidy's cheeks lost even more colour, if that were even possible. She felt a fuzziness engulf her head and her vision clouded over as if someone had dropped a veil across her face.

Suddenly, a movement to DS Carmichael's side caught his eye. He tore his gaze away from the display of stomach contents and noticed the swaying figure standing several feet behind him. With a quick lunge, he leapt backwards and wrapped his arms around the slumped shoulders of DC Cassidy, stopping her falling at his feet and crumpling to the floor.

Tottering and swaying in his arms, DC Cassidy's body was like a dead weight. He looked down at the ashen face staring back up at him, her eyes wide open but the pupils disappearing up into the top of her head.

"Whoa, there you go." DS Carmichael took a few more steps backwards away from the bloody spectacle on the examination table, still holding tightly around DC Cassidy's shoulders. "Let's get you out of here."

With a quick nod at Dr Matthews, DS Carmichael scooped the young Constable's small frame up into his arms and carried her out of the examination room. As soon as he had backed out through the heavy swing doors, they were both greeted with a welcoming rush of cooler and fresher air. The stench of death not quite disappearing, but masked by the air conditioning of the corridor and reception area.

Turning away from the corridor that led to the front of the building, DS Carmichael made his way outside through a rear fire exit. Propping DC Cassidy up on a low wall by the back entrance, he gently pushed her head down between her knees and continued to hold onto her shoulders to keep her body steady.

The sun was now starting to dip behind the tall trees that encased the mortuary grounds, but the heat of the day was continuing to soar. Thankfully, the rear entrance was shaded from the intense glare and DS Carmichael noted from the cigarette butts littering the paved floor at their feet that this must be the designated smoking area for the mortuary staff, taking a well-earned break from the stresses of their uniquely necessary and yet ultimately horrifying job. As much as he hated smoking, he couldn't begrudge them this small act of normality.

"Nice deep breaths now," he murmured, patting DC Cassidy's shoulders. "Nice deep breaths."

Very slowly, DC Cassidy felt her vision clear, everything that had been blurred and out of focus was now swimming back into shape. Clarity returned and she saw that she was staring down at a baking hot, dusty pavement and not a red plastic bucket filling with blood and guts. A repeated wave of nausea washed over her which made her retch, her shoulders rising sharply. She fought once more to keep the contents of her breakfast down in her stomach, not wanting to embarrass herself even more than she had already. The hot, acrid taste of bile at the back of her throat burned. She could feel a pair of strong arms enveloping her, and as she slowly raised her head she came to focus on their owner.

A pair of black, beady eyes were watching her, cautiously. Eyes that she had previously associated with haughtiness and self-importance, she could now see housed something else. Was it concern? Compassion? Sensitivity? Even kindness? The longer she looked, the more she was convinced, once again, that there was something else beneath the cold, hard exterior they had been introduced to. She had seen a flash one time before, in the car returning from visiting the home of the Dales. And now she saw it again. The voice belonging to the eyes then spoke.

"Are you OK?" It was a soft tone that echoed the concern and compassion of the eyes. "You look a bit pale. Shall I get you some water?"

DC Cassidy shook her head and found herself smiling, gratefully, up at

DS Carmichael. "No, it's fine. Thanks. Just give me a minute."

"You had me worried there for a moment." DS Carmichael released his grip of her shoulders, and once he was satisfied she was not about to collapse, he moved to the side and sat down on the low wall next to her. "Why don't you stay out here. I'll go and finish up in there."

DC Cassidy nodded her gratitude, and took in a deep breath of fresh air, feeling the stale odour of decay finally leaving her lungs. "Thanks. That would be great."

DS Carmichael nodded, and pushed himself up off the wall, heading back towards the rear door.

"Carmichael?" DC Cassidy called out just as he was reaching for the door. "Can we...er...can we keep all this to ourselves?"

DS Carmichael turned to face her, his hand resting on the door handle. "All what?"

DC Cassidy nodded at the mortuary building in front of them. "What just happened....in there."

DS Carmichael paused for a moment, before pulling the fire door open. "What happened? I don't know what you mean." He gave a small shrug of his narrow shoulders. "Nothing happened, did it? Nothing that I can recall anyway." With a quick flash of a smile, he disappeared back inside the mortuary.

* * *

Time: 4.30pm
Date: Monday 23rd July 2012
Location: Metropolitan Police HQ, London

"CCTV, show me what we've got so far." Jack sat down next to DS Cooper in the computer suite and nodded at the screen. The room was dark, the lights dimmed to help the officers as they scoured through hours and hours of CCTV coverage.

"It's not great, boss," murmured DS Cooper, as he manipulated the mouse and let the cursor dance over the screen. "Amanda and Carmichael have been through most of it. It hasn't thrown up many leads."

Jack glanced at his watch. "When did they say they would be getting back from their jaunt to the mortuary?"

DS Cooper shook his head. "Not sure, boss. Anytime soon would be my guess. Dr Matthews doesn't normally hang around once he gets started."

"OK, so let me see what we have here while we wait." Jack nodded again at the screen in front of them and watched as DS Cooper brought up various images of CCTV footage.

"There are cameras on all the main roads around the three locations of the bodies. Inevitably some weren't operational, but we've pulled the images from every camera that was working." With another click of the mouse, DS Cooper brought up the first set of camera footage, black and white images that jumped and flickered. "The quality isn't great."

"You're telling me," sighed Jack, squinting through the dark to try and make sense of the poor quality, grainy images on the screen. "Anything useful?"

DS Cooper paused, clicking the mouse again. "From what Amanda tells me, none of the vehicles we see on the footage show up in more than one location. So, either none of the vehicles belong to the killer, or…"

"Or he has access to more than one car or van," finished Jack, nodding his head and sighing even more deeply. He had thought as much. They weren't going to be that lucky. If the killer does want us to catch him, as Dr Hunter seemed to be suggesting, then he wasn't going to make it easy for them. And he definitely wasn't going to make the mistake of being caught on CCTV.

"We are following up on all the drivers that are seen on camera in all three locations. Tracing them all is a big job, but Amanda has extra uniforms helping out on that as we speak. Everyone traced is going to be interviewed, see if they saw anything. Anything useful will be uploaded onto the system and forwarded to you directly."

Jack nodded. "Anything else?"

DS Cooper once again clicked the mouse and the grainy images in front of them changed. "Just this one, boss." He nodded his head at the screen where he had frozen one of the images on Berkeley Street in Mayfair, close to where Hannah Fuller had been found that morning. "It might be nothing, but Amanda has highlighted it as a potential line of enquiry. You see that van there?" DS Cooper pointed at the screen, his finger touching a blurred image of a dark coloured transit van. "The van behind the ambulance?"

Jack followed DS Cooper's finger towards the van and nodded. "Right kind of size for transporting a body. Have we run the plates?"

"It's bearing false plates, boss. That's why Amanda flagged it up before she went to the mortuary. It's the only suspicious thing the images have thrown up."

Jack peered more closely at the screen. "Can you enlarge it?"

DS Cooper clicked the mouse and the image grew larger, filling the entire screen. And sure enough, behind the London Ambulance Service vehicle was the blurred image of a dark-coloured, probably black, transit van. Two small windows at the rear appeared to have curtains pulled across. The registration plates were clearly visible MK12 YZK.

"And the plates are false?"

DS Cooper nodded. "Yep. Traffic have traced them to a silver Peugeot stolen in Greater Manchester last week."

"Do we have any images of the front?" Jack let his gaze linger on the fuzzy image of the van. "Can we see the driver?"

DS Cooper minimised the image and replaced it with another from a different angle, this time with a front end view. "Not much clearer I'm afraid."

Jack nodded and peered more closely at the screen. The front of the van looked slightly dented, with one headlight out. He sighed once again. The image was so blurred it was impossible to see anybody inside. "And it's not seen at any of the other two locations, just this one?"

"Just this one, boss," confirmed DS Cooper. "I know it's a long shot, and might not be related, but Amanda thought it suspicious enough to warrant further investigation."

"Yes, she's right. We are probably looking for a van....and there's no saying that this isn't the van our killer was driving, that night at least." Jack's eyes lingered on the image. "It's suspicious enough to need checking out. He may have just got lucky with the other cameras. See if you can get it to ping up on any other CCTV or ANPR systems across the capital." Jack paused and kept his eyes on the van. "Let's see if we can't trace where this son of a bitch went."

"DS Carmichael has been viewing CCTV from around the University," continued DS Cooper, leaving the image of the grainy van on the computer screen. "Only one decent camera at the entrance. Shows Georgina Dale leaving – but isn't really helpful as to what direction she went in. And no CCTV in or around The Briars Care Home."

Jack nodded and made to get up. "Anything yet from Patricia or Georgina's bank statements or cash point activity?"

DS Cooper began to follow Jack out of the computer suite and out into the corridor. "Nothing unusual for either Patricia or Georgina. No transactions after they went missing, as we would expect. The only thing they did have in common was a direct debit to London Life."

"London Life? What's that? Sounds like an insurance company to me." Jack held the door open for DS Cooper to follow him through to the stairs. "Message Amanda to get onto it – she must be back from the mortuary by now. Then we'll have a briefing before we go home for the night."

* * *

Time: 4.45pm
Date: Monday 23rd July 2012
Location: Metropolitan Police HQ, London

DC Amanda Cassidy's phone pinged while DS Carmichael parked the car in the rear car park. Having spent the journey back from the Westminster

Mortuary with the window down and a slight breeze caressing her face, she felt much better and far less queasy. The green tinge to her skin had paled. Glancing down at her phone, she noticed there was a message from DS Cooper.

"Chris wants me to check out London Life. You ever heard of it?" She glanced up at DS Carmichael as he turned off the engine. "The boss reckons it sounds like an insurance company."

DS Carmichael shook his head and released his seat belt. "No, never heard of it."

"He says both Patricia Gordon and Georgina Dale had direct debits with them." DC Cassidy slipped out of the passenger seat and joined DS Carmichael as he started walking towards the rear entrance. She felt a little light headed but jogged to keep up with him. "Looks like it's the only link between them so far."

DS Carmichael held the door open for DC Cassidy to enter, but remained outside, hovering on the top step. When he didn't follow her inside, DC Cassidy turned around and frowned at him. "Coming in?" she enquired. She watched as DS Carmichael looked down at his watch. "The team will be waiting upstairs."

DS Carmichael avoided her gaze and took a step backwards. "If you're feeling better and can make your way up on your own, I just need to pop somewhere. Cover for me?" Without waiting for a response, he turned on his heels and headed back towards his car.

Cover for me? DC Cassidy watched as he reversed out of the parking space and headed back out onto the road. How can I cover for you when I have no idea where you're going?

* * *

Time: 5.35pm

Date: Monday 23<sup>rd</sup> July 2012

Location: Metropolitan Police HQ, London

DS Cooper closed the door to the investigation room behind him and hurried over to the table where Jack was leafing through some of the victim's bank statements.

"Boss?" DS Cooper looked, hesitantly, back over his shoulder at the closed door. "I managed to do that digging about on our new friend, Carmichael?"

Jack's head snapped up. "Yes? Anything?"

DS Cooper shook his head and frowned. "It's all a bit strange, boss. You said he came from Sussex Police, yes?"

Jack nodded, slowly, fearing where this conversation might be going. "That's what the Chief Superintendent said."

"Well, nobody at Sussex has heard of a DS Carmichael. I even checked with Surrey in case the names got mixed up, Surrey and Sussex." DS Cooper paused, noting the look of confusion and concern creeping across Jack's face. "Still nothing."

Jack let the bank statements drop from his hands. "You're saying *nobody* has heard of him?"

"No one that I managed to get hold of, no. I even got someone to run the name through their database. Nothing. I then made a search for any DS Carmichael on the force throughout the country – the only DS Carmichael registered is from Strathclyde Police, and he's aged 67 and now long retired." DS Cooper leant against the table, once again glancing over his shoulder at the closed door. "It's like he doesn't exist, boss."

Jack absorbed the words in silence.

It's like he doesn't exist.

Just then, the door flew open and DC Cassidy breezed in, her gaze switching from Jack to DS Cooper and then back again. "Good, you're both here. It's about London Life – you asked me to find out who they were?"

"Good, you're back. How was the PM?" Jack rubbed at his temples in an attempt to massage away the threat of the impending headache about to engulf his brain.

DC Cassidy hesitated slightly, her cheeks pinking. "Fine. It was fine." She swallowed the faint taste of bile still lingering in her mouth.

"So, London Life?" continued Jack. "What have you managed to find out?"

"It's not an insurance company," continued DC Cassidy, stepping back to close the door behind her. "It's a dating site."

"A dating site?" Jack's forehead creased as his frown deepened. "What do you mean a dating site?"

"A dating site, Sir. It's how everyone mingles and meets people these days, what with social media and all that." DC Cassidy placed a print out of the London Life homepage on the table in front of both Jack and DS Cooper. "And both Patricia and Georgina belonged to it."

* * *

Time: 5.40pm

Date: Monday 23$^{rd}$ July 2012

Location: A cellar in London

He looked at his watch and grimaced. He was later than he had anticipated. It had been hard to slip away today; people would be missing him, noticing his absence. Filling the water bottle at the sink with tap water, he picked up the fresh packet of sandwiches and banana, placing everything inside a plastic carrier bag.

The door to the cellar was locked, as it always was. From the outside it looked like a door to a broom cupboard, somewhere you might keep your ironing board or vacuum cleaner. Somewhere to store muddy boots or a dog's lead. He chuckled to himself as he slid the metal bolt across and turned the heavy, wrought iron key in the lock, pulling the door towards him. It was strange how first impressions could deceive.

A cold rush of chilled air greeted him as he began to descend the stone steps. He passed a light switch and snapped on the overhead light which illuminated the stairwell with a dim glow. Reaching the bottom, he was faced with yet another door; once again the door was locked. Always locked. Even though he knew Carol could never escape, he couldn't take any chances. Carol was clever.

The key turned easily in the lock, the sound echoing against the stone walls. He gently pushed the door open with a foot, hearing the wood scrape noisily on the stone floor. Another rush of cold air enveloped him as he stepped forward over the threshold into the cellar.

Cold air tainted with something else.

What was it?

Fear?

Could you smell fear?

If you could, then this was almost certainly what it would smell like.

\* \* \*

Time: 5.45pm

Date: Monday 23<sup>rd</sup> July 2012

Location: Metropolitan Police HQ, London

"I want a list of all subscribers to this dating site." Jack nodded at the whiteboard where DS Cooper had loaded up the home page of London Life. Twenty or so thumbnails smiled out at them, picture profiles of lonely Londoners seeking friendship and goodness knows what else. Happy, smiling faces - welcoming faces; faces that wanted to be your friend.

Not the London I know, mused Jack, rubbing his chin and feeling the ever-growing prickles jabbing at his fingertips. "I want to know who they are, where they are, and I want to see their messages. I want to see who has been in contact with who."

"Not sure they will give that info out without a fight, Boss," sighed DS Cooper, scrolling through several pages of the website.

"Then a fight we will have, Cooper." Jack pushed himself up out of his chair and stretched, first feeling and then hearing his back creak. "Get onto the website and see what you can do. Get a warrant if they won't cooperate – and while you're at it, check if Hannah Fuller was a member too."

"Will do, Boss." DS Cooper scrolled back to the home page to obtain the dating site's contact information.

"Anyone seen DS Carmichael?" Jack made the point of looking around the room and noting the obvious absence of their new DS.

"He said he needed to be somewhere once we got back from the mortuary," replied DC Cassidy. "Said he would be back sometime later."

"Did he now." Jack was unable to hide the irritation in his voice as he headed towards the door. "How good of him. Right in the middle of an investigation and he goes AWOL. *Again.*"

"Give him the benefit of the doubt, Sir," continued DC Cassidy, gathering up the bank statements Jack had been poring over. "He seemed genuine. I don't think he's slacking off."

Jack hesitated at the door and cast a bemused look in Amanda's direction. "You've changed your tune," he commented, a hint of a smile playing on his lips. "You thought he was a creep yesterday."

"Yeah, well." DC Cassidy continued tidying up the bank statements, purposefully avoiding Jack's inquisitive stare. "Maybe he's not so bad after all."

Jack watched as DC Cassidy's pale cheeks began to colour. "Ok, well I need him here, first thing tomorrow for the briefing. As you're such good mates after your trip to the mortuary, I'll leave it to you to tell him – it's an eight o'clock start. No excuses." Picking up the jacket that he wasn't going to need to wear, Jack headed for the door. "Update the system with what's happened today, then get yourselves off home. We've an early start in the morning."

* * *

Time: 7.30pm
  Date: Monday 23$^{rd}$ July 2012
  Location: Isabel's Café, King's Road, London

Isabel stretched her legs out along the length of the sofa and lay back. Placing her plate and cup on the floor beside her, she closed her eyes and sighed.

Finally.

Peace at last.

Her legs ached. Her feet throbbed. Her back twinged every time she moved. Any thoughts she had of opening in the evenings when the Olympics started were unceremoniously thrown out of her head in an instant.

Just at that moment, Isabel felt a familiar furry bundle jump up from the floor to nestle into her lap. Opening her eyes slightly, she was greeted with the twitching, quivering nose and whiskers of her favourite tabby cat.

"Livi, sweetie," murmured Isabel, letting her eyelids close once again while stretching out a hand to begin to rub the cat's cheeks, just below her whiskers. "How was your day?" Isabel's question was greeted with a low, rhythmic purring, increasing each time she stroked underneath the tabby cat's chin. "Sleeping and eating? Eating and sleeping?" Isabel smiled to herself "You poor thing, you must be exhausted."

Livi rubbed her head up against Isabel's hand, her whole body vibrating with each purr. Isabel could feel the wetness of Livi's nose as she rubbed her furry head against her fingers. There was something quite comforting and relaxing about feeling the soft fur of a cat against your skin. Once Livi had tired of being petted, she set about giving her paws a good clean, flicking her tiny pink tongue in and out between her claws.

Isabel could sit and watch her precious tabby cat for hours. Having rescued her from a stray cat sanctuary when she was only seven months old, she had watched as the frightened, timid creature had slowly become accustomed to Isabel and then the busy café – now strolling around as if she were the one that was really in charge.

Isabel smiled once again as she continued to watch the tiny pink tongue darting in and out. She could remember watching Snowball perform the same cleansing ritual, amazed at how much time they devoted to keeping themselves clean. That and sleeping. And eating.

Snowball.

Isabel felt her stomach lurch, a heavy sigh rising and falling in her chest. My poor Snowy, she thought, casting her mind back to when the pure white bundle of fur was the centre of her world. Isabel knew she had taken Livi from the cat sanctuary as a way of filling the deep void that losing Snowball had left. She could never, ever, forget that wonderful fur-ball that loved to weave in and out of her legs and jump up onto her lap when she wanted attention.

Isabel could vividly remember the last time she saw Snowball. Well, not the very last time – she always tried to push that horrific vision out of her head and banish it to the darkest corners of her mind. That vision had no place in her memory. Instead, she remembered the last time she saw her, happily mewing and padding around their Cambridge home.

Such a long time ago, mused Isabel, casting her mind back; back to a time before Stuart and Jack MacIntosh had crashed into her life. Back to a time before her whole world had been turned upside down.

The newspaper advert.

It had all started with the newspaper advert.

Isabel's eyes flickered open towards the bureau nestling next to the bookcase. A bureau stuffed full of all sorts of important and not-so-important paperwork in a filing system only she would understand. Her eyes were drawn to the bottom drawer, and the contents she knew were filed away inside. It was a drawer she rarely opened anymore. She couldn't remember the last time she had. A drawer that contained a window to her past.

A draw that contained the Phoenix Project documents.

The media frenzy had calmed down a long time ago; the initial furore that had unravelled when she had made the contents of the documents public three years ago had subsided into a less than dramatic hum.

But she still kept them.

She would always keep them.

Her eyes now flickered towards the photographs of her parents and Miles that she kept on the bookcase. At one time, the very existence of those documents and their link to the fate of her parents and brother placed her life in danger. People were killed trying to destroy them. People were killed trying to save them. Now that the mystery of the Phoenix Project was out in the open, and the danger had subsided, Jack had tried to persuade her to keep them somewhere else; in safe storage, in an anonymous safety deposit box somewhere. Anywhere. Anywhere but here.

But Isabel wanted them near her.

She needed to keep them close.

To pack them away to a faceless, nondescript metal box somewhere, in an equally faceless and nondescript town, would be akin to boxing up her memories and forgetting them too.

And she would never forget.

She could never forget.

Jack didn't quite come out and say it, but Isabel knew that he was still concerned that Kreshniov was still out there, biding his time. Worried that he might come back into their lives.

But come back for what?

He had taken her money – what else was there left? He had his own copy of the Phoenix Project documents, he would have no interest in hers as well. Would he?

But Jack still worried.

Jack would always worry.

Stirring her from her thoughts, Isabel felt her phone vibrate on her lap. Picking it up and glancing at the screen, she felt a smile start to spread across her lips.

# SEVEN DAYS

\* \* \*

# Chapter Twenty Two

Time: 8.15am
Date: Tuesday 24<sup>th</sup> July 2012
Location: Metropolitan Police HQ, London

"Tell me about Hannah Fuller. The post mortem." Jack nodded towards both DC Cassidy and DS Carmichael, whom he noted were sitting together, close to the open window. Both fans were already humming, the sultry air overnight still laying heavily over them like a suffocating blanket. The sun outside promised yet another blisteringly hot day to come.

DC Cassidy flashed a look at DS Carmichael, her cheeks flushing once again. With a faint flicker of a smile, DS Carmichael returned the gesture with a curt nod.

"You take the lead on this one," he said. "I was only there as back up."

With her cheeks flushing a shade darker, she flashed a brief smile of thanks in DS Carmichael's direction and cleared her throat. "Well now we have a positive ID, I can confirm that Hannah Fuller died from strangulation. Missing Persons managed to get in touch with her next of kin – the family are from Leeds." She got up and walked over towards the whiteboard, clicking the mouse to bring up Dr Matthew's typed post mortem report. "Strangulation by ligature. So hard, it broke one of the bones in her neck." DC Cassidy paused while she scrolled down to the conclusion at the bottom of the report. She could almost taste the bile threatening to rise up into her throat once again. "No defensive wounds. Abrasions to one ankle. Indicative of being held in a restraint. No other injuries apparent. No sign of sexual assault." Clearing her throat again, she forced the imaginary bile back down. "Dr Matthew's commented on the lack of fibres or forensic material on the body. He felt the body had been cleaned or washed before being dumped."

Cleaned.

Jack felt the word echo around his head once again.

Cleaned.

"OK, thanks. So Hannah's post mortem report basically mirrors those of Patricia Gordon and Georgina Dale. The same cause of death. The same ankle abrasions." Jack paused, nodding his thanks to DC Cassidy. "And the same lack of forensic detail. We now have three murders definitely linked to the same man – and we need to find him before he makes it four."

Jack let his eyes stray to the blown-up colour photograph in the centre of the table; the black court shoe found close to Hannah's body. "The owner of that shoe is in significant danger."

"We could still do with making contact with Hannah's family, boss. Set up a family liaison." DS Cooper brought up a photograph of the seventeen-year-old onto the whiteboard screen. "Social services might help."

Jack nodded. "We have two tasks for this morning – Amanda and Carmichael, I want you both to concentrate on liaising with social services; get as much background as you can on Hannah. See if we can get any of the local force in Leeds to assist with the next of kin."

"Boss," nodded DC Cassidy, opening her notebook.

"Cooper and I are going to swing out to Camden and take a look at Hannah's room at the mother and baby unit. Everyone back here for another briefing at one."

* * *

Time: 10.30am

 Date: Tuesday 24th July 2012

 Location: Blackfriars Crown Court, London

"Ladies and gentlemen of the jury. I am now going to sum up the facts of the case and then direct you on some matters of law." His Honour Judge Geoffrey Campbell-Smythe paused and let his heavy-lidded eyes roam each and every member of the twelve strong jury sitting to attention at the side of Courtroom number one.

Sitting high up upon the bench, his bright red robes stood out against the dark mahogany wood panelling of the courtroom walls. As he shifted in his seat to pick up his legal notepad, the bench creaked beneath his ample weight.

"I want to start with the facts as set out by the prosecution in this case...."

Anthony Saunders stifled a yawn. Six weeks this trial had lasted and at last they were on the home stretch. He glanced at the old fashioned clock mounted on the wall behind His Honour, and calculated how long the summing up might take. With any luck, they could be out within the hour. Hopefully less if the old man hurried up. But His Honour Judge Geoffrey Campbell-Smythe was not renowned for being speedy.

The trial had gone well. His client, the defendant, stood a reasonable chance of a not guilty verdict. They had done their job well. Whether the defendant deserved a not guilty verdict was an entirely different matter, and not one that troubled Anthony Saunders. He had not become the experienced and well-thought of defence lawyer by troubling himself with minor details such as whether his clients were actually guilty or not guilty. The law was not about the truth. The law was not about justice.

It was about who could play the best game on the day.

And Anthony Saunders was backing his team.

Yes, there was circumstantial evidence that could possibly place his client at the scene, and yes, he didn't really have an alibi. And, unbeknown to the jury at this present time, due to the quirkiness of the English criminal law, he had a list of convictions as long as his proverbial arm. But did that make him guilty in this game we call the law?

Not if you played the game well enough, thought Anthony Saunders.

He began straightening up the loose papers on the table in front of him, trying to make as little rustling noise as possible. He quietly slipped his laptop back inside his shoulder bag by his feet, not taking his eyes off His Honour Judge Geoffrey Campbell-Smythe as he did so. The old man was carrying on with his summing up, moving on to the defence facts now. Not that there were many of those to trouble the jury. With nothing left to tidy away that wouldn't draw the disapproving scowl of the judge, Anthony Saunders picked up his pencil and began outlining a sketch on a spare page in his legal pad. Anything to pass the time. And we still had the judge's directions on the points of law to go.

The pencil made little or no sound on the blank white paper, nothing that could drown out the monotonous tones of His Honour. Anthony Saunders was immersed in his drawing, but kept an ear open to gauge the progress the judge was making to bring the case to a close. Moving onto points of law now. He groaned inwardly. This could take some time.

The law on theft in England had many constituent parts, each of which had to be proven by the prosecution beyond a reasonable doubt.

Beyond a reasonable doubt.

Anthony Saunders smiled to himself as he continued to sketch. Beyond a reasonable doubt was such a far reaching statement. Given long enough, most experienced and wily barristers could implant at least one seed of doubt into most juror's heads. And all it took was one simple seed. A seed that could then take root and grow.

The defence lawyer again glanced at the clock above the judge's bench and sighed. Forty-five minutes the judge had been summing up for now, and he didn't look like stopping anytime soon. He let his eyes sweep over the faces of the jurors, each one attentively hanging onto every word that emanated from the distinguished judge's mouth. He wondered what was going on inside each and every one of their heads right now. What questions were they asking themselves? What opinions had they formed about the defendant already? Were they even thinking about the case? He again let his gaze sweep over their faces. Maybe they were, like Anthony Saunders, merely passing the time until they could get out of the stuffy courtroom.

Anthony Saunders' pencil continued to skip silently over the paper, the drawing beginning to take shape. He liked drawing. Sketching. He had even been told he was quite good at it. There was talk of him going to art college when he was younger, something that had excited and appealed to him. But his overbearing father, the Right Honourable Bernard Saunders QC, was having none of that.

"You cannot make a living from colouring in, my boy," he had lectured. Anthony could hear his father's words echoing around inside his head. "No son of mine is going to be a penniless artist." And so, dutifully, Anthony had gone to university to study law; just like his father. All thoughts and ideas of pursuing his artist's dream were unilaterally extinguished. Although he excelled at university and achieved a 1:1, Anthony felt he never quite lived up to his overbearing father's expectations. Having chosen not to follow in his footsteps to the Bar, and instead choosing the solicitor route, Anthony felt his father's dismissive and disappointed demeanour every time they met for Sunday lunch. Which was not often. Which suited them both. But at least the Right Honourable Bernard Saunders QC didn't have a lay-about son at art college.

Fifty-five minutes now.

When would it stop?

Anthony studied the drawing in front of him and wrinkled his nose. Hmmmmm, not one of his best. He carefully and ever so quietly detached the page from his legal pad. It wasn't a masterpiece that he would be keeping. There was a glimmer of light at the end of the tunnel as His Honour Judge Campbell-Smythe closed the legal pad on his bench and cleared his throat.

"Ladies and gentlemen of the jury, you will now retire to consider your verdict."

With a nod of his head and an "all rise" from the Court Usher, everyone in the Courtroom rose to their feet and the jury solemnly filed out of court, one behind the other, to be ensconced in the jury room.

Anthony Saunders glanced again at the clock and mentally calculated what time he could get home. It would be tight, but he should just about make it. Technically he should wait at court with his client, as the jury could come back very quickly with their decision. But Anthony Saunders didn't intend to hang around for their verdict. There was a good chance they would get sent home for the night and resume again tomorrow. But even if they did reach a verdict before the end of the day, Anthony Saunders didn't feel the need to support his client with the guilty or not-guilty decision. The defendant had enough experience in front of the courts, as his lengthy previous convictions showed. He would be fine either way and didn't need his hand holding.

Anthony gathered up his things, ramming his court folder and legal pad into his bag and zipping it up. He swung his laptop bag up onto his shoulder and eased his way out from behind the counsel benches. He nodded his thanks to his defence barrister and hastily made his way to the exit, behind the throng of family members from the public gallery seats and several court reporters.

If he got a move on he would get back home in time.

* * *

Time: 11.45am
Date: Tuesday 24<sup>th</sup> July 2012
Location: St Joseph's Mother and Baby Unit, Camden, London

The room was small, with a tiny window tucked away above a chipped sink. A narrow single bed hugged one wall, with a smaller cot bed by its side. The walls themselves were bare, with the washed out pale grey paint peeling off in strips.

Jack stepped in, followed by DS Cooper, and they both cast their eyes around the inside of Hannah Fuller's room. The bed was unmade, as was the cot. Greying sheets and a stained duvet were rolled up in a heap on Hannah's bed; a smaller, milk-stained baby blanket had been tossed inside the cot.

There was no wardrobe, but a hanging rail ran along the opposite wall. A selection of clothes hung from the rail, but most were piled in a heap on the floor beneath. A separate mound of baby clothes and a selection of toys sat in the corner.

A small fridge hummed behind the door. Upon opening it, Jack only found a few cans of cheap lager and an unopened packet of cheese. On top of the fridge were empty cartons of baby milk and a sterilising machine.

The room had already been processed by forensics – working through the night. Fingerprint dust was still evident on the door frame, the door handles and other surfaces in the room. With no suggestion that Hannah had met her killer within these four walls, the examination had been concluded quickly.

"Not much here, boss." DS Cooper confirmed Jack's own suspicions. But before he could make any form of reply, a figure appeared in the doorway behind them.

"Felicity Walker." The figure stepped forwards and held out a hand. "I'm Hannah's social worker."

Jack shook the social worker's hand and stepped back to allow her enough room to enter the confined space of Hannah's bedroom. "DI MacIntosh," he greeted, and nodded towards his partner. "And this is DS Cooper. You knew Hannah well?"

Felicity Walker hesitated before giving a faint nod. "As well as anyone I guess. She wasn't always an easy person to get to know. She didn't trust people very easily, and she especially didn't trust anyone in a position of authority. So we had a fairly fraught relationship with her."

"And how long had she been here?" Jack nodded at the room around them.

"Since Hope was born." Felicity gestured towards the only personal item that seemed to be in the sparse room – a small photograph pinned to the wall above Hannah's bed. The photograph showed Hannah and a small baby, wrapped in a pink knitted blanket. "They came here straight from hospital – Hope would have only been a few days old."

"And what can you tell us about Hannah's time here at the unit?"

Again, Felicity hesitated before replying. "As I said, Hannah didn't trust easily. She had a very poor upbringing and things were not easy for her. The staff here at the unit tried their best with her – and for the most part, she was doing well. But then she would have lapses."

"Lapses?"

Felicity sighed. "At times she would forget to feed Hope. Or forget to wash her clothes. Sometimes forget to pick her up from nursery. Hannah had secured a place for Hope at a local nursery to allow her to look for a job. Everyone in the unit receive help with nursery funding to support them finding employment and eventually their own place to live." Felicity paused and shook her head. "But Hannah was so young – and she struggled."

"And she had no support from any family members?" Jack had already been told by DC Cassidy that Hannah's family had effectively washed their hands of her – and their grandchild.

Felicity continued to shake her head. "Hannah ran away from home at fourteen, her home life being very unstable. Her family are from Leeds and throughout her time here at the unit, none of them have wanted to become involved in her care." Felicity gave another sigh. "It's sad really. Hannah was just a child herself, trying to make her way in an adult world. She could have done with a lot more support than we were able to give her."

"Did she have any friends? Anyone she would see on a regular basis? You mentioned she might have been looking for a job?"

Felicity gave a wan smile and shook her head. "A seventeen-year-old mother living in a local authority unit isn't usually at the top of the interview shortlist. And as for friends? She was friendly with a couple of the other mothers in the unit, but beyond that no. There was no one else in her life other than Hope."

"So nobody saw Hannah in the company of anyone else recently?"

"Not that I know of. You can have a word with the staff here – I'm sure they would be happy to help. But no, I don't think so."

Jack nodded and began moving towards the door. "I don't think we need to take up any more of your time. Where is her daughter now? Hope, did you say?"

Felicity nodded. "Hope is being well looked after. She is in the care of one of our temporary foster carers at the moment."

Raising a hand as he departed, Jack stepped out into the corridor, the words 'temporary foster care' echoing around inside his head. Visions of himself and Stuart being taken to their first foster home flooded his brain. He wished Hope all the luck in the world, hoping that she followed his own path instead of that of his brother.

"Come on, Cooper," he breathed, stepping out of the front door. "Let's get back to the team."

* * *

Time: 11.45am
Date: Tuesday 24<sup>th</sup> July 2012
Location: Blackfriars Crown Court, London

Daphne Holbrook loved the quietness; first thing in the morning, last thing in the evening, or when a jury were sent out to the jury room. These were the times she revelled in the peace they left behind in her courtroom.

Because it was *her* courtroom.

Judges and juries came and went. Barristers and solicitors appeared and then disappeared with a flurry of robes and wigs. Defendants would sit in the dock, some nervously, others not, until their fate was decided. Then they, too, would be gone. Either home to their families, rejoicing in their liberty, or taking the solemn steps down to the cells beneath the court to await their transport to prison.

But she, Daphne Holbrook, Court Usher in Courtroom number one, always remained. And she ran a tight ship. Everyone who appeared in her court knew the behaviour she expected. Now the commotion surrounding the most recent case to be tried in her court had died down, and everyone had left, she could quietly survey the room around her and start to put it back into the condition and order she liked it to be in.

She tutted to herself as she picked up a discarded wig from the front bench of the prosecution. No doubt the barrister to whom it belonged would be frantically searching the robing room at this very minute trying to remember where he had left one of his most important pieces of courtroom attire. She placed it carefully back down on the prosecution bench. There was a chance the jury would return later that day and the wig would be needed.

She continued tidying counsel's benches, tutting once more at the number of pens and pencils that had been left discarded around the stone floor beneath. She picked them up and popped them into her pocket. She collected up the glasses and jugs of water from the benches and stacked them on the trolley by her side, ready to be returned to the kitchen. Fresh ones would be delivered if needed.

It was just as she was turning away, to push the trolley towards the door, that she saw it.

A discarded piece of paper that had floated to the floor behind the defence counsel's bench. She bent down as much as her arthritic hip would allow, and grabbed the wayward piece of paper. Running her enquiring eyes over it, she arched her eyebrows in wonder.

Unusual. Intriguing. Very intricate and detailed in parts. Shading in the right areas. Certainly a very good drawing.

But who would draw such a detailed picture of a shoe?

* * *

Time: 1.15pm
Date: Tuesday 24<sup>th</sup> July 2012

Location: Acacia Avenue, Wimbledon, London

Mac slid the package from the carry box on the back of his motorbike and removed his helmet. Customers often didn't like to be confronted by a biker with his helmet on – something about not being able to see their face.

He made his way up the short gravel drive, in-between high, well-tended leylandii hedges on either side, which gave it a private and enclosed feel. The gravel drive ended in front of an impressive looking house, with two large bay windows either side of the front door recessed into a porch area. Mac leant into the porch and rapped on the heavy wooden door using the well-worn brass door knocker in the centre. The sound echoed in the still air. Glass frosted panels either side of the door showed no signs of movement or habitation from within. Mac leant forwards once again and gave the door another rap.

The sound, once again, echoed emptily around him, but, just then, a different sound reached his ears which appeared to be coming from around the side of the house. It was the sound of a gate or door being swung open, followed by the definite tap-tapping of footsteps.

Mac stepped backwards and saw a narrow paved pathway leading around the side of the house towards what Mac assumed would be the back garden. Tucking the parcel under his arm, he began to walk along the path and around the corner, hoping to bump into the owner of the footsteps that he was sure he had heard.

The path did indeed lead towards the back of the house. As Mac rounded the corner, he noted a double garage with its roll-top door wide open, next to a gate that led into a beautifully well-tended back garden. Towering leylandii hedges again lined the edges of the garden. In front of the gate stood a man kitted out in gardening overalls and wearing ear defenders, a hedge trimmer grasped in his hands. As soon as he spied Mac heading along the garden path towards him, he pulled the ear defenders off and waved the hedge trimmer.

"Sorry. I can't hear a thing with these on."

Patrick stepped forwards, laying the hedge trimmer down at his feet, and took the proffered parcel from Mac's outstretched hand. "Thanks. I've been waiting for this."

Mac nodded. "No problem." He held out the electronic device for Patrick's signature. "You rent a space at Isabel's café, don't you?" Mac watched as Patrick scribbled his name. "In the art studio?"

Patrick looked up, a quizzical look on his face as he studied Mac's features. "Yes I do. So you must be....?" He frowned, unable to put a name to the face in front of him, although it did look somewhat familiar.

"I'm Mac. I know Isabel from.... well, from a while ago."

"Ah yes," nodded Patrick. "I think I've heard her mention you. And I'm sure I've seen your face in the café. Your brother is that Detective Inspector, isn't he?"

Mac nodded, pocketing the electronic device Patrick had handed back to him. "That's right."

"So how is she doing? Isabel." Patrick picked up the hedge trimmer again. "She sometimes looks a bit down. Like she has the weight of the world on her shoulders."

"She's OK," replied Mac, turning to go. He still had another two deliveries to do before he could clock off for the day. "She's had a lot to deal with in recent years, but.... well.... she's getting there. She's going on a date tonight."

"A date?" Patrick raised his eyebrows. "Who with?"

Mac shrugged and started walking back down the path, calling back over his shoulder. "Some defence solicitor. Saunders. He's a bit cocky. Got some swanky apartment on the Embankment. I don't think he's right for her." Putting his helmet back on, he turned back towards Patrick. "There's something about him I don't like."

Raising a hand as a departing gesture, Mac left Patrick to attend to his hedge cutting. As he swung his leg over his motorbike and started the engine, he could hear the whine of the hedge cutter spluttering into action.

\* \* \*

Time: 1.30pm
Date: Tuesday 24<sup>th</sup> July 2012
Location Metropolitan Police HQ, London

"We're missing something." Jack rubbed his chin and felt the sharp stubble once again prick his fingers. He looked at the piles of paperwork on the investigation room table and sighed. The answer had to be in there. Somewhere. "Let's go back to the beginning. Victim number one – Patricia Gordon."

DS Cooper reached forwards and took the remote control, bringing up a picture of Patricia Gordon on the whiteboard screen. "Scene of crime have released their formal report. No evidence she met her killer at her flat. It's clean."

Clean.

Jack heard Dr Rachel Hunter's soft tones echo around the edges of his brain. "Your killer is very forensically aware." "No trace of any DNA or any other evidence on either body." "It is as though both victims were cleansed." He pushed the thoughts away and turned his attention back to the screen. "So, where did she meet him, Cooper? If not at her flat? Between leaving work on 6<sup>th</sup> July and her body being found a week later, where did she go that meant she crossed the path of our killer?"

"A date?" DS Cooper nodded back to the piles of bank statements and London Life paperwork littering the table. "We know she was a subscriber to London Life. Like the others." It had been confirmed while they were at the Camden mother and baby unit that Hannah Fuller also subscribed to the dating site.

Jack shook his head. "I don't think so. London Life are digging their heels in about releasing confidential information, but they do tell us she hadn't been active on the site for some time, and definitely not in the weeks leading up to her disappearance. Her last interaction on the site was back in April."

"Maybe it was someone she had met from the site before? And they messaged privately, rather than through the website?" DS Cooper shrugged. "Text messages, emails?"

"The forensic trawl of her mobile phone records doesn't flag up anything unusual." Jack nodded at another pile of paperwork. "She didn't text very often. Only the odd message to the care home about work, or to her ex-husband. And on the day of her disappearance, her phone was switched off."

"The ex-husband, then?" DS Cooper raised his eyebrows and clicked the remote control.

Jack looked up as an image of Frank Gordon filled the whiteboard screen. "I don't know. They seemed to get on well. Surprisingly well for exes." Jack thought back to when they had met Mr Gordon, the vision of the grieving ex-husband's face bathed in salty wet tears filled his head. Despite the son insinuating that all was not well with the separation, Jack increasingly felt that Frank Gordon was not their man. "No, I think those tears were real. And we can't link him to any of the other victims." He reached forwards and picked up the top copy bank statement of Patricia Gordon. "But we are definitely missing something. Something has to be in here that we've overlooked." He paused, and then nodded to DS Cooper. "OK, let's move on. Georgina Dale and Hannah Fuller."

Just then DC Cassidy burst into the room, DS Carmichael following in her wake.

"You'll never guess what, Boss," she breathed, slightly out of breath from hurrying along the corridor. "It's Anthony Saunders – the defence solicitor."

"What about him?"

"He subscribes to London Life."

"And?" Jack eyed the young DC as she approached the table. "Although interesting, I don't think being a member of a dating site is yet classed as a crime." Although maybe it should be, he mused silently to himself.

"Maybe not." DC Cassidy paused, a smile twitching at the corners of her lips. "But in the last six months, he has exchanged messages with all three of our victims."

# CHAPTER TWENTY TWO

\* \* \*

# Chapter Twenty Three

Time: 1.10pm

Date: Tuesday 24<sup>th</sup> July 2012

Location: Metropolitan Police HQ, London

DS Carmichael clicked the remote control and the whiteboard screen went blank. Picking up a whiteboard marker, he stepped forwards.

"So, here we have Saunders." DS Carmichael drew a box in the centre of the whiteboard. He then drew three lines at angles away from the box and wrote Patricia Gordon, Georgina Dale and Hannah Fuller next to each. "On April 2<sup>nd</sup>, 5<sup>th</sup> and 27<sup>th</sup>, he messaged Patricia Gordon. London Life are resisting making the content of the messages available, but will confirm that messages did occur."

Jack nodded, slowly, following DS Carmichael's pen as he wrote the dates next to Patricia Gordon's name.

"And then we have Georgina Dale, our second victim. Messages again from Saunders, on May 5<sup>th</sup>, 13<sup>th</sup> and most recently 27<sup>th</sup> June." Again, he wrote the dates next to Georgina's name.

"And lastly Hannah Fuller." DS Carmichael wrote June 6<sup>th</sup>, 18<sup>th</sup> and 30<sup>th</sup> next to Hannah's name on the whiteboard. "He messaged her three times too; the last one very recently."

Jack frowned at the whiteboard. "Are we seriously thinking he could be our killer? A solicitor?"

"I like him for it." DS Carmichael continued. "He has been in touch with all three victims. He knows police procedures; forensic procedures. He will know about DNA transference and how to keep a crime scene clean. And he's likely to know where the CCTV cameras are and how to avoid them. He's local – he knows London."

"But *seriously?*" Jack could feel the alarm bells ringing in his head. What DS Carmichael had outlined was true, but there was something gnawing at him at the back of his head. There was something about it that didn't fit. "I'm not so sure. What possible motive could he have?"

"Maybe there isn't one," replied DS Carmichael, the hint of irritation in his tone plain to all that were listening. "Maybe he's just a psycho."

"Well, we need more than this." Jack shook his head. "We don't have realistic grounds to arrest him based on the fact that he is a member of a dating site and has been in touch with all of our victims at some point. Without knowing what those messages actually said, it's not enough."

"But, boss." This time it was DC Cassidy stepping in. "He does fit a lot of the characteristics in the forensic profile."

*I* fit the profile, thought Jack, thinking back to his meeting with Dr Rachel Hunter. Christ, pretty much everyone in this building fits the profile. He shook his head again. "Still not enough. Bring me details of exactly what the messages said – lean on this London Life to disclose them; get that warrant served. Then, and only then, will I consider approaching Saunders."

After DC Cassidy and DS Carmichael had left with the task of extracting the information out of London Life, Jack let his eyes scan over the paperwork that was still littering the investigation table and sighed.

"We're still missing something, Cooper."

DS Cooper nodded and turned his attention back to the paperwork. "Patricia Gordon. If she didn't go out on a date, maybe she went out to a club or evening class? Or maybe she was just on her way to the shops?"

Jack picked up the bank statement that he had glanced at earlier. Casting his eyes down the columns he noted that she was a very careful spender. He leafed through some of the earlier bank statements over the preceding months. Always the same. Never went overdrawn. Always had a healthy balance in the account at all times. Jack scanned the regular monthly deposit from The Briars. Not much to live on once you take the regular bills into account, he mused. And the rent on the flat – it was in a nice area so wouldn't have been cheap. Jack let his eyes wander across the withdrawals column and noted what looked like the rent payment – confirming his suspicions that it would have been a big drain on such a modest income. And then there were all the furnishings in the flat – Patricia Gordon had a taste for good quality. None of it would have come cheap. Jack also remembered the credit card bills that were paid in full each month.

"Where did she get the money from?" Jack heard his thoughts spoken out loud.

"Boss?"

"Patricia Gordon," he repeated. "Where did she get her money from? She lives in a nice area. All the expensive furniture and gadgets we saw in her flat. She's never overdrawn. The care home doesn't pay much more than minimum wage. Where did it all come from?"

DS Cooper pushed himself out of his seat and came round to Jack's side of the table where they spread out the last six months of Patricia Gordon's bank statements. Together, two pairs of eyes scanned the figures.

It wasn't long until the answer presented itself.

"There." Jack pointed to the credit column on the page closest to them. "Cash deposit £200." He then stabbed a finger on another page. "And another. £200 cash deposit." He then indicated on each page the same regular cash sum, paid in every week.

£200 cash.

Every Friday.

Without fail.

Jack looked up at the bemused expression on DS Cooper's face. "Our victim had a second job, Cooper."

"A second job?"

"It has to be." Jack pointed again at the cash deposits on Patricia Gordon's bank statements. "She was earning two hundred pounds a week, cash in hand, for something."

DS Cooper flicked open his notebook. "Nothing came up in any of the reports from DC Anderson – neither the ex-husband or the son has mentioned anything about a second job."

"Maybe they didn't know." Jack got to his feet. "We need to find out what she's been doing for the extra cash – and more importantly, who she was working for."

Just at that moment, the door to the investigation room opened.

"DI MacIntosh?" A young PC's head peered around the door jamb.

"That's me," answered Jack, still focusing on the bank statements in his hand.

"Message from downstairs. You're needed over at Blackfriars Crown Court."

Jack looked up and frowned. "I'm needed where? Why?"

The young PC shrugged. "Sorry. The message was just that you needed to meet with QC John Fortmason – about the McArthur case. He will be outside court two in about thirty minutes."

Jack grimaced and let his shoulders sag. He nodded at the PC to let him know the message had been received and understood, and that he was dismissed. "Great," he muttered, as the door to the investigation room swung shut. "Just great." Pausing to grab his mobile phone, Jack turned to DS Cooper. "Right, while I'm away on this wild goose chase, I need you to collate everything we have on Saunders – ready for when Amanda and DS Carmichael return. If we seriously think it's him, I need to see everything we've got."

"Boss." DS Cooper sat back down at the investigation table and pulled what paperwork they had towards him. "And what about Patricia Gordon's second job?"

Jack headed towards the door. "Put that on hold - it's most likely a red herring. For now, we need to concentrate on Saunders."

\* \* \*

Time: 2.00pm
 Date: Tuesday 24<sup>th</sup> July 2012
 Location: Blackfriars Crown Court, London

As if I don't have enough to do, Jack muttered to himself under his breath as he jogged up the steps of the Blackfriars Crown Court. An urgent message from the prosecution QC in the McArthur case, and the only place they could meet was outside courtroom number two, while they were having an afternoon break.

A patrol car had been able to drop him off outside the court, so he wouldn't be away from the investigation for long, but Jack felt it was still time that could be spent more meaningfully elsewhere. Catching a serial killer, for example. The only good thing about the crown court on a day like today, however, was that it was cool. Its thick walls and air conditioning meant that the oppressive heat from outside stayed exactly there. Outside. Stepping over the threshold, Jack breathed in a lungful of cool air.

Courtrooms one to three were to the left, so after clearing the security checks, Jack walked briskly along the left-hand corridor. As he was approaching the first courtroom, the heavy oak panelled door creaked open and the court usher he knew as Daphne hurried out. Jack carried on walking towards courtroom two, further down the corridor, giving Daphne a brief nod of greeting as he did so. However, instead of returning the greeting she stood in front of him, barring his progress, waving a piece of paper in her hand.

"Oh, Detective," she began, still waving the piece of paper. "Have you seen the defence solicitor, Anthony Saunders, on your way in?"

"Saunders?" queried Jack, looking back over his shoulder. "No, sorry, I haven't. Is there a problem?"

"No, no, not a problem as such." Daphne shook her head. "He just left something behind in my courtroom." Jack heard the unmistakable 'my' in reference to courtroom number one and suppressed a smile. "I just wondered if he needed it. It is rather good."

Jack frowned a little and let his eyes fall to the piece of paper still being waved in the Court Usher's hand. "Something to do with the case? Evidence?"

Daphne shook her head. "Oh, no, nothing like that. Just a picture. A drawing. And a pretty good one at that. Have a look for yourself."

And so Jack did.

And suddenly his meeting with the defence QC slipped out of his mind.

"Do you mind if I take this?" Jack held his hand out for the drawing, which Daphne handed over without comment. At least she could now go back to her courtroom and resume her rightful position. Jack nodded his thanks and turned back towards the entrance. John Fortmason QC would have to wait.

\* \* \*

Time: 2.35pm
   Date: Tuesday 24th July 2012
   Location: A cellar in London

He bent down and picked up the discarded sandwich wrapper by the side of Jess's mattress. The sandwich had been eaten, but she had left the crusts behind and they were now hard and crispy beneath his fingertips.

Jess never liked to eat her crusts.

He smoothed and straightened the moth-eaten blanket over the top of the thin mattress. It looked flat and empty; empty and unloved, now that Jess was gone. Casting his gaze over his shoulder to the other side of the cellar, he saw Carol sitting up against the damp wall, a look of horrified resignation and panic on her pale face.

Poor Carol.

She looked so sad.

But it was all her own fault.

She had brought all this upon herself.

All of it.

He placed Jess's rubbish and the stale bread crusts into the plastic carrier bag he was carrying, and slowly crossed the stone cellar floor. As he approached, Carol seemed to shrink even further back into the wall. She hugged her knees up tightly to her chest, pulling the scratchy blanket taut around her legs. Her stockinged feet poked out of the bottom, raggedy holes allowing her toes to peek through.

"Now, now Carol, my dear." He spoke softly, kneeling down in front of her. "There's no need to be like that."

"What...what do you want from me?" Zoe's voice was barely audible, her lips hardly moving.

"Shush now, Carol. You just stay here and eat your dinner." He nodded at the as-yet untouched packet of sandwiches by her side – he had chosen prawn and mayonnaise this time. Nothing was too good for his Carol. "And drink your water. I don't want you getting ill."

Zoe shuddered at the thought of food, imagining it sticking in her throat and making her gag. But water. She needed water. Her mind was becoming fuzzy, as if she was in the middle of a dream, or at least a nightmare. Her limbs felt shaky, her heart pounded incessantly inside her chest. She reached out and grabbed the plastic water bottle, snapping off the lid and drinking thirstily.

"That's more like it, Carol. Not too fast now, you don't want to choke." He reached forwards to lay his hand on her wrist, pulling the bottle away from her lips.

Zoe physically recoiled from his touch. His fingers felt ice-cold against her skin. She could almost feel the evil transferring from his hand to hers. She began to retch.

"You see, Carol? You need to listen to me. Drink it more slowly. You never listen to me, Carol, and you know that is what used to make me so mad." There was a hard edge creeping into his hushed tones. "You need to listen, and do as you're told, Carol."

Zoe watched as he backed away towards the door.

Who was Carol?

And more importantly – what happened to her?

* * *

Time: 3.15pm
 Date: Tuesday 24th July 2012
 Location: Metropolitan Police HQ, London

Jack added the drawing to the pile and frowned.

Shoes.

Why was this case becoming all about shoes?

The door to the investigation room opened and DC Cassidy walked in, two bottles of chilled water in her hands.

"Chris has gone back down to the tech suite to see what more the CCTV has thrown up – and to get the guys to track that van through the ANPR system." She passed one of the bottles to Jack and switched on both floor fans.

Jack nodded and he gulped down several mouthfuls of water. "How did you get on with London Life?"

"Still refusing to answer. I've filled out the details for the warrant. We'll see what the response is."

"And Carmichael?" Jack noted the lack of DS Carmichael's presence in the room. He then noted the hesitation in DC Cassidy's response. "He is still here, isn't he?"

DC Cassidy perched on the windowsill by the open window and sipped her water. "He popped out a while ago."

"Popped out? What do you mean popped out?" Jack massaged his temples in frustration. "The man is never here."

"I'm sure he'll be back soon, guv. He said he wouldn't be long." DC Cassidy pushed herself off the window ledge and approached the table. "What's that?" She nodded at the sketch Jack had added to the paperwork.

Jack picked up the drawing and passed it to DC Cassidy. "That is a drawing of a shoe – sketched by none other than our friend Anthony Saunders."

"Saunders?" DC Cassidy took hold of the drawing, her eyes widening.

"He drew this?"

Jack nodded. "At court today. Left it behind as he rushed away."

"You think....?" DC Cassidy left the question unspoken.

"I don't know what I think right now." Jack rose from the table and made his way towards the door. "Get Cooper up here as soon as he's done with the CCTV and ANPR. And track down Carmichael. He's starting to get on my nerves with his disappearing acts."

\* \* \*

# Chapter Twenty Four

Time: 6.45pm
  Date: Tuesday 24th July 2012
  Location: Buckingham Street, Embankment, London

Isabel clutched the chilled bottle of Chardonnay in her hand and reached out to ring the doorbell. Flat 1b he had said. She looked at the brass plated keypad and gently pressed "Flat 1b – Saunders." No audible sound emerged and as she waited she raised her head to look up at the rows of windows stretching up towards the sky overhead.

The air had finally lost some of the oppressive heat of the day, a welcome breeze bringing some coolness to the early evening. Isabel bit her lip, nervously.

A date.

Was she really going on a date? When she had received the text from Anthony yesterday evening, it had seemed like a good idea. A harmless dinner date.

But a date?

Her stomach gave a few more involuntary flips as she waited, patiently, on the pavement outside. The flats were housed in a converted old grain merchant's building, a short step from the banks of the River Thames at Embankment. Sleek, energy-efficient windows had replaced the rotting wooden 18th century frames, but the original brickwork remained. "Ernest

Baker - Grain Merchant 1725-1899" had been chiselled into the solid russet-red bricks above the communal door.

After what seemed like an eternity, but in reality was no more than a few seconds, Isabel heard the intercom buzz.

"Come on in – push the door," it crackled.

Isabel's heart gave another leap, her stomach clenched into knots. She stepped forwards and tentatively pushed the heavy glass-fronted door, which clicked and swung open. She stepped over the threshold into a cavernous, wide open space, unable to stop herself gazing upwards at the high vaulted ceiling above.

A curved staircase to the right hugged the 18$^{th}$ century walls, and Isabel took several hesitant steps towards them. As she did so, a face appeared underneath the stairwell.

"Hey – I'm just through here."

Anthony Saunders' face beamed through at Isabel as she carefully walked past the curved steps, her three inch heels clicking with every step on the flagstone floor. She smiled, shyly, when she reached the entrance to Flat 1b, absent-mindedly smoothing her skirt down with her free hand.

"For you." She thrust the wine bottle out in front of her, hoping he would take it before the glass slipped through her fingers.

"Thanks," smiled Anthony, taking the bottle and glancing at the label. "A Chardonnay. Excellent choice." He flashed another smile, Isabel just noticing the faint dimple that appeared on his chin as he did so. "Just through here, follow me."

\* \* \*

Time: 6.45pm
   Date: Tuesday 24$^{th}$ July 2012
   Location: Metropolitan Police HQ, London

DS Carmichael took the stairs, two at a time. A glance at his watch told him that he had been gone too long this time. He hadn't accounted for the roadworks and diversion that had taken him out of his way, and added at least half an hour to his journey. It wouldn't be long before Jack lost his patience. The text from DC Cassidy had been brief, but to the point.

Get here. Now.

He jogged along the corridor towards the investigation room, straightening his tie as he did so. Despite the heat of the day, he continued to wear a shirt and tie – appearances were very important. Appearances were very important indeed.

Plastering a haughty expression on his face, DS Carmichael pushed open the door to the investigation room and breezed in. He was met by three pairs of eyes; two pairs that quickly lowered themselves to their coffee cups, and leaving one pair remaining to bore into him.

"Nice of you to join us." Jack didn't even bother to hide the sarcasm from his voice.

Seemingly unflustered, DS Carmichael took the remaining seat at the table, his eyes instantly drawn to the sketch that was still in the centre. "What's that?"

"That is a drawing of a shoe by Anthony Saunders," responded Jack, the sarcasm still evident. "Something you would have known about several hours ago if you had been bothered to be present. Where have you been?"

DS Carmichael ignored the question and reached forwards for the sketch. "Anthony Saunders drew this?" He looked up, all three pairs of eyes on him once again. "Anthony Saunders has an interest in shoes?"

\* \* \*

Time: 6.50pm
Date: Tuesday 24<sup>th</sup> July 2012
Location: Buckingham Street, Embankment, London

The first thing Isabel sensed was the intense, intoxicating aroma of garlic and rosemary wafting through the air towards her as she stepped inside. Her stomach flipped again – but this time it was more from a sense of hunger and anticipation of delicious food, rather than the nervous trepidation of going on her first date in over six years.

Anthony closed the door behind them and lightly touched her arm.

"I hope you don't think it's odd, but would you mind taking off your shoes?" He nodded down towards Isabel's feet.

Isabel felt herself glance down at her feet, noting that Anthony had already slipped off his brogues which were now neatly tucked away at the side of the plush door mat.

"Er, no.... of course not. Not at all." Isabel felt her cheeks colour with a hot pinkness as she bent down to unbuckle the thin straps around her ankles. She stepped down from the three inch heels and tidied them away by the side of the door.

"Sorry, it's just – new carpets." Anthony inclined his head towards the floor, nodding at the soft, deep-pile oatmeal carpet that stretched from the front door towards the rest of the flat.

"It's really no trouble," smiled Isabel, feeling the pink tinge to her cheeks begin to fade. "I would be the same."

Anthony nodded his thanks, his smile deepening alongside the dimple on his chin. He cast his eyes down to the discarded shoes. "Hey, nice shoes. They look like Christian Louboutin."

Isabel gave a small nod, her smile widening in surprise. "They are! I picked them up while I was travelling in France last year. I never really get the chance to wear them – I can't exactly wear them in the café."

Anthony bent down and picked up one of the shoes, turning it over in his hands. "These are really well made. The stitching on the leather is remarkable; it's so intricate." He trailed a finger along the delicate ankle strap, following the natural curve down to the elegant, tapered heel. "And these heels are exquisite. The French really do know how to make a good shoe!"

Isabel watched as Anthony continued to marvel at her shoe, turning it over and over in his hands, a look of wonder on his face. The feeling of hunger in her stomach subsided a little and allowed the underlying trepidation to resurface.

Why is he so interested in my shoes?

Anthony looked up and caught Isabel's confused gaze. He smiled, sheepishly, the dimple reappearing. "Sorry. Listen to me." He placed the shoe back down next to its partner and indicated for Isabel to follow him into the flat. "You must think I'm some weirdo, pouncing on your shoes like that. Come through. Let's open that wine."

* * *

Time: 7.00pm

Date: Tuesday 24<sup>th</sup> July 2012

Location: Metropolitan Police HQ, London

"There's enough here to pull him in." DS Carmichael leant against the windowsill in front of the open window, the faint breeze doing nothing to unstick his shirt from his back. Temperatures had risen all day once again, and the humid air did nothing to help lower them now the evening was settling in. Another long and sticky night was ahead. "The sketching of the shoe seals it."

Jack drained the dregs from his water bottle and rubbed his eyes; the high pollen counts all week were taking their toll. "It just seems..."

"Just because he's a solicitor doesn't put him above the law," interrupted DS Carmichael. "Or incapable of committing crimes."

"I realise that," replied Jack, trying to prevent the sarcasm and hostility he felt from returning to his voice. "I just...I just feel there's something missing, that's all."

"I say we pull him in." DS Carmichael folded his arms in front of him and fixed Jack with a beady stare. "Right now."

"I'd feel better if London Life had responded to our questions – I need to see the content of those messages."

"We won't get that until tomorrow, guv." DC Cassidy flicked open a page in her notebook. "They won't voluntarily provide the message details. I've tried, and so has Chris. They won't budge. The warrant won't get issued until the morning."

Jack shook his head at DS Carmichael. "I just need more."

\* \* \*

Time: 7.25pm
Date: Tuesday 24$^{th}$ July 2012
Location: Buckingham Street, Embankment, London

The wine was seeping effortlessly into her bloodstream, its numbing effect allowing the wave of relaxation to finally take hold. She leant back in the soft leather armchair she had sunk into. Real leather. She could tell. She sipped more of the intoxicating wine and glanced around Anthony's living room. It was elegant and stylish, nothing cheap or out of place. She could tell he must be doing well for himself. A sleek HD TV sat in the corner with some sort of surround sound cinema system. A towering bookcase hugging one wall was crammed full of DVDs and books. A large abstract painting adorned the wall opposite – something Isabel imagined wouldn't look out of place hanging in the Tate.

Anthony had lit several candles that glowed and glimmered, emanating a sweet, fresh fragrance. The blinds were drawn across the large floor to ceiling windows, keeping out the heat of the dying day and giving the room a fresh coolness. Isabel took another sip of wine and smiled. The scent of roasting lamb was stronger now, the rich aroma of garlic and rosemary filling her nostrils each time she breathed in. Her stomach was aching to taste it. The small galley-style kitchen was across the hallway, where Isabel could hear Anthony quietly humming to himself as he moved around the pots and pans.

Isabel pushed herself up out of the armchair and headed in the direction of the mouth-watering aroma. I should at least ask if I can help, she thought to herself - although she was very much enjoying just allowing herself to be enveloped in soft leather and letting the mellow alcohol work its way through her body, unwinding her taut muscles and wrapping her in a welcome cocoon of relaxation. She couldn't remember the last time she had spent an evening like this.

"Anything I can do?" Isabel entered the galley-style kitchen, sipping her wine as she did so. Anthony had just removed the roasting tin from the oven and was busy basting the succulent lamb with the cooking juices. The scent that hit Isabel was just as intoxicating as the wine in her hand. She breathed in deeply and quietly gasped. "My god, that smells divine."

"Fresh garlic and rosemary from the street market this morning," replied Anthony, flashing another smile, his dimple popping out once again. "Can't beat it." He drizzled the sizzling meat once more with the heady mixture. "And the meat came from that organic farm shop that just opened. Not too far down the road from you?"

Isabel nodded and took another gulp of wine. She swayed a little with the alcohol. If she had her Christian Louboutin heels on right now, she would have been tottering precariously. "Well, it smells gorgeous. Do you need a hand with anything?"

"All under control," replied Anthony, slipping the roasting tin back into the oven. "About another twenty minutes or so and it should be ready. You just make yourself comfortable." He picked up the nearly-empty wine bottle and poured another generous measure into Isabel's glass. "I'll be through in a moment. Just need to steam the vegetables."

Isabel giggled and obediently sipped more wine. "Ok. This wine is delicious."

"There's a cellar underneath the flats – I keep a few bottles down there for special occasions." He winked as he re-filled his own glass.

Isabel smiled, aware that she was starting to feel a little giddy. She stepped out towards the hallway. "Can I use your bathroom?"

Anthony nodded and pointed over her shoulder. "Sure. Door at the far end."

Isabel turned on her stockinged feet and left the heat of the kitchen, heading in the direction of the bathroom. It was, indeed, at the end of the hallway. Just as she was about to push the door open, she glanced across at the slightly open door adjacent to it. Sipping more wine and swaying a little, she glanced mischievously over her shoulder to check that Anthony was still ensconced in the kitchen. She then turned back towards the second door and tiptoed cautiously through.

* * *

Time: 7.30pm

Date: Tuesday 24<sup>th</sup> July 2012

Location: Metropolitan Police HQ, London

"He could be out there, right now," continued DS Carmichael, sleeves now rolled up to his elbows, beads of sweat visible on his brow. "Taking another victim off the street. We can't afford to hesitate on this one." He pushed away the cartons of takeaway Chinese that sat, mostly uneaten, before him.

"I do know that," replied Jack, tersely. "But we also have to make sure there is actual evidence before we wade in and arrest him."

DS Carmichael refused to give up. "He already has one in his clutches – he could be doing almost anything to her, right now. The consequences of us getting this wrong...."

"I'm well aware of the consequences," cut in Jack. He sighed and looked around the room, letting his eyes rest upon DS Cooper and DC Cassidy. "What do you both think? Is Saunders our man?"

\* \* \*

Time: 7.30pm
 Date: Tuesday 24<sup>th</sup> July 2012
 Location: Buckingham Street, Embankment, London

For a man's bedroom it was tidy. Extremely tidy. Worryingly tidy. Isabel thought back to her own bedroom in the flat above the café, and the tangle of bedclothes, nightwear and other clothing that seemed to occupy each and every surface and most of the floor space.

Anthony had a large double bed in the centre of the room, the duvet neatly smoothed, pillows plumped and straightened on both sides. A small bedside table housed an iPod docking station, a lamp and a glass of water.

Isabel found herself stepping further inside, sweeping her gaze a full three hundred and sixty degrees. Some tasteful prints were hung on the walls, low level lighting recessed into the ceiling with blinds covering the window to allow only a thin shaft of light to fall across the room.

As she was about to turn back and head for the bathroom, Isabel noticed a slatted door on the opposite side of the bed. It looked like some form of built in wardrobe, or maybe an ensuite. Isabel hesitated only momentarily, taking another sip of wine while listening to see if Anthony had ventured out of the kitchen yet. Hearing the gentle crashing of pans and the sound of the oven door opening and closing, Isabel turned back and padded silently across the bedroom towards the door.

\* \* \*

Time: 7.35pm
 Date: Tuesday 24<sup>th</sup> July 2012
 Location: Metropolitan Police HQ, London

"Do you really think it's him?" DC Cassidy directed her gaze towards DS Carmichael, who was still over by the window in search of what little breeze was available. "I mean, *really*?"

"Just because you fancy him, Detective Constable, doesn't mean he isn't our killer."

DC Cassidy felt her cheeks redden. "I don't *fancy* him, for your information," she retorted. "I was only asking you a question."

Jack held his hands up. "Look, less of the bickering. It's getting late and we're all hot, tired and grumpy."

"I'm hot and tired but I'm not grumpy," replied DS Carmichael, his face telling a different story. "I just need to know if we're together on this one. If we get this wrong and we leave him out on the streets..."

"If we go and pick him up I want full tactical support. *If* he is our man, and I stress *if*, then he's a killer of at least three women." Jack paused, holding DS Carmichael in his gaze. "I won't go without armed back up."

"So let's do it," urged DS Carmichael. "Put the wheels in motion now."

"*This* is what we will do." Jack paused to ensure he had everyone's attention. "First thing in the morning, we go to the Chief Superintendent. By that time London Life may well have coughed up the details about the messages that we need. You put your case before him, Carmichael. If he is in agreement, we go for it."

"But delaying it until the morning..."

"Is my *final* answer," interrupted Jack, hotly. "End of discussion."

* * *

Time: 7.35pm
    Date: Tuesday 24<sup>th</sup> July 2012
    Location: Buckingham Street, Embankment, London

Shoes.

Lots of shoes.

Isabel stepped into what was a small walk-in wardrobe of sorts. The small space was fitted with racking on either side, housing shelves upon shelves of shoes. She tentatively stepped further into the enclosed space, unsure if she should be feeling intrigued or slightly afraid.

The shoes appeared to be arranged in some kind of order, with colours grouped together and sizes from small to large. On the bottom shelves were racks and racks of black styles – ranging from ankle boots to delicate strapless stilettoes. From what Isabel could see, peering through the haze of alcohol that was now washing over her, the shoes all looked to be of good quality, many from well-known designers. She was sure she could see some Jimmy Choo, Louis Vuitton, Walter Steiger, even some Alexander McQueen.

Higher up the racks changed colour – groups of russet reds, bright blood-red scarlets, muted chocolate browns, pale pastels, verdant greens and sunburnt oranges. Cool ice whites and glistening silvers adorned a further rack. Isabel's curiosity drew her further forwards and she reached out to pick up the pair closest to her – a pair of plum purple velvet Gucci court shoes with a modest heel. She ran her fingers over the soles. They looked brand new. They smelled brand new.

Isabel hastily returned the shoes to the rack and backed away.

Taking a large sip of wine, she decided that she really did need the bathroom after all.

* * *

Time: 8.00pm
Date: Tuesday 24th July 2012
Location: A cellar in London

Zoe had eaten the prawn and mayonnaise sandwiches – hunger had eventually taken over from the fear. She also noticed that he had left a further packet together with a banana and apple by her side, so at least he wasn't starving her. Her stomach rumbled once again, but the thought of more food made her feel sick.

The cellar felt deathly quiet without Hannah. Although the pair of them hadn't talked much, now it was just Zoe on her own she felt the crushing silence suffocating her from all sides. The only sound was the occasional scrape of the metal chain as she changed position, or stretched her legs. She had tried shouting for help earlier, but the thick walls around the cellar seemed to merely swallow her words. Tired and hoarse she had succumbed to the dark and the silence once again.

What time it was, she had no idea. The gloom of the cellar dissolved time.

With a shuddering sob, she turned over and faced the damp wall. Closing her eyes, she welcomed sleep to block out the fear and terror she felt inside.

* * *

Time: 8.00pm

Date: Tuesday 24<sup>th</sup> July 2012

Location: Buckingham Street, Embankment, London

"You don't mind, do you?" Anthony Saunders paused, his fork midway between his plate and his mouth. "Eating in here? I don't really have a dining room."

Isabel shook her head, slowly chewing and savouring a particularly moist and mouth-watering piece of well-cooked lamb. She swallowed and washed it down with another sip of wine. They had moved on to their second bottle of warming red Merlot.

"Not at all. I always eat with a tray on my lap at home." Isabel smiled from the sofa. "And usually a cat."

Anthony returned the smile and resumed eating. "Maybe I should get a cat," he mumbled, chewing his way through the lamb morsel from his fork.

"It can get quite lonely rattling around here on my own."

Isabel cut a slice of roast potato and dipped it into the garlic and rosemary gravy on her plate. She popped the crispy forkful into her mouth and let her eyes wander around the room again. She had given the room a good once over earlier while Anthony was cooking, noticing there weren't many personal possessions or mementoes on the surfaces of the bookcase and shelving. All she could see were a handful of photographs, and they were all of one person.

And one person only.

"Is that your daughter?" Isabel nodded at the photograph closest to them on the bookcase. The photograph was in a simple silver-plated frame, showing a young girl of approximately seven or eight years of age sitting astride a pony. Her joyful face full of delight grinned towards the camera, while she was supported either side by whom Isabel assumed were Anthony and his ex-wife.

Anthony placed his fork down onto his plate and turned his head towards the photograph. Although the wine was turning her vision a little hazy around the edges, Isabel thought she saw his eyes cloud over, their usual brightness disappearing like a dying ember on a burnt out log fire. After a while, he simply nodded.

"Yes, she was about eight when we took that." He paused and the smile returned to his lips. "Always loved her ponies."

"Does she live with her mother?" Isabel wasn't quite sure why she was asking. She took another large gulp of Merlot, hoping she hadn't put her foot in it and trodden unceremoniously onto painful territory.

Anthony flicked his gaze back to Isabel and nodded. "Yes, she's with her mother. I don't see much of them anymore." His eyes, still subdued and misty, lowered to his plate where he began slowly cutting through another piece of tender meat.

Isabel averted her gaze and cast her eyes around the rest of the photographs on the bookcase. One was of a small baby with an all toothy grin; a saliva encrusted chin, and rich, rosy cheeks from teething. One next to it was of a toddler, being pushed along on a tricycle. The same toothy grin, the same saliva encased chin.

Isabel instantly found herself thinking back to her own trusty tricycle that she had loved from the very day she received it for her fifth birthday. She could remember her fifth birthday like it was yesterday. The party in the garden with her mother's homemade buttercream biscuits, and the homemade birthday cake in the shape of a star, topped with pink icing and jelly sweets. She could remember falling off her new tricycle as she came hurtling down the slope in the garden, and scraping her knee on the pedal. She could remember being whisked up into the arms of her Uncle.

Except he wasn't her Uncle.

Isabel shuddered and shook the thoughts from her head. She sipped again at the wine in her hand. Next to the photograph of the toddler on the tricycle was one of an older girl – possibly a teenager – sitting on a bench next to a life-size Mickey Mouse. Isabel inched forwards in her seat a little, her eyes searching the young girl's face. She had her father's smile, that was evident; the signs of a small dimple on her chin. She was dressed in jeans and a sweatshirt with a large letter J in the centre, her hair scraped back off her face and into a high pony-tail.

The "J" matched the "J" Isabel had seen on a signet ring on Anthony's left hand. She usually didn't like jewellery on a man, but this seemed different.

"She's very pretty," Isabel heard herself saying, casting a glance back at Anthony who was staring sombrely into the remains of his dinner, appetite gone. "You must be very proud of her."

Anthony looked up, the cloudiness of his eyes still apparent. Slowly he nodded.

"Always," he said, simply.

\* \* \*

Time: 1.45pm
  Date: 21st November 1997
  Location: The Forest of Dean, Gloucestershire

"Come on, slowcoaches!" Jess hurried on ahead, shrieking with delight every time she jumped over a fallen tree branch. Her laughter filled the still air, echoing and bouncing off the trees that lined their forest path. "Race you to the river! Last one there buys the ice-cream!" Her voice tailed off as she disappeared out of sight.

Jess's mother lengthened her stride and picked up the pace, following in her daughter's footsteps. She swung the rucksack a little higher up onto her shoulder, feeling it bounce rhythmically between her shoulder blades as she paced.

"Come on, Carol. Don't be like this." His voice was strained and had the hint of long suffering impatience bubbling underneath like the babbling stream that flagged their route.

"Me?" she thundered, feeling her own anger bristling. "I'm not being like anything." She continued striding ahead, her walking boots making light work of the moss covered pathway. The weather had been kind to them so far – the late autumn Indian summer they had been promised had extended into November, meaning that their week's holiday in the Forest of Dean had been full of trips out for forest walks, exploring deserted caves and even some wading in the rivers.

"Carol." This time his voice was hard. Hard and threatening. He picked up his own pace and strode quickly behind her, easily matching her stride for stride. He deftly made a grab for her arm, catching her tightly around the wrist and pulling her roughly to a stop.

"Ow, stop it! You're hurting me." Carol tried to wrestle her arm free of his grip, but he was too strong for her. "Let go. Jess might see."

"Stop fighting, Carol. Just calm down." He made no attempt to loosen his grip, if anything it tightened even further. "You know why things are like this. You know what you did."

Carol flashed him a hot look, full of hatred, and once again tried to twist herself free. She dug the heels of her walking boots into the dirt-track underfoot and twisted her body violently in towards his. Caught momentarily off guard, he stumbled and lost his footing.

It was enough to break free.

This time.

\* \* \*

Time: 00.15am
  Date: Wednesday 25<sup>th</sup> July 2012
  Location: A cellar in London

The hardest part was negotiating the steps. They didn't look very steep when you were climbing up and down, with the bannister to help, but dragging a body to the top always made him sweat. He paused halfway, resting against the handrail, and wiped the sweat from his brow with the back of his hand. He hadn't remembered Carol being so heavy before. Maybe she had been putting on weight without him realising.

She hadn't been listening to him.

Again.

Carol never listened.

Breathing in deeply, he placed his hands once again between her shoulders and began hauling her up the final few steps. Her legs bounced against the roughly hewn stone, but Carol remained quiet and didn't utter a sound. Once they reached the top, he placed her onto the kitchen floor and glanced at his watch. The sun would be coming up soon – he needed to get moving if he wanted the protection of darkness to mask Carol's final journey.

But first she needed to be cleaned.

They always needed to be cleaned.

He dragged her towards a small utility and washroom at the rear of the kitchen. The walk-in shower cubicle had everything he needed – nailbrush, antibacterial washes and wipes, bleach. He knew if he moved quickly he could be loaded up within half an hour. He set the shower to "hot" and began washing Carol's body, being careful to don a pair of rubber gloves as he did so.

It needn't take long.

He had done this before.

\* \* \*

# Chapter Twenty Five

Time: 6.05am

Date: Wednesday 25<sup>th</sup> July 2012

Location: Battersea Park, London

The early morning dew clung to the bright blue plastic overshoes Jack had snapped onto his feet. As he shuffled along the hastily constructed walkway, his white protective suit rustling as he did so, Jack felt the all too familiar feeling of déjà vu envelop him. The call had come through to Jack's mobile at 5.04am. They had another one. The early morning discovery made by a jogger in Battersea Park.

It was always a jogger.

Or a dog walker.

That was why Jack avoided outdoor exercise and had never owned a pet.

The now-traumatised jogger had stumbled across the body as it lay unhidden, lying in the centre of an open space flanked by mature trees. It was daring. It was brazen. Jack glanced over his shoulder, noting that the main road, a busy arterial route across the river towards Chelsea, was not far away.

The all too familiar white tent had already been erected to screen the grisly discovery from prying eyes, and Dr Philip Matthews was already in attendance. He exited the tent just as Jack approached the end of the walkway.

"DI MacIntosh. We must stop meeting like this." Dr Philip Matthews nodded his head back towards the tent flaps behind him.

"Morning, Doc," replied Jack, noting once again how impeccably turned out the pathologist was, even at this early hour. He must have received the dawn-chorus phone call at the same time as Jack, but yet seemed to have been able to don an expensively cut three-piece suit, cravat and also polish his shoes. Jack had barely managed to run a hand through his bed-hair. "What have we got?"

"We have a young female. Approx. age thirty-five to forty-five. Hair colour- dark. Still clothed; positioned on her back." Dr Matthews paused. "And yes, ligature marks around the neck."

"Same as before," stated Jack. It was not a question.

"Same as before," concurred Dr Matthews.

"Restraints?"

"Same as before," conceded the pathologist. "Abrasions to the left ankle."

"Any idea how long she has been here?"

"I can't answer that, Jack. But not long, not long at all. Let me get her back to the mortuary. It was a warm night. Time of death might be difficult to pinpoint even with further tests."

Jack nodded and waved Dr Matthews on his way. Stepping forwards, he peered inside the flaps of the tent, needing to see for himself.

The body lay just as Dr Matthews had described. Her eyes were open, staring up at what would have been a cloudless sky was it not for the hastily erected tent acting as her tomb. What did those eyes see at the very end? mused Jack. What face had filled her last moments when the life was being choked out of her? What secrets would she never tell?

The woman was pale skinned, slim and well dressed. Her legs were bent modestly to the side, but Jack could see all he needed to see.

One shoe.

She was wearing only one shoe – a black court shoe with a low heel.

Jack already had the other in an evidence bag back at the station.

Stepping backwards, Jack felt his heart beginning to sink; that familiar gnawing feeling gripping his stomach. He nodded to DS Cooper who was hovering in his wake, plastic evidence bag in hand. Then the pair of them began scouring the immediate vicinity.

Looking for a shoe.

A shoe belonging to the next victim.

*  *  *

Time: 6.45am

Date: Wednesday 25th July 2012

Location: Isabel's Café, King's Road, London

Angus McBride peered in through the window, cupping his hands across his brow as he squinted in the early morning sunshine. He raised his hand and rapped his gnarled knuckles against the glass.

CLOSED

The sign hanging up in the front door confirmed his suspicions, but a deep frown creased his forehead. Isabel's was never closed at this time. Not on a Wednesday morning. He let the heavy Royal Mail postbag sink to the pavement by his feet and took a step back. After quickly glancing up and down the street, wondering if he would spot a slightly harassed figure rushing towards him, apologising profusely for making him wait but she had just run out of milk and had to make an emergency dash to the corner shop further up the street.

But there was no such figure, harassed or otherwise.

Angus then glanced up at the window above the café entrance, which he knew was the flat where Isabel lived. The small window that overlooked the road gave nothing away. The curtains were open, but the window itself remained closed.

An unsettling feeling began to creep into Angus's stomach, replacing the rumbling hunger pangs that had begun when he thought about the mouth-watering warm and freshly-baked sausage roll he would be having for his breakfast.

He once again stepped forwards and peered through the window into the café. But nothing had changed. The closed sign was still hanging. The lights were still off. The counter deserted.

Isabel was nowhere to be seen.

* * *

Time: 6.50am
Date: Wednesday 25<sup>th</sup> July 2012
Location: A cellar in London

Isabel's eyes fluttered open as she stirred from her slumber. Her head felt groggy, her tongue felt dry. As she tried to focus on her surroundings, her vision remained blurry, as if her eyelids were still glued together.

How much did I have to drink last night, she wondered, as a snapshot of several glasses of Merlot washed over her. One bottle? Two? More? She saw Anthony's face flash in front of her, and the smell of roasting lamb and rosemary filled her nostrils.

Except she couldn't really smell lamb.

She couldn't smell rosemary.

She could smell.... what was it? Vomit? Sweat? Urine?

Isabel's eyes snapped open. She was fully awake now. A quick glance around her confirmed that she was not at home. With her heart beating fast inside her chest, she pushed herself up into a sitting position, while memories started to come flooding back, all jumbled together like a badly fitting jigsaw puzzle. Anthony. The meal. The photographs. The shoes. The photographs. Anthony.

Isabel let her eyes wander across to the other side of the cellar, towards the identical threadbare mattress opposite. Hadn't there been someone else here before? Isabel frowned, trying to make sense of the foggy memories jostling for position inside her head. There had been a woman, she was sure of it. But now she was gone. She took in the empty blanket draped over the mattress. Had she spoken to her? Isabel was sure that she had. She was sure that she had said her name was Zoe.

But Zoe was no longer there.

Isabel wracked her brains to try and remember what had happened, how she had ended up here, in a damp cellar. Alone. She couldn't remember leaving Anthony's; everything was such a haze. How had she got down here? Had she been drugged?

Isabel tried moving her legs, and as she did so, a loud, scraping sound accompanied the movement. Looking down she saw that her left ankle was encased in a heavy, metal clasp with a chain snaking its way into the darkness and beyond, in the direction of a rusty radiator on the wall. She also noticed that one of her shoes were missing.

\* \* \*

Time: 7.00am

Date: Wednesday 25<sup>th</sup> July 2012

Location: Isabel's Café, King's Road, London

Once he had exited the tube station, Dominic practically sprinted along the King's Road. He was late. And he was *never* late. His heart was thudding in his chest, partly from the exertion of running, but partly from his fear of being late. He knew Isabel wouldn't mind, and probably wouldn't even comment on it at all – but Dominic *hated* being late.

He was meant to arrive at the café at 6.30am.

It said so in his notebook.

And his notebook was never wrong.

He clutched the notebook to his chest as he ran the last one hundred metres along the pavement towards the café. Even before he arrived, Dominic sensed that something was wrong. The café looked the same, from a distance, but Dominic could see that it was not the same at all.

He slowed to a jog as he approached the front door, immediately noticing the "closed" sign hanging in the window.

Isabel had forgotten to turn it over.

Just as she had forgotten to turn on the lights.

Dominic tentatively stepped forwards to push the door – it was locked.

Isabel had also forgotten to unlock the door.

Except she hadn't.

Dominic knew in an instant.

Isabel wasn't there.

Panic started to well up inside him. He side stepped, from foot to foot, clutching his notebook as if his life depended on it. After what seemed like an eternity, but which in reality was only a few seconds, Dominic thrust his hand into his jeans pocket and brought out his key.

His emergency key.

For use in an emergency.

*This* was an emergency.

He forced the key that he had never had to use before, into the lock and twisted it clockwise, hearing the heavy "click" as he did so. Pushing the door open, he stepped over the threshold and peered into the dim café.

"Isabel?" he called out, hesitantly, his voice even quieter than the stillness of the sleeping café. "Are you there?"

"She's not there, sonny."

Dominic whirled round to see Angus McBride hovering outside on the pavement, a concerned look on his wrinkled face. His greying beard twitched as he spoke, his slate-grey eyes having lost their usual twinkle. "I came for my usual coffee and sausage roll - but there's no sign of the lass."

Dominic nodded, taking another small step into the silent café. No hissing sound of the coffee machine warming up; no humming sound from the ovens as they baked their first batches of the day. No sound. No sound at all. Everywhere was deathly quiet.

"I've been coming here at quarter to seven every day for three months, sonny," continued Angus, depositing his Royal Mail bag at his feet on the pavement. "Never has the wee lass not been here to open up."

Dominic nodded and reached for his phone.

* * *

Time: 7.15am

Date: Wednesday 25<sup>th</sup> July 2012

Location: Islington, London

Mac was about to put on his motorbike helmet when he felt his phone vibrating in the inside pocket of his heavy leather jacket. Momentarily considering to let it ring out, he sighed and placed his helmet at his feet. It might be work – cancelling or rearranging one of his deliveries. Better to answer it.

He shrugged out of the jacket and reached inside for his phone. Glancing at the screen, he almost hit the ignore button – an unknown number. An unknown number at this time of day usually meant a PPI call, or someone insisting he had been involved in an accident within the last three years. His finger hovered over the top of the red button; he was already late for work as it was.

But what if it was important?

What if something had happened to Jack?

He hit the green button and brought the phone to his ear.

But it wasn't a PPI call. And it wasn't a claims company asking about his recent accident. Neither was it anyone from work, and it wasn't about Jack.

It was Sacha – from the café. She spoke very quickly, panic evident in her tone. Dominic had found Mac's number in Isabel's address book upstairs in her flat.

The café and the flat were empty.

Isabel was missing.

\* \* \*

Time: 7.20am

Date: Wednesday 25<sup>th</sup> July 2012

Location: Metropolitan Police HQ, London

Jack eyed the ever-increasing pile of files and papers on his desk before slipping into his chair. Various other open investigations still needed his attention – but Operation Genevieve had to be his priority. He ran a finger around inside his shirt collar, feeling the stickiness of the day starting already. It had taken two long, cool showers to rid himself of the cold sweat ingrained into his skin from yet another restless night. He had had another vision of the door; the door to the kitchen. The door that led to the discovery of his mother. At 3am he had given up and taken the first of the showers, relishing in the feeling of the water drumming repeatedly against his back and shoulders. He didn't know how long he had remained under it - it could have been five minutes; it could have been fifty-five. His next water bill would most probably be able to tell him.

He had then sat in the lightening dawn, listening to the world waking up outside – everyone slumbering into action after another hot and sticky night. Until the call came through just after 5am that the killer had struck again. Another quick cold shower and he had finally pulled on some clothes – noticing the increasing volume of clothes in the washing bin that he was wilfully ignoring. He was down to his last shirt. And yesterday's trousers would have to do. Again.

At least he smelt good. Two showers and a liberal encasement in deodorant made sure of that.

Deodorant was another item the shops were never running out of. Cold beer and deodorant. Electric fans, yes. Dehumidifiers, yes. Air conditioning systems, yes. But deodorant and cold beer, there was plenty of that to go around.

Jack drained the dregs of his black coffee and nodded his thanks to DS

Cooper, who swiped the mug out of his hands and took it to the small sink in the corner of the office. Jack thought of his own kitchen sink at home – he had eventually cleared it of all the dirty dishes last night, not wanting another repeat of the smashed dinner plate. It had taken him a good half an hour, up to his elbows in soapy suds, but he had found it quite a therapeutic experience. He had used the time to let his mind wander. Would that count as part of the meditative therapy he was meant to be trying before his next session with Dr Riches? *If* there was going to be a next session, that was. Jack had yet to make up his mind.

For that half an hour, he had felt quite calm and serene. He could almost feel his cares and worries floating away on top of the soap suds. Perhaps he had invented a new meditative technique.

But this morning he felt anything but calm and serene. He got to his feet, ready to add a fourth victim to Operation Genevieve. DC Cassidy was on her way in, and Jack had set a briefing for eight o'clock. Where DS Carmichael was, nobody knew.

Moving the files and papers marked "urgent" to one side, Jack was just about to follow DS Cooper out of the office when his phone rang. He saw from the screen that it was Stuart. He glanced at the time – Stuart should be at work by now, weaving in and out of the congested commuter traffic.

"Hey, Stu?" Jack answered the call on the third ring. "What's up?"

\* \* \*

Time: 8.15am
  Date: Wednesday 25<sup>th</sup> July 2012
  Location: Metropolitan Police HQ, London

Jack paced backwards and forwards by the open window, the sickness in his stomach growing by the second. Stuart had emailed him a photograph of Isabel, which was now uploaded onto the whiteboard. Jack could barely look at it. He nodded at DS Cooper to begin.

"Isabel Faraday. Age thirty-two. Presumed missing since yesterday evening." DS Cooper clicked the mouse and enlarged a picture of the shoe Jack had found at the murder scene less than two hours ago. A shoe, nestling in the grass some fifteen to twenty metres away from the gruesome early morning discovery. "This shoe was found this morning – her friend Sacha Greene has verbally confirmed that Isabel owns a pair just like it."

"Isabel is said to have gone to Anthony Saunders' house last night for dinner." Jack found his voice, recalling his brother's panic-stricken and garbled conversation with him earlier. "She failed to open her café this morning and reports say her bed hasn't been slept in."

"Saunders." DS Carmichael flashed a dark look in Jack's direction. "I told you it was him. If we had picked him up last night..."

"That's enough, Sergeant," clipped Jack, returning the dark look. "Get the evidence we have on Saunders together and meet me at the Chief Superintendent's office in twenty minutes."

# Chapter Twenty Six

Time: 8.45am
  Date: Wednesday 25<sup>th</sup> July 2012
  Location: Metropolitan Police HQ, London

Chief Superintendent Dougie King exhaled noisily. He drummed his fingers on his desk, a pensive look darkening his features. His eyes bore into Jack, holding his gaze without blinking, before doing the same with DS Carmichael. Neither Jack nor DS Carmichael had sat down in the vacant chairs – they hadn't been asked to. Instead, they both stood to attention in front of the Chief Superintendent's desk, awaiting their fate like a schoolboy awaits his punishment from the headmaster.

"And you're sure about this?" Chief Superintendent Dougie King flashed another penetrative look at Jack. "This is our man?"

Jack hesitated, about to open his mouth to reply when DS Carmichael stepped in.

"Absolutely, Sir. One hundred percent."

Chief Superintendent King transferred his gaze back to DS Carmichael. "Talk me through the evidence once again. We have to be more than sure on this one."

Jack nodded at DS Carmichael to take the lead, feeling unable to speak. How could he have put Isabel's life in danger like this? Through his own inactivity and indecisiveness, Isabel's life now hung in the balance. It made him feel physically sick. DS Carmichael cleared his throat before addressing the Chief Superintendent.

"Firstly, he fits the demographics of the profile. Right age. Right background. He's educated. He's intelligent. He's charming – so the women say." DS Carmichael held up a hand and began to count the points of evidence with his fingers. "He lives in the right area. He has knowledge of London. He's single. And he has an expert knowledge of forensics." He paused, making sure he had the Chief Superintendent's undivided attention. "He's a subscriber to a dating site that the first three victims also subscribed to. He's sent messages to all three of them. We obviously haven't got an ID yet for the woman found this morning, but checks will obviously be made to see if she has had contact with him too. Miss Faraday had a date with him last night and hasn't been seen since; her mobile phone was last active at his home address. And lastly, the shoe found at the scene this morning has been confirmed to closely resemble one Miss Faraday herself owns."

Chief Superintendent King sat back in his chair, the leather creaking under his weight. He nodded, thoughtfully, weighing up the evidential points described by DS Carmichael.

But DS Carmichael hadn't finished. "And we have one final piece of evidence that proves we have the right man." DS Carmichael held his hand out towards Jack. "Jack?"

Pausing only briefly, Jack nodded and brought out the plastic evidence bag he had clasped behind his back.

"In here, we have a drawing made by the suspect." DS Carmichael leant forwards and handed the evidence bag to the Chief Superintendent. "It's an intricate drawing, a sketch, of a shoe." DS Carmichael nodded towards the evidence bag.

"I can see that, Sergeant," replied the Chief Superintendent. Dougie King let his eyes rake over the pencil sketch drawing, his mind ticking and whirring as he did so. "And we are saying this is evidence of....?"

"Our killer has a shoe fetish, Sir," continued DS Carmichael. "The shoes at the scene. Our suspect, here, clearly has an unusual interest in shoes. It makes him our man."

"It shows he has an interest in drawing, Sergeant, not necessarily in shoes." The Chief Superintendent handed the plastic evidence bag back across the desk towards DS Carmichael. "What's your view on it all, Jack?"

The sickness in Jack's stomach continued to spread. He could almost taste the acrid stomach acid in his mouth as he swallowed. Isabel. When he had taken Stuart's phone call this morning, he felt the axis of the world shift.

They had to find her.

*He* had to find her.

"Is Anthony Saunders our man?" The Chief Superintendent continued to stare at Jack, his eyes boring into him. "You do know who his father is?"

Jack took a deep breath and nodded. "He certainly does fit the profile, Sir. DS Carmichael is quite correct about that."

"I know he fits the profile, Jack, but does he fit the evidence? Do we even have any evidence? Real evidence?" He paused, shifting his gaze between Jack and DS Carmichael. "Enough for me to authorise an armed response to arrest him?"

Jack opened his mouth again, but hesitated. Images of Isabel flooded his head. She was out there, somewhere, being held against her will. Kidnapped. Or worse. He had to do everything within his power, and beyond, to find her. And find her before it was too late. "He's the only suspect we have, Sir. And if we don't act now, we may have another murder on our hands." The words stuck in his throat as he uttered them.

The killer was clearly escalating – the time between the last two victim's bodies being found was reducing, and reducing fast. They may not have much time left.

"So, yes, Anthony Saunders is our man."

* * *

Time: 10.45am

Date: Wednesday 25th July 2012

Location: Buckingham Street, Embankment, London

"Flat 1b." DS Carmichael led the team of four armed officers to the front of the converted grain merchant's building. A quick call to his office had confirmed that Anthony Saunders was working from home that day. "I want two of you around the back entrance, in case he makes a run for it, and two of you remain out here."

Two officers, kitted in their heavy police armed response protective gear, nodded and immediately jogged around to the rear of the building, their Glock 17 pistols held loosely but firmly by their sides. Radio communications crackled in their earpieces as they disappeared out of sight. "Jack?" DS Carmichael glanced back over his shoulder to the pavement where Jack was standing with DS Cooper and DC Cassidy. All three had bulky police issue stab vests. "You ready?"

DS Cooper and DC Cassidy cast concerned looks in Jack's direction, noting how he remained motionless by the side of the police van, his forehead knotted with an ever deepening frown.

"Boss?" DS Cooper broke the silence. "We're going in?"

Jack ran a finger around the neck of his stab vest. It was beginning to chafe and irritate his skin. He remained firmly planted by the kerbside, his eyes flicking from the armed police flanking the entrance to DS Carmichael and back again. His vision swam in and out of focus.

None of this felt real.

He had hoped that it was just another one of his nightmares – and that he would wake up in a cold sweat, feeling nauseated. And Isabel would be safely tucked away in her café, serving her early morning customers.

But standing outside Anthony Saunders' flat, Jack knew that this particular nightmare was only just beginning. And if Isabel was inside, they needed to find her.

So Jack gave the nod. "Sure. Let's do this."

\* \* \*

Time: 10.50am
  Date: Wednesday 25<sup>th</sup> July 2012
  Location: A cellar in London

Isabel could feel the hard concrete beneath the mattress, as if she were lying directly on the floor. She had no idea what time it was – her phone and watch had been taken from her; when, she didn't know - but when she had woken up, they were gone. She pushed the coarse blanket off her legs; it was making them feel itchy. For a moment she lay there in the semi-darkness, feeling twinges of pain shooting through her aching back and limbs with every slight movement she made.

She knew that she mustn't panic. She mustn't shout or scream, that was right wasn't it? She needed to keep her head; to keep her self-control, only then would she be able to find a way out. She lay back against the thin mattress and stared up at the ceiling, which appeared as dark as the night sky.

A memory suddenly crept into her head, stowed away long ago in the depths of her subconscious.

\* \* \*

Time: 11.50pm
  Date: 25<sup>th</sup> June 1985
  Location: The Glade, Church Street, Albury, Surrey

Isabel wriggled on the thin mat, feeling the lumps and bumps from the grass beneath. As she wriggled, she thought she could feel a stone digging in between her shoulder blades, and the more she wriggled the more it dug in.

"There's a worm at the bottom of the garden," sang Elizabeth Faraday, in a gentle sing-song voice. "And his name is Wiggly-Woo!"

Isabel screeched with delight as her father's hands tickled her beneath her ribs.

"And all that he can do is, wiggle all night, and wiggle all day..." Christopher Faraday watched as more screaming came from Isabel's lips, her squeals of delight causing her to roll around on the mat.

"Stop it!" she cried, clutching her sides with laughter. "You're making me too wiggly!"

"Like Wiggly Woo!" laughed Christopher Faraday, wiping tears of laughter from his own eyes.

Isabel turned over onto her tummy, her face screwed up with merriment. "You're so funny, Daddy!" she yelped, rolling out of the way of his tickling hands.

Just then, Elizabeth Faraday turned her eyes skywards. Whereas a few moments ago they had all been lying back on their camping mats, staring up at the star studded sky, Christopher passing around his telescope and marvelling at the clearness of the night, now she noticed a huge black cloud sweeping across and starting to deposit heavy, fat raindrops on them from above.

"It's raining!" yelled Isabel, still rolling around and giggling. "It's raining!"

"Let's get back inside the tent," said Christopher Faraday, getting to his knees. "Hopefully it'll pass soon." He nodded towards the small two-man tent that they had erected in the back garden – the aim being to spend the night outdoors before Isabel's fifth birthday the next day.

"Or how about we go into the summer house and I go and make us some hot chocolate with marshmallows!" said Elizabeth Faraday, standing up as the raindrops increased in their frequency and size. "Last one there is a wiggly worm!"

\* \* \*

Time: 10.50am

Date: Wednesday 25th July 2012

Location: Buckingham Street, Embankment, London

"Mr Saunders? My name is Detective Sergeant Carmichael from the Metropolitan Police. We need to speak to you. Open the door."

Silence.

"Mr Saunders. If you don't open the door I have authority to force entry." DS Carmichael paused, listening to the continued silence. "If you do not open the door in the next ten seconds, it will be forced open."

More silence.

Again.

Just as DS Carmichael was about to give the nod to the two accompanying officers to use the "enforcer", a sharp buzzing sound filled the quiet street,

The outside door was open.

DS Carmichael motioned for the two armed police officers to enter ahead of him towards flat 1b. He radioed his command to the armed officers stationed outside at the rear of the building to hold their ground and be ready.

Jack, together with DS Cooper and DC Cassidy, followed on behind, each with their uncomfortable and bulky stab proof vests weighing them down. Stab proof, mused Jack, as he moved ahead of DC Cassidy. He eyed the Glock 17 pistols in the hands of the armed officers up ahead. Stab proof, but not bullet proof.

"Mr Saunders, it's the police. Open up." DS Carmichael's voice echoed outside flat 1b. "You have ten seconds; otherwise armed officers will break down the door. I repeat. Open up, Mr Saunders. You have ten seconds."

Jack held his breath for what seemed like longer than the aforementioned ten seconds, but a discernible click was heard almost as soon as DS Carmichael had finished giving the command. The door to flat 1b swung open.

Immediately, DS Carmichael motioned for the armed officers to enter. He flattened himself against the outside wall, and indicated that Jack, DC

Cassidy and DS Cooper should follow suit. Only when the confirmatory 'clear' was heard emanating from the flat did they move towards the door and enter the flat.

DS Carmichael strode into the hallway of flat 1b to see an ashen-faced Anthony Saunders standing facing a wall with his hands raised above his head. Dressed in a loose-fitting dressing gown, and shampoo suds still clinging to his hair, it appeared that the raid had interrupted the defence solicitor's morning shower.

"Anthony Saunders," spoke DS Carmichael, stepping further into the flat. "I am arresting you on suspicion of murder. You do not have to say anything. But it may harm your defence if you do not mention when questioned something that you later rely on in court. Anything you do say may be given in evidence." DS Carmichael glanced back at Jack, DS Cooper and DC Cassidy who had followed him into the hallway. "Someone cuff him."

\* \* \*

Time: 12.15am
Date: 26<sup>th</sup> June 1985
Location: The Glade, Church Street, Albury, Surrey

Isabel scooped up a huge, globby marshmallow with her spoon and deposited it into her mouth, squealing with delight at the same time. A dribble of frothy chocolate trickled down her chin and dripped onto the picnic table.

The sound of the rain hammering on the roof of the little summer house was the only sound they could hear. Elizabeth Faraday sank back into her husband's arms, cradling her mug of hot chocolate in her hands. The drumming and vibrations from the raindrops was almost soothing, almost meditative. She allowed her eyes to close.

"Mummy, Mummy, Mummy, wake up!" screeched Isabel, her eyes shining. "It's my birthday!"

"So it is, sweet pea," murmured Elizabeth Faraday, glancing at her watch and smiling contentedly at her beaming daughter. "Happy birthday my darling."

Isabel's eyes were widening by the second. She took another gulp of hot chocolate, her lips and chin stained milky brown. "And today is my party!"

"Happy birthday, sweetheart," echoed Christopher Faraday. "You're such a big girl now!"

Isabel swung her legs from her picnic chair, noticing how her feet almost reached the ground. She was getting bigger! She was five now, and five was almost grown up!

"Will there be party games, Mummy? And a cake? And lots of presents?" Isabel could barely contain her excitement, swinging her legs so frantically that she almost toppled off the side of the chair.

"I'm sure there will be all of those things," smiled Elizabeth Faraday, stifling a yawn as she pushed herself up. "But you won't get to enjoy any of it if you're too tired. I think it's time we went to bed, don't you?"

"And when you wake up, it will be your party day!" added Christopher Faraday, collecting up the mugs of hot chocolate and joining his wife by Isabel's side.

Between them they carried the excitable five-year-old back into the house.

* * *

Time: 11.10am
Date: Wednesday 25<sup>th</sup> July 2012
Location: Buckingham Street, Embankment, London

"Let's get him shifted back to the station for interview," said DS Carmichael, taking control. He nodded at Anthony Saunders who had now been allowed to put on something more appropriate than a flimsy dressing gown before being transported to a police station. "We'll get the forensics lot to go over the place."

Jack watched as the defence lawyer was led away by DC Cassidy. Was he watching the man who had kidnapped Isabel? The man who held the secrets as to where she was and the killer of four other women?

Jack hoped so.

He really hoped so.

The Chief Superintendent could then breathe a sigh of relief and the Olympics could unfold as planned, untouched and unscathed. And the quicker they could get Anthony Saunders talking, the quicker they could find Isabel.

Before it was too late.

As Anthony Saunders disappeared outside to the waiting police van, DS Cooper emerged from the bedroom at the far end of the corridor. "Full of shoes, boss." He nodded behind him. "A wardrobe full of shoes."

Jack returned the nod, but the nausea he felt in his stomach had now been joined by something else.

Fear.

If Anthony Saunders was their man, where was Isabel?

\* \* \*

Time: 11.30am

Date: Wednesday 25th July 2012

Location: A cellar in London

Isabel ran her tongue over her dry, chapped lips. She could almost taste that marshmallow. And the creamy hot chocolate that only her mother knew how to make. Her mother made the *best* hot chocolate in the world.

Isabel felt the familiar heave in her chest.

Every time she drank a hot chocolate she thought of her mother. She did extra special hot chocolates in the café – topped with cream, caramel, marshmallows – just about anything you could want. And every time she made one, every time she even smelt one, she thought of her mother.

Isabel shuddered even though the air in the cellar had taken on a warmer, stickier feel. Was this what it was like? Was this what it felt like; waiting to die? Was this how her parents had felt when...?

A lump formed in Isabel's throat and she choked it back. Had they known they were about to die in that cottage? Isabel had always wondered but had been afraid to ask the question.

Correction.

She had been afraid to hear the answer.

She hoped that they had not known; hoped they had been oblivious to what was coming, and it had happened quickly and quietly, without them knowing.

Unlike Isabel.

She read the papers.

She knew what this man was capable of.

And she knew what was coming.

* * *

# Chapter Twenty Seven

Time: 12.30pm

Date: Wednesday 25th July 2012

Location: Metropolitan Police HQ, London

"Patricia Gordon; how do you know her?" Jack fixed Anthony Saunders with a searching stare. Interview room one was a small and stuffy windowless space – the submarine grey walls flecked with drips of long discarded coffee and other stains Jack did not wish to dwell on. The previous occupant's body odour issues lingered in the stagnant air.

Anthony Saunders sat with a straight back on an uneven legged wooden chair. His eyes widened at the question posed to him. "I...I don't.... I don't know who that is." He reached forwards for the plastic cup of water that he had asked for; although warm and chalky-tasting, he needed something to lubricate his increasingly dry throat.

Jack watched the defence lawyer's demeanour alter slightly at the mention of the first victim's name. He let the question hang tantalisingly in the air for a moment or two longer than necessary before continuing. "Really? The evidence begs to differ." Jack nodded at DS Cooper, who slid an A4 sized document out from a thin folder in front of him.

"You are being shown item reference CC-001 – a message inventory from London Life." DS Cooper passed the piece of paper across the table towards Anthony Saunders.

The defence lawyer took the document in his hand, his eyes immediately scouring its contents.

"For the sake of clarity, Mr Saunders," continued Jack, casting his eyes down to an identical piece of paper sitting in front of him, "this document reference shows an itemised list of messages sent by you on the dating site London Life – the recipient of those messages is Patricia Gordon."

Jack let the information hang in the space between them, jostling for room amongst the stale body odour and an ever increasing tension that electrified the air around them. "I put it to you again, Mr Saunders. How do you know Patricia Gordon?"

Anthony Saunders let the document fall back onto the table, and lifted his gaze to meet Jack's. "And I repeat my earlier response, Detective Inspector. I don't know her."

Jack began to detect the wariness and nervousness Saunders had initially exhibited upon being arrested and thereafter read his rights, was now slowly being replaced by a self-assuredness bordering on the cocky. The shift was subtle, but even the humid and heavy air of the interview room couldn't mask it from Jack.

"This document would appear to suggest otherwise." Jack nodded back down at the paperwork. "A total of three messages sent to Patricia Gordon between 2$^{nd}$ and 27$^{th}$ April this year. How do you explain that, Mr Saunders, if you do not know her?"

Anthony Saunders leant back in his chair, the uneven legs causing it to wobble, and folded his arms across his chest. A flicker of a smile crossed his lips as he took another sip of the warm water in his cup. "And what do these messages say?" he enquired, theatrically raising an eyebrow and giving a small shrug. "You don't seem to have a print out of the content of these co-called messages."

Jack shifted in his seat and caught DS Cooper's eye. They had anticipated this question coming up during their hastily arranged interview strategy meeting in Jack's car on the way back to the station. But not quite this early on. Jack eyed the man sitting across the table – Anthony Saunders, ever the seasoned defence professional, was clearly no pushover when it came to police interviews. He would have sat in on enough of them to pick up more than an adequate knowledge of police tactics.

Jack hated interviewing lawyers.

And he was beginning to hate interviewing this one more than most.

Clearing his throat, Jack continued. "We are requisitioning the content of these messages as we speak." London Life had been approached but had politely declined to disclose the content of its members' private messages. They had gone on to quote a number of privacy and data protection laws, at which time Jack had switched off and stopped listening. Without a warrant, they would disclose nothing.

Something Anthony Saunders obviously knew.

The warrant had been served that morning and DC Cassidy was monitoring London Life's response from the room next door.

"But as yet, you don't have them," the defence lawyer stated, continuing to rest back in his chair. The cocky, edginess to his tone was growing. "Shall we move on?"

"You don't deny that you have sent messages to Patricia Gordon three times between 2nd and 27$^{th}$ April?" pressed Jack, refusing to let the lawyer gain the upper hand. "The evidence is there in black and white."

"Indeed it is, Detective Inspector," replied Saunders, nodding slowly. "But I send messages to lots of women." A smile crossed his face. "Between you and me, I'm known to be a bit of a flirt." He winked across the table at Jack. "Is this all you have? Some messages?"

Jack felt the tell-tale sensation of his hackles rising on the back of his neck. The heat of the interview room was doing nothing to help keep a lid on his increasing temper. He avoided the lawyer's taunting gaze and slid the document from London Life back into his folder, at the same time as pulling out two more. He nodded silently at DS Cooper.

"You are now being shown two further documents with item reference CC-002 and CC-003." DS Cooper handed two almost identical documents across the table towards Anthony Saunders.

"These documents contain further evidence from London Life showing messages between yourself and Georgina Dale and also Hannah Fuller."

Jack paused, allowing the defence lawyer time to scan the print outs. "Bit of a coincidence, don't you think? These two women, plus Patricia Gordon, have all been abducted and murdered within the last twelve days. And you have been in contact with all three of them. I'll ask you one more time – how do you know these women?"

Anthony Saunders flicked through the two documents, casting his eyes down each list of dates. Jack could see a film of perspiration forming on the lawyer's upper lip, the first sign that he was becoming agitated. Saunders placed the two pieces of paper back down on the table and resumed his stance with arms folded across his chest, hands tucked away out of sight – hands that Jack sensed were beginning to show a slight tremble. "I've never met any of these women before."

"But you have messaged them." Jack tapped a finger on the documents in front of him. "It says so right here."

Anthony Saunders merely shrugged. "If it says I did, then I did. But I refer you to my previous answer. I've messaged lots of women on this site. But I don't necessarily meet any of them. And I don't keep records."

Jack conceded the point. "Duly noted. It's a good job someone does though, isn't it? As soon as London Life respond to the warrant and disclose the content of these messages, I'm sure we will return to it." Both Jack and DS Cooper returned documents CC-001 to CC-003 back inside their folders. "Forensics, Mr Saunders," continued Jack, changing the subject entirely. "You have a lot of inside knowledge of police procedures with regards to the collection of forensic evidence at crime scenes, don't you??"

"Are you asking me or telling me?" Anthony Saunders remained seated with his arms folded, but began to shift slightly in his chair.

"I will rephrase." Jack noted an element of hostility creeping into the defence lawyer's tone of voice. "What is your knowledge of police procedures for the collection of forensic evidence at crime scenes?"

Anthony Saunders shrugged. "I have a basic working knowledge. It comes with the job."

"A basic knowledge, Mr Saunders?" Jack interrupted, raising an eyebrow. "I put it to you that you have a much more in depth knowledge than just the basics."

Another shrug in response. "Where are you going with this, Detective Inspector?"

"On March 18<sup>th</sup> this year you attended a conference held in Birmingham – the content of that conference was "Police procedure and the collection of crime scene evidence – the defendant's perspective.""

"Indeed I did." A darkness began to descend across Anthony Saunders's features. "Along with several hundred others."

"So you must concede that your knowledge is a little more than the basic level you intimated to us before?"

"Must I?" Anthony Saunders levelled his gaze at Jack. "If I recall correctly, the conference was a little disappointing, with nothing more than any half-decent defence lawyer would already know, or any fan of the CSI programmes on TV these days. I left early."

"But you do know how to keep a crime scene forensically clean?" Jack knew he was pushing it with this line of questioning, but as Anthony Saunders had waived his right to any legal representation, he thought it worth the risk. Anything was worth it if they could find Isabel alive.

A throaty chuckle emanated from Anthony Saunders as he shook his head from side to side. "An interesting line of questioning, detective. One that will be automatically thrown out if this goes any further. But yes, in answer to your pathetic question – obviously I am aware of what evidence can incriminate a suspect at a crime scene, and I am therefore aware of how to avoid it. Was that the answer you wanted?"

Jack glanced up at the video camera blinking in the corner of the room. Being unsure exactly who might be watching, and not wanting to attract unwanted attention, he changed his tactics.

"Isabel Faraday. How do you know her?"

* * *

Time: 1.00pm

Date: Wednesday 25<sup>th</sup> July 2012
Location: A cellar in London

Isabel had drained the last of the water from the plastic bottle some time ago. How long had he been gone? When was he coming back? Time meant nothing in this deep, dark cavern.

Isabel felt herself begin to shake. I need to get a grip, she told herself. I need to stop panicking. They will have noticed that I wasn't at the café; someone would have raised the alarm by now. Poor Dominic would have arrived for work and found that she wasn't there; the café would have been empty and locked. Isabel could imagine the panic that would have overtaken him. Surely he would have said something to someone?

Surely someone was looking for her?

\* \* \*

Time: 1.10pm
Date: Wednesday 25<sup>th</sup> July 2012
Location: Metropolitan Police HQ, London

"I met Isabel at her café – on the King's Road."

"And subsequently?"

"She came to my flat for dinner last night." Anthony Saunders unfolded his arms and leant forwards onto the wooden table. "Why?"

"When was the last time you saw Isabel Faraday?" Jack watched as the cockiness and over-confidence that had been adorning the defence lawyer's face began to slowly recede. It was replaced by an uneasy expression, a hesitant frown crossing his brow.

"When she left my flat." Anthony Saunders' voice was controlled and his tone levelled. Gone was the mocking distaste at Jack's line of questioning. "I don't know exactly, about half past eleven, maybe quarter to midnight I guess. I had had a little too much to drink. Why are you asking?"

"Isabel Faraday did not open her café this morning, and as far as we can tell she did not return home last night." Jack paused, watching the lawyer's reaction, trying to read the man behind the façade. "What can you tell us about that?"

"Nothing!" exploded Anthony Saunders, eyes that had previously been full of self-assuredness were now widened in shock. "I told you, she left to go home about half eleven, or just after."

"So you say," pressed Jack. "Were there any witnesses to that effect?"

"Witnesses?" Anthony Saunders ran a hand through his hair, visibly flustered. "What are you getting at? I thought this was about me messaging women on a dating site."

"Witnesses," repeated Jack, continuing to hold the increasingly uncomfortable looking lawyer in his stare. "Did anyone see Isabel Faraday leave your flat last night?"

"No, of course not. It was late. But she got into an Uber. I know, because she went outside to meet it."

"An Uber?" Jack frowned and looked between Saunders and DS Cooper. "What the hell is an Uber?"

"It's a taxi – they're new." DS Cooper tried to suppress the smile from his lips as he watched Jack's bemused expression. "You book them with an app on your phone."

"So, she got into a taxi, or whatever an Uber is," continued Jack, shaking his head. "You have any idea who picked her up? You have the number?"

Anthony Saunders shook his head. "No...no....she used her own phone."

"You have CCTV outside your flat?"

Another shake of the head. "No, it's never been necessary."

How convenient, thought Jack. "OK. Let's try something else." He opened his folder and slid a photograph across the table. "Tell me who is in this picture."

Anthony Saunders took a hold of the photograph, a slight tremble visible as he did so. The perspiration on his top lip remained. "That's a photograph of my wife – and my daughter."

The photograph showed a young woman with her arms lovingly enveloped around a girl of approximately eight years of age.

"And these?" Jack slid three more photographs across the table.

Anthony Saunders picked them both up, the tremble increasing in its severity. "Again, there's a photograph of my wife and I, with our daughter on a pony. Another of her at Disneyland." He traced a finger over the image of his daughter sitting next to Mickey Mouse in her favourite sweatshirt with the letter "J" emblazoned across the front. "And that one there is a photograph of my son, just after he was born."

Jack watched as the defence lawyer's face drained of colour, his ashen skin losing its tone – his eyes glassed over as the memories provoked by the photographs invaded his senses.

"Mr Saunders. Where are your wife and children now?"

* * *

Time: 6.15pm
Date: Friday 12<sup>th</sup> June 1998
Location: Arundel, West Sussex

"Jess, go to your room." His voice, deep and stern, almost caused the plates to vibrate on the dinner table.

Jess looked up from her plate, fork hovering over the as yet untouched chicken casserole. The tension in the dining room had instantly evaporated any feelings she had of hunger, the gnawing in her stomach more as a result of fear than of being empty. She glanced warily from her father's thunderous face to her mother's pensive one, her own heart quickening inside her chest.

"I said, go to your room," he repeated, emphasising each word clearly. "Now!"

Jess let the fork crash down onto her plate, specks of gravy peppering the ice-white tablecloth. She leapt from her chair and ran from the room.

She had known this was coming.

She always knew.

Dad had had "that look" on his face ever since Mum had come home from work. And when he had "that look" .... Jess shuddered and ran up the stairs, two at a time.

After mum had got home from work, Jess had excused herself and run down to the bottom of the garden, pretending to feed the chickens even though she had already fed them that morning, hoping that their clucking and scrabbling around for feed would drown out the argument that she knew would be coming.

Now up in her room, Jess could feel her father's deep-throated booming voice vibrating up through the floorboards from the dining room below. She curled up on her bed and reached for the tatty teddy bear that sat by her pillow. She hugged it tightly to her chest and began to cry.

Silent tears cascaded down her flushed cheeks, dripping onto Tatty Teddy as she pulled him closer and closer with each sob. The sound of dishes crashing to the floor beneath her made her clamp her hands over her ears and pull the duvet over her quivering body. She wanted to wrap herself up and disappear. Sobs escaped her mouth as she gulped in air in between each shudder, her pillow quickly sodden with her salty tears.

Although she was hiding underneath her duvet with her head buried under a pillow, nothing could drown out the blood-curdling scream and thud that followed.

Jess sat bolt upright in bed hardly daring to breathe.

* * *

Time: 1.20pm

Date: Wednesday 25<sup>th</sup> July 2012

Location: Metropolitan Police HQ, London

"So, where are they?" repeated Jack, watching Anthony Saunders' expression as he continued to hold the photographs in his hand. "Your wife? Your children?"

"We don't live together anymore." Anthony Saunders' reply was blunt, and he dropped the photographs back onto the table.

"We know that. That's not what I asked." Jack nodded back down at the photographs. "I want to know where they are now."

Anthony Saunders breathed in deeply and raised his gaze. "Can I have some more water, please?"

Jack felt a flash of annoyance cross his face. "In a moment. I want you to answer the question, Mr Saunders. Where are your wife and children?"

"I really need some water." Saunders averted his gaze from both Jack and the photographs. "And then maybe I need that lawyer after all."

* * *

Time: 7.30pm
Date: Friday 12<sup>th</sup> June 1998
Location: Arundel, West Sussex

Jess crept downstairs to find her father on his hands and knees clearing away the broken crockery from the dining room floor. She hovered in the doorway, unsure if she had the courage to step through. She glanced around the room.

Where was Mum?

He must have sensed her presence, because within seconds he had turned around and plastered his face with a reassuring smile. "Oh, Jess. It's you." He motioned for her to come forwards. "Mind your feet. We had a bit of a spillage."

Jess flashed a quick look at the dining table and noticed the casserole dish that had housed the homemade chicken casserole was missing – she could only assume that was what her father was attempting to clear up from the floor beneath. Large ceramic shards littered the floor, in between gooey lumps of chicken and vegetables.

Jess also noticed that the water jug and glasses lay smashed to smithereens in another corner of the room. Her father saw her shocked expression.

"Ssshhh, it's OK," he soothed, beckoning her towards him. He pushed himself up off his knees and held his arms out wide. "Come here."

Jess took a hesitant step towards her father, her terrified eyes still glancing frantically around the room.

Where was Mum?

"Sssshhhh, it's OK," he repeated, taking a step forwards, carefully sidestepping the broken casserole dish and closing the gap between them. He wrapped his arms around her shoulders and pulled her close. "Everything is all right now."

Jess stood rigidly in her father's arms.

Where was Mum?

* * *

# Chapter Twenty Eight

Time: 4.00pm
Date: Wednesday 25<sup>th</sup> July 2012
Location: Metropolitan Police HQ, London

"For the purpose of the tape, Mr Anthony Saunders now has legal representation." Jack cast his eyes across the table once they were all seated. "Please introduce yourself."

"Caroline Beachcroft – from Messrs Ogden, Peters and Staff."

Jack nodded towards the middle-aged, seasoned lawyer who sat opposite. In her early fifties, with greying fair hair clasped neatly behind in a loose bun, she had an unblemished face, adorned with a smattering of sun-kissed freckles across the bridge of her nose and cheeks. He knew Caroline. Liked her even. Knew her to be fair, with no hidden agendas. And she was smart too; she knew her stuff, and certainly knew her way around a police interview. She had been a very wise choice on behalf of Anthony Saunders. He certainly knew what he was doing.

"You have now had a lengthy break to consult with your solicitor. Before the break, we were asking you about your wife and children," began Jack, picking up where they had left off before Saunders had summonsed his lawyer. A fresh round of water, chilled this time, had furnished the table, with coffee for both Jack and Caroline Beachcroft.

"My client will not answer questions about his family, Inspector," interjected Miss Beachcroft, her voice light and crisp. "There is no relevance that has been disclosed concerning the basis of his arrest."

Jack was forced to suppress the smile that teased his lips. She was good. She was very good. He eyed Anthony Saunders across the table, noting that he refrained from catching anyone's eye and merely stared down at the table in front of him. "Then we shall move on," Jack conceded, opening the folder once more. "Mr Saunders. A further woman was found murdered in the early hours of this morning. During the break, I was informed that she has just been identified as Zoe Turner. Do you know someone by the name of Zoe Turner, Mr Saunders?"

Anthony Saunders continued staring at the table, refusing to meet Jack's eyes.

"These four women all went missing on 6th July, 12th July, 19th July and 21st July. Please tell us where you were on each of these dates. Let's start with 6th July."

Anthony Saunders raised his eyes and then turned his attention to Miss Beachcroft sitting next to him. She gave him a discreet nod, at which he returned his gaze to face Jack and DS Cooper. "I'm afraid I can't tell you; I don't know."

"It was a Friday, if that helps at all," added Jack, after consulting the folder.

Anthony Saunders's face remained impassive. He merely shook his head slowly from side to side. "I...I don't remember. Without my work diary I can't possibly...."

"Well, it's a good thing that we have already checked with your employers and got a copy of your diary, isn't it?" interrupted Jack, pulling out a piece of paper and sliding it across the table towards Anthony Saunders.

"Item reference CC-004," confirmed DS Cooper, pulling out his own copy from his folder.

"This document, Mr Saunders," continued Jack, "confirms that on the afternoon of Friday 6th July you cancelled a conference with Counsel at Pump Court Chambers, which had been due to take place at 4pm, plus a meeting with a new client beforehand at 2pm. Your employers confirm you left your office at 1.45pm. Where did you go, Mr Saunders?"

Anthony Saunders stared at the copy of his work diary entry for Friday 6<sup>th</sup> July, while Caroline Beachcroft hastily cast her eyes over the damning entries. Silence filled the stuffy interview room – the break for refreshments having done nothing to extract the stale odours of the air around them.

Jack glanced across at DS Cooper and then turned his attention back to Saunders. "Well? Where were you going that was so important that you had to cancel an important barrister's conference at such short notice and clear the rest of your diary?"

Anthony Saunders carried on shaking his head, accompanied this time by a small shrug.

"Surely you would be able to remember something like that?" pressed Jack. "It wasn't that long ago, Mr Saunders. What was so important that you had to cancel all your engagements that afternoon?"

The silence continued.

"The suspect has not provided an answer," stated DS Cooper, eyeing the tape recorder sitting at the side of the table.

"I...I just don't remember," stuttered the defence lawyer, still shaking his head. Jack noticed that Saunders was jiggling his leg up and down under the table. A sign of agitation, he mused. A sign that he is uncomfortable with this line of questioning.

A line of questioning that Jack fully intended to continue with.

"Let's try another." Jack reached back inside the folder and retrieved another document. "How about the 12<sup>th</sup> July? Where were you that day?"

Anthony Saunders looked up, eyeing the piece of paper in Jack's hand. His leg continued to jiggle uncontrollably beneath the table. He glanced at Caroline Beachcroft who, once again, gave a curt nod towards her client. He opened his mouth, then closed it again without a sound, his obviously increasing agitation not being quelled by the calming influence of his legal advisor.

"Mr Saunders? The afternoon and evening of 12<sup>th</sup> July. Where were you?" Jack paused. "Again, if it helps, it was a Thursday."

More silence.

Saunders continued to fidget in his seat, whether it was from the uncomfortable silence or the uncomfortable wooden chair, Jack could not be sure. To prolong the agony, Jack sat back in his chair and fixed the increasingly worried looking defence lawyer with his best penetrative stare. He noticed that Caroline Beachcroft was still casting her expert gaze over the extracts from Saunders' work diary, her expression giving nothing away.

Jack waited a few more seconds before deciding to turn the screw a little more.

"Again we have been in touch with your employers, and obtained a copy of your diary for the day in question." Jack nodded once more towards DS Cooper who promptly handed over another sheet of A4 paper.

"Item reference CC-005," DS Cooper announced. "Desk diary entry for Thursday 12$^{th}$ July."

Once again, the now established pantomime of Anthony Saunders staring at the diary entries and the questioning glances towards his solicitor, played out in interview room one. And Jack was happy to sit back and watch, once again leaning back in his chair and letting himself start to enjoy the now obvious displeasure that his tactics were causing.

"Where did you go? Why did you cancel your commitments again that afternoon?" Jack nodded his head towards the document on the table. "Once again, more client meetings cancelled at short notice. What was so important?" Jack's questions were met by more silence.

"Again, the suspect has not given an answer." DS Cooper reached back into his folder and passed two more documents across to Jack.

"How about 19$^{th}$ and 21$^{st}$ July? A Thursday and Saturday respectively."

"Item reference CC-006 and CC-007," confirmed DS Cooper. "Desk diary entries for both dates."

"I again ask you, Mr Saunders, to account for your movements on both of these dates." Jack tapped a finger on the copies as he slid them across the table towards Saunders and his solicitor.

The accustomed silence prevailed.

Jack could almost hear the ticking and whirring of the tiny wheels and cogs inside Anthony Saunders' head, as he either tried to remember his movements or tried to concoct a suitable sounding alibi.

Neither was forthcoming.

"As before," continued Jack, "we have approached your employers, who confirm that you cleared your diary on Thursday 19<sup>th</sup> July at short notice, without explanation, cancelling meetings. Tell us where you were, Mr Saunders."

\* \* \*

Time: 1.00pm

Date: Thursday 19<sup>th</sup> July 2012

Location: Blackfriars Road, London

Anthony Saunders glanced at his watch and then at the traffic inching, nose to tail, along the Blackfriars Road, heading towards the Thames. The heady smell of diesel fumes from the idling buses snarled up in the early afternoon traffic began to infiltrate and irritate his nostrils. He could feel a headache coming on.

The heat didn't help either. The temperature had continued to climb all day, the non-existent breeze meaning there was no respite from the incessant heat beating down onto the parched bone dry pavement beneath. Pedestrians went about their business with increasingly uncomfortable frowns on their faces, clutching bottles of water and fanning their faces with their hands.

There was no chance of hopping onto a bus, he mused, as he again took another glance at the crawling traffic. It would take too long. With a sigh he headed towards the underground station – the thought of even a short journey cooped up in a stifling carriage with tightly packed, sweaty bodies made him shudder.

But he needed to get home.

And fast.

He had things to do.

His secretary had pursed her lips when he had told her to clear his diary for the rest of the day. Again. This is becoming a bit of a habit Mr Saunders, she had muttered through her tightened jaw, peering disapprovingly at him over the rim of her spectacles. But he pushed her image from his thoughts and concentrated on negotiating the steps down into the Southwark underground entrance.

* * *

Time: 4.30pm
   Date: Wednesday 25th July 2012
   Location: Metropolitan Police HQ, London

"Tell me about your wardrobe, Mr Saunders," continued Jack, returning the extracts from the lawyer's work diary to his folder.

"My wardrobe?" Anthony Saunders stared blankly at Jack. "What about my wardrobe?"

"The one in your bedroom with all the shoes in it." Jack was passed a photograph from DS Cooper's folder, and slid it across the table. The photograph showed multiple shelves stacked full of shoes in a variety of styles and colours.

"Item reference CC-008," announced DS Cooper, taking out an identical copy for himself.

Anthony Saunders continued to stare blankly down at the photograph.

"Tell me why you have so many pairs of women's shoes in your wardrobe, Mr Saunders."

"Relevance, Inspector?" Caroline Beachcroft peered closely at the photograph, a frown crossing her freckled face. "How is this connected with the murder of four women, the basis of your arrest of my client?"

Jack took in a deep breath. They had managed to keep the fact of a shoe being found at each murder location out of the press so far. A feat in itself considering the propensity to internal leaks springing up sporadically during even the lowest profile investigations. But Isabel was still missing, and potentially alive, so Jack considered now was the time to place all their evidence on the table. Plus, Caroline Beachcroft was no pushover; unless they divulged the relevance of their line of questioning she would advise her client not to answer.

"A shoe was left at each scene by the killer," confirmed Jack. "A shoe belonging to the next victim. *That* is the relevance of the shoes, Miss Beachcroft."

"This is new information, Inspector. You haven't disclosed this in any of the press releases so far and you didn't disclose it as part of the discovery when I arrived today." Caroline Beachcroft raised her head and fixed her pale blue eyes on Jack. "How do we know this is even true?"

As much as Jack liked and respected Caroline Beachcroft, he was starting to become irritated. He reached for his coffee, but realised that it had now become tepid with a film of stagnant milk on the surface. Instead he turned his attention back to the defence solicitor across the table.

"As you will be well aware, Miss Beachcroft, certain details, *pertinent* details, during a murder investigation can and are often kept out of the press for operational reasons." Jack opened the folder and took out a series of four photographs, each depicting an abandoned shoe at one of the crime scenes.

"Item reference CC-009 to 012," confirmed DS Cooper, handing out identical copies.

"These shoes were found at the sites of the discovery of the bodies of Patricia Gordon, Georgina Dale, Hannah Fuller and now also Zoe Turner this morning. So my question still stands, Mr Saunders. Why have you got a wardrobe full of women's shoes?" Jack tapped a finger on each of the photographs, feeling his pulse rate quickening. "I need an answer."

* * *

Time: 1.45pm
Date: Thursday 19<sup>th</sup> July 2012
Location: Buckingham Street, Embankment, London

Anthony Saunders breathed a sigh of relief as he climbed the steps to his flat. He was on time. The tube journey had been just as horrific as he had anticipated - hot, stuffy, and smelly. He had shared a far too intimate space with a heavy-set man covered in body hair and tattoos; neither of which ordinarily bothered him, except the dense covering of body hair was a haven for odour heavy droplets of sweat to be captured, releasing their toxins freely into the enclosed carriage space. Mixed with the stomach churning aroma of greasy, fried chicken and onions that had been left behind in a discarded takeaway box, Anthony Saunders couldn't wait to be released into the relative fresh air of the ground above.

He reached the entrance to his flat and couldn't open the door quickly enough, shuddering at the memory of the tube journey. Once inside, he wrenched off his sweat sodden shirt and tie, wriggled out of his suit trousers and underwear, and headed straight for the bathroom. Leaving his clothes strewn across the floor, he stepped into the shower and turned the dial to cool.

A few minutes later, cleansed and freshened, he gathered up his discarded clothes and rammed them straight into the washing basket. He padded through to the front room with a towel wrapped around his waist, letting the last of the shower's water droplets dry naturally on his skin.

Just at that moment the doorbell buzzed. He picked up the intercom and immediately pressed the button releasing the main door.

At last.

He had been waiting for this all week.

A short, sharp rap on his front door followed, and Saunders pulled it open to take delivery of the large parcel that had been manhandled through the entrance by a frazzled and pink-cheeked delivery man.

"Parcel for Saunders," the man announced, breathlessly, from behind the parcel.

"Sure thing, thanks." Saunders took the parcel from the grateful delivery man, scribbled a rough signature on the proffered delivery note, and backed away towards his front room.

His eyes gleamed.

This was the one he had been waiting for.

This was the one that was going to make all the difference.

He skilfully sliced through the parcel tape using a knife that he had abandoned on his breakfast plate earlier that morning. Folding out the flaps of cardboard, Anthony Saunders' face glowed with delight. He reached inside and picked out an elegant ruby red stiletto, the ankle straps adorned with diamond-like stones.

They were exquisite.

They were perfect.

* * *

Time: 4.45pm
Date: Wednesday 25<sup>th</sup> July 2012
Location: Metropolitan Police HQ, London

Anthony Saunders buried his face in his hands, and a shuddering sigh escaped his mouth. He tried to suppress the sobs that were gathering in his throat, but it was a battle he was always going to lose.

The time had come.

He would have to explain.

He would have to tell all.

He had no choice.

Raising his head, he breathed in the deepest breath he could muster and settled his focus on Jack. Slowly, he gave a nod.

"Ok, I can explain." Saunders' voice was shaky, and he nervously wrung his hands together in his lap. "I know I've done wrong, and that it may have consequences for me."

Jack and DS Cooper exchanged an expectant look. Were they now about to finally get their long awaited confession?

"I've done wrong, I admit," continued Saunders, locking eyes with Jack across the table. "But I'm no killer." He paused again, taking in another deep breath. "I really have never met any of those women. And Isabel really did leave my flat alive and well last night. I swear."

\* \* \*

Time: 11.35pm
   Date: Tuesday 24<sup>th</sup> July 2012
   Location: Buckingham Street, Embankment, London

Isabel hovered over the threshold of the door to flat number 1b. She felt a little tipsy from the wine they had drunk, and then the "one for the road" brandy afterwards. She swayed a little as she stepped back into her shoes and smothered a giggle behind her hand.

"Oops," she laughed, steadying herself against the door frame.

"Let me." Anthony Saunders knelt down and gently buckled the ankle straps around Isabel's slim ankles. "These really are lovely shoes."

"Well, thank you, kind Sir," Isabel chuckled, straightening her shoulder bag across her chest.

"Thank you for coming," replied Saunders, the smile on his lips triggering the boyish dimple on his chin. "I had a great time."

"Me too," smiled Isabel, her cheeks colouring as she tucked a stray lock of hair behind her ear. "Dinner was lovely."

"Are you sure you don't want me to wait outside with you?" Anthony motioned towards the door. "When is your taxi coming?"

Isabel glanced down at her phone. "It says it's two minutes away. I'll be fine." She turned on her heels and began to totter across the flagstone hallway.

"Well, if you're sure." Anthony gave another dimple-smile and watched as Isabel carefully made her way past the stairs, holding onto the banister as she did so - the red wine still having its effect. "Call me sometime."

Isabel raised a hand in reply, concentrating on putting one foot in front of the other. The evening had been great, the food and wine had been divine; the company, she had to shyly admit, had been even better. The last thing she wanted to do was round off such a perfect evening by turning a somersault and landing in an ungracious heap.

She pulled open the outside door and felt the welcome rush of cool evening air hit her face. Carefully stepping over the front step, she glanced back down at her phone to check the location of her taxi.

"Damn," she muttered, as the screen suddenly turned to black. "And now you choose to die on me." She pressed a few random buttons in the hope of injecting some hidden power, but all they did was confirm to her that her battery had died.

She stepped out onto the pavement outside the converted Ernest Baker Grain Merchants building, and looked along the road to where she hoped she would see the taxi emerging in a moment or two. The evening air was balmy and she quietly hummed, happily, to herself as she waited.

It wasn't long before two headlights approached from the end of the road and headed in her direction.

\* \* \*

Time: 5.30pm
Date: Wednesday 25<sup>th</sup> July 2012
Location: Metropolitan Police HQ, London

"Interview recommenced with Anthony Saunders at seventeen thirty." DS Cooper started the tape recording.

After requesting a short break to consult with his solicitor, Anthony

Saunders returned to his seat and nodded he was ready to continue. A fresh cup of water was placed in front of him, from which he took a sip and cleared his throat.

"I swear. She got into that taxi."

"But you didn't actually see her, did you?" Jack eyed the defence lawyer across the table. "You weren't actually outside with her."

"No," admitted Anthony Saunders, glumly. "She left my flat and the last I saw of her was when she stepped outside to wait for her taxi."

Jack nodded. A search of Isabel's phone records had confirmed her last location was Buckingham Street when the battery had died or the phone had been switched off. The last activity on her phone had been accessing the Uber website. In the last ten minutes, DC Cassidy had checked with the taxi company and they had confirmed one of their drivers had shown up at Flat 1b, but there had been nobody at the address to pick up. After waiting for a few minutes, they put it down to a crank call and the taxi was reallocated elsewhere.

"Ok, go on." Jack nodded at Saunders to continue.

"The shoes; I can explain the shoes. It's not what you think." Saunders paused and drew in another deep breath. "I buy and sell women's shoes. Larger sizes for the transgender and transvestite community. I have a website."

"Details, Mr Saunders." Jack motioned to DS Cooper to take a note of the address.

"Um, its *www.biggershoes.co.uk*." Saunders again buried his head in his hands, his shoulders shuddering as he fought back the tears that were again threatening to engulf him. "I know this is going to mean trouble for me. And my father...he...." Saunders broke off, shaking his head. "God knows what my father will say. But I swear to you, that is all I do with the shoes."

Jack frowned. "Why will buying and selling larger sized women's shoes mean trouble for you, Mr Saunders? As far as I know, that hasn't been made illegal."

Anthony Saunders glanced up at Caroline Beachcroft by his side, and she again gave a small nod, giving her silent permission for her client to answer.

"I may not buy them from the most authorised of channels."

"Meaning?" probed Jack, although he thought he knew what the answer would be.

"OK, so some may be stolen." Saunders hung his head.

"Some?" Jack raised his eyebrows.

"OK, so most of them."

Jack exhaled loudly and caught DS Cooper's eye. They both looked down at the photograph from Saunders' wardrobe.

And then the penny dropped.

It had stared them in the face and they had both been blind enough to miss it.

Pairs of shoes.

*Pairs.*

Anthony Saunders wasn't their man.

"But, why, Mr Saunders?" Jack rubbed his chin, pushing away the ever increasing sense of panic within. "You're a successful defence lawyer; you work in a prestigious law firm in central London. You must be pushing a pretty decent salary. You come from a privileged and moneyed background. Your father...."

"Yes, I know who my father is," interrupted Saunders, hotly. "You don't need to tell me."

"So why?" Jack shook his head, standing his ground in his line of questioning. "I don't follow. Why would you get involved in this kind of business on the side; buying and selling stolen goods? What is worth taking such a risk for?"

Anthony Saunders avoided both Jack's and DS Cooper's penetrating stares, and instead he reached for the pile of evidence that had slowly been accumulating on the table in front of him. He leafed through the documents and placed some to the side. Spreading the rest out on the table, he selected the series of photographs showing his daughter riding the pony, sitting on the bench at Disneyland and the one of his newborn son.

"Them," replied Saunders, his voice barely above a whisper. "I do it for them."

* * *

Time: 8.00pm
    Date: Tuesday 24<sup>th</sup> July 2012
    Location: Buckingham Street, Embankment, London

"I'm sorry," breathed Isabel, softly, taking another sip of Merlot. "I didn't mean to upset you."

Anthony Saunders shook his head and hastily wiped away a solitary tear that was sliding down one cheek. "No, I'm the one that's sorry. I'm being all soppy and maudlin and we're meant to be having a good time!" He raised his wine glass and took a large mouthful of the deep burgundy wine, thankful for the intoxicating and anaesthetic effect of the alcohol. He had drunk more since the children had been born; a lot more.

"Well, I'm sorry anyway," repeated Isabel, giving what she hoped was a sympathetic smile in his direction. "She looks really pretty."

Anthony nodded, and let his eyes fall onto the photograph Isabel had been looking at - his beaming daughter riding on a pony.

"She loved ponies – always did from when she was small. Still does." He smiled at the memory that seeped into his thoughts. "And despite her condition, and her problems, we did everything we could to make her feel like any other child; to give her the same experiences and opportunities."

Isabel felt a frown forming. Her condition? Her problems? She looked once again at the photograph on the bookcase, this time looking more closely and more intently than her earlier cursory glance had allowed. And it was then that she saw it.

She still saw the same happy, grinning child sitting astride a brown and white pony, an unmistakable look of glee on her heart-shaped face – but what Isabel hadn't seen the first time around were the callipers on her legs, and the small, thin tube leading to her nostrils. Isabel followed the tubing to an oxygen cylinder being supported in the crook of her father's arm.

Both parents, one either side, had steadying hands around their daughter's waist, helping her to sit high and proud atop her pony.

Just like any other child.

Isabel felt her eyes begin to swim with newly forming tears. As she silently brushed them away, she watched as Anthony's face crumpled around the edges with the still evident pain and emotion washing over him, yet his eyes were still full of love in amongst his own watery tears.

Letting her gaze drift across to the next photograph, Isabel again looked at the picture showing a slightly older girl of teenage years, sitting on the bench next to Mickey Mouse. At first glance, she had assumed it was merely a family photograph taken whilst on holiday in Disneyland – which it was. Except a closer look this time revealed much more than that. Much much more.

The girl in the photograph has the same heart-shaped face - the same warming smile beaming out towards the camera. Her teeth now sported braces, but the same hazel eyes twinkled with intense glee and happiness. Isabel looked more closely, and again saw the same callipers on her legs, the same oxygen tank attached to tubing that curled across the "J" on her sweatshirt, delivering oxygen to her nostrils.

Mickey Mouse was sitting closely up against her, close enough to offer the teenager the support she needed in keeping upright on the bench.

"Cerebral palsy." Anthony answered the unspoken question on Isabel's lips. "It was a traumatic birth. The cord was wrapped tightly around her neck. Her brain was deprived of oxygen for too long; she suffered severe birth asphyxia."

"I'm so sorry." Isabel didn't know what else to say, the words seeming so insufficient.

"She needs twenty-four-hour care. She lives with her mother." Anthony took another long swig from his wine glass. "We separated when she was small."

Isabel choked back the fresh tears that were forming and she, too, settled on another slug of wine. Across the top of her wine glass, she watched as Anthony got up and out of his chair, and refreshed both of their glasses with the rest of the Merlot. Before returning to his seat, he reached up to the shelf above and brought down another photograph that Isabel hadn't seen on her first inquisitive sweep of the room.

Sitting back down, Anthony held the photograph in his hands for a moment, silence filling the space between them. Isabel watched as the pain intensified across his features. Clearing his throat, he handed the photograph across to her.

"Sonny. He was Jasmine's twin brother."

Isabel brought a hand up to her mouth to stifle the gasp that was about to emerge.

"He also had the cord wrapped around him – but he didn't make it." Anthony's voice caught, and the rush of tears that he had been successfully damming up until now broke though. "Jasmine was born first, and they managed to resuscitate her. But by the time they got to Sonny..." He broke off for more Merlot to take away the pain. "This is our only picture of him."

Isabel glanced back down at the photograph in her hands and noted the tiny baby wrapped tightly in a blue blanket. He was firmly swaddled with just his face visible; his perfectly formed tiny face, eyes closed as if in peaceful slumber.

A slumber from which he would never wake.

Isabel rose from her seat and crossed over to where Anthony was slumped in his chair, placing a comforting arm around his shoulders.

"I'm so sorry," she repeated, once again. "I'm so sorry."

* * *

Time: 5.45pm
Date: Wednesday 25th July 2012
Location: Metropolitan Police HQ, London

"With Jasmine needing twenty-four-hour care, it doesn't come cheap." Anthony Saunders stared vacantly down at the photograph on the table.

"They live in the States. Nothing comes cheap over there. My wife – she's American. When we split, she went back home and took Jasmine with her. Hydrotherapy really helps with her mobility. But it's expensive. That's why I set up the website to try and earn something extra to help pay for all her medical bills."

Silence hung like a noose in the stale air of the interview room. Jack's mouth was devoid of words, and a quick glance across at DS Cooper beside him confirmed that his sergeant was equally as moved. DS Cooper passed Jack his mobile phone, logged into the *www.biggershoes.co.uk* website.

Across the table, Caroline Beachcroft dabbed at the corners of her eyes.

"Interview terminated at seventeen forty-five." Jack motioned for DS Cooper to turn off the tape recording. "Mr Saunders, you are free to go."

* * *

Time: 6.00pm
  Date: Wednesday 25<sup>th</sup> July 2012
  Location: A cellar in London

He cautiously shouldered open the heavy oak door and peered into the inky blackness beyond. He had left her for longer than he had intended, but events of the day had been spiralling. As he pushed the rest of the door open, a shaft of light illuminated a strip of the cellar floor, catching the edge of her mattress.

He could see a faint bundle at the far end, up against the wall. The metal chain from the radiator was pulled tight. She had been trying to push herself into the farthest corner of the room again, as far away from reality as possible.

They had all tried to do that, he mused.

But it didn't make any difference in the end.

He stepped forwards, his soft-soled shoes making no sound on the stone floor. He noticed the water bottle was empty and on its side by the end of the mattress, and it looked like she had at least tried to eat some of the sandwich.

Good girl.

Carol was finally starting to listen.

He brought a hand up to the side of his cheek where there were several red marks starting to show. Carol had been quite feisty when he had got her inside the car; when she had realised that she was not going home. That was most unlike her. Carol did not normally show such physical strength towards him. It was something he was going to have to watch – and control.

He placed the thin twine and masking tape that he had been carrying down by the side of the discarded water bottle, and bent down onto his knees. The others hadn't needed to be subdued like this – they had been good girls, compliant.

But this one was different.

* * *

Time: 6.05pm
Date: Wednesday 25th July 2012
Location: Metropolitan Police HQ, London

"Where is DS Carmichael?" Jack shot down the corridor leading away from the interview rooms. "He's got some explaining to do."

DC Cassidy, who had been viewing the interview from the room next door via a two-way mirror, quickened her stride into a jog to keep up. "He's not here, Guv."

Jack came to an abrupt halt, causing DC Cassidy to almost run into the back of him. "What do you mean he's not here? We're in the middle of a murder investigation."

DC Cassidy shrugged, a worried look crossing her face. "He left soon after the break; when the solicitor arrived – once you started interviewing Saunders again. I....I don't know where he's gone."

"Jesus," muttered Jack, glancing at his watch and running a hand through his hair. "Everything goes belly up and he's nowhere to be seen. Arresting Saunders had been his idea, you know. He was the one pressing for it, convincing us all we had the right guy."

DC Cassidy merely nodded, unsure what she should say. They carried on along the corridor and just as they were approaching the main reception area, DS Cooper caught up with them from behind.

"Boss? Chief Superintendent King wants to see you."

"I bet he does," muttered Jack, knowing that the catastrophic farce that had just been played out in the interview room would have already been brought to the senior officer's attention. News like that never did take long to spread.

"Should we ring him?" asked DC Cassidy, bringing out her phone. "DS Carmichael, I mean. Find out where he is?"

Jack shook his head. "No, it's late. Leave him be. Wherever he is." He held the door open for both DC Cassidy and DS Cooper to walk ahead of him. "If I speak to him now I don't think I'll be responsible for my actions. He'd just better show his face tomorrow. You two get yourselves off home; there's nothing more we can do tonight."

\* \* \*

Time: 7.30pm
  Date: Wednesday 25<sup>th</sup> July 2012
  Location: A cellar in London

She had been surprisingly docile and compliant.
  The sedative in the water bottle had been a good idea.
  He glanced back down at the limp form stretched out on the mattress,

and placed the thin blanket over the top, tucking it in around the edges. It could get quite chilly down here at night time, despite the hot weather. And Carol always felt the cold.

He picked up the masking tape and remains of the twine, and backed away towards the door. Carol would sleep peacefully for a while now. As he reached the door and turned to head back up the stairs, he passed the empty mattress opposite and frowned.

He needed a new Jess.

* * *

# Chapter Twenty Nine

Time: 9.00pm
  Date: Wednesday 25th July 2012
  Location: Kettle's Yard Mews, London

Mac handed Jack another bottle of ice-cold Budweiser and sank down onto the sofa next to him. "I won't be able to sleep tonight, Jack. Not while she's still out there." Mac's voice cracked and he took another slug of beer to mask it.

Join the club, thought Jack.

"I don't think many of us will be sleeping tonight, Stu. You can crash here if you want. I'll be up early; I need to go and see the Chief Superintendent first thing. And that won't be pretty." Jack had avoided the repeated messages from Dougie King and managed to slip away from the station unnoticed. But he was going to have to face the music in the morning, that was for sure. The thought gnawed away at his insides.

Mac nodded, rolling the cool beer bottle across his forehead. "Thanks, Jack. But I feel I should be out there, you know, looking for her."

Jack shook his head. "We have officers on patrol all night. We're doing everything we can to find her." He heard his own empty promises echoing around the flat and took a mouthful of beer, momentarily closing his eyes. Had he really just said that banal statement out loud? The text book standard response you always gave to the worried family. "We're doing everything we can." It sounded so lame. So inadequate. So meaningless.

And it was.

"It really wasn't Saunders then?" Mac downed the rest of his beer in a second gulp. "Despite everything?"

"Nope." Jack gave another shake of his head. "He looked good for it on paper, but...there was always something about him that didn't quite fit. If I'd been more on my game..."

"Not your fault, Jack. You and your team, you've all been working like dogs on this...everyone can see that."

Everyone maybe except Chief Superintendent King, thought Jack.

"I just need to be able to do something. I hate just waiting around." Mac got up and padded back over to the fridge, pulling two more beers out. "I can't go to work. I can't go home. I can't do anything."

"Just stay here; keep your phone switched on. If she calls anyone, she'll most probably call you." Jack drained his bottle and accepted the fresh one.

"Me?" Mac sat back down on the sofa. "I doubt she'll call me, Jack."

"You think? Of course she would. You two are close; you'd be her first choice. You've been through such a lot together."

Mac could feel his eyes moistening. He turned away from his brother, blinking rapidly, and tried to shift the sob that was caught in his throat.

"I know how you feel about her, Stu," added Jack, his voice as still and soft as the sultry evening air outside. "It's obvious."

Mac leant forwards, elbows on his knees, still avoiding looking at Jack. "Yeah well, she's not likely to feel the same, is she? Not about me."

Jack frowned, and tried to catch Mac's eye. "I don't see why not."

Mac gave a throaty chuckle and turned his head. "You don't know why not? Why would someone like Isabel be even remotely interested in someone like me?"

"What do you mean – 'someone like me'?"

Mac shook his head and swallowed another mouthful of Budweiser. "Let's face it, Jack. I'm hardly the best prospect, am I? I've got a string of convictions, spent more time in young offenders institutions than I care to admit. Time in adult prison. I'm not exactly ticking all the boxes, am I?"

"That's all in the past, Stu. You were young. You've straightened yourself out now."

"But I'm damaged, Jack." Mac paused and hung his head. "I'm damaged."

"She doesn't see you like that. And neither do I."

"Yeah, well I do. It makes me ashamed…. of what I used to be." Mac paused, rolling the beer bottle between his palms. "Do you remember that day? In court? When I got sent down for the first time?"

Jack nodded, slowly. "Of course I remember."

"You want to know why I didn't look at you? The whole time, through the whole trial, I never once acknowledged you?" Mac paused, another lump forming in his throat. "I was ashamed, Jack. I was a hot-headed kid who thought he knew better than everyone. I gave the impression that I didn't care, Jack. But I was just ashamed. I couldn't look you in the eye because I was ashamed."

\* \* \*

Time: 3.30pm

Date: 31st October 1982

Location: Bournemouth Crown Court, Dorset

"All rise."

The Court Usher solemnly announced the return of His Honour Judge Charles Trowbridge. The wooden seats creaked as everyone in Court number two at Bournemouth Crown Court obediently got to their feet.

The judge shuffled in from the door that led to his chambers and sat heavily down in his seat behind the raised bench. He peered down over his horn-rimmed spectacles that perched on the end of his bulbous nose. Pale blue eyes peered out from behind the lenses. He gave a curt nod to the sea of heads in front of him, some bearing wigs, others not, and everyone obligingly sat down. Except for the defendants in the dock.

Jack resumed his seat with the others in the public gallery, flanked on one side by his foster mother, Mary, who gave his hand a reassuring squeeze. He had sat through every minute of the five-day trial, listening to the evidence that was going to spell the end of the life for his brother as he knew it.

"Members of the jury – will the foreman please stand." The Court Usher turned towards the twelve members of the jury, nodding as a gentleman from the front row got to his feet. "For each of the defendants, have you reached a verdict upon which you are all agreed?"

The foreman of the jury gave a slow nod. "We have."

The Court Usher then turned towards the four defendants standing in the dock. "In respect of the defendant Jason Alcock, on the charge of robbery, do you find the defendant guilty or not guilty?"

"Guilty."

"In respect of the defendant Jason Alcock, on the additional charge of manslaughter, do you find the defendant guilty or not guilty?"

"Guilty."

"In respect of the defendant, Stephen Byers, on the charge of robbery, do you find the defendant guilty, or not guilty?"

"Guilty."

"In respect of the defendant Kyle Williams, on the charge of robbery, do you find the defendant guilty, or not guilty?"

"Guilty."

"And in respect of the defendant Stuart MacIntosh, on the charge of robbery, do you find the defendant guilty, or not guilty?"

Jack held his breath.

But he knew what was going to be said before he actually heard the fateful word.

"Guilty."

Jack felt his stomach lurch, and the grip his foster mother had on his hand tightened. He felt hot tears pricking at the corners of his eyes, but he used his free hand to rub them furiously away. He mustn't cry. He told Stu that he wouldn't cry.

Jack watched as all four defendants remained standing in the dock. The jury were dismissed and thanked by the Judge for their dedication and professionalism over the last five days. His Honour Judge Trowbridge then turned towards the front bench of lawyers who were now all on their feet, wigs bobbing up and down in synchronicity.

The judge held up a hand to quieten the throng. "Jason Alcock, Stephen Byers, Kyle Williams, Stuart MacIntosh. You have all been found guilty of the crime of robbery – contrary to Section 8(1) of the Theft Act 1968. In addition, Jason Alcock – you alone have been charged and found guilty of the offence of manslaughter, contrary to common law. I will be deferring sentence for probation reports to be prepared on each of you. However." The judge paused and peered at each defendant in turn over the lenses on his spectacles. "I must warn you that the offences of manslaughter and robbery are serious crimes. You were sent for trial at the Crown Court due to the seriousness of these offences. And therefore it is certain that only a custodial sentence will be passed." He then turned his attention to the wigged lawyers still on their feet in front of him. "I trust there will be no applications for bail?"

It was more of a statement than a question; and not a question that the judge expected an answer to.

"Take them down." His Honour Judge Charles Trowbridge nodded at the security personnel flanking the defendants.

Jack craned his neck from his seat in the public gallery, straining to catch a glimpse of his brother before he disappeared. But try as he might to gain his attention, Stuart MacIntosh refused to raise his head, keeping his eyes cast downwards to the floor. He shuffled in line behind his three co-defendants, and disappeared from sight.

\* \* \*

Time: 9.15pm

Date: Wednesday 25<sup>th</sup> July 2012
Location: Kettle's Yard Mews, London

"You did your time, Stu. I know Isabel doesn't think anything less of you because of it." Jack wished he could turn back the clock and have forced his brother onto a different path - any path except the one that he took. "You just fell in with the wrong crowd – boys from that foster home. It was inevitable where it would lead."

"Didn't stop me though, did it?" Mac shook his head, a rueful smile crossing his lips. "I knew they were bad news. But at the time I didn't care. And to be honest, being banged up – even in that youth detention place – was better than that foster home." Mac took another large mouthful of beer to take away the memories.

"You were lucky only one of you got charged with manslaughter, though," added Jack. "The prosecution didn't seek to get you all under the joint enterprise law, which they could have. Easily. I'm surprised they didn't, to be honest."

Mac shrugged. "I don't feel lucky, Jack. That place taught me all I needed to know about crime – even when I got out I didn't stop."

Fair point, thought Jack.

"But, Isabel, Jack." Mac looked up and held his brother's gaze. "You have to find her. You just have to."

"I will, Stu. I promise."

A promise I hope I can keep, mused Jack, finishing off his bottle.

\* \* \*

Time: 10.45pm
Date: Wednesday 25<sup>th</sup> July 2012
Location: Metropolitan Police HQ, London

DS Cooper rubbed his eyes and forced his blurred vision to refocus on the screen in front of him. Again, the lights in the tech room were dimmed, giving the place a calm and serene feel. But DS Cooper was feeling anything but calm and serene. Isabel had been missing for almost twenty-four hours now and, with the release of Anthony Saunders, they were back to square one.

Where was she?

DS Cooper navigated the screen and again pulled up the CCTV images for all four victim locations. The images had been viewed countless times, but he couldn't help but feel that there must be another clue somewhere. Anywhere.

So far, the only credible lead the CCTV images had thrown up had been the black transit van with cloned plates. The registered owner of the Peugeot, the true owner of the registration plates, had been interviewed. A seventy-six-year-old partially sighted gentleman from Manchester, who was now bedbound after a recent stroke, was quickly eliminated from the enquiry. Whoever had cloned his registration plates wasn't known to him.

DS Cooper brought up the images of the black transit van and watched its progress, in slow motion, approaching the location of Hyde Park. No matter how many times they had enlarged the images, or looked at the van from other angles, there was no way of seeing into it. Whoever was inside remained hidden from view.

DS Cooper sighed and let the images play out. He had watched them so many times that he could now remember and recite the vehicle sequences in his sleep. The grainy progression played out before him once again. The black transit van passed by the location and turned right at the junction ahead, disappearing from view. ANPR checks had followed its route out of London and then lost it somewhere east of Oxford.

Just then, something caught DS Cooper's attention and caused his heart to momentarily flutter in his chest. What was that? He reached for the mouse and started the CCTV sequence from the beginning once again. The usual progression of vehicles commenced – the white Ford, followed by the dark BMW, then the mini with two motorbikes in close proximity behind. A gap then until the ambulance came into view, followed by the black transit van with the cloned plates. Once the transit van had turned right, the next vehicles to enter the CCTV screen were the Land Rover followed by the VW Golf. All as expected. All checked out and eliminated, other than the stolen black transit van.

But this time DS Cooper had noticed something that had escaped him before. A slight flicker on the screen as the vehicles moved through the sequence. So slight it was almost undetectable.

But it was there.

DS Cooper rewound the scenes once again and noted the clock in the lower right hand corner of the screen giving the timings for the images. He let the scene play out one more time, finishing with the Land Rover and VW Golf.

And there is was.

Again.

The clock had jumped forwards by approximately one-hour in-between the Land Rover and the VW Golf passing through the camera.

There could only be one explanation.

* * *

Time: 11.00pm
Date: Wednesday 25$^{th}$ July 2012
Location: Kettle's Yard Mews, London

Jack rose from the sofa and collected the empty Budweiser bottles from the coffee table. Stuart had managed to sink a fair few before passing out, and Jack couldn't really blame him. He watched his brother's sleeping form, curled up at one end of the sofa - mouth open and a faint snore rumbling from his nostrils. Hopefully he would sleep all night – putting off the nightmare that would greet them both in the morning.

Despite craving sleep, Jack hadn't felt like drinking – waving away the third bottle Stuart had offered him. He needed to keep himself alert, and alcohol would not be his friend tonight.

He padded over to the sink and placed the empty bottles in a bin bag. Just then, his mobile phone began to ring. Returning to the sofa where he had left it, Jack noticed that the ring tone had failed to disturb the sleeping Stuart.

"Yep," answered Jack, noticing DS Cooper's name flashing up on the screen. "What's up?"

\* \* \*

Time: 11.45pm

Date: Wednesday 25<sup>th</sup> July 2012

Location: Metropolitan Police HQ, London

Jack threw the door open and hurried into the tech room. "Cooper, show me what you've got." He grabbed a chair and sat down.

DS Cooper quickly navigated the screen with the mouse and brought up the first set of grainy CCTV images.

"I was running through the images, looking for the black transit van, when I spotted it. Hyde Park on the evening of 20<sup>th</sup> July. The images run through as expected until 21.04." DS Cooper let the screen play out before them, pausing the last image at precisely 21.04. "The last vehicle to pass through is a Land Rover. Registration BM09 AVW." He nodded at the screen and Jack saw the aforementioned vehicle steadily trekking across the camera's view. "But when I resume the recording, note the time in the bottom right hand corner."

Jack's gaze flickered to the digital clock in the corner of the screen and gave a quick nod for DS Cooper to continue the sequence. As DS Cooper clicked the mouse, and the screen jumped into life with the VW Golf jerkily crossing the scene, Jack saw the time jump – to 22.05.

"Show me again, without the pause."

DS Cooper rewound the images and let them play. Once the VW Golf had exited the screen, he paused the images. "So, as you can see, we have an hour of missing footage between the Land Rover and the VW Golf."

"Plausible explanation?" Jack could almost feel the colour draining from his face as he asked the question.

"It's possible there could have been a technical problem with the camera," began DS Cooper, closing down the CCTV images for location two.

"But?" Jack could sense there was a but coming. He knew his DS too well. Cooper would not have called him so late at night to tell him one of the CCTV cameras was faulty.

"But, after seeing that, I went back and looked at the CCTV for the other locations too."

Jack almost didn't need to ask. "And?"

"There is missing footage on all of them." DS Cooper paused, navigating more CCTV images on the screen in front of them. "I'm no technical expert, boss, but looks to me like someone has been deleting evidence."

\* \* \*

# Chapter Thirty

Time: 7.30am

Date: Thursday 26th July 2012

Location: Metropolitan Police HQ, London

Chief Superintendent Dougie King forcibly threw the newspaper onto his desk, narrowly missing a tumbler of ice cold water. Jack felt himself flinch.

"Jesus, Jack," he breathed, easing himself back into his chair and nodding at Jack to take a seat. But Jack remained standing. "It's all over the front page."

Jack nodded, eyeing the front page of the Daily Mail and Jonathan Spearing's exclusive report on the wrongful arrest of a prominent London defence lawyer. "Yes, Sir."

"You told me he was our man," continued the Chief Superintendent, turning his head away from the newspaper print. "You both stood right there before me, and swore blind that he was our killer."

Jack hung his head and lowered his eyes to the floor. He could almost physically see the frustration and disappointment seeping out of the Chief Superintendent. He had no words to justify their actions; no words to explain the almighty cock-up that occurred under his watch. It wouldn't serve any purpose to mention how he had had his own doubts at the time, how he knew there was something wrong with Anthony Saunders being their man. It was his investigation. He was the senior officer. He was in charge. And he had given his backing to the arrest.

And now look where it had gotten them.

"Tomorrow, Jack," continued the Chief Superintendent. "Tomorrow is the Opening Ceremony. And I've promised that we will have the killer in custody before then. Please tell me you have a plan B?"

"I know." Jack found his voice. "And we're working round the clock, I promise." Jack knew it was a feeble and empty gesture, but he didn't really have anything else to give.

"This has created such a back-lash upstairs, Jack. Thankfully I'm having dinner tonight with the Rt Honourable Bernard Saunders QC, our wrongly accused's father. And he is not a happy man, Jack. Not a happy man at all. Hopefully I will be able to smooth things over a little and repair the damage that has already been done. Prevent any future embarrassment. But it is not going to be pretty." Chief Superintendent Dougie King exhaled loudly again and closed his weary eyes. "I need you to get the right man, Jack. And fast."

"Sir."

"But first, you need to warn this reporter off." Chief Superintendent King pushed himself out of his chair and started pacing behind his desk, coming to a halt by the window. He gazed out at the more than uninspiring view of the rear staff car park. "I don't know where he is getting his information from, but this needs to stop. Now."

Jack nodded. "I'll have a word." His eyes fell to the newspaper still sitting on the Chief Superintendent's desk - the newspaper report that had leaked the fact that the killer was leaving shoes at the scenes of his crimes; taunting the police. Staying one step ahead.

"Make sure you do." The Chief Superintendent turned back to face Jack across his desk. "I can't have the Daily Mail printing things that not even our own officers are party to. The shoes at the scenes – that was evidence we were suppressing. If there's a leak, Jack, you need to plug it. And quickly."

"Sir." Jack knew Jonathan Spearing relatively well. They had had their run-ins in the past, but he was a decent reporter. He was old school and respected the work of the police, most of the time. If he was receiving information from a source within his own team, Jack needed to get to the bottom of it. And in the words of the Chief Superintendent, he needed to do it fast.

"He's still out there, Jack." Chief Superintendent King tapped the glass in the window frame with the tip of his finger. "Our killer. It's embarrassing enough to have arrested the son of a prominent QC. It's not like you to be so off your game, Jack. You need to pull this all together." He paused and turned back to hold Jack in his gaze. "Our killer is still out there in my city, Jack. And I need you to find him."

* * *

Time: 8.00am
Date: Thursday 26<sup>th</sup> July 2012
Location: Metropolitan Police HQ, London

"I'll go." DS Carmichael held up a hand, silencing any protests. "I'll go and warn off the reporter."

"I'm not sure that's a good idea, Sergeant," replied Jack, closing the blinds to block out the early morning rays of sun that were causing the investigation room's temperature to soar. He rolled his shirt sleeves up and undid the top button of his shirt, feeling the sweat bristling underneath his collar. "I think you could do with keeping a low profile for now."

DS Carmichael shook his head and rose to his feet. He picked up his suit jacket that had been slung across the back of his chair. "No, I really need to do this. I ballsed up. I admit it. Jumped to the wrong conclusions – and took you all down with me." He paused and gave Jack a weak attempt at a smile. "I need to make amends."

Jack exhaled and rubbed his eyes. He could still feel the wrath of the Chief Superintendent, his superior's anger at the wrongful arrest of Anthony Saunders still piercing his heart. They had messed up.

Correction.

Jack had messed up.

This was his investigation, and he would carry the can.

And now the whole world knew, too.

The Daily Mail had led with the story first thing that morning. How they had got their information was anyone's guess – the Metropolitan Police could be a leaky ship at the best of times, and working out how to plug it would be a fool's errand. They were on a damage limitation exercise now. And the first step in that exercise was to silence the reporter who had broken the story.

An hour after Anthony Saunders had been escorted from the building, London Life had responded to the warrant asking them to disclose the content of their members' messages. The messages Saunders had sent to each of the women were scrutinised – and found to be harmless. Advertising messages regarding his outsize shoes website; nothing more, nothing less. As soon as Jack had read the documents, he screwed them into paper balls and vented his frustration on the waste paper bin. If they had received this information earlier, maybe they wouldn't have gone in all guns blazing and arrested Anthony Saunders.

And they wouldn't be in the mess they were in now.

And they wouldn't have wasted vital time in the search for Isabel.

"I don't know, Sergeant. We can't afford for anything else to go wrong. The Chief Superintendent is not a happy man. We have the threat of a wrongful arrest lawsuit hanging over us now." Jack paused and sighed. "I should go myself."

DS Carmichael continued to walk towards the door, slipping his suit jacket on as he did so. He shook his head. "No, I *really* need to do this. You need to let me try and repair the damage."

Jack exhaled another sigh, but before he could reply DC Cassidy stood up and began to cross the room. "Maybe give him a break, boss? Let him go?" She had been sitting, quietly, in the corner by the window, trying in vain to get the benefit of what little air was seeping into the hot and humid investigation room. "Might be for the best in the circumstances?"

Jack opened his mouth to protest, but found DS Cooper was also nodding in agreement. "Go on, boss. We need you here. We still have an investigation to run." DS Cooper flashed a look at DC Cassidy, a look that only the two of them would understand. But it did not go unnoticed by their Detective Inspector. "And we need to run through the CCTV again with you."

Jack tried to catch the eye of DS Cooper, but found his sergeant avoiding his gaze. Hadn't they sat through the CCTV late last night? What else could there be to see? Jack raised his hands in defeat and gave DS Carmichael a nod. "OK, OK, off you go. You know where to go and what to say?"

DS Carmichael nodded and patted his breast pocket. "Got the address right here. I'll call when I'm on my way back."

"All right. But you come straight back. No more vanishing tricks."

Jack gave a dismissive wave to DS Carmichael's back as he slid through the investigation room door and disappeared. He then turned to the rest of his team, eyeing DS Cooper and DC Cassidy curiously. "So, what's so urgent with the CCTV that I need to see it - again?"

* * *

Time: 9.15am
Date: Thursday 26th July 2012
Location: Home of Jonathan Spearing, London

DS Carmichael pulled up outside Jonathan Spearing's home address. He checked his watch. The drive hadn't taken as long as he had thought, and he had made good time. Flicking the blue lights and sirens on from time to time had helped. Leaving the car at the side of the road, he made his way up the short, paved garden path that was flanked by welcome bursts of colour in the flowerbeds. Bright yellow rudbeckia mirrored the scorching heat of the sun overhead. Spiked spears of red hot pokers interspersed with clumps of lilac and salmon pink petunias softened the edges of the path. The heady, sweet smell of the potted geraniums tickled DS Carmichael's nose as he approached the front door.

He rang the doorbell, hearing the faint tinkling sound echoing into the depths of the house beyond. Sources at the Daily Mail had confirmed Jonathan Spearing was working from home that day, and it wasn't long before DS Carmichael could see the faint outline of a figure approaching the door through the mottled glass panel.

The door opened to reveal a lean-framed man dressed in casual tracksuit bottoms and a faded REM t-shirt. "Can I help you?"

DS Carmichael held out a hand showing his warrant card. "DS Carmichael, Metropolitan Police. Are you Jonathan Spearing?"

The man glanced at the warrant card, a faint frown creeping onto his forehead. He nudged his spectacles further up onto the bridge of his nose. "Yes, yes I am. What's this about?"

DS Carmichael pocketed his warrant card and nodded over the reporter's shoulder, towards the hallway. "Maybe we could step inside?"

Jonathan Spearing allowed his frown to deepen, slightly, and a shadow of suspicion tinged with curiosity edged into his features. "Well, I was just on my way out, Sergeant, so if you don't mind I think it's best that we do this here?" He paused and looked directly into DS Carmichael's eyes, a flicker of a smile dancing on his lips. "Whatever *this* is?"

DS Carmichael nodded. Great. A defensive reporter, that's all he needed. And he was supposed to be trying to make things better, not stirring up another hornet's nest and making things worse. The last thing he needed was to appear on the front page again in tomorrow's early edition.

"Of course, Mr Spearing. Here is fine. I'll try not to keep you too long."

The reporter kept his eyes on DS Carmichael as he stepped out onto the porch and pulled the front door closed behind him. DS Carmichael instinctively took a step backwards.

"I'll be frank, Mr Spearing. I'm here concerning a newspaper article that appeared in this morning's edition of the Daily Mail. An article that contained some fairly classified information." DS Carmichael paused, watching to see the reporter's reaction. There was none. He continued with his non-committal blank expression. "Information that could be damaging to an ongoing murder enquiry."

A smile crossed Jonathan Spearing's face and a small chuckle escaped his lips. "Has DI MacIntosh sent you to rap me across the knuckles, Sergeant? Do his dirty work for him?" The smile widened, reaching his eyes that twinkled in the glare of the overhead sun.

DS Carmichael cleared his throat and continued. "As you can appreciate, the leaking of sensitive information to the press......"

"Are you admitting you have a leak, Sergeant?" Jonathan Spearing folded his arms across his chest and rocked back on his heels. "Tut, tut. Oh dearie me."

DS Carmichael bristled underneath his suit jacket and fixed the reporter with a hard stare. "At times like this, we need the national newspapers to work *with* us, not against us. Reporting sensitive information could have a detrimental effect on our investigation – you could be responsible for allowing a serial killer to remain at large, putting more women at risk."

"Oh I think you are managing to keep this serial killer on the streets all on your own; you don't need my help. You arrest and question an entirely innocent man?" Jonathan Spearing shook his head and allowed another chuckle to form. "Surely that has a far more damaging effect on your investigation than me simply reporting the truth? I think the bigwigs at the Metropolitan Police are getting all hot under the collar because they now face a wrongful arrest suit – could cost them a pretty penny, too. Especially if daddy QC wades in."

DS Carmichael drew in a deep breath, fighting against the bait Jonathan Spearing was dangling in front of him. He needed to maintain his composure and not lose it with a reporter who wouldn't think twice about making him tomorrow's headline news. "It would be very much appreciated if such classified information was left that way – classified. Let us get on with our jobs."

Jonathan Spearing took a step forwards, the smile slipping from his lips. "Look, it's not my problem if you've got a leak in your department. I only report what I'm told. Maybe you should concentrate on arresting the right people in the future."

DS Carmichael nodded his head and took a matching step forwards towards the reporter. The two men stood face to face, another inch and their noses would have been touching.

"I'm not sure if you quite heard me." DS Carmichael's inky-black eyes bore into the reporter's equally stony stare. "If any more classified information reaches the front pages, then things could become very difficult for you. Take this as a friendly warning."

Jonathan Spearing held DS Carmichael's beady gaze for a few seconds before taking a step backwards and nodding. "Friendly warning received and understood, Sergeant."

DS Carmichael returned the nod and mirrored the retreating step – the space between the two men restored. "Then I'll be on my way." As he turned to leave, a figure approached from the roadside, heading up the garden path towards them.

"Ah." Jonathan Spearing bent down to retrieve a parcel that had been sitting on his porch by the geranium pots. "Parcel for you; delivered while you were out"

The reporter stepped past DS Carmichael with the large box held out before him. DS Carmichael obligingly stepped out of the way, watching as the box was delivered to its rightful recipient.

"Thanks, Jon. They always deliver when I'm not at home. Thanks for taking it in."

"No problem. Anytime. See, Sergeant." Jonathan Spearing watched as his neighbour turned to go back down the garden path. "I can be a responsible neighbour. You plug your leaky ship and I'll be a good boy and only report on things I'm meant to."

DS Carmichael grunted in response and followed the reporter's neighbour and his parcel back down the garden path, heading for his car. Slipping into the driver's seat, he watched Jonathan Spearing head back inside his house and close the door behind him. Had the message been received and understood? He hoped so. He really hoped so. He could ill afford to make any more mistakes.

Taking his notebook out of his pocket, DS Carmichael updated his notes on his confrontation with the reporter. Slipping it back inside his jacket, he glanced at his watch. He just had enough time to take a detour on his way back to the station.

* * *

Time: 9.15am
  Date: Thursday 26<sup>th</sup> July 2012
  Location: Metropolitan Police HQ, London

Jack followed DS Cooper into the darkened tech suite. DC Cassidy was already seated and getting the footage ready to view.

"Neither of us could sleep last night." DC Cassidy eyed DS Cooper and gave a half-hearted smile. "What with everything that happened yesterday. So Chris called me and we stayed late - had another look through the CCTV. He showed me where the scenes had been deleted." DC Cassidy nodded at the screen in front of her as Jack and DS Cooper took their seats. "We had the tech guys work on the images overnight too."

"They find anything?" asked Jack, more out of hope than anything else.

"Well, don't ask me how, but they've managed to recover the deleted scenes from all four locations. They worked through the night; gave us the results early this morning." DC Cassidy clicked the mouse and the first set of grainy images flooded the screen. "This is from the first location. The deleted scenes were between 21.30 and 22.45." She let the frames play out, cars and vans making their way through the camera's view. At 21.47, she paused the screen.

At the centre of the monitor was a dark coloured Ford Mondeo, registration plate clearly visible. AK09 BVZ. DC Cassidy let the image remain on the screen for several more seconds before clicking the mouse and bringing up a different set of images.

"These are from location number two. Hyde Park. Deleted images were between 21.04 and 22.05." As before, she let the images play out before pausing the screen at 22.01. The same dark coloured Ford Mondeo, registration AK09 BVZ, hovered in the centre, caught on camera.

Jack's eyes widened as the realisation began to hit home.

"And locations three and four?" His voice was taut.

DC Cassidy nodded, loading up the CCTV images for location number three. "Deleted scenes were between 21.20 and 23.00." The scene played out until 21.44 when the Ford Mondeo graced the screen once again. She quickly followed suit with the most recent murder location, at Battersea Park. "And finally, we have the fourth location from yesterday's discovery. Deleted scenes were again found between 21.25 and 22.58 of the night before." After playing on for a few seconds, the image of the now familiar Ford Mondeo was frozen in the centre of the screen.

Jack sat back in his chair, his heart thumping. This was it. This was the break they had been searching for. The black transit van had been a costly red herring. *This* was the guy they were after.

Ford Mondeo AK09 BVZ

"Please tell me they aren't cloned or stolen plates," breathed Jack, not taking his eyes from the image of the suspect's vehicle in front of him. "Please say we can trace him."

DC Cassidy paused, and flashed a look at DS Cooper. Cooper gave a discreet nod – but not so discreet that it escaped Jack's attention. Eyeing his two detectives, he frowned, swapping his gaze from DS Cooper to DC Cassidy, and then back again.

"What? What is it?" The tension gave Jack's voice a gravelly hoarseness. "What is it you're not telling me?"

DC Cassidy took in a deep breath before clicking off the computer screen. The room darkened even further as Ford Mondeo AK09 BVZ disappeared from view.

"We can trace the vehicle, boss," she replied, keeping her voice even and controlled. "That's not a problem. We even know where it is right now."

Jack let out the breath that he hadn't been aware he was holding. "Well that's good news, right?" He continued to eye his junior officers' faces, not liking the expressions they were trying their hardest to hide. "Right?" he repeated.

"Vehicle AK09 BVZ is a Metropolitan Police pool car, boss." This time it was DS Cooper who cut through the silent tension.

"It's one of *ours*?" Jack's face froze. "A pool car?"

DS Cooper nodded, catching the gaze of DC Cassidy out of the corner of his eye. He felt his lips and mouth go dry. "And we traced who it's booked out to." He paused, his brain struggling to form the words that needed to be said. Taking a deep breath, he dropped the bombshell Jack knew was about to land. "Currently, vehicle AK09 BVZ is booked out to DS Carmichael and has most recently been tracked to the address of the Daily Mail reporter, Jonathan Spearing."

\* \* \*

Time: 9.50am
 Date: Thursday 26th July 2012
 Location: St James's University, London

Dr Rachel Hunter opened the door and greeted Jack, stepping aside to let him into her office.

"We could have dealt with this over the telephone, Inspector," she began, closing the door behind him. "I have an appointment in 10 minutes."

Jack nodded, out of breath from the rushed journey from the station. "I know, I'm sorry. I just need to say what I've got to say, in person."

Dr Hunter nodded her acquiescence, and motioned for Jack to take a seat in the comfortable chairs by the coffee table. "Glass of water?" She inclined her head towards the iced water machine nestled next to the coffee. Despite the ever increasing heat and humidity, Dr Hunter looked impeccably cool and unflustered.

Jack shook his head and remained standing. "Could it be a police officer?"

He came straight to the point, seeing little or no sense in beating around the bush. "Our killer. Could he be a serving police officer?" The words seemed to stick in his parched throat.

Dr Hunter paused, seating herself behind her well-organised and un-cluttered desk. Jack found himself comparing it to his own desk which seemed to visibly groan under the weight of files and paperwork being deposited on it with relentless regularity. He shook his head to rid himself of the distraction. He watched as Dr Hunter reached into the top drawer and pulled out the thin manila folder Jack recognised from their initial meeting. Opening the folder, she slid out the single sheet of paper that listed the characteristics she had compiled for the investigation. She ran a well-manicured finger down the headings.

"A police officer, you say?" Dr Hunter paused and then slowly let her gaze flick up to meet Jack's. "You have someone in mind, or are you just talking theoretically?"

"Let's say theoretical, for now," replied Jack, nodding his head towards the list in her hand. "Is it possible though?"

Dr Hunter returned her attention to the list of characteristics. "Well, if your *theoretical* police officer is male, aged 30-55, is single or has difficulties making relationships, is charming, intelligent, forensically aware with no criminal record......." She paused and held Jack in her gaze. "Then I would say you have a potential match."

\* \* \*

Time: 10.30am
   Date: Thursday 26th July 2012
   Location: Metropolitan Police HQ, London

"He's on his way back." Jack looked at the message on his phone before glancing up at DS Cooper and DC Cassidy. "We need to be ready for him."

"Are you going to arrest him, guv?" DS Cooper asked the question that was on both his and DC Cassidy's lips.

Jack shook his head. "No, not at this stage, Cooper. He's got some questions that we need answering, that's for sure. If he cooperates…"

"And if he doesn't?" DC Cassidy let the question hang in the air.

Time was ticking to find Isabel. The time interval between victims was shortening all the time. Dr Hunter had given Jack information on serial killers and how they may escalate their behaviour, ultimately killing more quickly and more often. The initial euphoria felt after each kill lasting for a decreasing amount of time. The information did nothing to calm the disquiet and unease he felt. If DS Carmichael knew anything about Isabel's disappearance, then Jack was going to get it out of him one way or another. DS or no DS.

He had shared his impromptu meeting with Dr Hunter with both DS Cooper and DC Cassidy as soon as he had returned to the station. Predictably, neither seemed willing to believe the killer could be one of them.

"But, one of us, boss?" DS Cooper had responded, face ashen. "Surely not?"

"Is he, though? One of us?" Jack raised a questioning eyebrow. "You did the searches yourself, Cooper. We have no idea where the hell he's from – or even if he *is* a police officer. You found no trace of a DS Carmichael – anywhere."

Jack had gone through each and every characteristic of the criminal profile, and both DC Cassidy and DS Cooper had to admit that he seemed to fit. Everyone was still stinging from the rebukes their arrest of Anthony Saunders had caused from the higher echelons of the Metropolitan Police; this time they had to get it right.

\* \* \*

Time: 10.30am

Date: Thursday 26<sup>th</sup> July 2012

Location: A cellar in London

The masking tape across her mouth made it difficult to breath. She could feel herself hyperventilating underneath the scratchy blanket he had lain across her. She tossed her head from side to side to try and rid herself of the coarse material that itched her skin, and to get her head out into the open air.

It seemed to still be dark. But that meant nothing down here. She had no idea what time it was, or what day it was. Her stomach rumbled. She couldn't remember the last time she had eaten. Yesterday? She saw that the packet of sandwiches that had been by the side of her mattress had been removed, the water bottle replaced.

So he had been back to see her. But when that was she couldn't even begin to guess. Her mind felt foggy, her thoughts jumbled and incoherent. She tried to sit up but found her arms had been tied behind her back, wrapped at the wrists with some sort of thin twine. It cut painfully into her flesh every time she tried to move.

So, eventually she stopped moving.

\* \* \*

Time: 11.30am

Date: Thursday 26<sup>th</sup> July 2012

Location: Metropolitan Police HQ, London

DS Carmichael walked briskly through the main entrance, smiling at his good fortune at securing a privileged parking space out front rather than the rear car park, and within a split second knew that something was wrong.

To his immediate left, he saw Jack stood alongside DS Cooper, their faces pale and tense. He flashed his gaze to the right where the lobby was flanked by a further four officers, the two closest to him noted to be armed, with steady well-trained fingers hovering millimetres above triggers. The faces that belonged to the fingers trained on his every move; the eyes within those faces boring into him, watching and waiting.

DS Carmichael's stride faltered. He froze, standing stock-still in the centre of the entrance lobby, his feet sticking like glue to the parquet floor below. Feeling his pulse quicken, he took a backwards glance at the doors that had swung shut behind him. Two more armed officers had appeared, blocking off any retreat.

DS Carmichael returned his gaze to meet Jack's, raising his eyebrows questioningly. "Jack? Is everything all right?"

Jack's eyes momentarily flickered to the armed officers who had now entered the lobby at Carmichael's rear. With every movement, the creak of their body armour seemed to echo in the still air.

"Jack?" repeated DS Carmichael, edging away from the gun barrels pointed in his direction. "What's happened, Jack?"

"You need to step this way, Sergeant," replied Jack, motioning with his hand for Carmichael to move forwards. "Nice and steady, no sudden movements. You know the score." Jack nodded at the two armed officers flanking Carmichael, each one taking a synchronised step towards him. DS Carmichael whipped his head to the side, his eyes widening.

"What's going on? You're starting to scare me now, Jack." DS Carmichael felt his arms raise slowly into the air, palms up, instinct taking over as he continued to sense the barrel of a gun inching towards him. "Let's not do anything rash."

"Time to come with us, Sergeant." Jack indicated to Carmichael that he should follow him towards the custody suite behind them. "Let's not make this any harder than it needs to be."

DS Carmichael took another hesitant step forwards, noting the armed officers behind him were following suit. They were so close he could almost feel their hot breath on the back of his neck. "Make what harder, Jack? What's going on?"

Jack paused, waiting for Carmichael to catch up. He placed a light yet firm grip on his fellow officer's elbow. "I think you know. You've got some questions to answer."

# Chapter Thirty One

Time: 11.45am

Date: Thursday 26<sup>th</sup> July 2012

Location: Metropolitan Police HQ, London

"The time is eleven forty-five AM. Present in the room are DS Cooper and myself, Detective Inspector Jack MacIntosh." Jack paused and looked up, his hollow eyes meeting Carmichael's. "State your name and rank for the purposes of the tape."

DS Carmichael remained wide-eyed, his coal-black pupils flicking from Jack to DS Cooper. "Seriously? We're really doing this?"

"Don't make it any harder than it already is, Sergeant." Jack eyed the video recorder tucked away in the top corner of the room, the red dot winking on and off. "Your name and rank."

DS Carmichael licked his lips, suddenly feeling how dry they had become all of a sudden. He reached forwards and took a sip of water from the plastic cup, grimacing at the lukewarm liquid. He gave a discernible shake of his head before replying. "Detective Sergeant Robert Carmichael."

Jack let a sigh escape his own lips. "You are not under arrest, but remain under police caution. Do you understand?" He avoided Carmichael's stony stare – it was never easy interviewing one of your own.

DS Carmichael mirrored Jack's sigh, but his own now exhibiting a degree of exasperation tinged with an edge of growing hostility. "Yes, I understand the difference between being under arrest and under caution. I'm a police officer."

Jack felt the heckles prickle at the back of his neck, but refused to rise to the bait. "And you have been offered legal advice and the opportunity to have legal representation, but have declined. Is that correct?"

"Why would I need...?" But DS Carmichael was cut short.

"Is that correct, Sergeant?" Jack's own voice was now straining to keep civil and emotionless. He could feel the anger welling up inside him; the man opposite him could be responsible for Isabel's disappearance, and the deaths of four women.

Anger that he had to keep in check.

Anger wasn't going to get him the answers he needed

Anger wouldn't get Isabel back.

"Yes, that is correct," replied DS Carmichael, icily. He sat back in his chair, his black beady eyes boring into Jack. "I don't need legal assistance as I've done nothing wrong."

We'll see about that, thought Jack, as he opened the folder in front of him.

\* \* \*

Time: 9.00pm
Date: Friday 12<sup>th</sup> June 1998
Location: Arundel, West Sussex

Jess had stayed in her room for the rest of the evening. She could hear her father continuing to clear up the mess in the dining room. He had placed the broken shards of the casserole dish into the outside bin, and swept up the shattered water jug and glasses. She then heard the mop and bucket being taken out of the understairs cupboard.

But she didn't dare go downstairs again.

Not yet.

She had yet to hear anything from Mum. Dad had said that she got upset and it had brought on one of her migraines, so she needed to go and lie down. She got a lot of those these days. Migraines.

But Jess hadn't heard her mother come upstairs to lie down. She hadn't heard her parents' bedroom door open or close. All there had been was silence.

* * *

Time: 11.50am
Date: Thursday 26th July 2012
Location: Metropolitan Police HQ, London

DS Cooper slid a series of four, seven inch by five inch, black and white grainy images across the table. "For the purposes of the tape, item reference AC 001 to AC 004 are being shown to DS Carmichael."

Jack leant forwards in his seat, resting his elbows on the table. "Recognise the vehicle in each of these images, Sergeant?" Jack nodded at the stilled frames from the CCTV pulled by DC Cassidy, isolating the vehicle registration AK09 BVZ.

DS Carmichael's gaze lowered to the four photographs that had been placed in front of him. Jack watched intently from the other side of the table, physically watching the colour ebbing away from Carmichael's cheeks. His skin took on a clammy, pallid tone, and if Jack was seeing things correctly, a few beads of sweat had popped up on his forehead.

Now we are getting somewhere, he thought. "Sergeant?" repeated Jack, nodding once again at the images. "The vehicle?"

DS Carmichael's eyes travelled from one image to the next, his lips thinning and the muscles in his jaw tightening. He looked up to meet Jack's questioning look.

"No comment."

The two words all police officers hated to hear echoed around the bare walls of interview room number two.

"Are you saying that you don't recognise the vehicle in these images, Sergeant?" Jack nudged each of the photographs a few centimetres closer to Carmichael. "Why don't you take a closer look?"

DS Carmichael shook his head. "What I am saying, Inspector, is no comment." His voice was as hard and steely grey as the walls of the interview room.

And just as unyielding.

"The interesting thing is, Sergeant," continued Jack, unmoved by his fellow officer's refusal to cooperate. "This vehicle was seen at all four locations of our victims, merely hours before their bodies were discovered. How do you explain that?"

DS Carmichael let a flicker of a smile tease at his lips. "I know what you're doing, and it won't work. I don't have to answer your questions, and you know I don't." He paused and nodded back down at the photographs. "If what you really want to ask me, is did I have anything to do with the deaths of these four women, then the answer is simple. No I did not." DS Carmichael broke off, more colour seeming to drain from his face. "And I can't believe you are really asking me that, I really can't."

"This car is a Metropolitan Police pool car," continued Jack, tapping one of the images with his finger. "And as of Wednesday 4th July, who do you think it was booked out to?"

DS Carmichael maintained his silence, merely turning his head to the side and upwards to glance at the video camera, its red recording light still blinking.

"I'll tell you, shall I?" Jack carried on. "As of Wednesday 4th July, vehicle registration number AK09 BVZ was booked out to a Detective Sergeant Robert Carmichael. Your good self."

"Item reference AC 005," announced DS Cooper, sliding a copy of the pool car documentation across the table.

"So, here we have it, Sergeant. A car seen at each location, merely hours before the bodies of the victims were discovered. And said vehicle is booked out to yourself. How do you explain that?"

"No comment."

"Did anyone else have the use of your vehicle, Sergeant?"

"No comment."

"Where were you going on each of these dates, Sergeant?"

"No comment."

"Still you choose no comment." Jack failed to keep the irritation out of his voice. "We have the life of another young woman at stake here, for god's sake. If you know anything...." He broke off, his voice catching at the back of his dry throat. "You need to tell us where she is."

DS Carmichael shook his head, more urgently this time. "You're barking up the wrong tree here, Jack. Completely. Shit, you're in completely the wrong forest."

"Another interesting fact, Sergeant," continued Jack, clearing his throat, "is that these images of *your* car, were found to have been deleted from the system. At each of the four locations. How much of a coincidence is that?"

DS Carmichael shrugged and avoided Jack's penetrating look. "No comment."

Jack raised his eyebrows. "From where I'm sitting it looks like a senior police officer has tampered with evidence. Evidence that incriminates him in four murders and a kidnapping."

DS Carmichael rubbed his hands over his face. "No comment," he replied.

"Luckily for us," continued Jack, "the tech guys managed to retrieve it all. Who knew that was even possible, eh?" Jack let the question hang in the air. "So, I'm going to ask you again, one more time. Why is the vehicle that is booked out to you found to be at each of the four murder locations? And why were the images deleted?"

DS Carmichael pushed the images back across the table.

"No comment."

* * *

Time: 9.55pm
  Date: Wednesday 25th July 2012
  Location: Metropolitan Police HQ, London

DS Carmichael closed the door to the tech suite behind him. He closed the blinds at each window and made sure the lights were off, just in case. He was pretty sure no one else was around, but being pretty sure wasn't good enough. He knew Jack had gone home, but he hadn't seen DC Cassidy or DS Cooper leave.

He sat down at one of the computer stations and powered up the monitor. He glanced at his watch. He needed to be in and out of here as quickly as possible – someone could come in at any moment. The monitor sprang into life, casting a hypnotic glow out into the dimness of the suite.

Quickly, he pulled up the first set of CCTV images for the location of Patricia Gordon's body. Following the time line through, he paused the screen when Ford Mondeo AK09 BVZ filled the screen at exactly 21.47. With a quick look over his shoulder, unsure who he was really expecting to see, DS Carmichael entered the commands into the keyboard exactly as he had been shown.

"Are you sure you wish to delete this file?" The box flashed up in the centre of the screen.

DS Carmichael hit "yes."

\* \* \*

Time: 12.05pm
  Date: Thursday 26th July 2012
  Location: Metropolitan Police HQ, London

"Are you married, Sergeant?" Jack's change of direction caught DS Carmichael momentarily off guard. A faint frown crossed his brow, his already coal-black eyes seeming to darken further.

"I'm sorry? What's that got to do with anything?" He glanced from Jack's expressionless face to DS Cooper, then back again.

"I'm interested. Are you married?" Jack made a show of consulting one of the pieces of paper inside the manila folder still sitting on the table in front of him – Dr Hunter's criminal profile. "Maybe divorced? Wife run out on you?"

"I don't think that's any of your business," cut back DS Carmichael, a hotness creeping into his voice.

"Oh, it's my business all right," continued Jack, closing the folder. "When I'm investigating four murders and at least one kidnapping, *everything* is my business."

"And while you're asking me senseless questions, you're wasting valuable time in tracking down the killer."

"I'll decide whether my questions are senseless or not," interrupted Jack, inclining his head towards the table where DS Carmichael had placed both his hands. "Looks like you have a mark where a wedding ring used to be."

DS Carmichael instinctively covered up his left hand with his right, and flashed a warning look at Jack. "No comment."

\*\*\*

Time: 5.45pm
　Date: Friday 12<sup>th</sup> June 1998
　Location: Arundel, West Sussex

He stared at the third finger on her left hand, the all too familiar feeling of irritation and annoyance bubbling to the surface like a hot geyser. "You've taken your wedding ring off."

There was no response.

"Carol. I said, you've taken your wedding ring off."

Carol whipped her head around in his direction, her eyes red hot and brimming with tears. She tipped the saucepan full of vegetables into the casserole dish with the chicken. "Can you blame me? After what you said to me last night?" She rubbed at her wet cheeks with the back of a hand, her vision misting over with fresh tears. "What you accused me of?"

He still couldn't take his eyes off the third finger of her left hand. "Everything I said last night was true, Carol. Deny it if you want, but I know a lying bitch when I see one." His voice began to rise, the tone thick with condemnation and what sounded to Carol like pure and unequivocal hatred. "You've been lying to me for a long time. Do us all a favour and just admit it."

Carol glanced at the closed kitchen door behind them, praying that the thick oak panels would absorb the rising tempo of their latest argument. She bit her bottom lip, wondering if any door, any wood, could ever really be thick enough.

"Would you keep your voice down?" she urged, her voice low. "Jess might hear. She's only upstairs."

He either didn't hear her, or he didn't care.

Maybe it was both.

"Perhaps she needs to know the truth about her precious mother," he replied, the venom in his voice spilling out into the early evening air that was seeping in through the open kitchen window. "Perhaps she would be better off knowing what a lying, cheating whore her mother truly is."

A trembling hand flew up to cover Carol's mouth, as she tried to gulp back her sobs. "I've told you so many times – you're wrong. There is nothing going on between me and Brian. There never was." She rubbed again at her wet cheeks, trying to stem the steady flow of fresh, hot tears that continued to leak out of the corners of her eyes. "Why won't you listen to me? It's all in your head."

Enraged, he jumped to his feet, the wooden chair scraping violently behind him on the flagstone floor. "Don't you dare tell me I'm imagining it, Carol. I've *seen* you. I've seen what you're like together. You don't even have the decency to hide it."

Carol slammed the casserole dish into the oven and sat down at the kitchen table made from roughly-hewn railway sleepers, back in the days when her husband would lovingly create anything for his growing family. She could barely remember those days now. Just like she barely recognised the man in front of her as her husband.

When had it all changed?

When had it all started to go wrong?

Before Jess was born?

After?

Carol's memory was as hazy as her tear streaked vision. Accusing her of having an affair with someone at work had been the final straw. The weeks and months of bickering and fighting had culminated in such a showdown last night that Carol had ripped off her wedding ring and flung it across the bedroom. As far as she knew, it was still lying in the dusty corner underneath the Victorian chest of drawers upstairs.

And the way she was feeling right now, that's where it could stay.

She heard him stomp across the kitchen towards the door, feeling him bump roughly against the back of her chair as he passed by.

"Don't forget we are meant to be going out for the day tomorrow," she murmured, her head in her hands. "Jess has been looking forward to it for ages. She can't see us like this."

She felt him pause by the door, and waited for the acid-laden retort to escape his poisonous mouth. Instead, his voice was quiet and calm – if anything, that worried her more.

"Jess won't see us fight. I won't let you hurt her the way you have hurt me. Jess won't see a thing."

\* \* \*

Time: 10.35pm

Date: Friday 12<sup>th</sup> June 1998

Location: Arundel, West Sussex

Jess mustn't see.

He shut the door that led to the back garden and turned the lock.

Jess mustn't find her.

Things had not gone to plan.

They were meant to have been having a talk, a calm discussion about the future. Their future.

But now?

This was not supposed to have happened.

But it wasn't his fault, was it?

None of this was his fault.

*She* had been the one to start lying to him.

*She* had been the one to start going behind his back.

*She* had been the one to blame.

*She* had driven him to it.

And what had now happened, *she* had been the one to make him do it.

It was her fault.

It was all her fault.

The remnants of the broken casserole dish were now in the bin, and the dirty floor had been mopped. He had swept up the shards of shattered glass – everything was back to how it was before.

Except for one thing.

Carol.

He stepped out into the hall and glanced up the stairs, just in time to hear Jess's shrill voice cut through his muddled thoughts. "Dad? Where's mum?"

* * *

Time: 9.05am
Date: Saturday 13<sup>th</sup> June 1998
Location: Arundel, West Sussex

"Isn't Mum coming too?" Jess slid into the passenger seat and fastened her seat belt. She glanced back over her shoulder towards the house. "The fresh air might do her good?"

He smiled and started the engine. "Mum has one of her migraines, Jess. It's best she stays home and rests for a while. But we can still go and have fun, right?" He flashed another smile at his daughter – one that almost reached his cold, lifeless eyes.

Almost.

But not quite.

Jess returned the smile, but quickly glanced back at the house again as the car moved off the drive. "OK. It's just that I haven't seen her since yesterday, at dinner. Is she all right?"

"I told you, Jess," snapped her father, tightening his grip on the steering wheel. "She has one of her migraines. She needs to lie down in the dark and not be disturbed. Now can we please stop talking about your mother."

Jess shrank back into her seat and clasped her hands together in her lap, quietly kneading them together to steady herself. She hated it when Dad got angry. It frightened her when Dad got angry.

And Dad got angry – a lot.

\* \* \*

Time: 12.10pm

Date: Thursday 26th July 2012

Location: Metropolitan Police HQ, London

"Seriously, Jack, you're wasting time." DS Carmichael turned round in his chair to face the video camera. "How long are you going to let this carry on for?"

"If you could address your answers to me, Sergeant."

"This is such a joke. A sick joke." DS Carmichael closed his eyes and shook his head. "Why won't you listen to me?"

"Was that why you were so keen to arrest Anthony Saunders?" continued Jack, leaning back in his chair and fixing Carmichael with his eyes. "A useful diversion? Pin the crimes on someone else?"

"You're not listening," replied DS Carmichael, continuing to shake his head. "You've got this all wrong."

"Something else you might be able to help us with, Sergeant. When you arrived here on my team, you claimed to have come from Sussex. So how is it that no one from Sussex has ever heard of a DS Carmichael?" Jack waited for a response from the other side of the table.

The muscles in DS Carmichael's jawline tensed and he flashed another look up at the video camera which was still blinking at them. Jack frowned slightly - it appeared that Carmichael was mouthing something to the camera behind the cover of one of his hands. He cleared his throat to regain Carmichael's attention.

"It's like you don't exist – anywhere." Jack folded his arms across his chest and fixed DS Carmichael with a stony stare. "Why is that? Where are you really from?"

DS Carmichael sighed once again and shook his head. "No comment."

Jack tried not to let the exasperation he felt infiltrate his voice. "Are you even a police officer?"

DS Carmichael covered his face with his hands and rubbed his palms into his tired eyes. "Jack – you're not listening to me. You're wasting time asking me absurd questions, when you should be out there looking for Isabel. We all should be. Instead, you've got me cooped up in here asking damn stupid questions about nothing."

"I may be asking damn stupid questions, as you so eloquently put it, Sergeant, but you are not answering them." Jack felt his hackles prickle once again, and balled his hands into fists. "*That* is wasting us time."

DS Carmichael felt his own patience snap. "Look, turn that bloody tape recorder off and let's get out there and find him." He nodded at the tape recorder at the side of the table by DS Cooper, the counter still ticking round marking each second of the interrogation. He kicked back his chair and rose to his feet, leaning forwards with his hands on the table. His face inched closer and closer to Jack's. "Isabel won't thank you for being holed up in here, when her life could be ebbing away as we speak."

Jack sprang to his feet and, before he knew it, one balled fist that had been resting loosely by his side suddenly thundered forwards and smashed into DS Carmichael's face. The force of the impact sent him reeling backwards, tripping over his own feet where he landed, sprawled on the floor.

"Don't you dare bring Isabel into this," roared Jack, his hand stinging sharply from its contact with DS Carmichael's nasal bones. The pain shot up his arm and into his shoulder. "She is worth a million of the likes of you."

DS Cooper leapt to his feet, and made his way around to the door, to either summon help or get the hell out of the interview room – he hadn't quite made his mind up which. He reached for the door handle and wrenched it open, only to be confronted by the imposing figure of Commander Adam Forsyth.

The Commander strode into the room, closely followed by a harried looking Chief Superintendent Dougie King.

"DI MacIntosh." Commander Forsyth's booming voice echoed around the walls of the interview room. At a little under 6' 6" with broad shoulders to match, he seemed to instantly fill the snug confines of interview room two. His closely cropped dark hair, greying at the temples, sat atop stern and scowling features – features that were being directed wholly at Jack. "Stand aside. Wait for me in Chief Superintendent King's office." He paused, his ice-blue eyes jabbing hotly towards Jack's. "Now, Inspector!"

Jack jumped as if given a bolt of electricity and strode from the room, his cheeks burning and his fist throbbing. As he exited the interview room and made his way out into the corridor, he heard the Commander's voice continue in his wake.

"DS Carmichael, you are hereby immediately released from caution. Get somebody to see to your nose." DS Carmichael scrambled to his feet, nodded and headed towards the door, the Commander's tone following him. "And somebody turn off this bloody tape!"

\* \* \*

Time: 1.15pm
  Date: Thursday 26<sup>th</sup> July 2012
  Location: Metropolitan Police HQ, London

"Shit, Jack. What in God's name has got into you?" Chief Superintendent Dougie King ran a hand over his closely cropped wiry hair, beads of perspiration clearly visible on his worried brow. "I have no idea how to unpick this unholy mess – and with the Commander watching too." He shook his head and exhaled loudly. "Shit, Jack," he repeated.

Jack frowned. "Why was the Commander watching anyway?" He couldn't help but remember the furtive glances Carmichael kept making towards the video camera. Had he been aware all along that they were being watched? "That's not routine."

"Nothing about this is routine, Jack," replied the Chief Superintendent, exhaling noisily yet again. "Assaulting a fellow officer? On tape? Jesus, Jack..."

"But why was the Commander watching," pressed Jack. "I don't understand."

"You think that is your main concern? That the Commander was watching?" Chief Superintendent Dougie King wiped the sweat from his brow and nodded at the vacant chair in front of his desk. "I think you better sit down for this one."

Jack stepped forwards and began to lower himself into the visitor's seat.

"On your feet, Inspector," boomed Commander Forsyth, striding into the room and sending the door crashing into the wall behind. Jack almost jumped out of his skin as he leapt to his feet, clasping his hands behind his back. He winced as the fist that threw the punch continued to throb.

"You've got some explaining to do, but first you are going to listen."

Commander Forsyth nodded curtly at Chief Superintendent King to step aside, and deftly slipped himself into the vacant swivel chair behind the desk. A snug fit for the Chief Superintendent's ample frame, the chair was dwarfed by the Commander's imposing stature. He once again fixed his ice-blue eyes upon Jack, but did not indicate that he should resume his seat. Jack remained standing, planting his feet in a wide enough stance to withstand what he expected to be the mother of all ear-bashings from his superior officer.

"Before you give me your account, Inspector, of just *how* you came about to assault one of our own officers – and if he escapes without a broken nose I should be very surprised – you need to listen and listen well. Understood?"

Jack fixed his gaze on a section of the wall above the Commander's left shoulder. He knew better than to try and return the stony stare that was boring into him. He gave a slow nod.

"You are one of my best officers, DI MacIntosh," began the Commander, speaking in a low and level tone, the initial anger having abated. "And for that reason I am possibly going to overlook the serious errors of judgment you have displayed just recently." He paused, and flicked his ice-blue eyes towards Jack. "Detective Sergeant Carmichael has been seconded to our division by the Major Crime Unit at Sussex."

Jack tore his eyes away from the section of wall he was fixing his gaze upon and found his mouth starting to open. But any retort or reply he was forming was silenced by the Commander's raised hand.

"Yes, I'm well aware, Inspector, that your own investigations drew a blank concerning there being a DS Carmichael attached to Sussex Police. Or anywhere else for that matter." The Commander's voice, although now devoid of anger, had still lost none of its frosty tone. "And there is a very good reason for that, if you had stopped to think before rushing in, all guns blazing."

And then the penny dropped.

Almost at exactly the same moment that the words tumbled out of the Commander's mouth.

"DS Carmichael is working as an undercover officer on Operation Evergreen. The reason his vehicle was captured on your CCTV was by pure coincidence. And the subsequent deletion of the images was authorised by myself. There was no ulterior motive connected to your case. Carmichael is not his real name, for obvious reasons."

"Undercover?" The cog wheels inside Jack's brain slowly started turning. "But how does that fit...?"

"It doesn't, Inspector," interrupted Commander Forsyth, getting to his feet. "His brief with Operation Evergreen is to investigate historic child cruelty and the possible sexual assault of children in local authority care, dating back to the 1970s and 1980s. He is investigating possible police involvement and possible corruption of high ranking police officers in association with these cases of child abuse. He is working with our anti-corruption unit from the top floor."

"The ghost squad?" Jack raised his eyebrows.

Commander Forsyth, flashed an irritated look at Jack and continued. "A new, much larger, investigation is due to be launched later this year, Operation Yewtree. Yewtree will be investigating child abuse claims involving some of the country's highest profile figures of the entertainment industry. It is going to be one of the biggest, if not *the* biggest, investigation the Metropolitan Police has ever launched. It is going to be huge, Inspector. Unprecedented. DS Carmichael's investigation is going to be working in tandem with Operation Yewtree." Commander Forsyth paused, noting Jack's confused and bewildered expression. "As you can imagine, Inspector, confidentiality is of extreme importance. Hence why nobody knew of DS Carmichael's true identity – not even the Chief Superintendent here, before you start casting aspersions in that direction."

Jack glanced across at Chief Superintendent Dougie King, whose own bemused features mirrored his own.

"Only senior officers with the rank of Commander or above have been privy to this information, DI MacIntosh," continued Commander Forsyth. "Your little antics in there a few moments ago has meant that such confidential information is now required to be disclosed to yourself – and, no doubt, the rest of your team." The ice-blue eyes again sought out Jack's gaze. "For Operation Evergreen, and ultimately Operation Yewtree, to succeed I need you and your team to keep this information to yourselves. Under no circumstances can any of the conversation within these four walls leak out. Do I make myself clear?"

"Crystal, Sir," replied Jack, nodding his head curtly and flashing another look at the Chief Superintendent. "You can rely on my team's discretion, Sir."

"Hmmmm." Commander Forsyth pushed the swivel chair back and strode purposefully towards the door. His towering frame filled the doorway where he paused and turned back towards Jack. "You need to make your apologies to DS Carmichael, DI MacIntosh. And quickly. He is a mighty fine officer and will be a credit to your investigation. And I could do without the complexities of an internal enquiry and criminal proceedings for assault taking up our valuable and already stretched resources."

And with that, he was gone.

"Did you....?" Jack half-turned towards Chief Superintendent King, who was resuming his place behind his desk. He raised a hand and cut Jack off midsentence.

"No, I did not, Jack. You heard the Commander." He eased himself into the newly vacated chair. "Only ranks of Commander and above were privy to the information surrounding Operation Evergreen. It's all news to me."

"This Operation Evergreen, and Yewtree..."

"Is not your concern right now, Jack." The Chief Superintendent nodded towards the door. "You need to be gone. You're needed elsewhere. Go and apologise to DS Carmichael and then go and catch my killer, Jack. You have until tomorrow. The clock is ticking."

Jack sped down the corridor in the direction of the investigation room.

\* \* \*

# Chapter Thirty Two

Time: 1.45pm
Date: Thursday 26<sup>th</sup> July 2012
Location: Metropolitan Police HQ, London

"One more time, Cooper." Jack rubbed his roughened chin – shaving was his least favourite grooming routine at the best of times, but he failed to remember the last time a razor had graced his skin. "What are we missing? Give me a run down on what we have so far. Again."

DS Cooper wakened the sleeping whiteboard and clicked the remote-control. The screen flickered into life, giving off a faint hum, and the images of the four victims were brought up in quick succession.

"Patricia Gordon, age forty-five, last seen on Friday 6<sup>th</sup> July. Body discovered at St James's Park on Friday 13<sup>th</sup> July. Cause of death, strangulation by ligature. Restraint marks on one ankle. Worked at The Briars Residential Care Home as a housekeeper. Had an evening job - we haven't located where that was yet."

Jack nodded. "We still need to find that evening job." He motioned for DS Cooper to continue.

"Georgina Dale, age twenty-one, last seen on Thursday 12<sup>th</sup> July. Body discovered at Hyde Park on Friday 20<sup>th</sup> July. Cause of death also strangulation by ligature. Again, restraint marks on one ankle. Full-time student at St James's University, studying English. No known part time jobs."

"And a shoe belonging to Georgina was found at the first location," added DC Cassidy, "suggesting that both were held captive at the same time." She nodded at the blown up photographs of the shoes found at the various scenes, spread out in the centre of the table.

DS Cooper flicked over a page in his accompanying notebook. "Hannah Fuller, age seventeen. Last seen on Thursday 19th July. Body discovered at Green Park on Monday 23rd July. Cause of death the same as for the first two victims, strangulation by ligature. Same restraint marks to one ankle. Unemployed; full time mother."

"And a shoe belonging to Hannah was found close to Georgina's body," added DC Cassidy, once again.

"Again, suggesting the two women were held captive at the same time," mused Jack. "Where is he keeping them? He needs somewhere with space for two to be kept at the same time."

DS Cooper continued. "Final victim, Zoe Turner, age thirty-nine. Last seen on Saturday 21st July. Body discovered only yesterday morning. Dr Matthews has verbally confirmed likely cause of death is strangulation by ligature, but a formal PM report is to come. He also confirmed similar marking on one ankle the same as the others. News just in states she worked at a company that is due to move into The Shard. No other information yet – next of kin are still being traced. Visual ID made by her boss – he reported her missing when she failed to turn up for work."

"Her shoe was found close to Hannah's body." DS Cassidy tapped the image of a black court shoe. She hesitated for a moment, before continuing, flashing a look at Jack. "And the final shoe found close to Zoe's body yesterday has been identified as belonging to Isabel Faraday – current whereabouts unknown."

Jack swallowed past a lump that had formed in his throat at the mention of Isabel's name.

"Do you want to run through the psychological profile again, guv?" continued DC Cassidy, reaching out for the manila folder next to the photographs of the shoes where Dr Hunter's report was housed.

Jack shook his head. "We've gone off on two separate wild-goose chases on the back of that report – let's leave it where it is. We need to find a link between the victims – there has to be one. He's too clever to be that random. It's buried, but it has to be there." He rose from his chair and headed towards the door. "I'm going back to The Briars to find out where Patricia Gordon's evening job was. While I'm gone, get all the crime scene photos together – and go through them. Again. We're missing something."

* * *

Time: 2.45pm
> Date: Thursday 26<sup>th</sup> July 2012
> Location: The Briars Residential Care Home

"Sorry to bother you again, Mrs Masters." Jack nodded and smiled at the matron, easing himself into a chair in the small office. He noted the desk was still piled high with paperwork, much like it had been on his first visit. It bore a striking resemblance to his own desk buried in paperwork back at the station. Jack pushed the thought from his mind.

"Not at all, Inspector," replied Mrs Masters, once again squashing her ample frame into her swivel chair. It creaked beneath her weight. "How can I help you?"

"It's really just some more background information on Patricia Gordon. During our investigations, it's come to our attention that she may have had another job? A second income?"

Mrs Masters nodded. "Yes, yes, that's quite correct. She did."

"You don't happen to know what that would be?" Jack raised his eyebrows. "We noted from her bank statements she had a regular deposit each week, but it was in cash so we can't trace where it came from." He paused. "Another care home, maybe?"

Mrs Masters shook her head. "No, not a care home, Inspector. She worked in the evenings, Monday to Friday, as a cleaner."

"A cleaner?" Jack frowned. "Would you happen to know where that was?"

\* \* \*

Time: 3.00pm
  Date: Thursday 26<sup>th</sup> July 2012
  Location: A cellar in London

A pair of hands grabbed her roughly by the shoulders and lifted her into a sitting position. She must have dozed off; her eyes squinted in the dark, trying to make out the shapes in front of her. Without warning, the masking tape was ripped from her mouth and she felt something bang against her teeth.

It felt like a bottle.

She opened her lips to feel the cool rush of water fill her mouth. She opened her mouth wider, greedily gulping the liquid as fast as she could.

"Slow down, slow down," he hushed, a faint chuckle to his voice. "You'll choke."

Isabel coughed and spluttered as the water went down the wrong way, but it didn't stop her thirstily draining more from the bottle. Water had never tasted so good. She felt as though she hadn't had a drink in days. So thirsty. So thirsty.

But it didn't last.

The bottle disappeared and the masking tape reappeared once again.

"Not long now, Carol – we'll soon have you out of here."

\* \* \*

Time: 3.30pm
  Date: Thursday 26<sup>th</sup> July 2012
  Location: Metropolitan Police HQ, London

Jack handed DS Carmichael another tissue. "I guess saying sorry again doesn't really cut it."

DS Carmichael took the proffered tissue, throwing the blood-tinged one in his hand into the waste-bin by his side. He dabbed the fresh tissue at his nose, the blood flow showing signs of abating. He shrugged and shook his head.

"You had your reasons, Jack. Forget it."

Jack gave a somewhat rueful smile. "Maybe. But I should never have hit you. I don't do that. I don't know what came over me."

"She's your friend. A good friend," replied DS Carmichael, dabbing at his top lip where Jack's fist had split the skin on its upward trajectory towards his nose. "You guys are tight. I get that. Amanda told me. It's fine, honestly. I'll live."

"Not broken then?" Jack nodded at DS Carmichael's nose. He received a shake of the head and a faint grin in response.

"No, badly bruised and swollen I think was the verdict. And I still have all my teeth." He raised his split lip, wincing in pain as he showed Jack the open wound still oozing blood.

Jack grimaced and passed him another tissue. "And I shouldn't have said those things about your personal life." His eyes flickered towards DS Carmichael's blood stained hand – the faint mark of a wedding ring band still visible. "You were right; it was none of my business."

DS Carmichael flexed his left hand and gave another shrug. "We're police officers, Jack. Since when did any of us retain the ability to maintain a stable relationship? Show me a happily married police officer and I'll let you have another go at breaking this nose."

"Fair point." Jack rose to his feet and headed towards the door. "When you've finished pampering yourself, we could do with you back upstairs. We've still got a killer to catch."

\* \* \*

Time: 3.40pm
  Date: Thursday 26<sup>th</sup> July 2012
  Location: Metropolitan Police HQ, London

As Jack returned to the investigation room, the wall of heat hit him square in the face. DC Cassidy was busy trying to make the standing floor fans provide more than a weak wave of air movement; trying but failing. The only window in the room was open as wide as health and safety would allow, and the blinds were drawn to shut out the direct sunlight that was beating down from outside. Despite this, the heat of the day was still managing to seep into the room.

Jack ran a finger around the inside of his shirt collar and grabbed a bottle of water from the tray on the table. Although not chilled, it was better than nothing. "We need to go through the CCTV again," he announced. "There's got to be something we're missing."

DC Cassidy turned her attention away from the floor fans and reached for the remote control and mouse. The whiteboard screen juddered into life, the faces of the four victims frozen in time. "Not again," she breathed, tapping the mouse against the table. "This thing has been playing up while you've been gone. I think it's the heat."

"Ex-husband confirmed the evening job," said DS Cooper, rolling up his sleeves and discarding his tie. "An art gallery."

Jack nodded. "The Matron at the care home said the same thing. Gladwins Art Gallery on Buchanan Street. She's been working there in the evenings for quite a while, as far as they know."

DC Cassidy cursed under her breath and tried switching the screen off and on again; the usual suggested troubleshooting command for anything IT related. Why it worked, no one ever knew. However, when the whiteboard screen jolted back into life, the images were still frozen and starting to break up. "God give me strength..."

Just then, the door opened and DS Carmichael walked in, still dabbing a bloodied tissue to one nostril. "It's all going mad downstairs. The Wi-Fi is down, due to the heat." He glanced up at the stuttering and pixelated images on the whiteboard screen. "Looks like you know about that already, though."

Jack opened his mouth, about to welcome DS Carmichael back on the team, when a deafening bang penetrated the sultry air, sending waves of vibrations around the room. DC Cassidy almost flew out of her seat, dropping the remote control as if it were on fire. The whiteboard screen went black with a hiss and crackle; the overhead lights snapped off. The floor fans ground lazily to a halt.

"Power cut," announced DS Cooper, stepping over towards the door and popping his head out into the corridor. "Yep. Lights off everywhere."

Great, thought Jack. Just great.

"OK, Cooper. Let's bring DS Carmichael here up to speed." Jack nodded at the folder and paperwork still on the table. "I had wanted to go through the CCTV again, but...." Jack waved his hands towards the non-existent power supply. "Looks like that'll have to wait."

DS Cooper seated himself back at the table and reached for the manila folder.

"Why don't we go back to basics?" DS Carmichael strode over to the back corner of the room. "Time for a bit of old-school policing, eh Jack?" He looked back over his shoulder, while dragging out the abandoned pin-board that was still propped up against the far wall. "Sometimes, the old ways are the best, don't you think?"

Jack watched, a smile steadily creeping across his face, while DS Carmichael pulled the pin-board to the centre of the room. He then tossed a box of drawing pins onto the table. "Off you go then, Cooper."

\* \* \*

Time: 3.45pm
  Date: Thursday 26<sup>th</sup> July 2012
  Location: Metropolitan Police HQ, London

It wasn't long before DS Cooper had pinned up photographs of all four women, plus a time-line for each - from the last time they were seen, to the discovery of their bodies. Brief post mortem results and cause of death accompanied each photograph, as did their employment status and demographics such as age, height, weight and shoe size. Lastly, pictures of the shoes found at each location were pinned to the cork board.

Jack let DS Cooper run through the evidence once again for DS Carmichael's benefit, taking the opportunity to go over the facts one last time in his own head. Facts that bounced around inside his brain, but seemingly failed or refused to organise themselves into any logical sequence. At times like this, Jack often tried to get inside the mind of his suspect – delve into the inner workings of whatever depraved soul they were trying to apprehend. But this one – this one was different. Try as he might, Jack couldn't make sense of anything. None of the pieces fitted together like they should. It was like trying to complete a jigsaw puzzle without all the pieces, while blindfolded.

Something was missing.

Something was definitely missing.

"Cooper, bring up the CCTV images." Jack walked over to the pin-board and spun it around on its wheels, so a fresh board faced them. Fortunately, Jack had insisted that still images from the CCTV cameras should be printed off - still averse to relying solely on technology, he generally ignored the emails that clogged up his inbox, advising everybody they needed to do their bit to save paper. Jack was not against saving the environment, and proudly owned several "bags for life". But sometimes, technology could not replace good old fashioned paperwork. Unable to mask the faint smug smile that shadowed his lips, he watched as DS Cooper slid the photographs out of the file.

The grainy camera shots from each of the four locations were pinned to the cork board. Ford Mondeo registration AV09 BVZ, DS Carmichael's pool car, appeared in each image, along with other random cars and vans.

Four pairs of eyes scoured the photographs.

It didn't take long for the obvious to stare them full in the face. With the images pinned side by side across the pin board, it was impossible to miss.

"Shit," mouthed Jack, as the penny well and truly dropped. He could tell from the expressions of the other three pairs of eyes in the room that he was not alone.

"Shit," repeated DS Carmichael, stepping closer to the board. "How did we manage to miss this?"

"How to hide in plain sight," added DS Cooper, shaking his head.

In each of the images where DS Carmichael's Ford Mondeo registration AV09 BVZ was pictured, a single vehicle could also be spotted – sometimes in front, sometimes behind.

But there.

Always there.

The same vehicle.

In each location.

As clear as day.

A vehicle that would raise no suspicion.

A vehicle that would never register in anyone's memory as it goes about its lawful business.

A vehicle that as soon as it is seen, it is forgotten.

Invisible.

A perfect choice.

Jack joined DS Carmichael in front of the pin board, their faces mirrored in shock. The vehicle in question was a London Ambulance Service NHS Trust ambulance.


\* \* \*

# Chapter Thirty Three

Time: 3.50pm
Date: Thursday 26<sup>th</sup> July 2012
Location: Metropolitan Police HQ, London

"We need to find a sodding PC that's working." Jack scribbled the regis-tration number of the ambulance onto a scrap of paper. "Aren't we meant to have some kind of generator system up and running by now?" Jack could have sworn that during one of his many major incident training seminars that he had dozed off through, there was always the promise of a back-up generator if the worst should happen. Any widespread power outage, whether caused by accident, divine intervention or a terrorist attack, reassurances were abundant that the police's work would be able to continue.

But so far, he couldn't see, hear or feel anything kicking in.

Except panic and his own rapidly increasing heartbeat.

"On it, boss." DS Cooper leapt into action and headed in the direction of the door. "None of the internal phones are working, and I've got no mobile signal either. I'll head downstairs and see what's what." Before he reached the door handle, however, the door itself was flung open.

Jack's eyes widened at the sight of Mac rushing into the investigation room, followed by a harried and flustered looking police constable.

"Sorry, Sir," said the constable, still trying to get in front of Mac and bar his entrance. "The power cut has played havoc with all the security doors downstairs. And he wouldn't wait."

"I need to know what's happening, Jack." Mac's voice was taut and on the verge of breaking. "I'm going mad just waiting around for news." He shrugged off the clutches of the police constable who was still trying to guide him back into the corridor. "I need to know, Jack."

"OK, OK." Jack held up his hands to placate Mac and the flustered, pink faced police constable. "It's OK, Stu. Just calm down." He turned towards the police constable and gave her a reassuring smile, waving her away. "He's fine. Don't worry about it. Leave it with me. I'll escort him from the building when we're done." He flashed her another of his smiles, and saw the police constable's features relax, relief flooding her cheeks that she was now free from the responsibility of the unwanted intruder. She wasted no time in backing out of the investigation room and leaving them to it.

"Jack, I don't know what to do," continued Mac, pacing up and down by the window, his trembling hands raking through his unruly hair. "I can't... ..."

"Look, Stu. It's OK. Stop pacing up and down, you're making me dizzy." Jack reached out and grabbed hold of Mac's arm, bringing him to a halt and guiding him towards a chair. "Just sit down. Now really isn't a good time, Stu. You can't be here, you know that."

"Where else am I meant to go, Jack?" Mac looked up into his brother's eyes, unable to hide the moist tears that were threatening to squeeze themselves out of the corners of his own. "We can't lose her. *I* can't lose her..." His voice cracked and broke off.

Jack placed what he hoped was a comforting hand on Mac's shoulder. "I know. But we're a bit busy here right now, Stu. Now *really* isn't the time." Jack flashed a worried look at the pin board, nodding towards the CCTV images that were still displayed. "We've got to try and track down an ambulance when all our computer systems are down. You need to let us get on with it."

Instantly, Mac whipped his head up, his eyes drawn to the pin board. "Did you just say ambulance?"

\* \* \*

Time: 1.15pm
 Date: Tuesday 24<sup>th</sup> July 2012
 Location: Acacia Avenue, Wimbledon

While the customer took hold of the hand-held electronic device and scribbled his signature, Mac raised his eyes over the man's shoulder towards the double garage behind him. The up and over garage door was open, showing the interior. One side of the garage appeared to be a workshop area, with a wooden bench running along the left hand side. Mac squinted through the sun, seeing what looked like a variety of hand tools hanging from the wall above the bench. Hammers, several saws, and what appeared to be a power drill with its various attachments.

The right hand side of the garage, however, housed a vehicle. Mac let his eyes run over the unusual occupant of the building. Not that the vehicle itself was unusual. It was pretty standard. Just not the type of vehicle you would normally expect to see in a suburban double garage. Its signature yellow and green colouring reflected the sun's rays, shining brightly as if recently washed and polished.

\* \* \*

Time: 3.55pm
 Date: Thursday 26<sup>th</sup> July 2012
 Location: Metropolitan Police HQ, London

"I need that address, Stu," barked Jack, making a grab for the same piece of paper that he had scribbled the ambulance registration number on.

"I'm.... I'm not sure I remember it exactly." Mac looked from Jack to the other three pairs of eyes in the room. "I would need to check back with work."

"Think, Stu. Just think. Anything you can remember about it – the road name, the post code. Jesus even just the area of London would be a start." Jack picked up the internal phone that was housed on the table, and grimaced as it confirmed the systems were still down. "Where's this sodding generator?"

"It was in Wimbledon. That's all I can remember. The road.... maybe something Avenue?" Mac broke off and shook his head. "But surely you don't think it's him?"

"Him?" Jack frowned at his brother. "What do you mean *him*?"

"Patrick."

"Patrick who?" A sinking feeling began to creep into Jack's stomach. "Who are you talking about?"

"Patrick," repeated Mac, pausing while the others caught up with him. "The guy who rents space in Isabel's art studio. It was his house that I saw the ambulance at. In his garage. I was delivering a package to his address."

Jack stood stock still, his eyes widening in shock. It was several seconds before he managed to find his voice, seconds that seemed to drag on for hours. "*Isabel's* Patrick? Are you sure?"

"Absolutely, no question," nodded Mac. "I even mentioned to him that I recognised him. From the studio."

"Whoa, let's back up a minute," interrupted DS Carmichael, who had been leafing through his pocket notebook, frantically flicking the pages until he found the one he wanted. "Would this have been Acacia Avenue, Wimbledon, by any chance? Corner house, flanked by huge leylandii trees. Just down the road from the White Hart pub?"

Mac nodded. "Sounds like the place. There was definitely a pub close by. Patrick Mansfield lives there. Big double garage."

DS Carmichael snapped his notebook shut and shook his head, his throbbing nose and bleeding lip pushed from his thoughts. "No he doesn't. But Peter Holloway does."

\* \* \*

Time: 9.15am

    Date: Thursday 26<sup>th</sup> July 2012

    Location: Acacia Avenue, Wimbledon

"Ah," called out Jonathan Spearing, bending down to retrieve the parcel that had been sitting on the porch by the geranium pots. "Parcel for you; delivered while you were out."

The Daily Mail reporter stepped past DS Carmichael with the large box held out before him. DS Carmichael obligingly stepped out of the way, watching as the box was delivered to its rightful recipient.

"Thanks, Jon. They always deliver when I'm not at home. Thanks for taking it in."

"No problem. Anytime."

DS Carmichael followed the man and the parcel down the garden path, heading for his car. Patrick. Patrick Mansfield. DS Carmichael had taken a quick glance at the address label on the parcel. Patrick Mansfield it had said.

As the box had been handed over, DS Carmichael and Patrick Mansfield had caught each other's eye. Only fleetingly, and just for a split second.

But it had been enough.

Enough for DS Carmichael to know that Patrick Mansfield was not who he said he was. There was something about those eyes. He had seen them before. Hollow eyes. Devoid of emotion. Eyes that DS Carmichael would never forget.

\* \* \*

Time: 4.00pm

Date: Thursday 26<sup>th</sup> July 2012
Location: Metropolitan Police HQ, London

"I felt there was something wrong about it," continued DS Carmichael. "But I couldn't put my finger on it at the time. It was over in a matter of seconds. That reporter, Jonathan Spearing, handed him the parcel, and then he was gone. But not before I glimpsed into his eyes. And something registered. I'd seen them someplace before. I just couldn't remember where. And when I saw the name Patrick Mansfield on the address label on the parcel, it grated with me. I just didn't know why at the time." DS Carmichael paused, flashing Jack an urgent look. "It came to me on the drive back, but when I got here we were kind of distracted. He's not Patrick Mansfield. He's Peter Holloway."

"Peter Holloway?" Jack felt the air around him thicken, the oxygen being squeezed from it until he felt unable to breathe. His throat felt scratchy and in desperate need of hydration. He swiped at the bottle of water once again and gulped down the lukewarm fluid inside, grimacing as he did so. "Talk to me. Who is he?"

DS Carmichael grabbed an A4 sheet of paper from the manila folder on the table and rushed over to the pin board. He stabbed two drawing pins into it before swiping up a marker pen.

"Peter Holloway. When I worked at Sussex Major Crime, his wife and daughter disappeared. The summer of 1998. I was just a rookie PC, but he was always suspect number one in my eyes. But there was nothing we could stick on him. He came out squeaky clean and played the devastated husband and father very well."

"You didn't believe him?" Jack moved closer to the pin board.

"Not a chance. He did it. I was sure of it."

"Details. Now."

DS Carmichael wrote as fast as his shaking hands would allow. "Peter Holloway. On a Sunday in June 1998, he reported his wife Carol and daughter Jess missing. He said they had failed to come home after a shopping trip."

"And they were never found?"

"Never." DS Carmichael shook his head. "At the time they were living out in the Arundel area of West Sussex. We took that place apart, the garden too. No sign."

"Isabel told me that Patrick talked about his wife and daughter to her." Mac had risen from his chair and made his way over to the pin board, standing by Jack's shoulder. "He told her that they both died in a house fire. So he could empathise with her own loss."

"There was no house fire. The guy was a serial liar," continued DS Carmichael. "I wouldn't believe a word that came out of his mouth. He's evil. Pure evil."

\* \* \*

Time: 5.15pm
Date: Sunday 14<sup>th</sup> June 1998
Location: Arundel, West Sussex

Peter Holloway clicked the padlock into place and turned his back on the shed. Walking briskly back towards the house, he glanced at his watch. He would need to move them soon; they couldn't be found here.

But before that, he had things to do.

Entering the kitchen by the back door, he immediately strode over to the American style fridge housed in the corner, next to the gleaming Aga. It had been Carol's choice. The fridge. He hated it. Too big. Too cumbersome. Too American.

But Carol had got her way.

As she always did.

But not anymore.

Pinned to the fridge, in amongst the shopping lists and photographs, was the calendar Carol used to plan their lives. Supermarket deliveries, hair and doctors' appointments, coffee mornings, school parents' evenings, hockey club for Jess, riding lessons on a Saturday morning, Carol's shift patterns, Carol working late.

Yes, Carol working late.

He knew exactly what that had meant.

She could deny it all she wanted.

But he knew the truth.

He grimaced as he cast his eyes over the latest entries. He hated the way his life was mapped out for him. Every minute of every day was planned and accounted for. What time was he going to work? What time would he be home? Was he going to take the car for its MOT next week? Questions, questions, endless questions.

But not anymore.

Peter picked up the marker pen Carol used to annotate the calendar. In small, neat handwriting, mirroring Carol's, he added an event to Sunday 14th June.

"Mum and Jess – London shopping. Back late."

The marker pen squeaked on the cheap, glossy calendar paper and felt clumsy in his latex-gloved hands. He stretched his fingers, the tight-fitting material making his hands feel hot and sweaty. But he couldn't remove them.

Not yet.

He still had things to do.

A quick scan of the front room located Carol's handbag. Inside, he deposited her purse, glasses, house keys and mobile phone. Luckily for him, the phone had been switched off – nothing to suggest she had not been in London for the day with her daughter as the calendar indicated. He picked up both coats from the coat-stand by the front door, and bundled everything together into a black bin liner.

He picked up his own mobile phone from the sofa, ripping off one latex glove so he could access the keys more easily. He typed a quick message.

"What time will you be home, love? Do you want me to pick you up from the station?"

Sent.

To Carol.

A message she would never receive.

He glanced again at his watch. Quarter past five. He had a few hours until he would become worried about his wife and daughter's whereabouts; concerned that they had not been in touch and hadn't yet returned home. Concern that he would dutifully pass onto the local police station – not 999 – I mean, it's not an emergency is it, officer? They're just out late, enjoying the day shopping. It's nothing to worry about, really, is it? It's just, well, it's getting late now, officer, and my wife's phone seems to be switched off.

Peter Holloway snapped the latex glove back on his hand.

Three hours.

He would ring in three hours.

That would be enough time.

Time enough to clean the car and empty the shed.

\* \* \*

Time: 4.10pm

Date: Thursday 26th July 2012

Location: Metropolitan Police HQ, London

Suddenly, the overhead lights flickered into life, the fluorescent bars humming and buzzing. The floor fans whirred and picked up speed, ruffling the papers pinned to the cork pin-board.

"Looks like the generator has kicked in, or the power is back on," mused DS Cooper. "What do we do first, boss?" He nodded at the annotations and information on the board that DS Carmichael had hastily added only moments ago.

"Get me a search on the address in Wimbledon. I want to know who owns it." Jack paced up and down by the window. "And then we'll need a back-up team – two teams – one for Isabel's café in case he's there, one for the

Wimbledon address...." Jack broke off mid-sentence, his eyes falling on the scattered crime scene photographs on the table in front of him.

And then it hit him.

It was there.

The link.

The link they had been searching for all along.

Jack spread the photographs out, separating them into four sections.

"Patricia Gordon." Jack pointed at the batch of photographs of her neat and tidy one-bedroomed flat. "We now know she had an evening job – at the Gladwins Art Gallery. Who fancies betting a certain artist frequented that gallery?" Jack cast his eyes around the room. Everyone's gaze, including Mac's, was trained on him.

* * *

Time: 6.00pm

Date: Friday 6th July 2012

Location: Gladwins Art Gallery, Buchanan Street, London

Patricia Gordon pushed open the door to Gladwins Art Gallery and smiled at Roger, the security guard, standing to attention by the front window.

"Evening, Roger," she breezed, heading straight for a door at the rear of the ground floor gallery, towards the back offices and store cupboards. "Still hot out there today."

"Certainly is, Mrs Gordon," replied Roger. "Not looking forward to the journey home tonight."

Patricia smiled over her shoulder as she disappeared through the door, emerging a few moments later with her mop and bucket, pulling a cleaning trolley behind her. She had placed a plastic apron over her clothes and swapped her shoes for a comfy pair of trainers. She headed for the lifts, usually starting her cleaning routine on the upper floors of the three storey gallery, cleaning the exhibit rooms on level three first.

The lift pinged and the doors opened. With a final smile in Roger's direction, Patricia pulled the cleaning trolley into the lift and hit the third floor button. It only took a matter of seconds to reach the top floor, the doors opening once again onto level three. This was where the gallery exhibited its most prized and valuable paintings and sculptures. Most of the exhibitors were local artists, but there was the occasional Damien Hirst or David Hockney to be found, which would draw in the crowds from time to time.

As she stepped out of the lift, Patricia noticed a slightly built man heading her way, a large canvas painting under his arm.

"Oh, hold the lift would you, my dear," he called, breaking into a faster walk, the canvas banging against his leg. "This thing is very awkward to carry."

Patricia hurriedly turned back towards the lift doors and hit the button, but just as she did so the doors closed and the lift started its journey back down to the ground floor.

"Sorry." Patricia turned round, apologetically, and hit the button once again to recall the lift. "Just missed it."

"No problem, my dear," he replied, coming to a halt by the lift doors and resting the canvas at his feet. "I'm in no rush."

Patricia smiled and turned to be on her way, picking up the mop and bucket with one hand and starting to push the cleaning trolley with the other.

"Patrick. Patrick Mansfield." The man held out his hand towards her, his watery green eyes twinkling. "I'm not sure we've met."

"Oh, er, Patricia. Patricia Gordon." Patricia stepped back towards him, placing the mop and bucket back down at her feet. She politely took hold of his hand, noting it felt smooth and cool in her grip. "I'm just the cleaner."

"Never just a cleaner, my dear," cooed Patrick, continuing to smile at her as the lift doors pinged once again. "You're just as important as the artists on show here."

Patricia returned his smile and once again turned to leave.

"You remind me of someone," Patrick continued, ignoring the waiting lift and stepping in front of the mop and bucket. "I think it must be your eyes."

"Oh really, who?"

* * *

Time: 4.15pm
    Date: Thursday 26<sup>th</sup> July 2012
    Location: Metropolitan Police HQ, London

"Georgina Dale – University student. It just came to me now; where I'd seen it before." Jack jabbed a finger at the photographs of Georgina's small bed-sit in the halls of residence at St James's University; and at one photograph in particular, taken from her student desk. Amongst the open copy of Daniel Defoe's Journal of the Plague Year, and the half-finished essay, was a scrap of paper pinned to a post-it notepad.

Evening Language Tuition – Italian, French, German,
    Portuguese, Russian, Japanese, Mandarin
    All abilities – contact Patrick on 07876 544239

Jack's mind was instantly cast back to his first, and last, abortive attempt at hypnotherapy.

* * *

Time: 9.25am
    Date: Saturday 21<sup>st</sup> July 2012
    Location: Dr Evelyn Riches, Psychotherapist, St James's University,

London

Jack emerged from the therapist's office, blinking rapidly as the full glare of the morning sunlight flooded in through the curtain-less windows. Although Dr Riches had assured him that he was out of whatever trance-like state he had slipped into, he still felt somewhat groggy, a little soft around the edges.

He wasn't convinced this was working, but he had promised Stuart. And the Chief Superintendent. With the dreams picking up in their intensity over the last few months, he knew that something had to give. Work was draining him, and the sleepless nights were taking their toll.

"Same time in a fortnight," Dr Riches had said as her parting shot. "And remember to practice the meditation techniques in the meantime. Access those websites." He had nodded his head, obediently, taking the leaflet on the "step-by-step guide to meditation" and forcing it into his back pocket. "We will get there, Jack," she had added. "We will."

Jack remained unconvinced. He walked over to the chair where he had left his suit jacket, folding it over his arm as he had no intention of wearing it on what promised to be another scorching hot day. The clock on the wall told him he needed to be at work.

Squeezing these fifty minute sessions into an ever decreasing window in his work day was going to be tricky enough – but with a live murder investigation underway it was likely to become untenable. Maybe he would knock the sessions on the head for a bit – until things calmed down. He could always try the meditation in the meantime.

Jack felt a rueful smile cross his lips.

Yes. Jack MacIntosh. The Meditator.

Or not.

Jack knew that the crumpled leaflet in his back pocket would most likely stay there.

Heading for the door, he glanced at the notice board adorning the wall as he passed – covered in motivational quotations.

Difficult roads lead to beautiful destinations.

Don't wait for opportunity. Create it.

Don't try to be perfect. Just try to be better than you were yesterday.

The pain you feel today is the strength you will feel tomorrow.

Other posters contained website addresses for mindfulness techniques and meditation, self-help groups and publications. Jack noticed several more posters that contained adverts with detachable strips of paper. One was calling for volunteers for a research study into the effect of playing computer games on the brain.

Are you aged 18-30? Regularly use computer games?

Take part in our research study and earn £50 per session.

Call Mark on 07656 109387

The next was calling for volunteers to assess the effectiveness of meditation techniques in giving up smoking.

Are you a smoker? Want to give up?

Take part in our research trial investigating meditation techniques

Earn £25 per session

Call Andrea on 07892 085482

Hmmm, thought Jack. Seems like there's more money to be made in computer games than giving up smoking. Figures, he thought to himself as he reached the door. One final advert caught his attention.

Evening Language Tuition – Italian, French, German

Portuguese, Russian, Japanese, Mandarin

All abilities – contact Patrick on 07876 544239

* * *

Time: 4.20pm

Date: Thursday 26<sup>th</sup> July 2012

Location: Metropolitan Police HQ, London

Patrick.

"I knew I'd seen it before." Jack stabbed a finger at the photograph from Georgina's student desk. "I'm betting that's our man. He was into languages, wasn't he?"

Mac nodded, standing at Jack's shoulder and peering at the photograph. "He definitely was. I overheard him saying he was teaching that young lad, Dominic. The one who helps Isabel in the café? Was teaching him all sorts, I think."

* * *

Time: 11.45am

Date: Thursday 12<sup>th</sup> July 2012

Location: St James's University halls of residence, London

Georgie dropped her biro onto the, as yet, unfinished essay on her desk and rubbed her eyes. She had studied Daniel Defoe's Journal of the Plague Year for 'A' level English several years ago – but it was like reading it for the first time again. She was struggling to concentrate, and the thump thump thump from the guy playing drum and bass in the room above wasn't helping either.

She got up and went to open the mini fridge next to her bed. Three cans of Red Bull and a half eaten sausage roll. Sighing, Georgie considered ringing home – she was sure they would be glad to see her. And she would get fed. And get her washing done. And she would be able to relax in a hot bath rather than make do with the lukewarm dribble from her en suite shower room.

Tempting as it was, Georgie settled for a Red Bull and returned to her desk. She closed the Daniel Defoe book – she would give it another go after a shot or two of caffeine. The summer classes she had signed up for were, on the whole, interesting – and she didn't regret choosing to stay on in her halls of residence over the summer break. She would be paying the rent on the room anyway – or at least her parents were.

Taking another long gulp of the fruity, fizzy liquid, Georgie waited for the caffeine buzz to enter her bloodstream. She smiled at the way her life had been turned around – when now the strongest substance she took was either caffeine or the occasional vodka and coke. She didn't even smoke anymore.

She glanced at her notepad and the post-it note stuck in the corner. She had placed it there as a reminder the day before; she needed to give Patrick a call. He had cancelled their lesson last week, due to some family crisis or other, so she needed to rearrange. They had been working on some basic Mandarin, and she was keen to keep at it.

Reaching for her mobile phone, Georgie drained the last of her can of Red Bull and dialled the number. It was answered quickly.

"Georgie, my dear – how good to hear from you. I was only thinking about you a moment ago."

Georgie smiled into the receiver. "Hi, Patrick. Wondered if I could rearrange my lesson with you? Are you free over the weekend?"

Patrick confirmed that he was, indeed, free at the weekend but as he had a few hours spare later on today, would that be acceptable? Georgie readily agreed; anything to get out of her stuffy room and have a change of scenery. Her essay could wait another day.

After arranging to meet later on that afternoon, Georgie ended the call and deleted the call history.

Patrick was quite insistent on that.

And cash payments.

Something to do with how he wasn't declaring his language tuition earnings to the tax man – so everything had to be done under wraps. Cloak and dagger. Secretive. No paper trail.

Georgie smiled.

She liked that about Patrick.

It felt exciting.

It felt dangerous.

At that moment in time, Georgie didn't realise just quite how dangerous it was.

* * *

Time: 12.30pm

Date: Monday 23$^{rd}$ July 2012

Location: Isabel's Café, King's Road, London

"Mandarin." Patrick beamed at Dominic and pushed a piece of paper and pen towards him. "Let's start with some basic characters and sounds."

Dominic's eyes widened as he saw the list of Chinese symbols expertly and artfully drawn onto the paper that was now in front of him. "Mandarin? Really?! Isn't that really difficult to learn?"

"Nonsense," scoffed Patrick, his green eyes twinkling as he studied Dominic's wary expression. "It's a language spoken by the most people in the whole world – over a billion at least."

"Yes, but..."

"No buts, young man. You have a talent for languages. I can tell." Patrick picked up the pen and drew another character onto the paper. "If you put your mind to it, I'm sure you can accomplish anything. Wouldn't you agree, Erik?"

Erik paused, paint brush in hand. He leant his head to one side and cast his eyes over the half-finished painting on his easel. After a few more seconds deliberation, he looked over at Patrick and Dominic, a smile crossing his lips.

"Absolutely. Nothing is impossible."

* * *

Time: 4.30pm
   Date: Thursday 26<sup>th</sup> July 2012
   Location: Metropolitan Police HQ, London

"What background do we have on our third victim?" Jack focused his gaze on the only photograph they had of Hannah Fuller. Said to be a fairly recent picture, it showed a very slim, waif-like young girl, with her blonde hair scraped back into a high pony tail. "Has anything come in yet from the family liaison officer?"

"Still a bit sketchy," answered DC Cassidy, reaching for the remote control. "Some information was uploaded overnight." The whiteboard flickered into life. "She was estranged from her family; ran away from home aged fourteen. They don't really know that much about her recent life at all; and to be honest, they don't really appear to be that interested. The social worker was more helpful."

DC Cassidy used the mouse to navigate her way around the screen, pulling up a series of internal reports. "Ran away at fourteen. Lived on the streets, or sofa-surfing with friends. Minor drugs offences. Some shoplifting. Gave birth to a daughter in 2011 – when she was sixteen." DC Cassidy clicked on some images, showing Hannah together with her newborn baby. "Placed in a mother and baby unit soon after birth. The baby, Hope, has been the subject of several interim care orders. Hannah had been given one last chance to sort herself out, clean up her act, or her daughter was going to be removed from her care." DC Cassidy paused while bringing up some separate documents onto the screen. "Hannah was diagnosed with a personality disorder before she ran away from home; her GP records show several overdoses and self-harm attempts. Her current address is still given as the mother and baby unit – attends weekly sessions with her social worker, Felicity Walker."

"What's that?" Jack turned his attention to something written at the very bottom of the whiteboard screen. "The addendum at the bottom, there."

DC Cassidy enlarged the screen and read out the entry from the bottom. "Attends Art Therapy at the local community centre, one evening a week."

Art therapy.

* * *

Time: 8.00pm

Date: Wednesday 18<sup>th</sup> July 2012

Location: Walton Road Community Centre, Camden, London

Hannah loaded the paintbrush heavily with thick, black paint and scored several wide, angry lines across the paper. Paint flicked onto her t-shirt and across her cheeks. She brandished the brush as if it were a sword and she were fighting for her life.

In a way it felt like she was.

With her other hand she picked up a smaller brush, loaded it with a shimmering, metallic gold, and began stabbing and jabbing the paper in ferocious strokes. In amongst the smears of paint across her cheeks, angry tears trickled hotly from her reddened eyes, and dripped from the bottom of her chin. She rubbed them away with her arm, causing dark smudges of black and gold to smear across her face.

She loaded both brushes again. More paint. More smudges. More tears.

Her anger was at boiling point, ever since her five o'clock appointment with Felicity, her social worker. Hannah was trying, really trying, but whatever she did it never seemed to be quite good enough. She wasn't keeping her room tidy enough; she wasn't washing Hope's clothes often enough; she wasn't feeding Hope the right food; she was smoking too much around Hope; she was drinking too much. Everything was just too much.

Hannah attacked the easel with the black paint brush once again. Everyone expected so much of her, but offered her so little help. Mum and Dad were nowhere to be seen; not interested in helping to raise their only grandchild. Hannah knew she was struggling, but was determined not to give up. They could threaten to take Hope away as much as they liked. But she would never give up.

"Now, now Hannah." Patrick Mansfield appeared at her side and placed a calming hand on her shoulder. He could feel the tension in her muscles through the thin fabric of her t-shirt. "Carry on like that and you'll go right through that paper."

Hannah shrugged Patrick's hand from her shoulder and resumed her stabbing strokes, more black and gold paint flicking towards her.

"I'm not done yet," she replied, fiercely, her eyes squinting towards her easel. "You can't stop me."

"No, no I can't," answered Patrick, his voice low and soothing. "And neither would I want to." He edged away from Hannah's easel and opened a nearby cupboard. "Here – you might be needing these."

Hannah watched as Patrick deposited two fresh pots of paint on the table next to her – one black, one gold. Plus, two extra paintbrushes. He nodded at her to continue, closing the cupboard door as he did so. Turning to leave her to it, he leant in close to her ear and whispered.

"You remind me of my daughter."

Without another word, he merely winked and turned away.

\* \* \*

Time: 4.40pm

Date: Thursday 2th July 2012

Location: Metropolitan Police HQ, London

"Art therapy," confirmed DC Cassidy, nodding at the screen. "Social Services have confirmed the sessions were run by local artist, Patrick Mansfield."

"Do they not do any background checks for these kinds of things?" questioned Jack, his eyes drawn back to the pin board by his side. Hannah

Fuller's seventeen-year-old face stared back out at him.

"If they did, unless he has a criminal record I guess nothing would have flagged up as unusual," commented DS Cooper. "He wasn't using his real name."

Jack shook his head and eyed his watch. Time was ticking away. "How long will those cars be, Cooper?" He walked over to the window and parted the blinds, the sun streaming in and momentarily blinding him. Despite the window being open, the air remained hot and still. He stepped back and stood in front of one of the floor fans.

"As soon as, Boss," replied DS Cooper. "They'll let us know."

"While we wait – what have we got on yesterday's victim? We now have an ID?" Jack went back to the pin board and tapped the crime scene photograph of Zoe Turner's body lying in the grass in Battersea Park. "What do we know about her?"

DC Cassidy turned back to the whiteboard screen. "Dr Matthews emailed through a preliminary post mortem report just an hour or so ago. Same cause of death – strangulation by ligature. Same abrasions to one ankle, consistent with being restrained. Approximate time of death – between ten o'clock Tuesday night and the early hours of yesterday."

"Anything else?" Jack resumed his seat at the table, squinting at the whiteboard and Dr Matthews' draft report. "I guess it's too early for reports on her last known movements. Have next of kin been contacted yet?"

"Next of kin are being traced," replied DC Cassidy. "She was from Barnstaple originally, so we are liaising with the force in North Devon on tracing her family. She was reported missing by her boss when she failed to turn up to work yesterday morning, and he was worried due to the press coverage about the previous murders. She was single. Lived alone. A well respected advertising executive, based in offices on London Bridge – due to relocate to the new Shard as soon as practical."

"The Shard?" Mac had been slumped in a chair close to the fan, his t-shirt clinging uncomfortably to his chest, his leather motorbike trousers sticking to his skin. "She worked at The Shard?"

"Well, not yet," said DC Cassidy. "The company she worked for had agreed to lease offices on one of the floors. But they hadn't actually moved in yet, building work still being finished off." Clicking the mouse, she brought up Zoe Turner's employment details. "Crawford Advertising Agency. Due to move into The Shard towards the end of the year or early 2013 – currently working with designers to kit the place out."

"He was working for someone at The Shard." Mac got to his feet and moved closer to the whiteboard. "Patrick. I'm sure of it. Isabel mentioned he had some big commission or other – some advertising agency wanted him to design paintings for their reception area."

* * *

Time: 12.35pm

Date: Saturday 21$^{st}$ July 2012

Location: The Shard, London Bridge Street, London

Patrick watched as Zoe Turner quickly stepped across the road, shielding her eyes against the glaring sun. She reminded him so much of Carol. His Carol. The trim figure. The sleek black hair. The air of confidence that seemed to surround her.

He headed after her, timing it to perfection so that they met on the pavement.

"Ah, Ms Turner," breezed Patrick, a welcoming smile flashing across his face. "Fancy bumping into you here." He held out his hand in greeting.

Zoe Turner hesitated, her stride faltering while she tried to place the man standing in front of her. A slight frown crossed her features until recognition finally filtered through. "Mr Mansfield. Patrick," she replied, taking his hand in hers and giving it a momentary shake. "What brings you out this way?"

"Nothing in particular, Ms Turner," replied Patrick, gesturing for Zoe to step to the side as two workmen carrying a heavy metal barrier sought to get past them on the pavement. "It's all happening around here, isn't it?" He nodded towards The Shard, where a flurry of activity was still evident. Workmen in bright orange fluorescent tabards were dragging barriers and concrete blocks across the entrance, others were seated in cranes hauling heavy materials into place.

"Yes, indeed it is." Zoe pointed towards the skyscraper. "Our offices are to be on the seventh floor. I've just been allowed up to review the floor designs and office layout. I took your portfolio with me; I hope you don't mind. Our artistic director was there and he was most impressed with your work. He can't wait to see what you come up with for our reception area."

Patrick smiled. "Well, I'm going to make it my best work yet. I should have something for you to view in the next fortnight or so."

"That's super. We look forward to it." Zoe Turner turned to go, but found that Patrick had inched himself across her path.

"If you have a few minutes – we could grab a cold drink? They do a nice iced tea in that café over there." Patrick nodded back towards the vegan restaurant he had vacated only minutes before; his quinoa noodles no doubt still warm in the bin.

Zoe hesitated for a moment and looked at her watch.

Patrick noticed her delicate wrists, her slender fingers.

So much like Carol.

"Well, yes, I suppose I could do with something cool. An iced tea would be perfect." Zoe nodded her agreement and followed Patrick back across the road in the direction of the restaurant.

Patrick smiled to himself.

Carol had always liked iced tea.

* * *

Time: 4.45pm
Date: Thursday 26<sup>th</sup> July 2012

Location: Metropolitan Police HQ, London

"What about Isabel?" DC Cassidy nodded at the pin board where an additional photograph had been hastily tacked next to the four other victims. "Where did her path cross with this Patrick's?"

"Could've been anywhere," mused Jack. "They knew each other well – he rented space in her art studio and was there most days."

"Well it had to be sometime soon after she left Anthony Saunders's flat," replied DC Cassidy. "And before she arrived home."

\* \* \*

Time:11.35pm

Date: Tuesday 24<sup>th</sup> July 2012

Location: Buckingham Street, Embankment, London

Isabel stepped onto the pavement outside the converted Ernest Baker Grain Merchants building and looked along the road to where she hoped she would see the taxi emerging in a moment or two. The evening air was balmy and she quietly hummed, happily, to herself as she waited.

It wasn't long before two headlights approached from the end of the road and headed in her direction.

Isabel took a step closer to the kerb so that the Uber driver would be able to see her, and she raised a hand in greeting. The headlights drew closer, momentarily blinding her as they swung across the road to pull up in front of her.

As she made to reach for the rear passenger door, the driver stepped out into the dark stillness of the night.

"Oh," exclaimed Isabel, stopping in her tracks. "I didn't expect to see you!"

Patrick Mansfield smiled and gestured along the road behind them.

"There's an accident not far from here – the road is completely closed. Traffic is backing up all over. I thought I'd head down and rescue you. If you've ordered a taxi, there's no way they will be getting through."

Isabel returned the smile. "That's extremely kind – but how did you know where I would be?"

Patrick shrugged. "Lucky guess? Your friend, the motorbike delivery guy, he mentioned you had this date tonight...didn't take long to look up your lawyer friend in the phone book."

Isabel slowly nodded, and reached again for the passenger door. She was still feeling a little tipsy from the alcohol and needed to get her shoes off.

"Hey, come around the front." Patrick took hold of Isabel's elbow and guided her around to the passenger side of the car. "You'll be much more comfortable up here with me."

Isabel was in no position to protest and soon found herself folded into the front passenger seat. She heard the heavy clunk of the door as Patrick got in, and then the click of the central locking. Feeling a little queasy as the car drew away from the kerb, Isabel felt a chill flutter through her veins.

"If my taxi can't get through, how come you did?"

\* \* \*

Time: 4.50pm
  Date: Thursday 26<sup>th</sup> July 2012
  Location: Metropolitan Police HQ, London

Jack looked up at the four other faces that were now surrounding the table.

"I don't think we have any doubt that he's our man," he confirmed, nodding at each and every one. "He's our killer."

The internal phone rang, DS Cooper snatching it up on the second ring. He listened intently to the voice on the other end, briefly nodding his head.

"Good. Fine. OK." He gave another nod. "I'll let him know." Replacing the receiver, DS Cooper reached for his jacket and turned towards Jack. "Two tactical teams will be in the rear car park in five minutes. Plus squad cars."

Jack nodded his thanks. "Stu?" He looked towards his brother's haunted face. "You stay here. Don't go anywhere. And leave your phone on." After seeing Mac slowly nod his head, Jack turned to the rest of his team. "Let's go. Let's go get our killer."

\* \* \*

# Chapter Thirty Four

Time: 5.00pm

Date: Thursday 26<sup>th</sup> July 2012

Location: Metropolitan Police HQ, London

Jack dived into the passenger seat and slammed the door behind him. "Go, go, go!" he yelled, using one hand to wrench his seatbelt across his body and click it into place. In his other hand he pressed his mobile phone to his ear. "Cooper? As soon as you get there, I want a status report. If this guy Patrick, or Holloway or whoever the hell he is, is there, I want to know. And fast."

He snapped his phone shut and thrust it into his pocket. Steadying himself against the front dashboard, he felt the patrol car swerve around the exit of the rear car park and out onto the main road. It would take them approximately thirty minutes to reach Wimbledon. His stomach clenched and churned as he tried not to think about what they might find when they got there. Part of him hoped Patrick was there, part of him didn't. Maybe DS Cooper would find him at Isabel's café, innocently working in the art studio, and all of this would be unnecessary.

But Isabel needed to be found. And if he had her, Jack wanted to find her. No matter how traumatic that find might be. He picked up the police radio that had been sitting on the front dashboard, selecting the agreed radio frequency. "ETA thirty minutes," he informed the squad cars following in their wake. "Keep in formation." One further high performance patrol car

390

and an armoured police van were tailing him with blue lights flashing and sirens blaring. Worried road users hastily got out of their way, pulling over to the side of the heavily congested road, buses slowed down and waved them through. Taxis tended to carry on regardless.

The rapid response driver in control of Jack's vehicle concentrated intently on the road ahead, barely flinching as he sped through red lights and onto the opposite carriageway to reach their destination as quickly as possible. Jack could feel beads of sweat forming on his brow, but PC David Lyons was as cool as the proverbial cucumber. His eyes fixed, his face taut with concentration, both hands loosely on the wheel as he guided the car through a one-way system at 60 mph. Jack's own hands gripped his seat, the whites of his knuckles showing.

Jack's radio crackled into life. He risked taking a hand off the seat and grabbed it, knowing it would be DS Cooper with an update.

"Just arriving on scene, boss. Update to follow."

The radio then went silent.

* * *

Time: 5.00pm
Date: Thursday 26<sup>th</sup> July 2012
Location: A cellar in London

The huddled frame beneath the thin blanket was still; deadly still. Motion-less. Despite the heatwave soaring outside, the thick walls of the cellar kept the air cool and dank – no heat penetrated.

No heat to warm the limbs that rested beneath the blanket. No heat to bring colour to her wan cheeks. No heat to warm the blood coursing through her veins.

She remained cold.

She remained still.

She remained motionless.

Not even her breath could be heard.

* * *

Time: 5.15pm

Date: Thursday 26<sup>th</sup> July 2012

Location: Isabel's Café, King's Road, London

The King's Road was curiously empty for the late afternoon rush hour. Maybe it was the heat keeping people indoors, or the excitement of tomorrow's Opening Ceremony causing workers to take time off work. The patrol car carrying DS Cooper drew up in a bus lane on the opposite side of the road, fifty metres away from the front entrance to Isabel's café. From his front passenger seat position, DS Cooper scoured the entrance using a pocket-sized set of binoculars. The door was closed but he could see the "open" sign hanging in the centre.

A quick sweep of the front windows showed a young mother sitting in a window seat, sipping a wide-rimmed cup of coffee, with her baby nestled on her lap. She appeared to be alone at the table, a bulging baby-changing bag occupying the seat opposite. On the other side of the door, the other window seats appeared to be empty.

From previous visits to Isabel's, DS Cooper knew that there was a back entrance. Not an accessible entrance as such, the patio doors leading out onto a small, walled courtyard garden, but a means of escape nonetheless.

"We'll take the front entrance. Cassidy, you and your guys take the back." DS Cooper's radio transmission was greeted by an affirmative confirmation, and looking in the rear view mirror, he noted the second patrol car behind them discharging its occupants. A further police van, housing yet more armed officers, came to a halt close to its bumper.

DC Cassidy, dressed in protective clothing, exited the front passenger seat of the second patrol car, while two armed officers emerged from the rear. The group quickly jogged across the two lanes of traffic and headed down a narrow alleyway between an organic wholefood shop and another premises selling retro second hand clothes. Both shops were open for business, but trade was light; the heat of the day was keeping people away. Therefore, nobody seemed to notice the procession of heavily armed police officers heading down the shaded alleyway to the rear of the properties.

Each property along the passageway had a rear wall – some with access gates, others without. DC Cassidy took the lead, heading down the narrow alley until they came to a neat, well-maintained red-brick wall topped with ornamental spikes. There was no means of access to the walled garden beyond, but DC Cassidy knew this was the one they were looking for. She stopped and nodded at the wall in front of her.

The two armed officers at her rear scaled the wall as if it were a mere foot high inconvenience, avoiding the lethal looking spikes, and silently dropped themselves down into the courtyard below. Taking up positions either side of the rear patio doors, hidden in the shadows, they held their weapons steady, listening for further command while training them at the closed door.

Three more armed officers had followed them along the alleyway from the back-up police van, and with the help of two conveniently located rubbish bins, they were now also training their loaded weapons on the rear entrance to Isabel's café.

Receiving a nod from each of the armed officers positioned on the wall in front of her, DC Cassidy brought her police radio to her lips. "In position – rear entrance secure."

* * *

Time: 5.25pm
Date: Thursday 26th July 2012

Location: Wimbledon, London

A text message from DS Cooper confirmed that the second unit were in place at Isabel's. They would be storming the café at any moment. Jack's stomach clenched even tighter as he looked out of the passenger window, watching the nameless streets with their nameless occupants flash by.

The blue lights and sirens had afforded them an uninterrupted run towards Wimbledon. The tightly packed streets of central London, with their terraced houses, one-room bedsits and two-up-two down maisonettes, had now given way to much wider streets – mature leafy trees lining the pavements, on-street parking without restrictions. The properties facing these streets were now spacious semis, or roomy detached houses sporting front and back gardens. Private driveways housed gleaming Range Rovers and shiny Mercedes. The street lighting looked as though it actually worked, dustbins remained hidden in back gardens until bin day, and not a mini-cab firm or kebab shop in sight.

Welcome to suburbia, thought Jack, as they took a left and headed down yet another tree-lined avenue. He had a distinct feeling that they were not in Kansas anymore. The patrol car slowed down outside the White Hart public house - a well-maintained pub that sported a generous car park to the rear, wooden picnic-style tables outside the front entrance complete with umbrellas, and ceramic plant pots filled with sweet-smelling summer blooms either side of the arched wooden front door.

Jack's patrol car swept into the virtually deserted car park, pulling up next to a brand new BMW. The following patrol car and police van did the same. Almost before the car engine had died, Jack pulled himself out of the passenger seat and quickly scanned the car park and beyond. He noticed the walls of the pub were graffiti free, no broken bottles littered the ground, and no piles of dried up vomit decorated the front steps. It was as far removed from the city as Jack could imagine.

There was only one couple sitting outside on one of the wooden picnic tables, nursing cold glasses of cider, plates of recently consumed late lunchtime salads and sandwiches discarded to the side. The procession of police vehicles, and then the heavily armed officers wearing bulky protective clothing that emerged from within them, afforded a raised eyebrow from the couple on the picnic table. However, Jack noticed that they continued to sip at their ciders, content to watch the scene play out before them.

As they passed by, Jack raised a hand and put a finger to his lips.

* * *

Time: 5.25pm

Date: Thursday 26<sup>th</sup> July 2012

Location: Isabel's Café, King's Road, London

Three pairs of wide, panic-stricken eyes stared at the barrel of the Glock 17 weapon, their hands rising instinctively in the air.

"H...he's not here," stammered Sacha, in response to DS Cooper's question, her voice quivering in harmony with her hands. She didn't take her eyes off the gun, but reached out with one hand to clutch at Dominic who stood frozen to the spot next to her. "I...I've not seen him...not for a few days. Dom?"

Dominic shook his head, letting his mother grip onto his forearm. "N..no.....not since yesterday."

DS Cooper nodded, casting his attention to the third set of wary eyes still trained on the armed police officer in front of them. "And yourself?"

Erik Neumann flickered his gaze from the gun barrel to DS Cooper, his face passive. He didn't seem to show the same fear and panic at having armed police officers storm in, brandishing loaded weapons and bellowing instructions on not to move. Both Sacha and Dominic had instinctively screamed when the patio door had exploded in front of them; Sacha dropping the tray of freshly baked cookies onto the floor as she emerged from the kitchen, Dominic falling to his knees and hiding behind the art studio table. Fear coursed through their bodies, turning their legs to jelly.

Erik had been sitting at his easel and merely put down his paintbrush, rose to his feet and showed his open hands to the armed officers. He looked as though his heart had barely skipped a beat. And if DS Cooper wasn't very much mistaken, a hint of a curious smile had crossed the German's tight lips.

"We have only met a few times," answered Erik, shrugging his narrow shoulders. "I do not know him very well. I think I last saw him on Monday."

"H...have you found her?" Sacha's voice trembled, her grip tightening on Dominic's arm. "Isabel?" Coarse tears began to trickle down her pale face, her lips quivering.

DS Cooper shook his head, turning to the armed officers behind him and indicating they could stand down. He raised the police radio to his lips. "Stand down. I repeat stand down. Suspect absent from the premises." Turning back towards Sacha and Dominic, he tried a reassuring smile. He wasn't convinced it was working, as both mother and son still clung to each other in shock. "No, not yet," he replied, nodding once again at them both that they could now relax. "Take a seat. Sorry we had to shock you like that."

The two armed officers who had burst through the patio doors retreated into the back courtyard, stepping through the jagged glass that had been shattered in order to gain entry, their weapons lowered.

"Why are you looking for Mr Mansfield?" enquired Erik, resuming his seat at his easel and picking up his paintbrush. "Has he done something wrong?" The hint of a smile DS Cooper had thought he had seen earlier was still toying with his lips.

"He's a person of interest in a current investigation," replied DS Cooper. He wasn't sure he liked the glint that was shimmering in the man's eyes.

A shaking hand whipped back up to cover Sacha's mouth. "Oh my God, you don't think...." She choked back the question. "H...he's not involved.... with Isabel? Is he?" She exchanged a shocked look with Dominic, who was leaning back against a stool, his eyes still trained on the retreating gunmen. "He.... he can't be, surely? *Patrick*?"

"As I said. He's a person of interest in a current investigation." DS Cooper glanced over towards the café, where the young mother who had been sitting in the front window seat was still rocking on the spot, cradling her baby in her arms. She was looking towards him, pale faced, confusion and fear etched in amongst her already sleep-deprived features. He tried another reassuring smile. "I'm sorry...once again. For alarming you all." He began walking across the café floor, towards the front door, and glanced at his watch. "And we'll get someone over to repair the door."

"But..Isabel?" Sacha had followed DS Cooper into the café, Dominic trailing in her wake. "You think he.... Patrick.... has something to do with her going missing?"

DS Cooper paused at the door. "At the moment, we don't know. We just need to find him. Jack is heading over to his house in Wimbledon as we speak." He took in the worried looks washing over both Sacha and Dominic's faces. "We'll let you know as soon as we have any information," he added. "Sorry, I need to get going and call DI MacIntosh."

Just as DS Cooper was about to pull open the front door, Dominic stepped forwards out of his mother's shadow, holding his notebook in his hand. "Officer?"

\* \* \*

Time: 5.30pm
   Date: Thursday 26th July 2012
   Location: Acacia Avenue, Wimbledon

DS Carmichael recognised the imposing leylandii trees from his last visit. They had been recently trimmed, but still afforded cover as he and Jack approached the house from the side. Two armed officers stealthily inched their way up the gravel path and around the side of the house towards the back garden. The windows into the house gave no hint of life within.

Jack, with DS Carmichael at his side, followed in the wake of the armed officers, their protective body armour hanging heavily from their shoulders, making them sweat profusely in the incessant heat. Every movement they made seemed to generate a deafening creak, in the otherwise stillness of the surrounding air. The only other discernible sound was of birds chirping in the surrounding trees and the distant noise of a tinny radio.

Two further armed officers brought up the rear, four more remaining out at the front of Acacia Avenue, loaded weapons trained on the front door. The heavy military style boots of the officers leading the procession crunched lightly on the gravel as they made their way towards the back gate. The gate was shut, but unlocked. Looking through the wooden slats, the first armed officer gave a curt nod towards Jack.

Their man was at home.

* * *

Time: 5.30pm
Date: Thursday 26<sup>th</sup> July 2012
Location: Acacia Avenue, Wimbledon

Kneeling on a padded garden mat, Patrick Mansfield was busy clipping back the straggling, sun-singed tentacles of his perennial geraniums, depositing the clippings into a nearby recycling bin. The garden was well-tended and neat, the lawn freshly mowed, the flowerbed edges trimmed. He had spent some of the morning dead-heading all the patio containers that adorned the paved area outside the kitchen door, and was now tending to the bushes that had sprung up and grown over the summer despite the intense heat and lack of rain.

He hummed to himself as he worked. When he was finished, he would make a fresh pot of coffee and relax in a garden chair. Maybe start a new painting or sketch. The sun was sinking slowly towards the horizon, but its heat still beat down on to the back of his neck. He could feel a trickle of sweat making its journey down his back, in between his shoulder blades. Maybe a cool shower first?

He sensed their presence before the announcement came. The sweat on the back of his neck was accompanied by a prickle – the unmistaken sense of being watched.

"Armed police – put your hands in the air where I can see them."

\* \* \*

# Chapter Thirty Five

Time: 5.40pm
  Date: Thursday 26<sup>th</sup> July 2012
  Location: Acacia Avenue, Wimbledon

"Nothing." DS Carmichael emerged from the back door of Patrick's house. "No sign of anyone inside."

The initial search of the house had revealed nothing untoward. A standard three bedroomed house. Kitchen. Lounge. Dining room. No secret doors. No secret passageways. No basement or cellar. Nowhere to keep the kidnapped women. And no Isabel.

The outbuildings hadn't shown up anything either. The double garage did, indeed, house a refurbished London Ambulance. A quick search had revealed that the registration number AK01 RPG was legally registered to a one Mr Patrick Mansfield.

Jack had not allowed a detailed search inside the ambulance – wanting to wait for the forensics team to arrive and do a thorough job without any allegations of contamination. The rest of the garage housed a workshop – with the usual tools and paraphernalia that went with it. A cursory look around had revealed there were no secret spaces underneath the concrete floor; no secret steps down to a cellar or basement. And nothing in the loft space above.

Just a regular three bedroomed house with detached double garage.

Jack slowly began to feel deflated. He had been so certain, so sure that they were finally onto the real thing; that Patrick was their man and he was going to lead them to Isabel. But now the all too familiar feelings of doubt were creeping in once again. This could be the third wrong suspect they had targeted in as many days, and Jack did not fancy having to explain that fact to the Chief Superintendent – not after last time.

"He recognised me as soon as he saw me." DS Carmichael followed Jack as they began walking back along the garden path and around the side of the house towards the front. "He realises I know who he really is."

"Holloway? You really think he's him?" Jack approached the front patrol car, nodding at the driver that they were about to leave. Patrick Mansfield sat solemnly in the back seat, handcuffed.

"No doubt in my mind," replied DS Carmichael, pausing to peer into the rear window. "I'd never forget that face. Never in a million years."

* * *

Time: 2.45pm
Date: Thursday 18<sup>th</sup> June 1998
Location: Sussex Police

Peter Holloway nursed a cup of hot coffee, his hands curled around the sides, letting the heat spread through his fingers.

"Is there anything else we can get you, Mr Holloway?" Senior Investigating Officer DCI Michael Broadbent sat down on the opposite side of the table.

"No, thank you. This is fine." Peter Holloway's voice was calm and steady. He managed a small smile.

"Well, I won't keep you long. I'm sure it's been a long enough day for you already."

Peter Holloway nodded and took another sip of his coffee. It tasted bitter and sour at the same time, as if the milk was on the turn. He wished he had asked for sugar now.

"You reported your wife and daughter missing on Sunday 14<sup>th</sup> June - can you just run through the events of that day one more time for me? Just for our records."

Peter Holloway dutifully nodded, placing his cup of coffee back down on the battered and scarred interview table. "It was about seven or eight o'clock that I started to get worried. They had been out shopping all day, but were due back by seven at the latest. I even texted Carol to ask if she wanted picking up from the station."

DCI Broadbent nodded, noting the correlation with the phone records in his possession. "Indeed. And then what?"

"Well, I waited a little longer – as you do. But when my further texts went unanswered, I think I sent at least two more, I rang her mobile. Carol's mobile. But that went to voicemail." Peter Holloway paused, breathing in deeply to compose himself. "So I then went out in the car and headed down to the station to see if I could meet them from the last train."

"And they never arrived?" DCI Broadbent watched as Peter Holloway shook his head, sadly.

"No. I waited until the last train, tried Carol's mobile one more time, and then contacted the police."

"Were there any difficulties in your marriage, Mr Holloway?" DCI Broadbent raised his gaze and looked directly into Peter Holloway's eyes. Eyes that were unemotional. As hollow as his name. "Any recent arguments?"

"Arguments?" Peter Holloway frowned, and shook his head. "No, none. We were very happy."

DCI Broadbent nodded and added a note on the piece of paper in front of him. He glanced sideways at the two-way mirror where he knew the hastily arranged investigation team were watching. There was more to the disappearance of Carol Holloway and her daughter than Peter Holloway was telling them. Of that they were sure.

"And what about your daughter, Eleanor? Was she happy at home? Any problems at school?"

"No, no problems at school," replied Peter Holloway. "Jess – she hated her first name. Preferred her middle name, Jessica – she was a perfect student. And perfect daughter." He raised a hand to his eyes and made to brush away a stray tear – a tear that DCI Broadbent was sure was fake.

DCI Broadbent made another note on the piece of paper in front of him. "So, the two of them disappearing like that, without taking any clothes or personal items with them, would be completely out of character?"

"Completely." Peter Holloway leant back in his chair, his coffee cup abandoned in front of him. He flicked his eyes to the side, noticing the two-way mirror. He knew what it was the minute he walked into the room. He wasn't stupid. He had watched enough detective dramas to know that behind it would be a bank of officers watching his every move, listening to his every word. Watching his reaction. Waiting for him to slip up.

He smiled to himself.

Peter Holloway didn't slip up.

He knew that one of the officers behind the mirror would be the new PC he had spoken to first of all – he had forgotten his name, but he would never forget those beady, bird-like eyes, and narrow bird-like nose. He had asked him much of the same questions DCI Broadbent was asking just now – but he detected something in the young officer's voice. Something in his tone.

That beady eyed PC suspected him; he knew it.

He would have to watch him.

He could be trouble one day.

\* \* \*

Time: 5.45pm
  Date: Thursday 26<sup>th</sup> July 2012
  Location: Acacia Avenue, Wimbledon, London

"It has to be him. He owns an ambulance." DS Carmichael rounded the patrol car to get into the rear passenger seat.

"I'm not sure that's enough; there's no law against owning an ambu-lance," replied Jack, making his way to the front passenger side door.

"But it appears in all the CCTV footage?"

"So do you, if I remember rightly."

"Yes, well, that's different. Holloway is a killer. I know he is."

"I know; I agree. It's him." Jack's mobile phone beeped, the text message confirming that DS Cooper and DC Cassidy were about to leave Isabel's café. He opened the passenger door to the patrol car while dashing off a quick reply.

Seeing Patrick Mansfield in the back of the car did not quieten the fear still growing inside Jack. If anything it made it worse.

Where was Isabel?

If Patrick was their man, why wasn't she here?

* * *

Time: 5.45pm
Date: Thursday 26th July 2012
Location: Isabel's Café, King's Road, London

"What is it, Dom?" Sacha took a hesitant step towards Dominic, a flash of concern on her face. "What's the matter?"

Dominic stepped from one foot to the other; left then right, left then right. He continued to grip his notebook firmly in his hands.

"Dominic?" DS Cooper stepped away from the front door. "Is there something you need to tell me?"

"If...if you're looking for Patrick." stammered Dominic, swallowing past the lump that had formed in his throat. "I...I just wondered if you.... if you knew about the other house?"

"The other house?" DS Cooper's eyes briefly met with DC Cassidy. "What other house, Dominic?"

"His.... his mother's house. In Fulham." Dominic held out his notebook, open on a page with several neat, dated and timed entries. "There." He nodded at the open page.

DS Cooper took the notebook and glanced down at a section towards the bottom of the page.

12.51pm Tuesday 3rd July

Patrick telephoned plumber

To repair a broken shower.

At 12 Homefield Avenue, Fulham

"And this.... this is his mother's house? In Fulham?"

Dominic shrugged. "I guess. He told me his mum used to live in Fulham, before she died."

DS Cooper handed Dominic back his notebook and reached for his phone. "Shit."

* * *

Time: 6.00pm

Date: Thursday 25th July 2012

Location: Metropolitan Police HQ, London

Chief Superintendent Dougie King slid into the back seat of the unmarked Bentley and sighed. The day had gone from bad to worse. News of the arrest, and then the subsequent release, of Anthony Saunders, had hit the news headlines across the capital and beyond. The press and public relations department had been inundated with calls from reporters up and down the country, forcing them to switch all their telephone lines to answerphone while the furore died down.

And then the incident with Jack and DS Carmichael.

And the subsequent assault.

What a mess.

And all witnessed by Commander Forsyth.

A hastily arranged press conference later that afternoon, to which the Chief Superintendent expressly forbade Jack or DS Carmichael from attending, had done little to dampen down the disquiet. It had been short and sweet, the Chief Superintendent addressing the media personally. After a concise statement, he had refused to answer questions and had exited as quickly as his size nine's would allow.

Sighing once again, he looked out of the window into the early evening. It wasn't like Jack to be off the boil like this. He knew his Detective Inspector had recently resumed some long overdue psychotherapy; maybe that was affecting his usually pin-point judgement. If Jack didn't pull himself together voluntarily, he suspected that they may have to go down the route of Force approved psychological assessment once again. But Dougie King pushed that thought from his mind.

Tonight he had bigger things to worry about.

The air conditioning in the car was a grateful release from the heat of the day, heat that wasn't all down to the weather, and Dougie King relaxed back in his seat.

"Heavy traffic out there tonight, Sir." Charles Crosier, the driver, glanced in his rear view mirror as he pulled out onto the main road. He caught the Chief Superintendent's eye. "There's a dinner and speech at the Mansion House."

"Great," muttered Dougie King, settling further back into the soft leather upholstery. "Just what we need." He glanced at his watch. He was meant to be meeting the Right Honourable Bernard Saunders in approximately thirty-five minutes. It was already going to be an awkward drinks and dinner engagement, thanks to the arrest of the eminent QC's son. But if the Chief Superintendent showed up late as well, it would be like adding further insult to the already painfully inflicted injury. "I don't suppose there is a quicker route?"

Charles Crosier shook his head. "Sorry, Sir. It's grid-locked everywhere. The Mayor of London is delivering his pre-Olympics speech – followed by drinks and dinner. Should be a grand occasion judging by the looks of the traffic. I bet there are dignitaries coming in from all over. And the road traffic units will be out soon setting up diversions and road closures in readiness for the Opening Ceremony tomorrow."

Chief Superintendent King again looked out of his side window at the nose to tail traffic barely inching along. "All this for the Mayor of London?" he muttered, shaking his head. "Honestly, who do they think he is? The Prime Minister?"

Charles Crosier indicated left and peeled away from the worst of the traffic, although the road he pulled onto seemed almost as bad. "You wait, Sir. When he *is* Prime Minister, you won't be able to get anywhere."

The Chief Superintendent snorted in response. "Boris Johnson as Prime Minister? Like that would ever happen"

* * *

Time: 6.30pm

Date: Thursday 26th July 2012

Location: 12 Homefield Road, Fulham, London

With the wrought iron key hanging innocently on the wall next to it, the broad oak cellar door was opened without force. Armed officers, guns ready, flooded the darkness with bright light from their head torches, quickly securing the shadowed space. Once it was ascertained there were no threats lurking in the cobwebbed corners, they then trained their weapons on the motionless mound beneath the threadbare blanket.

"Clear." The command everyone was waiting to hear echoed back up the cellar steps to where DS Cooper and DC Cassidy were waiting, behind another bank of armed officers. Once the all clear had been raised, the wall of officers parted and they immediately ran towards the steps, descending as quickly as they could.

DS Cooper reached the entrance to the cellar first, and motioned for DC Cassidy to stay back. His eyes were instantly drawn to the huddled form on the mattress. Cautiously stepping forwards, his police baton outstretched in front of him, he crouched down next to the lifeless form. Four Glock 17 pistols were still trained over his shoulder, watching for the slightest movement, making his heartbeat quicken inside his chest.

Without touching the mattress or blanket itself, DS Cooper nudged the thin covering with his baton, lifting it away from the inert mound beneath. As the blanket peeled away, he recognised Isabel's pale face. Her eyes were closed, thick masking tape covering part of her nose and mouth.

With a careful flick of his baton, the blanket fell away, exposing Isabel's motionless body.

Breaths were held.

Hearts pounded.

Eyes were trained for any signs of life.

And then they saw it.

Isabel's chest rising and falling.

She was alive.

\* \* \*

Time: 6.45pm
Date: Thursday 24th July 2012
Location: Metropolitan Police HQ, London

"Peter Holloway – you are under arrest for the murders of Patricia Gordon, Georgina Dale, Hannah Fuller and Zoe Turner. In addition, you are under arrest for the kidnapping and false imprisonment of Isabel Faraday. You have already been cautioned, but I will remind you again – you do not have to say anything. But it may harm your defence if you do not mention when questioned something that you later rely on in court. Anything you do say may be given in evidence. Do you understand this caution?"

Peter Holloway stood mutely at the custody desk, handcuffed at the wrists, and merely nodded.

"Is there anything you wish to say at this stage?" The Custody Sergeant tapped the details into the computer in front of him.

Peter Holloway remained voiceless and shook his head.

"Your detention has been authorised and you will now be taken to a holding cell, where preparations will be made to interview you. You have the right to consult with a solicitor − if you do not have your own, one will be appointed for you. Do you wish to consult with a solicitor, Mr Holloway?"

Another silent shake of the head followed.

"If that should change, please make your request known to the interviewing officers and arrangements will be made." The Custody Sergeant nodded at Jack and DS Carmichael. "Cell three."

* * *

Time: 7.15pm
Date: Thursday 24<sup>th</sup> July 2012
Location: 12 Homefield Road, Fulham, London

DS Cooper watched as Isabel was helped into a waiting ambulance. She had roused not long after the armed officers had arrived, asking for water for her parched throat. Although DS Cooper was not a doctor, she appeared to be unharmed − if a little dehydrated. Due to her drowsiness, paramedics suspected some form of sedation and hooked her up to some IV fluids, but they wanted to take her to the nearest hospital for some further tests.

Despite her protests, DS Cooper managed to persuade Isabel to get into the ambulance, on the pretext that if there was nothing wrong then she would at least get a lift home.

Once the door to the ambulance was closed, he pulled out his mobile phone and dashed a quick message to Jack.

"Isabel safe. On way to hospital (under protest)."

* * *

Time: 8.45pm
  Date: Thursday 24<sup>th</sup> July 2012
  Location: Metropolitan Police HQ, London

"A full confession." Jack walked into the investigation room where DS Cooper and DC Cassidy were waiting. "He wants to see a solicitor, and make a full confession."

"That's great news, Boss," replied DS Cooper, sharing a grin with DC Cassidy. "How come he's caving in so quickly? He's only been here an hour or so."

"Well, I think the evidence against him was pretty compelling." DS Carmichael followed Jack into the room and closed the door behind him. "He'd have been a fool to have tried to deny any of it."

"Even so," continued DS Cooper. "That doesn't usually stop them."

"The ambulance recovered from his Wimbledon home – several false plates were found underneath the front seat and forensics have lifted various samples from the back." Jack sat down in one of the vacant chairs by the window. "The Fulham address is currently cordoned off for a detailed forensics search – but even now reports are coming in with positive results. There's even a full paramedic's uniform in one of the wardrobes. We'll know more tomorrow."

"Has he given any reason why?" DC Cassidy turned her head to the pin board which was still in place – all four women's pictures were still staring out at them. "Why he did what he did?"

"I guess his confession statement will tell us." Jack reached across and turned off the floor fan which was still blowing across the room. "But he has mentioned a few things already – each victim reminded him of his wife and daughter. The ones that disappeared back in 1998. He mentions his wife being unfaithful with a police officer."

"At the time, when they disappeared, he couldn't sing his wife's praises enough." DS Carmichael joined Jack by the window. "The perfect marriage, according to him. I never believed him then, and I don't believe him now. His wife, Carol, was part of the forensics department at Sussex. I never met her but everyone said she was the kindest, most loyal person. I can't see her having an affair."

"Well, at least we now have the link to his knowledge of forensics," added Jack, casting his mind back to Dr Hunter's criminal profile.

"You think he'll explain the relevance of the shoes?" DS Cooper nodded his head towards the photographs of the shoes that were also still pinned up on the board.

"Maybe. Maybe not." Jack shrugged. "My bet is they're a red herring. A way of playing with us, teasing us. Leaving us clues that weren't really clues. Dr Hunter was probably right – he wanted us to catch him, but he wanted to make us work for it."

"Is it me or is the weather turning?" DC Cassidy got to her feet and went to close the open window. "It feels cooler somehow. You reckon there might be rain?" She peered out into the evening light.

Before anyone could reply, the door to the investigation room opened and a PC popped his head in.

"DI MacIntosh? There's a message for you. From the forensics team at the Fulham house?"

Jack felt his stomach lurch. "What message?"

The PC shrugged. "Just that you need to call the crime scene manager. Something about bringing in machinery to lift the patio. The dogs are going crazy – they think there's something buried under there."

SEVEN DAYS

* * *

# Chapter Thirty Six

Time: 12.30pm

Date: Friday 27<sup>th</sup> July 2012

Location: The Duke of Wellington Public House, opposite Metropolitan Police HQ, London

"Pint?" DS Carmichael glanced at Jack while raising a hand to attract the barman's attention.

Jack nodded. "Thanks. I'll have a Guinness." He scanned the rest of the pub and noticed a spare table in the far corner of the room, nestled in between the fireplace and the dartboard that was, thankfully, not being used. "I'll go and grab us a table."

Jack headed over to the spare table and waited until DS Carmichael brought over the two pints of Guinness, plus a bag of salt and vinegar crisps.

"Cheers," nodded Jack, picking up his drink and taking a sip. "Although it really should be me buying you a drink. You got us onto Patrick, or whatever his real name is, pretty quickly." Jack returned his glass to the table, noting the stickiness from its previous occupants' drinks plus tell-tale crumbs from a hastily consumed lunch.

"Well, that young lad from the café put us onto the Fulham address – I'm not sure we would have found it so quickly if it wasn't for him."

"Dominic's a good lad." Jack paused and then nodded at DS Carmichael's face. "And I need to say sorry for your lip."

DS Carmichael smirked and took a sip of his own drink, wincing at the still raw cut on his upper lip. "It's OK, boss. No real harm done." He put his drink back down on the beermat in front of him and opened the packet of crisps, offering Jack the packet. "And I probably did kind of ask for it."

Jack shook his head and waved away the packet. "I'm not your boss in here. Call me Jack."

"I hear they've found human remains underneath Holloway's rear patio." DS Carmichael took a long sip from his Guinness.

Jack nodded. "I heard the same. Two sets of remains. Too early to say for definite."

"There's no doubt in my mind, Jack. It's Carol and Jess. It has to be."

"You're most probably right," conceded Jack. "But we'll wait for the formal identification. Then we'll charge him with two more."

DS Carmichael nodded and shifted his weight back in his chair, watching Jack sink another few mouthfuls of his drink. "I admire you, you know."

Jack paused, glass poised at his lips, and locked eyes with DS Carmichael across the rim of his drink. "You admire me? For what reason?"

DS Carmichael regarded Jack for a few more seconds, taking in the roughened, unshaven detective's appearance, but knowing that the eyes behind the less-than immaculate appearance were sharp and never missed a beat. "I admire you as a DI, I admire you as a leader – you lead your team with strength and vigour. And a passion for the job that shows. There was never any doubt that you would catch the killer."

Never any doubt?

Jack was not so sure.

"You played a part too, you know. Your background information on Patrick - Holloway - led us to him more quickly. Without it the result might have been very different." Jack gave an involuntary shudder. The alternative consequences did not bear thinking about. Instead he took another deep mouthful of his Guinness.

"But I also admire you as a person," continued DS Carmichael. "As a man."

Jack found himself holding DS Carmichael's gaze, noticing probably for the first time how the eyes he originally thought were cold and uncaring, actually had a depth to them. Eyes that had seen trauma. Eyes that had seen sadness and undeniable grief. Eyes that he recognised.

"Go on," Jack found himself saying. "I'm intrigued."

DS Carmichael glanced at his watch. "You need to be anywhere right now?" He fixed Jack with a questioning look, raising his eyebrows slightly.

Jack shook his head. "No, not for a while."

"Then drink up." DS Carmichael nodded at the half full glasses on the table. "I need to show you something."

* * *

Time: 1.30pm
Date: Friday 27th July 2012
Location: 7 Palace Mews Road, London

As they pulled up outside the house in Palace Mews Road, Jack felt the unnatural stirring of déjà vu wash over him. The property looked the same as he remembered. The same neat front garden. The same well-tended lawn. The same well-stocked and well-weeded flowerbeds bursting with summer colour. The same silent net curtains hanging in each and every silent window. It had been four years since Jack had last been here, but it felt like yesterday.

Jack glanced, curiously, across at DS Carmichael in the driving seat, and tilted his head to one side. He regarded the Detective Sergeant sitting next to him, watching how he was avoiding Jack's inquisitive gaze. Eventually Jack broke the silence.

"What are we doing here, Carmichael?" Jack again glanced out of the passenger window at number seven, fleetingly wondering if it was a face at the window that he could see. If it was, it disappeared as quickly as it had appeared.

DS Carmichael paused before he turned to his superior officer. "I'm taking you inside to meet one of the most important people who have ever shaped my life." Another pause before he continued. "There's a lot you don't know about me, Jack."

* * *

Time: 1.35pm
  Date: Friday 27<sup>th</sup> July 2012
  Location: 7 Palace Mews Road, London

DS Carmichael had barely finished knocking before the door swung open. "Robert! How lovely to see you!" Mrs Tindleman hesitated slightly before stepping forwards to embrace the lean Detective Sergeant.

Jack hung back in DS Carmichael's shadow, confused thoughts flooding his head - thoughts that would not slow down to wait for his brain to catch up. What were they doing here?

It wasn't long before his presence was noticed.

"And this is DI Jack MacIntosh," announced DS Carmichael, stepping to the side so that Mrs Tindleman could have a full view of the detective inspector lurking in the shadows. "A colleague of mine."

Mrs Tindleman let go of DS Carmichael and stepped forwards towards Jack. She held out a hand in warm acknowledgment. "I know who he is," she replied, her smile reaching the corners of her eyes. "We've met before."

* * *

Time: 1.55pm
  Date: Friday 27<sup>th</sup> July 2012
  Location: 7 Palace Mews Road, London

The room looked exactly the same as before. The same floral curtains hanging in the window. The same low coffee table sitting in the centre of the room. The same mantelpiece with the same polished, silver framed photographs.

But although it looked the same, it felt different. It felt very different. No longer was the air heavy with grief and despair; no longer did the house seem to echo with quiet sobs and cries for a lost loved one. Grief no longer shrouded this room. Instead, it felt light. It felt airy. It felt happy.

Jack glanced at Mrs Tindleman. She was exactly the same as he remembered her. Her fair hair tied loosely in the nape of her neck; the same grey eyes searching his own. But again, although she looked the same, she wasn't the same. Gone was the burden of grief weighing down her narrow shoulders; gone was the darkness in her red-rimmed eyes, darkness that had snuffed out the light, suffocating any hint of happiness. Gone was the weariness and hopelessness that she had worn like a shroud at their last meeting.

Instead she looked happy.

Radiant even.

"I'm not sure I understand," began Jack, watching as both Mrs Tindleman and DS Carmichael sat next to each other on the sofa opposite him. Two pairs of eyes stared across the coffee table at him; two pairs of twinkling eyes. Two pairs of eyes that held a secret Jack did not seem to be part of. "I'm a little lost," he admitted.

DS Carmichael smiled, and for the first time, Jack noticed the smile actually reached his eyes. Eyes that continued to twinkle, mischievously. "And you call yourself a Detective?" The smile turned into a laugh, while he turned towards Mrs Tindleman and gave her a quick nod. "You tell him."

Mrs Tindleman reached across and squeezed DS Carmichael's hand before turning her attention to an increasingly bemused Jack. "Inspector, this man here is my son." She let the statement hang in the air, the silence only disturbed by the rhythmic ticking of the mantelpiece clock. "And very proud of him I am too." She gave another squeeze of DS Carmichael's hand.

Jack let his gaze switch from DS Carmichael to Mrs Tindleman, and then back again, the confusion still evident on his face. "But...?"

It was DS Carmichael's turn to now reach across and take hold of his mother's hand. He mirrored her motherly squeeze, but this time did not let go. "When I was seven, these incredibly wonderful and kind people took me in and raised me as their own. My real mother was an alcoholic and drug addict; my father was serving life in prison for murder. I had been sent from pillar to post in various different foster families until the Tindlemans came to my rescue." DS Carmichael paused and gave his mother's hand another gentle squeeze. "They are my heroes."

For one of the rare moments in his life, Jack felt speechless. Various words were forming in his head but they refused to leave his mouth in any coherent form.

"They formally adopted me when I was twelve," continued DS Carmichael. "I changed my name to Tindleman by deed poll." DS Carmichael reached into his jacket pocket and removed his warrant card, flipping it over so that Jack could see his photograph and details.

Jack leant forwards in his seat, still trying to formulate a response from the tangled web of thoughts encircling his brain. DS Robert Tindleman, the warrant card read.

"Carmichael was my birth name. I kept it for undercover work – I guess I couldn't quite let go of the past no matter how much I might have wanted to."

Jack shook his head, the bewilderment still sticking like glue.

"Charles and I couldn't have children of our own." Mrs Tindleman's gentle tone filled the void. She let her eyes wander towards the mantelpiece where there was a photograph in a silver plated frame of her and Charles Tindleman on their wedding day. Jack felt his gaze follow hers, coming to rest on the same photograph. A photograph he remembered seeing on his last visit. "But we so wanted a child in our lives. And Robert has made us both so very happy and so very proud."

Jack let his eyes focus on another photograph on the mantelpiece. This one was of Charles Tindleman with his arm around his grown-up son; his grown-up son dressed in his policeman's uniform, not long after graduation. The young PC Tindleman had the same inky black eyes that Jack could feel boring into him from across the coffee table. The look of pride on Charles Tindleman's face could be seen from every angle. Jack wasn't sure if he had seen this photograph before, on his last visit. Had it been there? Had he seen it and not realised its connection to the DS that walked through his investigation room door some four years later?

\* \* \*

Time: 4.15pm
  Date: 17<sup>th</sup> November 2008
  Location: 7 Palace Mews Road, London

"Have you got everything you came for?" Mrs Tindleman had not moved from the sofa. Her eyes were still hollow and red raw from crying. Her skin still transparent and paper thin, looking as though she could crack at any moment from even the smallest gust of wind.

Jack tucked the buff coloured envelope he had taken from Charles Tindleman's desk under his arm and nodded. "Yes, yes thank you, Mrs Tindleman. It's most kind of you to let me have a look around." Jack was making his way across the darkened living from, the curtains still drawn and blocking out what light was trying to get in. "Are you sure you don't need me to stay? I could make you another cup of tea?"

Mrs Tindleman shook her head slowly and glanced up at Jack through water-filled eyes. "It's fine, Inspector. My son is due here any moment." She nodded at the mantelpiece; at the photograph of Charles Tindleman hugging his newly-qualified police constable son.

PC Robert Tindleman.

\* \* \*

419

Time: 2.00pm

Date: Friday 27<sup>th</sup> July 2012

Location: 7 Palace Mews Road, London

"I had no idea." Jack finally managed to find his voice. He turned his gaze away from the photograph on the mantelpiece to fix his eyes on DS Carmichael. "No idea that you had come through the foster care system too."

DS Carmichael shrugged. "Why would you? You should know, Jack, it's not usually something that you shout from the rooftops."

"No, maybe not." Jack sipped the hot tea that Mrs Tindleman had insisted on making, but he held up a hand to refuse the wedge of fruit cake on offer.

"I was lucky," continued DS Carmichael, affording his mother a smile. "I found the most wonderful people and they gave me a fantastic childhood – for which I will be forever thankful." He paused. "Not everyone is so lucky."

No, they're not, thought Jack.

* * *

Time: 1.30pm

Date: Saturday 10<sup>th</sup> September 1977

Location: St Bartholomew's Boys Home, Christchurch

The sound of the heavy oak door slamming shut behind him caused his heart to thump painfully inside his chest. His knees felt weak, his breath coming in rapid gasps. He felt sick. So very very sick.

And he wanted Jack.

A hand grabbed him roughly by the shoulder, fingers digging deeply into his skin. The hand pulled him forwards, making him trip over his untied shoe laces and fall to his knees onto the cold, tiled floor beneath.

"Stand up, boy!" growled the voice that belonged to the hand.

Stuart MacIntosh felt himself being dragged to his feet, the hand clawing deeper and deeper into his shoulder, the pain spreading down through his arm and into his quivering hand. Another hand appeared and clasped him around his wrist.

"And don't start with any of that crying," continued the voice. "I can't bear children who cry."

Stuart dared to look up into the face that was now inches from his own. A round, moon-like face that housed deep-set eyes; eyes which burrowed into a craggy covering of leathery skin. Aged lines bore deep into the man's forehead, carving deep ravines from temple to temple. Coarse grey hairs protruded from his bulbous nose, mirrored by identical growths emerging from each ear. As he spoke, his cavernous mouth sneered at Stuart, giving a glimpse of stained, chipped and uneven teeth. A rotten stench of stale cigarette smoke mixed with boiled, watery cabbage hit the young eight-year-old full in the face.

He recoiled backwards, trying to shrink as far back as he could into the dusty shadows of the huge hall, but the man's grip on his shoulder and wrist stopped him in his tracks. Stuart felt his bottom lip begin to tremble and the threat of tears stabbed at his eyes.

Suddenly, a sharp slap stung his cheek.

"I said no crying, you miserable little boy!"

A deep, red welt began to form on Stuart's left cheek, halting his tears before they were fully formed.

"Now, follow me. And don't make a sound."

The man started striding towards a door at the rear of the hall, dragging Stuart by the wrist in his wake. The door opened out into a narrow corridor, the walls damp with crumbling brickwork and covered with cobwebs. Stuart found himself stumbling into a run to keep up with the man's lumbering stride, the pain from the grip around his wrist causing him to choke back more unshed tears.

After a few turns, the corridor ended in a flight of uneven stone steps. The man did not break his stride, merely continuing to climb the steps while dragging his charge behind him. Three flights of stairs led them to room fifteen.

The man halted, loosening his grip slightly on Stuart's wrist, and turned his face towards him. More stale smoke and rotten cabbage wafted across Stuart's face.

"Don't get any funny ideas about running away, boy," snarled the man. "You stay right where you are and don't move an inch. Don't even breathe."

The man released his talon-like grip on the young boy's wrist and pulled out a large, rusty set of keys from his pocket. Selecting a heavy iron key from in amongst what looked like a dozen other identical iron keys, the man slid the key into the lock and turned.

"In you go." The man pushed the door open, the heavy wood grating on the stone floor. Once open, he pushed Stuart in the small of his back, causing him to stumble forwards.

Three pairs of solemn eyes looked up at him from unwashed, tear-stained faces. Even at the age of eight, Stuart could recognise sadness when he saw it.

Sadness and fear.

None of the eyes moved. Not even to blink. It seemed like the owners of the eyes dared not to move. Or breathe. Stuart felt the rough hand once again push him further into the room, and the door swing nosily shut behind him, the heavy echo bouncing off the damp stone walls. The grating sound of the lock being turned caused Stuart's skin to prickle.

The man was gone.

Stuart looked up once more at the owners of the three pairs of sad eyes, now noticing the bruises of varying degrees and ages littering their bare arms and legs. Bare arms and legs that were thin and pale, starved of sunlight and nourishment. The threadbare mattresses upon which the boys were cowering were stained and dirty, barely offering any comfort from the hard stone floor beneath.

The tears that had threatened to spill from his eyes were now released.

And for the first time in six years, Stuart MacIntosh wet himself.

* * *

Time: 2.10pm

Date: Friday 27<sup>th</sup> July 2012

Location: 7 Palace Mews Road, London

"My brother," said Jack, simply. "He was one of the unlucky ones."

"You were separated?" Mrs Tindleman eyed Jack with kind eyes, her face full of motherly concern. "They didn't keep you together?"

Jack shook his head, slowly, taking another sip of his cooling tea. "At first they did. We went to a foster family in the countryside; they took us both on. But the placement was only temporary, and it didn't last. Stuart was...." Jack paused, setting his teacup back on its saucer, and felt a smile cross his lips. "Stuart was just Stuart." Sighing, he let his eyes rest on the photograph of Charles Tindleman with his fatherly arm proudly encircling his policeman foster son. "They split us up when I was six, and Stuart was four. He kind of went off the rails a little after that. Foster family after foster family. Ended up in a children's home.... before he made the career choice of an approved school and youth detention." There was no hint of bitterness to Jack's voice; if anything there was pity. Pity and sorrow for the choices they had both made and the different courses their lives took.

DS Carmichael released his mother's hand and looked at his watch. "We best be making a move, Jack." He leant forwards and gave Mrs Tindleman a brief kiss on the cheek before rising to his feet.

Jack nodded and placed his empty cup and saucer back on the coffee table. "Nice to see you again, Mrs Tindleman," he smiled, following DS Carmichael towards the door. "We'll see ourselves out."

Mrs Tindleman nodded and smiled at the departing police officers. DS Carmichael pulled the front door of his childhood home closed behind them before making his way down the path and towards the car.

"The children's home your brother was in – was it local to where you grew up?" DS Carmichael unlocked the doors and slid into the driver's seat.

"Christchurch, wasn't it?"

Jack climbed into the front passenger seat and nodded, frowning slightly. "St Bartholomew's. How did you know that?"

DS Carmichael shrugged. "You must have mentioned it. Or somebody did." He put the key in the ignition and fired up the engine, pulling away from his childhood home. "Is that the massive Victorian place, out near Hinton? Falling down now?"

Jack nodded, clicking his seatbelt into place. "Yes, that's the one."

\* \* \*

Time: 2.15pm

Date: Sunday 10<sup>th</sup> June 2012

Location: St Bartholomew's Home for Boys, Christchurch

"It looks smaller." Mac stepped back and stared up at the red-brick Victorian building. "Much smaller."

Jack's gaze followed Mac's to take in the sweeping gravel driveway that was now littered with overgrown weeds. The cast iron gates at the roadside had yielded without protest to their touch, the ancient rusted hinges coming away from the crumbling brickwork that housed them, extracted like rotting teeth.

They made their way further up the driveway, stepping over knee-deep stinging nettles and sharp thistles. They stepped in-between discarded beer cans and takeaway boxes, and skirted around black bin bags spilling their rotting contents. The building itself still stood, but barely. Empty, gaping holes replaced the windows; any panes of glass still standing were jagged and broken, others had been boarded up. The front door hung limply off its hinges, inviting visitors to step inside – although their passage would have been hampered by the green ivy clinging to every available surface surrounding the porch.

A rusty sign hung at an odd angle on the broken brickwork next to the door.

No admittance – Private Property
  Trespassers will be prosecuted.
  24 hours CCTV Security
  Bulldog Security Systems Ltd
  (01425) 755999

Somehow, Jack didn't think that Bulldog Security Systems were all that interested in the security breaches at St Bartholomew's Home for Boys. He glanced up at the front façade in search of the promised CCTV coverage – and smiled, ruefully, when not a single camera could be seen.

Mac slowly ascended the three stone steps to the front door, again noting how much smaller everything was than he remembered. He could recall as clear as day, as if it were yesterday, his eight-year-old self being dragged up these same stone steps. To him, the door had seemed of giant proportions, the walls never-ending as they stretched skywards. In reality, as Mac paused on the threshold, the door was little bigger than himself, and the building only three storeys high.

He gave an involuntary shudder as he reached forwards and tentatively pushed at the dilapidated front door. The remaining hinge that held the door in its lop-sided position, gave way to Mac's touch, silently opening up the entrance to St Bartholomew's Home for Boys.

Mac hesitated momentarily before taking a footstep across the threshold and into the cavernous hallway. Breathing in, he imagined that he could still smell the stale cigarette smoke and rotten cabbage of the breath of his initial captor.

Mr Wakefield.

That had been his name.

Caretaker at St Bartholomew's.

Although the role of caretaker insinuated that the job required him to take care of his charges.

And that certainly had not been the case.

Mac shuddered once again before pushing the fragile door fully open. Jack hung back on the steps outside, letting his brother take this step – this important step – on his own.

As it had to be.

He had entered this monstrosity of a building on his own as a child. Alone And as a man he had to do the same.

* * *

Time: 3.00pm

Date: Friday 27th July 2012

Location: Metropolitan Police HQ, London

"So, what do I call you now?" Jack tore his thoughts away from Stuart and St Bartholomew's Home for Boys, and back to the present. "Should it be DS Tindleman?" He reached forwards to switch on the air conditioning, relieved to feel a blast of ice-cold air hit his face.

DS Carmichael smiled and shrugged as he pulled into the rear car park of the station. "Either is fine," he replied, glancing over his shoulder as he reversed into a narrow space between two patrol cars. "Officially, I'm a Tindleman – but my undercover ID is Carmichael."

"Not so undercover anymore, though," mused Jack, releasing his seatbelt. "You've been rumbled."

"Well, I won't tell if you won't," he grinned, switching off the engine and affording Jack a mischievous wink. "It can be our little secret."

They crossed the rear car park and Jack was about to push the back entrance door open when his phone rang. He was debating ignoring it until he saw the name flash up on the screen.

"Stu?" Jack paused on the step, holding up a hand and signalling for DS Carmichael to wait. "Everything all right?"

As Jack listened to Mac's reply, the frown crossing his tired brow increased the more he heard. Nodding his head, he let the door swing back shut and turned around, motioning to DS Carmichael to follow him back towards the car. "OK, OK, we're on our way."

* * *

# Chapter Thirty Seven

Time: 4.10pm
Date: Friday 27<sup>th</sup> July 2012
Location: Isabel's Café, King's Road, London

Jack and DS Carmichael stepped into Isabel's café and were greeted by the warming smell of cinnamon, coffee and sweet pastry. Jack felt his stomach growl, unsure when he last had anything to eat. Maybe he should have taken Mrs Tindleman up on her offer of a generous slice of fruit cake. But all thoughts of food disappeared from his mind when he saw the anxious look on Mac's face as his brother hurried across from the art studio at the rear.

"Jack. Glad you're here."

"Stu? What's up?" Jack frowned. Mac hadn't made much sense over the phone, some garbled message about Isabel being unnerved by something at the café and that he was worried about her.

"I'm not sure. I think you need to see for yourself."

Jack and DS Carmichael followed Mac back into the art studio at the rear of the café. Jack saw Isabel sitting on one of the stools by an artist's easel. Although she had been checked over by a doctor and declared fit enough to return home after her ordeal yesterday - in fact she had insisted, refusing to stay overnight in hospital - the experience of the last few days was clearly etched onto her face. Her skin was a deathly shade of white, her eyes sunken and full of fear. Dark smudges encircled her eyes.

"Isabel?" Jack stepped forwards and placed a concerned hand on her shoulder. She shrunk back at his touch. "Are you OK?"

Isabel glanced up, the whites of her eyes showing, her pupils round and dilated.

"What's happened?" pressed Jack, the feeling of disquiet he had been so familiar with lately returning to his stomach. "Tell me."

"Erik has left," interrupted Mac, nodding at the wall behind Isabel. "Just upped and left without saying anything. Left all his paintings behind for Isabel."

Jack glanced up at the wall where several large canvases now adorned the space. A quick look confirmed they all depicted some bridge or other, mostly watercolours and one pen and ink drawing. Jack seemed to remember Isabel mentioning that her new artist seemed to specialise in drawing and painting bridges.

"And?" Jack frowned at the paintings. They weren't exactly to his own taste, but they weren't half bad he supposed. This Erik chap was quite a talented artist. Whatever floats your boat, he mused, as he turned his attention back to Isabel. "What's the problem? Did he leave owing you money?"

Isabel managed to shake her head, still looking as white as a sheet.

"Look at this one." Mac stepped forwards and pointed at one of the paintings nearest to him. The painting was an intricate picture of a bridge, expertly created with light watercolours bringing the whole scene alive.

Jack stepped closer. "What exactly am I looking at?" The painting was pretty good, if that was your thing.

Isabel slid off her stool and came to stand at Jack's elbow. "It's the mathematical bridge in Cambridge. I used to live nearby, just around the corner," she breathed, her voice shaking. "It's my most favourite place in the whole of Cambridge. I used to go there a lot, sometimes every day in summer." She took a small step closer to the painting. "See how the bridge is made up of short sections of timber; back in the 18$^{th}$ century when it was built, it was revered as a mark of genius in its engineering and design."

Jack looked back at the painting, taking in the expertly re-created wooden timbers spanning the quiet waters of the River Cam. He gave a small shrug. "It's a good painting; if you like bridges. But I don't understand. What's the problem?"

Isabel raised a shaky hand and pointed with a delicate finger at an image on the bridge. The watercolours made the image look a little blurry around the edges, but by squinting Jack could make out that it was the image of a person. A woman. A woman resting against the bridge. Jack felt another shrug forming, but fought against it. Instead he repeated, "what's the problem?"

"It's me," whispered Isabel, her eyes darting back to Jack. "The person on the bridge is me."

Jack peered more closely at the painting. He took in the outline of the figure, blurred as it was. Yes, it did look like it could be Isabel, but then again the watercolours were so hazy at the edges that it could be anyone. "It looks a *little* bit like you..."

"It *is* me." Isabel's voice was now more definite, the strength returning to her. "I'm sure of it."

"OK...." Jack's voice tailed off while he glanced between Mac and Isabel, feeling like he was missing something. "Does someone want to explain... .?"

"Erik. He's been there. Cambridge. He painted me on that bridge. He must have followed me." Isabel's gaze never left the painting as she spoke. "Erik must have seen me when I lived in Cambridge."

Jack raised a hand and frowned towards Mac, who merely returned his gesture with a shrug. "Right, let's rewind a little here. Maybe that is you in the painting, Isabel. But maybe he just painted the bridge from a picture, from the internet or something, and added you onto it? This doesn't mean that he was watching you, or stalking you, if that's what you're worried about."

Isabel broke her gaze and fixed Jack with a hard stare. "No, maybe not. But this does." She handed him a note with a parking ticket attached. Jack took the note and scoured its neat handwriting.

"Isabel. Thank you for your hospitality. I'm sorry I couldn't stay longer. Please accept my paintings as my parting gift to you. My favourite is the Mathematical Bridge. I know it is your favourite too."

Pinned to the note was a parking ticket from May 2009

"You see," repeated Isabel. "He was there."

* * *

Time: 12.30pm

Date: 30<sup>th</sup> May 2009

Location: Green Park Parade, Cambridge

He sat behind the wheel of his nondescript hire car and quietly hummed to himself, intermittently tapping his fingers on the leather steering wheel. Adjusting his dark sunglasses, he peered out of his side window and across the road.

A woman he guessed to be the wrong side of seventy, judging by the lines mapping her face, was shuffling along the pavement, a floral quilted dressing gown loosely wrapped around her. Her silver-grey hair was bundled up in an assortment of mismatched curlers, a translucent shower cap encasing her scalp. As she shuffled along, she occasionally stooped over to scatter small pellets onto the pavement, making a strange squeaking and sucking noise as she did so.

"Smokey," she called, inching along the kerbside. "Come on, sweetie." More pellets were dropped to the ground and more squeaking emanated from her lips.

He then noticed a movement out of the corner of his eye, coming from one of the bushes flanking the pavement. Suddenly, a tortoiseshell cat with four white paws leapt from within the tangle of leaves and branches, and quickly made a bee-line for the tasty offerings the old lady had dropped to the floor.

Treats, he mused, resuming his tapping and humming. He continued to watch as the cat followed the Hansel and Gretel trail back up the stone steps and disappeared inside with the help of the old lady shooing it from behind.

The door behind them closed, and he didn't have long to wait until the true object of his observations emerged from next door. He glanced at his watch and smiled.

A creature of habit. Every day at the same time, she would emerge from her house and make the short walk around the corner. Every day for the last three weeks, including the weekend. He nodded, appreciatively, to himself.

He liked that about Miss Isabel Faraday.

And just like every day for the last three weeks, he waited until she was out of sight before sliding out from the driver's seat, placing his parking ticket on his dashboard, and silently following in the young woman's shadow.

He didn't need to rush. He knew exactly where she would be going. The same place, every day. He tucked his sketch book underneath his arm, his box of charcoal pencils and watercolours stowed away in his small knapsack, and whistled tunelessly into the late-Spring air as he made his way towards Queens College.

And the Mathematical Bridge.

* * *

Time: 4.20pm
Date: Friday 27th July 2012
Location: Isabel's Café, King's Road, London

"He was there," she repeated, taking a step backwards to sit back down, the whites of her knuckles showing as she gripped the sides of the stool to steady herself. "He was watching me. All this time, he was watching me."

Jack read the note again and stared at the parking ticket, his cluttered mind furiously trying to connect the dots to catch up with what his instinct was telling him. "Why would Erik have been following you?" was all he could muster. "When he arrived, did he give you any indication he had met you before, or seen you before?"

Isabel shook her head, still grasping the sides of her stool as if letting go would cause her to collapse to the floor. "None." She paused, her face losing even more colour. "And there's more."

"More?" Jack exchanged another bewildered look with Mac. "What do you mean there's more?"

Without a word, Isabel went over to a bureau by the patio doors, pulling open the top drawer. After rummaging for several seconds she brought out a postcard, holding it gingerly between her fingers. She returned and handed it over to Jack.

"It's the Mathematical Bridge, in Cambridge," she explained, her voice shaking. "The same as in the painting."

Jack looked at the glossy postcard in his hand and then up again at Erik Neumann's painting. "I don't understand," he frowned. "What has this got to do with anything?"

"I received that postcard in the post just after I opened the café." Isabel's voice was small and faint. "It has no message."

Jack flipped the postcard over to confirm the back was, indeed, blank.

"It has a Cambridge postmark," she continued. "It's from him. It has to be. It's from Erik. He's known about me all along."

Both Jack and Mac continued staring at the parking ticket and postcard. Jack gave a faint shrug of his shoulders and handed them both back to Isabel. "I don't know what else to say, Isabel. I truly don't. I have no idea why a German artist would have been stalking you; it makes no sense."

"He wasn't German." Dominic's hesitant voice carried through from the archway leading into the café. Jack turned around to see him hovering at the entrance, a tea towel in his hands as if he had just finished the washing up.

Jack frowned. "Sorry? We were just talking about Erik – the visiting artist from Germany?"

Dominic shook his head again and nudged his spectacles further up onto the bridge of his nose, a slight smudge of icing sugar on one cheek. "I know who you mean – but he wasn't German."

"He was from Hamburg – he told me." Isabel's faint voice could barely be heard. "He was born there. He kept on about how many bridges it had…. more than Venice…." Her voice tailed off as an unexplained sickness spread through her stomach. "He told me."

"But he wasn't German," insisted Dominic, taking a tentative step forwards into the studio, twisting the tea towel in his hands. "He was Russian."

"Russian?" Jack's frown deepened, and he exchanged a confused and worried look with Mac, who was now standing by Isabel's side, a steadying hand on her shoulder. "How come you think he was Russian, Dominic?"

Dominic swallowed, nervously, as all four pairs of eyes seemed to be trained on him. He glanced behind, giving an apprehensive look at Sacha who had followed him in from the kitchen, a tray of freshly baked pastries in her hands. She too had a dusting of icing sugar in her hair.

"It's OK, Dom," she whispered, giving a reassuring nod. "Tell them what you know."

"I…. I…," stuttered Dominic, turning back to face the inquisitive stares still focused in his direction. "I…Patrick…. he was teaching me some languages. He was good at those." He paused and hurriedly reached into his back pocket to bring out his notebook. "We started off with some simple Spanish phrases…. then some Portuguese, as it's quite similar. Then some Mandarin, but I didn't get on too well with that." Dominic flicked through the pages of his notebook, methodically stepping from side to side as he did so. His hands began to shake as he turned the pages.

"But the Russian, Dominic," prodded Jack, feeling the knot in his stomach twisting more and more as the seconds ticked by. "You mentioned Russian?"

"Yes." Dominic looked up, starting to nod animatedly. "Yes. Patrick started teaching me some Russian. Just the basics. But that was how I came to realise that Erik wasn't German. He never spoke German; he spoke Russian." Dominic glanced, nervously, at Jack. "I…I overheard him talking on the phone a few times. And he was speaking Russian. Not German.

*Russian.*"

Jack didn't need to look up to feel Mac's gaze boring into him. "How sure are you?"

"One hundred percent," replied Dominic, firmly. He handed his notebook across to Jack. "He said some of the key phrases Patrick had been teaching me. I...I wrote down what he said. And then translated it."

Jack took the notebook and scoured Dominic's neat handwriting. He saw almost a page full of what he could only assume was Russian – as it made no sense to him. But then again, languages had never been his strong point, giving up the obligatory French lessons at school and replacing them with woodwork at the earliest opportunity.

Jack flicked the page over and saw what he then deduced was Dominic's translation. He felt Mac appear at his side, his brother's hot breath brushing his cheek as he peered over Jack's shoulder.

Mac followed the neat translation down to the end of the page.

"Face/off," murmured Mac, nodding at the extra notes Dominic had made at the end. He had noted the FACE and OFF written in small capital letters at the end of the translation. "That's a good film – one of my favourites." He nodded at no one in particular. "John Travolta, wasn't it? And Nicholas Cage?"

Dominic shook his head. "No, not the film. Just FACE. OFF." He motioned towards his own face. "Face off," he repeated. "Like Mrs Doubtfire."


\* \* \*


Time: 5.30pm
Date: Tuesday 24<sup>th</sup> July 2012
Location: Isabel's Café, King's Road, London


Isabel had locked up the café, and was upstairs in her flat. But she could come down at any minute so he had to be quick. He stepped through to the washroom at the side of the art studio – a small space with a wash basin and toilet. He looked up at the mirror on the wall and smiled.

Erik Neumann smiled back at him.

Lifting his chin up slightly, he carefully peeled away the almost invisible line beneath his jaw. The rubbery prosthetic mask began to lift and separate from his underlying skin. Working carefully, yet quickly, he peeled away the rest of Erik Neumann until he was left staring blankly, once again, at the mirror.

The real me, he thought, the smile returning to his lips.

Boris Kreshniov carefully stowed the delicate prosthetic mask of Erik Neumann into a specially adapted metal case, and slipped it into his holdall, zipping it up tightly, away from prying eyes.

He splashed some cold water onto his face, his own face, and patted it dry with a towel.

It's good to be back, he thought to himself, as he backed out of the narrow washroom and into the studio. A quick glance into the café confirmed that he was still alone. Grabbing his jacket off one of the art stools, he swung his holdall onto his shoulder and headed for the patio doors. A quick scale of the brick wall surrounding the courtyard garden, and he could lose himself in the back alleyways.

Isabel would never know.

Dominic watched him leave from the shadows of the café, peering out from behind one of the sofas. After seeing Erik in the washroom, he had dived behind the nearest sofa just in time to remain hidden from view. He held his breath as he watched Erik disappear over the garden wall. Not quite sure what he had just witnessed, Dominic pulled out his notebook and began to write.

FACE.

OFF.

* * *

Time: 4.30pm

Date: Friday 27<sup>th</sup> July 2012
Location: Isabel's Café, King's Road, London

Jack followed Mac's gaze back to the paintings on the wall. In perfect synchronicity, they both stepped forwards and squinted more closely at the signatures in the bottom right hand corner of each canvas.

Erik Neumann, the signatures read.

But that wasn't what was catching both of the brothers' attention. It was the symbol carefully etched into the canvas next to each swirling signature.

A prism.

Erik Neumann and a prism.

The tension that had now descended on the art studio was broken once more by Dominic's hesitant voice. "I looked it up – his name. And what it meant." Dominic once again picked up his notebook which Jack had dropped onto the bench in front of them. He again flicked through the pages until he found what he was looking for. "Erik – means eternal ruler, in Danish. And Neumann..." Dominic paused and looked up. "It means...."

"New man," breathed Jack, mirroring the words as they left Dominic's mouth. "New man." He exchanged a look with Mac that required no words.

Kreshniov.

Boris Kreshniov had been back.

And now he was gone.

Again.

"Can someone tell me what's going on?" enquired DS Carmichael.

* * *

# Chapter Thirty Eight

Time: 9.00pm
Date: Friday 27<sup>th</sup> July 2012
Location: Metropolitan Police HQ, London

"Take a seat, Jack." Chief Superintendent Dougie King motioned towards the vacant seat opposite his desk, squeezing himself into his own leather swivel chair, sighing as he did so. "This won't take long."

Jack did as he was bidden, watching as the Chief Superintendent reached for his desk drawer.

"Well earned, Jack, I think."

Jack didn't object as two glass tumblers, followed by a half-full bottle of single malt, landed in front of him.

Chief Superintendent King handed a good measure of Highland Park across the desk. "You came through for me, Jack. Well done."

Jack accepted the drink and took a sip. "It was a team effort, Sir. They all did me proud."

"Even our friend, DS Carmichael?" A small smile teased the Chief Superintendent's lips as he swirled the contents of his glass tumbler, before taking a large mouthful and savouring the warmth. "You two friends now?"

Jack hid his own smile behind his glass. "He proved his worth in the end, Sir. I think we all underestimated him when he first arrived – maybe jumped to a few conclusions that we shouldn't have."

"Indeed. And not just you, Jack." Chief Superintendent King refilled his glass, offering the bottle to Jack who placed a hand over the top of his. "I'll hold my hands up and admit I wasn't sure about him myself."

"If we had known the facts when he arrived, Sir..." Jack let the question hang in the air.

"Then we could have avoided a lot of misunderstandings. I know."

"Why was it such a secret?" Jack took another sip of the Highland Park, feeling the hot, fiery sensation slip comfortingly down his throat. "Me and the team could have been trusted with the truth of why he was really here – and who he really was."

"That was Commander Forsyth's decision." The Chief Superintendent barely hid the grimace behind his whisky. "Way above my head, Jack. The powers that be insisted on anonymity - the IPCC don't like unwarranted attention being focused on them. Investigations into potential corruption, corruption by police officers, is a hot topic. And as DS Carmichael was only investigating the *possibility* of police collusion with crimes against children, it seemed like a reasonable request in hindsight."

"Fair enough," acknowledged Jack. "I guess we'll be seeing a bit more of him now – DS Carmichael, I mean. Or Tindleman. I'm not sure what I should be calling him."

Chief Superintendent King smiled. "I hear he took you on a trip down memory lane – visiting Charles Tindleman's widow?"

"Indeed he did, Sir."

"I had no idea of his connection to the Tindlemans," added the Chief Superintendent. "When I heard, it blew my mind. His connection to Charles, and therefore his connection to you – it shocked me, I can tell you."

Jack nodded again. "Me too, Sir."

"So, what are your plans now, Jack?" Chief Superintendent King leant forwards, his elbows on his desk, resting his chin on steepled fingers.

"Plans?" Jack frowned at the conversation's subtle change of direction. "I'm not sure I have any plans, Sir."

Chief Superintendent King nodded, thoughtfully, fixing Jack with his dark brown eyes. "What would you say if I suggested a bit of time off?"

Time off.

You need time off, Jack.

Jack wasn't surprised at the question, and if he was being honest, he had been expecting it. "I know I haven't been at my sharpest lately, Sir." He drained the last of the single malt in his glass and nodded at the further top up offered by his superior officer. He gazed down into the amber liquid, seeing his reflection mirrored back up at him.

A distorted reflection.

A reflection that wasn't him.

A reflection that wasn't Jack MacIntosh.

"I took my eye off the ball a few times in this investigation, Sir." Jack took another mouthful of whisky, distorting the reflection further. "I ignored my instincts. Let the facts get twisted. As a result, we went down too many blind alleys. If I had been thinking more clearly...."

"We all make mistakes, Jack." The Chief Superintendent shook his head and replaced the bottle of Highland Park in his desk drawer. "It wasn't an easy investigation...and with the time constraints I put you under..."

"That's no excuse, Sir," continued Jack, draining his glass. "I made too many mistakes. Mistakes I don't normally make. I mean, Saunders? I can't explain that."

Chief Superintendent King held up a hand. "No need to explain, Jack. I smoothed things over with his father. I'm not sure we'll be invited to the next Bar Council dinner, but it'll all be forgotten in time." He paused and caught Jack's eye. "You're a great DI, Jack. In fact, you're my best DI. I need you."

It was Jack's turn to shake his head. "It's still no excuse, Sir. And it wasn't just Saunders. I virtually arrested a fellow officer, accusing him of murder, and then physically assaulted him. That's not me."

"No, no, maybe not," replied Chief Superintendent King, nodding.

"So...I think your suggestion of some time off might be a good idea." Jack reached into his pocket and drew out the small business card for Dr Evelyn Riches. "You gave this to me some time ago, Sir." He held the card up. "I've had one session. I think I'd like to have more."

Chief Superintendent King smiled, his eyes softening as they lowered to read the business card in Jack's hand. "I thought you'd thrown that away a long time ago."

"I nearly did," admitted Jack, nodding at his own memory of throwing the card into the back of the drawer in his kitchen. "As I say, I've only had one session, but...she's different..."

"Different can be good, Jack." Chief Superintendent King inclined his head toward the card. "She does come highly recommended."

"So, if I were to take a period of leave...maybe a few months...?"

"That will be fine, Jack," confirmed the Chief Superintendent, smiling warmly. "I'll square it with whoever it needs to be squared with."

Jack nodded and made to get up out of his chair. He knew he needed a break. He knew he needed help. The nightmares were not going to disappear on their own, that was becoming acutely obvious. He was permanently exhausted, sleep being no cure. And now it was affecting his work. In his eyes, he had failed. And he had failed because his head wasn't in the right place.

He had to deal with it.

He had to deal with it now.

"Sir." Jack turned towards the door, already feeling as though a weight was beginning to shift from his shoulders. He had a way to go, he knew that, but it was a start. They always said acknowledging the problem was the first step.

"Thank you once again, Jack." Chief Superintendent King had also risen from his chair and joined Jack at the doorway. "Getting the arrest in time for the Opening Ceremony."

"Just."

"Just," conceded the Chief Superintendent, his eyes twinkling. "You did cut it a little fine."

"The Opening Ceremony should be underway as we speak, Sir."

"Indeed." Chief Superintendent King glanced at his watch. "James Bond and the Queen will be wowing the public any time now."

"Don't forget the corgis," smiled Jack, stepping out into the corridor.

"And the corgis," laughed the Chief Superintendent, raising a hand to Jack as he departed. "You take care now, Jack. And come back to me."

* * *

Time: 9.40pm
  Date: Friday 27<sup>th</sup> July 2012
  Location: Metropolitan Police HQ, London

DS Carmichael was leaning against Jack's Mondeo, watching as Jack left the rear entrance and crossed the car park towards him. As he approached, he stepped forwards and held out his hand.

"It's been good working with you, Jack. And the team. You got the guy in the end – I hope the Chief Superintendent gave you the praise you deserve."

Jack took the proffered hand, sliding his car keys into DS Carmichael's open palm. "You don't get away that easily, Carmichael. You're driving me home."

DS Carmichael frowned, taking the car keys and watching as Jack headed towards the passenger side door.

"The Chief Superintendent was *very* thankful," explained Jack, indicating with his hand that he had had one or two drinks. "On an empty stomach. I think it's best that you drive."

* * *

Time: 9.45pm
  Date: Friday 27<sup>th</sup> July 2012
  Location: Isabel's Café, King's Road, London

"I'm not taking no for an answer." Mac virtually pushed Isabel up the stairs to her flat, waving a tea towel in her wake. "You run yourself a hot bath. We'll finish up down here and lock up." Mac flashed a grateful look at Sacha and Dominic, who both disappeared towards the kitchen. "And then I'll order us a takeaway," he added.

"What would I do without you," came the reply, just as the door to the flat at the top of the stairs opened. "You really are the best."

Mac turned away from the stairs, feeling his cheeks beginning to burn. He checked the rear patio doors were locked and then went through to the café. He could hear Sacha and Dominic finishing up in the kitchen – the dishwasher being loaded and turned on, the oven doors wiped down ready for the morning's baking. He straightened a few cushions, placed half-read paperbacks and magazines back onto the bookshelves, and tucked the bar stools neatly under the counter.

After the discovery about Erik Neumann's real identity, Isabel had been shaken to the core. They had all stayed with her, Jack and DS Carmichael included, sipping strong coffee and reassuring her that all would be well.

Would it though? Mac couldn't be sure. And as he caught his brother's eye, he knew that Jack had his doubts too.

As he tidied, he couldn't help but think of how much Isabel had managed to achieve, despite the odds being set against her at times. She hadn't had it easy, not by a long shot. She had been through unimaginable grief, yet still she managed to function as a human being and create a business that was flourishing.

Mac sighed.

What had he managed to achieve in comparison?

He had progressed from an uncontrollable delinquent teenager to adult crime. Starting with approved schools and youth detention, there was then promotion to adult prison. A string of temporary, cash in hand jobs followed in its wake.

He was lucky the courier firm had seen past his less than encouraging history and given him a chance. Although he couldn't be sure, he strongly suspected a good supporting word from a certain Detective Inspector at the

Metropolitan Police may have held some sway.

But when he looked around at what Isabel had managed to create and achieve, he felt the all too familiar feeling of inadequacy creeping in. He sighed as he turned the sign on the door to 'closed', and straightened the menu hanging in the window.

"Stop doubting yourself, and ask her."

Mac swung round at the sound of Sacha's voice, watching as she switched the lights to the kitchen off and swung her handbag up onto her shoulder.

"I...I don't.... what do you mean?"

"Stop right there, Stuart MacIntosh." Sacha strode out from behind the counter and wagged a finger in his direction. "You know damn well what I mean!" She suppressed the smile that was forming on her lips. "Just sit her down and ask her out. It's painful watching you two sometimes."

If Mac's cheeks had been tinged pink before, they were now in danger of flushing scarlet. "I...I..." He shook his head and broke off. "She wouldn't be interested in someone like me. I'd be no good for her."

"Says who?" Sacha motioned for Dominic to follow her towards the door. "You've been there for her all this time; and you're still here for her now."

"But my past..."

"Who cares about the past? Isabel certainly doesn't." Sacha opened the front door and turned round to face Mac, her voice softening. "Look, she likes you. I know she does. And she can depend on you." Sacha reached forwards and gave Mac's arm a squeeze. "Be brave."

With that, she gave him a wink and both she and Dominic stepped out onto the pavement.

Mac shut and locked the door behind them, the bell tinkling overhead.

Be brave, Mac.

Be brave.

But brave was very far away from how he felt.

\* \* \*

444

Time: 10.35pm
  Date: Friday 27<sup>th</sup> July 2012
  Location: Kettle's Yard Mews, London

The Opening Ceremony was indeed well underway. Jack had felt obliged to watch, but had muted the sound after a while. There was only so much patriotism he could take today. With the images still flickering from the TV in the corner, he passed another bottle of Budweiser to DS Carmichael and sank back onto the sofa.

"Cheers." DS Carmichael held his bottle up in the air before taking a sip.

Jack returned the gesture with his own bottle. "Here's to the Olympics," he added, taking a mouthful of cold beer and savouring the taste. The weather looked like it was finally on the turn, with a cooler, fresher breeze starting to blow across the capital from the north. Clouds had been bubbling up all day – dampening the exhibition by the Red Arrows once the Ceremony had been officially declared open. If he listened closely enough, Jack reckoned he would be able to hear a collective sigh of relief across the country as electric fans could finally be turned off, and air conditioning systems could grind to a grateful halt.

"So, what's next for the team?" DS Carmichael reached for another slice of the meat feast pizza that had been delivered a short while ago. "I'm sure there must be plenty of other cases vying to fill the gap left by Holloway, now he's finally off the streets."

Jack nodded, reaching for some pizza himself. "The team will take on the next case allocated to them. They'll still have lots to do in building the case against Holloway – charging him is only the first step. We want a water-tight case come the trial date."

"I can't see him wriggling out of this one," commented DS Carmichael. "A signed confession within an hour of arrest? That's got to be some kind of record."

"Pretty much. But I never count my chickens, not when criminals are concerned. Been in the job far too long for that. I've seen signed confessions thrown out of court as being inadmissible one too many times. We need to make sure this one sticks fast."

DS Carmichael murmured his agreement. "And once they formally identify the bodies found under the patio in Fulham as being Carol and Jess – which they *will* do, I'm sure of it – he'll have two more murder charges to answer to."

"Let's hope we can finally get some closure on this, for the families at least – and for you, too." Jack sunk his teeth into the soft pizza base. "This case must have haunted you for years."

"I knew it was him, all along." DS Carmichael swallowed his pizza and washed it down with another mouthful of beer. "I just knew. But I was just a new recruit – it was my first case. There just wasn't any evidence – none whatsoever. They both literally just disappeared without trace."

"He certainly was a clever one."

"But maybe not quite clever enough," commented DS Carmichael, a rueful smile crossing his lips. "Nothing gets past Jack MacIntosh and his team. They're lucky to have you in charge."

Athletes were now parading through the Olympic Stadium - flags were being hoisted and waved, smiles directed towards the cameras. Jack watched as the Great Britain team entered the stadium to a huge roar – even with the sound turned down, Jack knew there would be a roar. He turned away from the screen and exhaled a sigh. "They're going to have to do without me for a while. I'm taking some time off."

DS Carmichael raised his eyebrows. "Time off?"

Jack nodded. "It's a long story – but I've a few things I need to sort out. Something's not quite right, in here." He paused and tapped a finger to the side of his temple. "A leave of absence is in order, and probably long overdue. I think if I didn't jump now of my own volition, I would probably end up being pushed at some point."

"Well, when you're back on the job – give me a shout. I'll still be around for a while."

"Operation Evergreen?"

"The one and the same."

"The Chief Superintendent said it was likely to be the biggest investigation the Met have ever handled."

"And he's not wrong." DS Carmichael placed his beer bottle back down on the coffee table. "Operation Yewtree will blow your mind. We're tagging Operation Evergreen alongside it, as there are some similarities that cross over between the two, but..." DS Carmichael paused and shook his head. "You will not believe some of the accusations that are going to come out. And the evidence to go with it. It's shocking."

"He mentioned something to do with TV personalities?"

DS Carmichael nodded. "It's all under wraps at the moment. There's a TV documentary that is due to be shown in the next couple of months - that will basically herald the start of Operation Yewtree. I can't say anything other than that. You need to watch it."

"I will."

"My investigation – Operation Evergreen – is more focused on local authority children's homes, foster homes, that kind of thing. But it ties in with the other investigation on some points."

"Children's homes?" Jack looked up from his pizza and caught DS Carmichael's gaze. "Was that why you were asking me about St Bartholomew's? Where my brother went?"

DS Carmichael hesitated before answering. He gave a brief nod. "Yes, yes it was. I won't lie, Jack. That home has come onto our radar."

"Are you saying...?"

"I'm not saying anything, Jack. The investigation has just started. But I will need to speak to your brother at some point, yes." The statement hung silently in the air, suspended in the freshening breeze that was wafting in through the open window.

Neither Jack nor DS Carmichael spoke for a while. Both their gazes fell onto the muted television. More athletes were now crowding into the stadium; some countries Jack had barely heard of, countries being represented by just one shot putter or a swimmer, but feeling just as important as the likes of the USA and Great Britain. And why shouldn't they, thought Jack. Why shouldn't they indeed.

Interrupting the silence, Jack's mobile phone pinged with an incoming message. "Speak of the devil," he murmured, seeing his brother's name flash up on his screen. "My brother, Stuart," he explained to DS Carmichael's unspoken question. "I invited him round for a beer tonight; thought he could do with some company."

Jack opened the message and then began to chuckle.

"Good news?" enquired DS Carmichael.

"Well, looks like he doesn't need any company from me tonight," replied Jack, typing out a swift reply. "Looks like he's got that covered, the dark horse."

Mac's message had been short and to the point.

STU: Won't be over tonight. Staying over at Isabel's.

\* \* \*

# Chapter Thirty Nine

Time: 11.30am

Date: 30<sup>th</sup> November 2012

Location: Dr Evelyn Riches, Psychotherapist, St James's University, London

"Think back to your safe place, Jack." Dr Evelyn Riches spoke in her soft, measured tone. "Today we are going to step forwards towards that door... .and if you feel like you want to, I am going to ask you to open it."

Jack sank back into the familiar leather armchair, head down with his chin resting lightly on his chest. His eyes were closed, his arms relaxed by his side.

"First of all, let's relax each and every muscle, each and every bone in your body. One at a time, from top to bottom." Dr Riches' voice floated through the air as if carried by an unseen force. "Starting from your head and neck, travelling down through your shoulders and arms, across your chest and abdomen. Down to your legs and feet. Feel those muscles relax, Jack. Feel how weightless you are."

Jack took in a deep breath.

He did feel weightless.

He did feel truly weightless.

"Now, let's descend the stairs once again, Jack. One at a time."

Dr Evelyn Riches watched from her chair opposite, noting how the muscles in Jack's face and neck visibly seemed to smooth and lose their tension. His shoulders sagged; his arms slumped on the arm rests. This was now their eighth session and she had been impressed with his progress. She admitted to being initially sceptical, having mentally made a wager with herself that DI Jack MacIntosh would not show up for his second session, never mind the rest of the course. His problems were deep and complex; and very much ingrained. She didn't sense the necessary commitment or resolve at their initial session; didn't detect the underlying determination that would be required to face up to his fears, and then beat them.

But she had been wrong.

For the first time in her professional life, she had been very wrong.

Detective Inspector Jack MacIntosh had surprised her – booking a full ten-week intensive course, plus requesting additional resources for meditation and mindfulness.

"That's it, Jack," continued Dr Riches. "Take the first step now. Slowly does it. One step at a time."

Jack felt his body descending the staircase in his mind; his body floating weightlessly above each step. The air around him felt light and airy; he felt he could breathe freely, each lungful he inhaled energised and refreshed him.

He took the first step.

"That's it, Jack. Ten steps to the bottom. Nice and slowly, a deep breath with each step you take towards your safe place."

Dr Riches knew that Jack's safe place was anything but.  She knew the battle he had with the demons from his past; understood how the nightmares of his childhood now locked and imprisoned him in his adult world. And she also knew that the only way to beat these demons was to take Jack back to the place where the nightmares had started.

The door.

The door that led to the kitchen of his childhood home.

The door that led to the discovery of his mother's body.

"Another step down Jack. That's it. Feel your body growing lighter with each step you take."

Jack felt himself descending further.  His footsteps felt so light, they felt like they were barely touching the floor. With every step he felt more relaxed, more toxins escaped from his muscles and more air filled his lungs.

He felt clean.

He felt pure.

He felt strong.

"Just a few more steps now, Jack. Your safe place is within reach." Dr Riches shifted slightly in her chair, pulling a notepad onto her knees. Jack had never reached further than this stage before. He had never managed to take that final step; never managed to step forwards towards the door; never managed to grip the handle and open the door into his past.

Dr Riches had attached a heart rate monitor to Jack before the session, and looking at the monitor beside her, his pulse was a steady sixty-five. Nice and relaxed. Nice and calm.

"You're almost at the bottom now, Jack." Dr Riches leant forwards to study Jack more closely, checking to see if he outwardly displayed any of the anxiety that she herself felt underneath. "Take one more step now, one more step and you are at the bottom." She held her breath and watched the heart rate monitor.

Sixty-five.

Sixty-four.

Sixty-three.

Jack's pulse rate was slowing.

"That's it, Jack. You've reached the bottom. Take a nice, deep breath and take a step forwards towards the door."

They were now in uncharted territory.

"When you feel ready, Jack, reach out and touch the handle of the door."

Jack felt himself float towards the door. He felt as if his body no longer belonged to him; feeling so light that movement was effortless. He felt his arm stretch out in front of him, gliding out into the blackness beyond him. He knew the door was in front of him, but he couldn't see it. Everything was black; there was no light, no illumination, no nothing.

One step forwards and he was at the door; he could feel it; he could sense it.

Sixty-three.
Sixty-two.
Sixty-one.
The door.
The door to the past.
The door he needed to open one last time.


THE END


Message from the Author

Thank you taking the time to read this book. I hope you enjoyed it!

As an independently published author, I would be really grateful if you could leave a review. Visit my book page on Amazon and click on "write a customer review".

As an author I love hearing from my readers!

There are various ways to get in touch:
  *www.michellekiddauthor.com – sign up for my newsletter*
  *www.facebook.com/michellekiddauthor*
  @AuthorKidd (Twitter)
  @michellekiddauthor (Instagram)

Thank you!

Printed in Great Britain
by Amazon